THE RACE

Brett Hoffmann has lived in Australia and Europe, and has spent much of his career at an international consulting firm. He is now based in Melbourne, and *The Race* is his second novel.

THE
RACE

BRETT
HOFFMANN

MICHAEL JOSEPH
an imprint of
PENGUIN BOOKS

MICHAEL JOSEPH

Published by the Penguin Group
Penguin Group (Australia)
250 Camberwell Road, Camberwell, Victoria 3124, Australia
(a division of Pearson Australia Group Pty Ltd)
Penguin Group (USA) Inc.
375 Hudson Street, New York, New York 10014, USA
Penguin Group (Canada)
90 Eglinton Avenue East, Suite 700, Toronto, Canada ON M4P 2Y3
(a division of Pearson Penguin Canada Inc.)
Penguin Books Ltd
80 Strand, London WC2R 0RL, England
Penguin Ireland
25 St Stephen's Green, Dublin 2, Ireland
(a division of Penguin Books Ltd)
Penguin Books India Pvt Ltd
11 Community Centre, Panchsheel Park, New Delhi – 110 017, India
Penguin Group (NZ)
67 Apollo Drive, Rosedale, North Shore 0632, New Zealand
(a division of Pearson New Zealand Ltd)
Penguin Books (South Africa) (Pty) Ltd
24 Sturdee Avenue, Rosebank, Johannesburg 2196, South Africa

Penguin Books Ltd, Registered Offices: 80 Strand, London WC2R 0RL, England

First published by Penguin Group (Australia), 2011

1 3 5 7 9 10 8 6 4 2

Text copyright © Brett Hoffmann 2011

Cover design by Dave Altheim © Penguin Group (Australia)
Text design by Karen Scott © Penguin Group (Australia)
Cover images by Anthony Marsland/Getty Images; Grant Faint/Getty Images; istock
Typeset in Fairfield by Post Pre-Press Group, Brisbane, Queensland
Printed and bound in Australia by McPherson's Printing Group, Maryborough, Victoria

National Library of Australia
Cataloguing-in-Publication data:

Hoffmann, Brett
The race / Brett Hoffmann
9781921518621 (pbk.)

A823.4

penguin.com.au

For my Italian connection, the Schiavos and the Sartoris
Grazie mille

23 May 2003 – Nice, France

'Look at it! It's fantastic!' Marcel Ganet called out. 'The gods have truly smiled on me today.'

'There's no need to shout,' the pilot said, tapping one finger on the headphones wrapped around his head. 'I need to keep the volume high to hear the tower.'

Marcel ignored him. He was even oblivious to the thumping roar of long blades spinning overhead as the small helicopter pulled higher into a perfect sky. Seconds after leaving the ground they were out over the sparkling blue water of the Mediterranean and as they climbed, the coastline came into view, all the way to the ruined castle on the headland. Marcel's eyes automatically flicked to the usual landmarks, marvelling at the lack of haze. It wasn't a hot day but the sun had the freedom of the sky, and the pebbly beaches strung out in front of the grand hotels on the Promenade des Anglais were already filling up. The light was almost ideal and Marcel's fingers itched to get at his cameras.

Fifteen kilometres along the coast, they passed by the entrance to the spectacular little harbour of the glamorous principality of Monaco. Marcel reached into the large bag under his legs and pulled out an enormous telephoto lens. He attached it to a Nikon body and loaded film in preparation for the only run he would get.

'Go slow,' he said to the pilot, who gave him a sullen nod and manoeuvred the helicopter back toward the coast. After checking the safety harness, he gave Marcel the okay to open the passenger-side door, which slid back and locked into place.

The green copper roof and baroque extravagance of the Monte Carlo Casino filled the viewfinder and Marcel clicked away happily in the knowledge that every shot was clear and sharp. He then took some close-ups of the Grand Hotel, the layered concrete affair hanging out over the sea that featured so heavily during the Grand Prix. Within a week, million-dollar machines would be negotiating the hairpin bend at the hotel's front entrance on the way down from the casino, before hurtling at breakneck speed through a tunnel under the hotel's guest and gambling wings.

Patiently, the pilot hovered over the tourist icons before slowly retracing his route along the coast until they were once again over the Promenade des Anglais. Marcel was still snapping away, first with long shots of the grand old hotels along the sweeping curve of the coast then focusing in on the pebbly beach, hoping to capture something like a topless sunbather for one of his postcard photos. It always made them more popular.

As they came closer to the airport – built out into the water of the bay – the pilot pulled the chopper away from the coast, following instructions received from the ground. They climbed and hovered back from the airport, awaiting clearance to return to the earth. Marcel continued shooting, twisting around in his seat to snap a few shots of the airport itself. It was an impressive sight, with terminal buildings and aircraft gleaming in the sun and the long runway dramatically surrounded on three sides by blue water. He would offer the photograph to airport management.

'We have to wait for a special,' the metallic voice of the pilot squawked in Marcel's ears.

'What sort?'

'Small private jet. Once it lands, there will be one more commercial take-off, two other choppers, then us, okay?'

'Sure, no problem.'

Marcel was happy to stay up here, his door open to the rushing wind and his big bag of cameras at his feet. He looked out to spot the incoming jet. Then he had an idea. From the side pocket of his camera bag he pulled out his most recent investment, a digital video camera. A spectacular sequence, like a swanky jet coming in to land right next to the sea with the beauty of Nice as the background, would be a sure winner with someone. The airport, Nice's city fathers, the owner of the private jet, perhaps. Somebody was sure to buy it.

'Antoine, can we go higher?' he called. 'I want to get a shot looking down at the plane landing.'

The pilot gave him a disapproving look but quickly flicked a switch to speak to the tower. Seconds later, they were climbing another fifty metres and the pilot had turned the helicopter so that the photographer had an uninterrupted view east.

'There,' he said, pointing past Marcel's nose at the sky. His experienced eye had picked out the speck of a small aircraft approaching at about a thousand metres. Marcel switched on the camera, thinking suddenly of his new baby daughter, whose arrival home from the hospital took up the first ten minutes of recording on the camera. He smiled at the thought of her, then flicked open the LCD screen and tried to zoom in on the descending jet. With the 120x digital zoom cranked up full the image was grainy, but as the plane came closer it grew in the frame and he knew the elegant beachfront in the background would soon come into focus.

With flaps fully extended and undercarriage locked down, the gleaming machine wobbled once as the pilot lined it up with the landing strip. The air behind the engines rippled with heat and Marcel hoped, even from this position, he'd be able to capture the dramatic puff of grey smoke marking the impact of rubber on concrete.

Barely 100 metres above the water, and 200 short of the long main runway, the small jet suddenly lurched in the air. A fraction of a second later, a ball of angry orange flame and billowing smoke ripped through the rear of the aircraft, tearing it in two. Spewing debris and black smoke, the engines and tail fell almost vertically into the Mediterranean Sea, where they entered the clear water with a great splash and clouds of steam. The wings and front two-thirds of the plane – including its passengers, or what remained of them – spiralled forward, burning furiously, smashing upside down into the ground just short of the runway. A deafening roar split the air as the jet and its contents disintegrated and scattered across the tarmac in small pieces. In just a few seconds, it was all over.

Hovering above the flames and smoke, Marcel Ganet sat stunned, his eyes fixed on the horror below, his video camera, still running but forgotten in his hand, pointing vaguely out to sea. He didn't even register the buffeting from the blast of the first explosion. The pilot reacted quickly to the shock wave and held the chopper steady. The two men looked helplessly down at the apron below, where emergency vehicles raced towards the scene of devastation and airport workers wisely ran the other way. Marcel could hear the panting breath of the pilot in his headphones and he realised that he, too, was sucking in oxygen.

'Shit!' was all he could think to say.

'Shit is right!' the pilot's voice crackled across the wire. 'Hey, keep that camera on.'

Marcel sat up in his seat as if he'd been slapped. He pulled the camera up with a shaky hand to point it at the scene below and cursed himself loudly. 'How could I be so stupid?' he said. 'I can't believe I forgot about the camera.'

'That's why you do tourism rather than journalism, I suppose.'

'What a waste!' Marcel smacked his own thigh sharply with his left hand. 'I bet I missed the whole damn thing.'

'Don't worry,' the pilot said grimly. 'Just thank God you weren't on that plane.' Then he took his hand away from the joystick briefly and pointed at the camera in Marcel's hand. 'And believe me, my friend, you have gold in there.'

1

Two men stood at the floor-to-ceiling windows of a modern office block, looking out at the square six floors below. Inside, it was cool and dark. Outside, the roadways – and the garden beds dividing them – were withering under the blazing summer sun. It was an ugly square by any standards, unusually so for central Milan. Oversized advertising hoardings topping many of the buildings only served to underscore the lack of charm. And it was a busy square, too, the hub for eight roads leading in all directions. Even today, when the city was just coming back to life after the annual August exodus of its citizens, the Piazzale Loreto flowed with chaotic traffic, spewing diesel exhaust into the humid air.

'You know, Jack,' the older of the two men said, 'you are now looking at a site of some historic note.'

Giorgio Borboli was a native of Venice, but part of his education had been in Great Britain and his English was near perfect, though he tended to overemphasise the vowel sounds. He wore a finely tailored suit, cleverly camouflaging the excess weight around his middle, and his face, though lined, was youthful for a man in his mid-sixties, especially as it was topped by a full head of grey hair.

'Really?' Jack Rogers said, and his eyes scanned the unexceptional view again, wondering what he had missed. When he hit his thirties Jack had rediscovered the satisfaction derived from being fit and strong. The years of regular exercise had earned him a body that could turn heads. At six foot, he stood about four inches taller than his client.

'Truly,' Borboli said. 'When the bodies of the dictator Mussolini and his mistress were brought back to Milan after their execution in 1944, they were displayed to the crowd down there, in the Piazzale Loreto. Perhaps you have seen the famous photographs?'

'That was here?'

Jack recalled the grisly fascination he'd felt as a boy when he first saw the black and white images of the Italian leader and his girlfriend hanging upside down above a baying crowd of jubilant Italians.

'Of course, the square has changed completely,' Borboli said. 'But this was the place.'

'A happy day for the Italian people,' Jack said.

Borboli shrugged and raised his eyebrows. 'There were many, including some in my own family, who were not so happy. Without the war, and the Germans of course, they would have been pleased to keep Mussolini in power. But, it is all history now. Thank God, we survived and prospered.'

He turned away from the window and moved back towards the quartet of low armchairs arranged around a square coffee table.

'Remind me, Jack, when did we first meet?' Borboli said as he reached down to pick up a glass of water from the table.

'Must have been about ten years ago, Giorgio. When I was still working in London for Deutsche Bank. About two years before I moved to the US.'

'I knew you'd do very well on Wall Street,' the older man said. 'But, I must say, I am a little disappointed with your accent now.'

Jack smiled. 'You have to talk like this to be understood in New York. Most people there think I have a quaint English accent, but when I'm in London they can usually tell I'm Australian. The family back in Sydney reckon I have a distinct American twang. I guess it depends on what you're used to.'

'And now you have your own business. Did you tire of working for somebody else?'

'A little. But mostly I just wanted to broaden the scope of my work. Everybody gets so specialised in those big firms. I need variety to stay interested.'

'And where did you find your partner? She is very impressive.'

'We worked at the same investment bank in New York. Actually, the business was her idea.'

'I am sure you will be successful. After all, you chose a Venetian as your business associate.'

Jack smiled. 'She's Australian like me, Giorgio, and proud of it. Her parents were Italian, but only her father comes from your part of the country.'

Borboli made a friendly, dismissive gesture with one hand. 'Pah! You can take the girl out of the Veneto . . .'

They shared a quiet laugh and then turned towards the door, where the subject of conversation was entering the office. Stella Sartori was tall and finely featured, with straight, dark, shoulder-length hair that glistened as she passed under a halogen ceiling light. She wore a short beige skirt cinched with a slim belt, and a simple white blouse open at the neck and highlighted by a fine gold chain. Her long legs were toned and tanned, but her face remained her best feature. Large eyes and a sensuous mouth were generally enough to fascinate – and intimidate – most men.

'Let me summarise,' she said, as they sat down in the armchairs once more. 'The Aretino Group is the Borboli Bank's largest client.

Your relationship with the company goes back many generations. The success of the bank has always been closely linked with the success of the Aretino family.'

'When an Aretino served as Doge of Venice in the seventeenth century,' Giorgio Borboli said, 'we were his closest advisors and supporters. And now, as the new millennium begins, we are still the family's most trusted source of funds.'

'But now,' Stella went on, 'the Aretino Group is a vast, diversified business. Whitegoods and furniture manufacturing, food processing and distribution, auto parts and detergents. Even wine, I think.'

'And the Formula One team,' Borboli said, gravely.

'Which the group has now owned for two years, is that right?'

The older man seemed uncomfortable at the mention of the team. 'This is their second season, yes.'

'And it has been financed largely by your bank?'

'Yes. The Italian economy has been flat for two or three years. Many of the Aretino businesses have struggled to maintain sales and profit margins. The Count decided a Formula One team would raise the global profile of the company and promote the opening up of new markets.'

'And I imagine,' Jack said neutrally, 'other banks weren't likely to offer the group a loan like that.'

A pained expression passed across Borboli's face. 'Perhaps not. Obviously, Count Aretino has relationships with other banks. We alone are not large enough to provide for all his needs these days. But you have to understand our unique relationship. It is not a simple matter to say no. Decade upon decade of mutual trust and profitability have set the tone for our dealings. The initial outlay seemed reasonable.'

'But it has you worried, Giorgio, doesn't it?'

'Yes, Jack, the F1 team has me worried. It has proved to be a bottomless pit. But my real problem is with other European financial institutions. It seems they regard our relationship with the Aretinos – and the team in particular – as an unsatisfactory risk. Our cost of borrowing has gone up substantially in the last few months.'

'Since the bombing of the Aretino jet?' Stella asked.

'Yes. Some in the banking community think it is part of a coordinated attack on the group. And, if the group goes down . . .'

'So does the Banco Borboli,' Jack said.

Stella tapped her notebook with a pen. 'Your relationship with the fifth-richest man in Europe should be seen as a positive, not a negative.'

'Indeed, but the Count guards his privacy closely. The secrecy and the lack of documentation do not sit well with my northern counterparts in these days of increased transparency and international standards. I believe a risk assessment report from a respected third party would go a long way to reassuring them.'

'Which is where we come in,' Jack said.

Borboli nodded.

'Do you think the group is under attack?' Stella asked.

The banker frowned. 'I don't think so, but it has certainly been a rough year or two for them. The terrible attack on the family jet is just the most obvious example. There have been fires at factories, labour disputes, cancelled contracts, unfounded claims of fraud and corruption in the media. And the racing team itself has been extraordinarily unlucky. Two key engineers defected to another team. A mechanic was crushed to death when a loaded container fell on him last month.'

His shoulders drooped as he recounted the litany of disasters. 'And, of course, when the plane went down they lost the team manager, the Count's brother.'

'Who would set out to undermine the company with such a

violent act?' Stella asked. 'Do you think it could be some corporate competitor?'

'No, but some bankers and bureaucrats here are not so sure. European companies can be very predatory if they smell blood in the water, and no terrorist group ever claimed responsibility. Count Carlo himself was meant to be on that flight. If he had been killed, it might have destabilised the whole group and, if the worst happened, we would stand in a much weaker position than other creditors. We have never asked the Aretinos for specific security on any of their loans, you see.'

Jack nodded coolly. 'So, Giorgio, what do you need from us?'

'First and foremost, Jack, I need you to be discreet. We have never turned to outsiders for assistance before and this is not an assignment I would take to one of the big firms. I need a strategic assessment of the Aretino Group's viability and the risks it is facing. I also need a frank and independent assessment of our own exposure.'

'Discretion is a given,' Stella said, 'but I hope you're not suggesting we conduct our analysis without the cooperation of Aretino Group management or access to their data. You said yourself, the Count is secretive. We're going to need all the information we can get.'

Borboli looked slightly embarrassed. 'Yes, of course, but it won't be as complete as you would like, I expect. I have already described the nature of our relationship with the Aretinos. We have never asked for detailed information in the way other banks might, not for this customer. I must admit we have been pulled a little out of our league by our largest client.'

Borboli prodded a phone on the table with his finger and spoke a few words of Italian. Within seconds the door to the office opened and his secretary entered, carrying a thick file of documents.

'Much of this is in Italian,' Borboli said, looking at Stella. 'I was assuming I would have to translate it for Jack, so it's a bonus to have you on the team.'

Stella smiled but was eyeing the file with disdain. There wasn't going to be enough in that one small stack of documents.

'Would it be possible for us to meet the Count?' Jack asked. 'Perhaps in a social setting. If he controls the group as tightly as you say, it would be helpful to know what sort of a character we're dealing with.'

'I agree,' Borboli said, 'and I anticipated your request. I have been invited to the team compound this Friday. If you join me as my guests, you can meet the family and get an insight into the operations of the Formula One team at the same time.'

'This Friday?' Jack said, his pulse quickening. 'You mean at the Italian Grand Prix itself?'

'Yes,' Borboli said. 'The circuit is in Monza, just north of the city.'

Jack grinned. 'Excellent,' he said, but to himself he added an exhilarating thought: This is going to be fucking cool.

2

The cab screeched to a halt, flinging Stella and Jack forwards uncomfortably. The ride from the bank had been a series of short, violent sprints between traffic lights, but the sense of speed was diminished by the impression that there was always some other Milanese driver nearby prepared to drive even faster.

Thankfully the journey was short. In Via Ravizza, Stella led the way from the cab to the tall iron gate over the arched opening at number 12. She exchanged pleasantries with the building's caretaker, who kept a suspicious eye on passers-by from his small office in the loggia. Through a wide doorway on the right and up a few steps, they moved into a dimly lit lobby where a broad stone staircase wrapped itself around the iron cage of an antique elevator barely large enough for three people.

With a disconcerting thump, the lift stopped abruptly on the third floor and Stella exited first and walked to the front door of the apartment, keys in hand. The apartment belonged to her relatives, who were away for three weeks on vacation. Jack's only complaint about their accommodation was the lack of air conditioning. A portable fan in the living room whirred furiously but made little impact. Once inside the front door, he was immediately pulling at his tie and shaking off his suit jacket. By the time he reached his bedroom, he was shirtless and tugging at his belt.

When Jack returned, in cotton shorts and a T-shirt, Stella was sipping bottled water in the kitchen while two plates of leftover pasta were reheating in the microwave. They took the food into the living room and headed for the long low sofa behind an enormous glass-topped coffee table. The table was already doubling as their makeshift office. Two laptop computers, notepads, pens and various printed pages and publications were in evidence. Stella's end of the table was neatly arranged. Jack's work area was messier, but not chaotic. Stella put down the file Giorgio Borboli had provided in the middle of the table, but didn't open it. The pasta was a higher priority.

Between mouthfuls, she said, 'This is the best job we've had so far, isn't it? Thanks for the lead.'

'It was a piece of cake. All I did was send Giorgio my new business card. I didn't expect him to fly us first class to Milan a few months later.'

'It won't be so easy getting it done, though. Italian family companies are notoriously secretive.'

'We'll get it done. We are the Stack Partnership, after all.'

She slowly nodded her head in uncertain agreement, then put down her plate to reach for the Borboli bank file. The first thing she noticed was a computer disk in a plastic sleeve.

'Aretino family press coverage,' she read from the label, and gave Jack a conspiratorial look. 'This might be juicier than plodding through a bunch of financial reports.'

'As good a place to start as any,' he said. 'Let's see what this cowboy Count looks like.'

'According to Giorgio, Carlo Aretino was always a conservative man, not a risk-taker at all,' Stella said as she inserted the disk into her computer. 'Federico was the one who loved all the trappings of wealth. He wanted the family to indulge in motor racing years ago, but Carlo blocked him until he thought it would work for the business. Carlo's definitely the brains of the outfit.'

'And Federico was the one killed in the plane crash?' Jack asked. 'Meaning the current Count was his younger brother?'

'Yep. Carlo inherited the title because Federico's only son was also killed.'

'Must be a powerful personality,' Jack commented, 'to have over-ridden his older brother to control the financial interests of the whole family.'

Stella shook her head. 'One reason the Aretino family has been successful for so long has been that control – the strongest of each generation leads the business and family interests.'

'The strongest man,' Jack suggested.

'Yeah,' Stella said, making a face, 'of course. Other men in the family seem to pursue the traditional paths, such as the church or philanthropy or the military. This is how it's been for centuries.'

Jack could see she was scrolling through a folder full of press clippings. She moved her wireless mouse to select the top one, which proved to be a newspaper article from the *Corriere della Sera*.

'"Aretino Plant Paralysed by Labour Dispute",' she read. 'This article is dated more than two years ago.'

The promise of juicy press coverage faded instantly. 'Let me know if you find any articles in English, or any good pics,' Jack said. 'While you're doing that, I'll get on the net and start building a profile of the group.'

She raised an eyebrow. 'Surfing Formula One sites, you mean.'

'Hey, somebody's got to do it. If it weren't for the issues with the F1 team, he probably wouldn't have called us in.'

'You're completely welcome to all the work on the car racing division. I find it astonishing that people are prepared to spend 200 million a year on a souped-up go-kart that some overpaid wanker is just as likely to smash into a wall.'

'We'll see how you feel after Friday,' Jack said knowingly, as he turned his attention to his computer screen.

Stella made a noncommital noise and scanned the first newspaper article, made a few notes, and moved on to the next one. She had more than sixty articles to review in this first folder, from a range of European publications, and all business-related. They appeared to divide almost equally between positive and negative stories. Certainly, there were reports of disputes, lost contracts and other business fumbles, but there were also articles about Aretino Group wins.

'Pretty typical stuff,' she said after a while, 'nothing to suggest a coordinated attack. They're so diversified that part of the business is almost bound to be on a downward spiral at any given time.'

In a second folder, she found a smaller group of articles covering the Aretino family themselves. The first file she opened was a scanned double-page spread from one of the ubiquitous Italian gossip rags. The colourful snaps of minor celebrities were enough to attract Jack's attention and he shifted closer to her computer screen.

'Tits and bums,' he said, 'all class. Which one is the Aretino?'

'This one,' Stella said, pointing to a very thin, evenly tanned, topless bather with her arms around a portly man who looked twice her age. 'Laura Aretino, twenty-eight years old, seen frolicking with notorious nightclub owner and playboy Ricardo Ponti. The headline reads "The Heiress and the Gangster" but this was taken last summer.'

Other excerpts from the gossip pages revealed candid snaps of Laura's two brothers – one of them a priest – and her cousin Stefano, who'd died in the fiery explosion over Nice. One file turned out to be a video clip from a TV talk show. A heavily made-up woman with pneumatic breasts was being interviewed by a comparatively tiny hostess. Jack couldn't follow the erratic conversation at all but he could tell they were discussing the Aretino family.

'Why do they put up subtitles whenever the guest says anything?' Jack asked. 'What language is she speaking?'

Stella smiled. 'She's speaking Italian, but not very well. They're not just subtitling her words, they're correcting them.'

'Who is she?'

'She's a reporter on one of these pap rags we've been looking at. She has to be English – that accent is diabolical. Here's her name on the screen now.'

'Victoria Cavendish,' he read. 'Sure sounds English to me.'

Stella was already moving on to the next set of files, most featuring the older Aretino generation in more conservative publications. Black and white pictures accompanied articles extolling the charitable works of Count Federico – who had had a great deal to do with the Catholic Church – and Carlo, whose generous donations had resulted in at least two hospital wings being named for the family.

'Rich, powerful and beautiful,' Jack summarised. 'Can't be too tough being an Aretino.'

The final folder was named 'Nice' and contained press coverage of the bombing of the Aretino corporate jet. Dozens of newspaper articles from around the world carried the dramatic story of the fiery crash.

Stella translated from an Italian article, 'French authorities believe a bomb was placed in the luggage compartment at the rear of the plane before it left Milan. The device was probably exploded by remote signal as it descended to Nice airport. Carlo Aretino, head of the Aretino group of companies – who was scheduled to be on the doomed flight – expressed the family's outrage and demanded that those responsible be brought to justice. Both the President and the

Prime Minister extended their sympathy and that of the nation to the Aretino family. In a statement from the Vatican, Pope John Paul II spoke of Count Federico's dedication to the faith and his tireless work for the sick as a Knight of the Order of St John.'

'I remember seeing the story on CNN back in May,' Jack said. 'Wasn't there some incredible shot of the bomb going off?'

Stella scrolled down. 'There are a couple of video files here.'

The screen of her laptop suddenly filled with the image of a serious-looking, middle-aged female anchor, who leaned aggressively towards the camera as she delivered the news with great intensity. As her report continued, the image on the television morphed to a frozen moment of horror – the instant when a ball of fiery energy blew apart the Aretino's luxury jet – and Stella was visibly shocked.

'My God,' she said, as she absorbed the bizarre contrast between the elegant coastal background and the aeroplane suspended forever at the moment of death and destruction. 'This must have been taken from a helicopter.'

'What a piece of lucky timing for the photographer.'

'A local photographer,' Stella said. 'According to the newsreader, he was in the air snapping postcard photos when this happened.'

When the clip ended, Stella replayed it and paused at the image of the bomb tearing into the plane. It was strangely compelling. Jack felt a shiver run down his spine. 'Christ, what a way to go.'

'You're right, though, it's an amazingly lucky shot.' Stella's head was tilted to one side as her eyes explored the photograph. 'It has to be a frame taken from a video, don't you think? Look at the pixelation here. It's definitely digital.'

'Surely it would have been broadcast. Footage like that would be all over the net by now.'

She made a thoughtful face. 'Not sure, entirely. But if a video sequence exists, the fact that it was never broadcast is interesting in itself. I wonder what the story is there?'

Before Jack could postulate a theory, she'd closed the file and opened another. Two younger presenters delivered a similar news broadcast but their interviewees included Victoria Cavendish, of *Peek!* magazine. On the screen, her lips moved but her words were inaudible as the male reporter paraphrased her comments.

Stella translated. 'Apparently she's talking about all the celebrities who are close to the Aretino family and speculating about who will come to the funeral.'

'Very tasteful,' Jack said, with his eyebrow raised.

'Oh, that's interesting.'

'What?'

'She's commenting on the Aretinos' financial position. Reckons they won't be able to afford a huge funeral and then she made some tacky remark about the price of new Learjets.'

'What a revolting woman.'

'She's an Aretino expert, Jack.'

He looked hard at Stella's face for a second. 'Are you suggesting we can use her?'

She leaned back on the couch. 'All I know is, as the only Italian speaker on the team, it makes sense for me to spend tomorrow working with Giorgio at the bank. That means you do all the background on the family and the Formula One team.'

'That's just how it turned out this time, partner. Can't be helped.'

'Maybe so,' Stella said, 'but if I'm going to be stuck in an airless office all day, I think it's only fair we get you and Victoria Cavendish together.'

3

'Oi, Jack, over here!'

Jack twisted his head to look, but the rows of tables arranged on the pavement in front of El Beverin were already crowded and he didn't recognise anyone. Nobody there would know him, anyway. Impeccably attired businesspeople sat at tables set with green tablecloths, shaded by huge rectangular umbrellas. Waiters in starched white jackets hurried down the rows collecting orders with practised professionalism.

'Jack Rogers!'

The female voice was louder now and several heads turned. He followed them with his eyes to the far corner of the outdoor seating area, where a woman was waving at him. That can't be Victoria Cavendish, he thought. She looks completely different. Her hair was dark instead of blonde and she looked years younger than the face he'd seen on TV. But as he moved towards her, she stood up and her hourglass figure was familiar.

She greeted him like an old friend. 'All right, Jack?' she said, her accent distinctively East London. 'I'm Vicky Cavendish, your blind date.'

He smiled and put out his hand. She took it, but then pulled him forward to plant a kiss on each cheek.

'You're in Italy now, love. It's very kissy-kissy here. Sit down, take a load off.'

Jack took the seat across from her. 'How did you know me?'

She smiled with a neat row of gleaming capped teeth. 'You're the only man here who isn't dressed like a poof. Look at 'em, in their pink shirts and designer ties. Milan must be the only town in the world where the boys care more about their looks than the girls.' She laughed loudly and earned a few annoyed glances from other tables. Lowering her voice slightly, she said, 'Just kidding. I looked you up. You're an investment banker, right? You were dating a fashion designer for a while, in New York. I found pics of you and her at a couple of shows. Nice-looking couple; very photogenic. You still together?'

Jack felt wrong-footed. 'No, I'm still based in New York. She lives in London now.'

'Single then, are you?'

He looked away. 'Yes.'

'Interesting.'

Vicky licked her lips and for a moment he felt like a cornered animal, until he was saved by the arrival of a waiter. Without looking at a menu, Vicky ordered 'the usual' in unrepentant English and the waiter seemed unfazed. Jack asked for a plate of whatever the chef recommended. A bowl of bread, cutlery and glasses were added to the table and, soon after, red wine and sparkling water arrived.

'Cheers,' Jack said, raising his wineglass, 'and thanks for seeing me at such short notice.'

Vicky waved her hand dismissively. 'I eat lunch here almost every day,' she said. 'If some handsome man wants to pay for it in exchange for a bit of gossip, I'll be there every time.'

'How long have you been living here?'

'Blimey, nearly five years. You'd think I'd be able to speak the bloody lingo better, wouldn't you?' Her breasts heaved as she laughed again.

'How does that work?' he asked, intrigued. 'How can you report for an Italian magazine if you don't speak the language?'

'I can read it and understand it perfectly well. Just can't get the bloody accent right, and the whole conjugating verbs thing. Not my forte, languages, as it turns out. Somebody at the mag fixes it all up for me.'

She smiled wistfully, but Jack's curiosity wasn't sated. 'But how on earth does a Londoner like you wind up working in Milan, of all places?'

Vicky chuckled. 'Like me? What do you mean by that?' She played with a piece of bread, apparently unsure whether she should risk eating it. 'Actually, it's not so strange. *Peek!* is owned by the same company I worked for on Fleet Street.'

Her tale was interrupted by their food, which the kitchen seemed to have churned out with remarkable speed. Jack was presented with a seared chicken breast. Vicky's choice was a piece of grilled fish, which she contemplated with little enthusiasm. 'I'm watching my weight,' she said, glumly. 'I'm doing some on-air pieces at the Grand Prix this weekend.'

'Really? I'm going to be there myself, on Friday.'

'Good for you. It's one of the hottest celebrity magnets on the calendar.'

'So that's why you came to Milan? Because it's celebrity central?'

Her bright-red lips formed a crooked smile. 'The Italians do love their star gossip, so it's a decent place for me to be, but the truth is I kinda shat in my own nest back in London.'

'Is that so? And I thought there weren't too many lines you could cross on Fleet Street these days.'

'There are some,' she said, with a twinkle in her eye, 'like when my boss's wife found out he paid for these.' She pointed at her chest with her knife. 'She seemed more upset by the tits than finding out I'd been doing her husband for years. Anyway, it was time to get out of town for a while and Milan seemed like a logical choice. I used to come here for the fashion shows every year anyway.'

She took a sip of water, leaving a lipstick stain on her glass. Then she fixed him with a quizzical look. 'You want to talk about the Aretino family, don't you? What's your interest in that lot? You keen on that skinny Laura bird, Jack? I wouldn't touch her with a barge pole, if I were you.'

'No,' he said, smiling, 'my interest is purely professional, nothing you'd find remotely interesting. There isn't a whole lot of information around about the Aretino Group. I want some insight into the key players, that's all.'

'You want to sell them something,' Vicky stated, her eyes narrowing.

'That's as good a reason as any,' he responded. 'Truth is, I'm lazy. I was looking for the fastest and simplest way to gather information on the family and somebody told me Vicky Cavendish is the undisputed expert.'

Nodding her head, she said, 'I do all the celebs, of course, but I specialise in blue bloods and politicians. They usually end up having the most spectacular falls from grace.'

'Has anything like that happened to the Aretinos?'

She dipped the piece of fish on her fork into the sauce on Jack's plate. 'They've had their ups and downs, but we should start at the beginning, don't you think? You get your notebook out, Jack, while I refill your wine glass.'

Three kilometres away, Stella was having much less fun than her partner was. She was in a sterile, air-conditioned meeting room, sitting at a wooden table spread with neat piles of documents. The remains of her lunch – simple sandwiches and bottled mineral water – were on a side table. In front of her, a computer terminal linked to the bank's mainframe seemed to radiate dry heat, while the spreadsheet on the screen of her own laptop was disturbingly incomplete.

She looked up from the document she was reading when the door opened. Giorgio Borboli was already sporting an apologetic expression, as if anticipating her dissatisfaction. 'Making any progress?'

With a sigh, she put the document down on the pile dedicated to the Aretino whitegoods division, pushed back from the table and stood up. 'Not really, Giorgio,' she said, stretching her arms as she moved to the window to observe the traffic melee below. 'We have bits and pieces of data and if I were a forensic accountant maybe, just maybe, I could construct a set of accounts for some of these businesses. But I'm not, and we need more than just the numbers, anyway.'

She strode back to the table and pointed to the spreadsheet on her computer screen. 'This is a list of the inputs we don't have.' Scrolling down, she showed her client a lengthy catalogue of omissions. 'And we need to gather this data for each part of the group, including the F1 team.'

Borboli leaned down to read the list. 'I think we will have some of this back at head office,' he said uncertainly, 'but not all of it.'

'Well, if we can't get most of it,' Stella said, 'I'm not sure we can help you. If you want our assessment of the Aretino Group, we're going to need a lot more information.'

The banker made a dismissive gesture. 'This is just your first day. I am sure we can dig up most of what you need. It may take a little time, that's all.'

'It would be much quicker,' she suggested, 'if we simply asked the Aretinos for the information.'

Borboli shook his head and smiled enigmatically. 'One step at a time, my dear.'

Jack finished his notes and put down his pen to take a drink from his wineglass. 'So you're not aware of any traditional enemies? No longstanding feuds between aristocratic clans?'

'None that I know of. If someone's out to get the Count, the motive is much more likely to be business or politics.'

'This will be helpful,' he said, flicking through the pages in his small notebook, 'when I meet them on Friday.'

'You're going to the Grand Prix with the Aretinos? You didn't mention that.'

'We'll be the guests of one of the team's sponsors.'

'We?' Vicky said, leaning closer.

'My business partner, Stella Sartori, and me.'

'Your business partner? More than just business, perhaps?'

Jack's face gave nothing away.

'Sorry,' Vicky said. 'I don't mean to pry but I can't help myself sometimes. Always tricky, mixing business and pleasure.'

'Tell me about it.'

Listen,' she added, sitting back in her seat, 'if you want to be really thorough in this little research project of yours, I reckon I've got a brilliant suggestion for you.'

Stella picked up the next document in her pile and started reading. Though she normally thrived on the details, her enthusiasm for this jumbled mess of Italian accounting and bank records was ebbing away. The second wind kickstarted by an espresso break did not last long. She thought of Jack, long-lunching at some gourmet restaurant in the heart of the old city while she was holed up in a soulless office building.

When her mobile phone rang and she saw who was calling, she smiled ruefully. Here we go, Mr Lucky is calling to rub it in. As she flipped open the phone, she stood up and moved to the window. A minor bingle below had spawned a screaming match. It was like watching reality television with the sound turned down.

'Hey there, Jack,' she said. 'Hope you're having a better day than I am. Can't wait to get out of here. How did you go with Ms Cavendish? Talk about anything interesting?'

There was a pregnant pause.

'Jack? What's wrong?'

'Nothing.' His voice sounded breathless. 'Sorry, I'm concentrating on where I'm going. I'm racing back to the apartment to pack a bag and head out to the airport. I'm hoping to make the 3.20 flight.'

'Airport?' she said, incredulous. 'What airport? The 3.20 flight to where?'

'Linate Airport,' Jack said. 'I'm going to Nice, via Paris.'

Christ, she thought, here we go again.

4

'Nuts?'

Before Jack could answer, the flight attendant placed a small packet next to the beer on his tray-table and moved on. He took a sip of the cool liquid as he reviewed his notes. Recalling some of Vicky's quotes made him smile as he glanced through his summary. 'Tosser, wanker, slut,' and, when asked, she'd assured him that she knew all the Italian equivalents.

They'd first discussed the current head of the family, Count Carlo Massimillio, though Vicky said he preferred to be known as Charles.

'They all speak English,' she'd said, 'even at home. He's married to an Austrian duchess who speaks English and not Italian, but I reckon it's also some kind of snob thing. Sets them apart from the hoi polloi.'

Under the Count's name, Jack had written: *58, rich, smart, influential, successful businessman, politically connected (Northern League), discreet (affairs suspected but no proof), married twice, religious, boring (until he bought F1 team). Dowdy, stay-at-home wife. Family villas in Venice, Mira and Milan plus property in London and*

Paris and a holiday mansion on Lake Garda. Top 5 on European rich list since brother's death.

'Serious bloke, mostly,' Vicky had said. 'Went to the best universities and was always going to be the one to take over the business side. His brother was a useless layabout in his youth, so I'm told.'

Jack flicked to the page headed 'Count Federico' and saw: *61, handsome, socialite, panty-chaser, gambler, party-goer (charities), mover and shaker in the Church but divorced first wife (childless) to marry much younger former TV presenter (mother of Stefano).*

Under Stefano's name, the notes read: *24, super playboy, tosser, aspiring car racer, friend to celebrities, dated pop stars and models, caught driving his Lambo drunk but let off.*

'I miss Stefano,' Vicky had said. 'Always bonking some new bird and buff as Brad in a swimsuit. His cousins aren't nearly as printworthy.'

Count Charles's eldest son was Giacomo, but Vicky said he answered to Jimmy. Under his name, Jack had noted: *35, born to Count's first wife (died of cancer many years ago), handsome, educated in England (LSE) and started out as stockbroker in London (Schroders?) then quit to become a priest (7 years ago), works in Rome, not seen very often.*

'He must have been working in the City about the same time as me,' Jack had said.

'Not quite so successfully, would be my guess. His younger brother is the golden-haired boy of business, hand-picked by Daddy to join him in the company while Jimmy was packed off to the seminary.'

Jimmy's younger brother was Alessandro, or Alex, and he was the eldest child of the Austrian Countess. The notes read: *33, fit, obnoxious, bit of a lad in his youth but got serious at uni (Harvard), business-focused but seen at A-list events and holidays at the best resorts, linked to Spanish movie star but regularly spotted with other women.*

Jack felt he already had some insights into the youngest sibling, Laura, and his notes only seemed to confirm them: *29, university dropout, party girl, two stints in rehab, clubber, likes older men.*

'Wasn't she linked to some shady character?' Jack had asked. 'I think he owns nightclubs or something.'

Vicky had just snorted. 'Which one? Truth is, Laura'll throw her leg over any old geezer, so long as he's got access to the good stuff.' She'd tapped her nose and winked. 'There were some raunchy snaps of her last summer with Ricardo Ponti, who's supposedly linked to the Mafia. But who the hell isn't in this country, I ask you? Since then, she's been pretty quiet. Actually, she's been out of the spotlight for months. Maybe you'll see her on Friday. Let me know if you do, would you?'

When they'd exhausted the gossip on individual family members, Jack had prodded her for business or financial scuttlebutt.

'I'm no expert,' she'd said. 'I do know it's been a tough couple of years, like it has been for everybody here. And our boys in sports reckon the Aretino racing team has been sucking money like a Russian whore. Rumour is, the Count's put some of the family's prize possessions up for sale. Vineyards, villas, classic cars, art, stuff they've owned for centuries. The man is clearly feeling the pinch.'

Jack had noted it all down. 'Any obvious enemies?'

'Only about a hundred business and political rivals, neighbouring landowners, cuckolded husbands, plus all the anarchists, communists, anti-royalists and sundry nutters this country seems to cough up. Oh yeah, and then there's the geezer who blew up his plane.'

And it was on the subject of the bombing that Vicky had offered her research suggestion. 'I've seen footage of the plane blowing up,' she'd said, quietly for once. 'The whole thing.'

'Stella suspected the image on the news was taken from a video.'

'Clever girl. Like half the publishing and broadcasting world, we tried to buy the footage, but the photographer had already sold it.'

'The photographer based in Nice.'

'Very good. Marcel Ganet.'

'Who'd he sell it to?'

'He wouldn't say. Part of the deal was absolute secrecy. He's just a provincial photographer doing weddings and the occasional postcard.'

'But you proved persistent.'

Vicky had adopted a satisfied smirk. 'I tracked down the pilot of the helicopter, who coughed up the truth for a few euros. When I confronted Ganet, he admitted taking the footage but claimed to have sold all the copies to a friend of the Aretino family who wanted to keep it out of the press.'

'And you believed him?'

'Well, the film never turned up, so part of the story is true, I suppose. But I didn't believe a bloke like that wouldn't keep a copy of the clip that made him a rich man.'

'And so you wore him down.'

'Yeah. It cost me a skinful of booze and a few quid, and I had to promise that I wouldn't let on to anyone. By then I just wanted to see it, even if we couldn't print it.'

'And was it worth it?'

'Christ, yes. It's spectacular, in a gruesome sort of way.'

'And you think he'll show it to me, too?'

'I have no idea,' she'd said, 'but it's been months and you're not looking to publish it, are you? He might be prepared to share for a small consideration.'

'Thanks, Vicky. I'll give him a call.'

'Back in May he had the world chasing him. You won't get

anywhere with a phone call – he's used to putting up the defences. A personal approach would be best, I'd say.'

Jack had hesitated.

'It's bugged me ever since,' Vicky had said, thoughtfully. 'Maybe the guy who bought the film was a good friend to the Aretinos, like he said. An honest man protecting the privacy of a noble family. On the other hand, the person who had the most to lose from that video was probably the scumbag who ordered the hit, wouldn't you say? In case it gave something away?'

Instantly, Jack had known he had to go. As the aircraft began its descent towards the French capital en route to Nice, he closed his notepad and looked out the window, resting his head on the plastic surround. In the distance, the Eiffel Tower was thrusting itself upwards with romantic arrogance and his mind suddenly filled with a vivid memory of a cool, sunny afternoon on the banks of the Seine. He was strolling with Stella in the shadow of Notre Dame, walking off a delicious lunch and chatting about the prospects for their new business. She was enthusiastic and excited. He was as content as he'd ever felt in his life. The future had seemed certain, and it was looking perfect.

Yeah right, he thought angrily, turning his head away from the window. Such reminiscences were still painful, though more than seven months had passed since that one and only romantic tryst with Stella. He preferred to block it out, not yet capable of thinking it all through rationally without falling victim to bitterness and embarrassment. And Vicky Cavendish hadn't helped, determined as she was to probe the hurt she'd somehow sensed in his psyche.

'I'd venture to guess you're not happy being single,' she'd said over coffee. 'Am I right? Does it have something to do with this business partner of yours? What was her name?'

'Stella,' he'd said, trying to keep his expression impassive.

But she'd seen something else in his eyes. 'You wince every time she's mentioned.'

'No, I don't!'

'Relax,' she'd said, briefly touching her hand to his. 'You should talk to me. I know about relationships. I can help.'

'I don't need help. And my love life is —'

'None of my business?'

'Not very interesting.'

'I wouldn't say that. I know for a fact that twelve months ago you were with that American designer and working for a bank on Wall Street. A few months later you've dumped the Yank and started a new business with a new chick. When did you first meet her?'

'It's been nearly a year now,' he'd said, reluctantly.

'And is she the reason you broke up with the other one?'

'No. Well, not exactly.'

'Not exactly,' she'd repeated, obviously intrigued. 'So how long was there between the last relationship and Stella?'

'Who says there was a relationship with Stella?' Jack had said stonily.

'I do. I'm guessing you bonked her and then decided to go into business with her. Then something went sour, right? On the personal front? Now you regret the whole thing.'

'That's not true,' he'd said, his cheeks heating up. 'We work very well together. I love the business we've started. We're going to do great things together.'

'But it's all work and no play now, isn't it? And that's not how you'd like it to be.'

He'd said nothing, but had felt his mouth tightening and Vicky read him easily. 'What happened?' she'd asked, watching his face intently. 'What did you do to screw it all up? You pushed too hard, didn't you? Typical man. You got a picture in your head of the perfect life with her and didn't stop to ask yourself whether she wanted the same thing.'

He'd given her a tight smile, hoping she'd leave it there. But she'd smelt blood in the water. 'Christ, Jack, what did you do?'

He'd had enough. Spotting a waiter a few tables away, he'd caught his eye and called out, 'Cheque, please!' Then he'd raised the last of the wine in his glass and said, 'Thanks, Vicky. It's been fun.'

5

After the crowded revelry in the narrow lanes of Nice's old town, Rue Cassini felt oddly wide and eerily quiet. The tourists did not venture this far after sunset. Jack was disappointed – he was hoping Marcel Ganet's studio would keep late hours during the summer season but this street of mostly residential apartments, with a few shops aimed at the locals, was locked up tight by nine p.m.

The dark thoroughfare sloped down towards the port and rows of masts bobbed in the distance. At the bottom of the hill Jack saw the familiar logo of the Kodak Company on a faded sign to his right. The glass windows of Ganet's shop exhibited samples of the man's work, including two weddings, three family portraits and a christening. The entrance itself was blocked by a metal security shutter.

Jack stepped back to look at the adjacent buildings and saw several levels of apartments above the shop, their windows hidden behind worn wooden shutters. The entrance was through a recessed door to the right of the studio, adjacent to a tarnished brass intercom panel. Next to one of the buttons, he found the name Ganet and pressed. When there was no answer, he tried again. No response.

With his stomach growling for food and his mouth anticipating a cold beer, he resolved to return in the morning. Turning away from the intercom to step back out into the street, he almost stumbled over the front wheel of a stroller being pushed into the doorway by a teenage boy.

'Sorry, pal, didn't see you there,' Jack said, reaching out an arm to steady himself.

The boy pulled the stroller back and mumbled an apology in French. In the stroller, Jack saw the sleeping face of a toddler. Their mother was still a few metres away, plodding up the slope from the port. With one hand she held a baby to her hip and with the other she carried several weighty shopping bags. In the weak light of the streetlamp, he could see that her face was worn.

Jack stepped aside as she trudged into the doorway and dropped her shopping bags on the pavement. With her free hand she reached into the pocket of her jacket for a set of keys.

'*Ici c'est la maison de Marcel Ganet?*' Jack said, taking a punt.

She looked at him as if he'd appeared from thin air. '*Oui. Je suis sa femme.*'

With hope in his voice, he said, '*Parlez-vous anglais?*'

'*Non,*' she said, turning her attention back to the lock, but as she pushed the door open she asked a question and Jack heard her say 'Aretino'.

Before Jack could answer, the teenager spoke. 'She asked if you are here about the Aretino tragedy.'

Jack turned to the boy. 'You speak English?'

'Yeah, pretty much.' The kid had a distinct American twang.

'What's your name?'

'Louis.'

'I'm Jack. Good to meet you. Please tell your mother the answer is yes, I'm here to talk to your father about his footage of the plane.'

'There is no footage,' Louis said, 'only one shot.'

'I know that's not true. I suspect you do too.'

Louis gave him a long look and then had an exchange with his mother. 'She wants you to come up.'

'Thank you.' Jack reached down to pick up the shopping bags before Madame Ganet changed her mind.

'How old are you?' Jack asked Louis as he led the way up the steep wooden staircase.

'Fourteen.'

'How come you speak such good English?'

'I watch a lot of movies and I chat on the net. In the summer, half the people in Nice speak only English.'

'But not your mother.'

'No. Well, she can speak a little, but she's not very happy with the Americans right now, so it's kind of a protest.'

'Because of Iraq?'

'Yeah, and they said some bad stuff about France.'

'I'm not American,' Jack said. 'I live there, but I'm Australian.'

'But your government still supports Bush and is sending in troops.'

'You're very well informed.'

Louis's narrow shoulders shrugged. 'My parents talk about it all the time.'

'Where's your dad tonight?'

'Out.'

The boy's tone suggested a nerve had been touched so Jack stopped talking until they'd climbed to the second floor, where the door to the front apartment hung open. Leaving the stroller at the entrance, Louis led the way down a dim hallway and through a neatly kept living room to an old-fashioned but clean kitchen. Following the boy's example, Jack put his shopping bags down on the central table. Madame Ganet came into the room, still carrying the baby.

She tore a blank sheet from a pad by the phone and put it on the table in front of Jack, next to a pen.

'She wants you to write down your name and the name of the company you work for,' Louis said. 'She's done this with all the other reporters and agents who've come knocking. She will give it to my father.'

Jack printed his name and his hotel on the paper and added a business card from his wallet. 'I'm not in the same business as the people who came earlier. I have no interest in publishing the pictures or the film.'

'Write that down, too,' Louis suggested.

'I'd really like to speak to your dad, if I could.'

Madame Ganet took the note and Jack's card and put them in her pocket without looking. Louis was climbing onto a stool to reach the high shelves in the pantry and asked Jack to pass up a shopping bag. His mother was speaking rapid French again and appeared to be holding out the baby for her son to take.

Louis muttered a few grumpy words for her benefit then switched to English. 'Would you mind holding Simone while my mother puts Michelle to bed?' he said, a jar of artichokes in each hand. 'I can do it if you don't want to.'

'No, I'll do it,' Jack said, offering the overworked mother a smile he hoped did not look as forced as it felt. He held out his hands to take the child but she hesitated and looked hard into his eyes before passing her daughter across.

'*Bonsoir,*' he said, in his best cutesy voice as he held the baby out in front of him. The infant's wide-eyed response could be interpreted as almost anything, including fear, so Jack pulled her to his shoulder and bounced up and down on the spot. Madame Ganet watched him with hawk eyes for a few seconds before leaving the room, which did nothing to improve his nerves.

'Don't cry, don't cry,' he pleaded quietly into the baby's ear but it seemed unnecessary, as she gurgled and cooed while exploring his ear with tiny fingers. Relieved, he continued flexing his knees with a steady rhythm while he waited for his shift to end. The next five minutes seemed interminable and when Madame Ganet returned to the kitchen, he moved to hand over the baby. But before he could, the infant rewarded his solicitous care by vomiting onto his shoulder and down his back.

Madame Ganet rushed forward, clearly embarrassed, and whisked the baby out of his arms. Jack held up his hands to indicate no harm was done, though the baby's dinner had quickly soaked through his thin shirt and was unpleasantly warm on his skin. He swallowed hard and helped himself to a wet cloth from the sink.

A smiling Louis grabbed another and helped pat down the shirt. 'My mother says you shouldn't have bounced her up and down so much,' he said. 'Sometimes it makes her hurl.'

Jack found himself chuckling and said, 'You can probably tell, babies terrify me.'

Louis laughed too and his mother joined in as the tension broke. The brief moment of merriment took years from her face and Jack glimpsed the thirty-year-old beauty she might have been in different circumstances. She indicated that he should sit down at the table and, without asking, took a bottle of beer from the refrigerator and placed it in front of him. While he savoured the cool ale and the almost instant buzz from drinking on an empty stomach, she did a more thorough job of removing the stain from his shirt.

Louis sat at the table too, baby Simone on his lap and a glass of Coke in front of him. He was staring at Jack. 'If you're not in the publishing business,' he said, 'what do you want with the Aretino film? Are you a policeman?'

Jack hesitated. 'No, more like an investigator. I'm a business consultant.'

Louis turned to his mother and had a conversation in French. She asked a number of questions and he responded.

At last, Louis switched back to English. 'Okay,' he said happily, 'we can go.'

'Go where?'

The boy stood up. 'I will take you to my father.'

6

'I should warn you,' Louis said to Jack as they walked side by side, 'he might be drunk.'

They were retracing the route Jack had taken from his hotel, heading back to the noise and lights of the old town party district.

'Oh, right. Is he celebrating something?'

'No, the opposite. He and my mother are having a huge fight. We spent the last two days with my grandparents in Marseilles and just got back tonight. My father thinks we're still away. They haven't been talking.'

'None of my business,' Jack said.

'No, but it has to do with that video.'

'The sudden arrival of big money often causes family trouble. I'm sure they'll sort it out.'

'Yes, I think so too,' Louis said with confidence. 'She came back, didn't she? Soon she'll be ready to forgive him, but I don't know if she'll let him keep the yacht.'

'Yacht?'

The teenager flashed a grin. 'Yeah, first my mother got mad

because she thought he'd sold the Aretino film for too little. Some of the photo agencies and reporters who turned up later offered heaps more. She wanted to put it all in a fund for our education and stuff. Then she found out Papa kept back 200 000 and bought a yacht with it. He's always wanted a nice boat.'

Jack whistled. 'I can see why your mum was upset.'

'I know. The worst thing is, he bought the boat two months ago but she only found out last week. I hope he gets to keep it,' the boy said wistfully. 'It's a beautiful boat.'

'You only talked your way into escorting me so you could see him, didn't you?'

Louis's look was unapologetic. 'I just want to see he's okay and tell him we're home.'

'If you've been away,' Jack asked, raising his voice over the hubbub, 'how do you know where to find him?'

'He only goes to one place.'

Around several corners and down a quieter alley, they came to an establishment so quintessentially French it scared off all but the bravest tourists. Heavy wooden furniture was out on the pavement, and wide arches in pink stucco led to a dark, atmospheric interior.

As soon as they passed under the arches Louis headed towards a table in the rear where a thin, unshaven man with dark hair was sitting alone, his feet resting on a chair. When he saw the boy approaching his face lit up and his arms flew wide as he stood up to hug his son tightly.

Jack slowed his approach to allow them time to reconnect. After a frenetic exchange of news, Louis disentangled himself from his father's arms and waved Jack over. As he made the introductions, Marcel Ganet stuck out his hand and said in clumsy English, 'You help my wife. Thank you.'

Close up, his inebriation was obvious. His eyes, teary from the joy

41

of reunion, were unsettled and unfocused. His body swayed slowly on shaky legs and as soon as he'd given Jack's hand a perfunctory shake he plopped back down in his seat and took a long drink from a straight-sided glass half-filled with a cloudy liquid.

'Sit, sit,' he said, and Jack took a chair

Louis said, 'My mother said I must come straight home, so I'll say goodbye now.'

Jack stuck out his hand. 'Thanks for all your help.'

The teenager's handshake was far more convincing than his father's. 'Please, Mr Rogers,' he said quietly, 'I know it is not fair to ask, but if my father gets too drunk . . .'

'You want me to see him home? I can do that.'

Louis smiled gratefully. 'Thanks. Sometimes, on nights like this, he ends up in the police cells.'

With a last kiss for his father, the boy disappeared back into the street and Jack was left facing the drunken photographer. 'I need food and drink,' he said.

Ganet clearly approved, because he grinned lopsidedly and pulled himself up in his chair to call for service. Soon Jack had a generous bowl of steamed mussels in front of him, accompanied by a basket of crisp, thick fries. Crusty bread and a tall glass of tap beer arrived too, along with a fresh Pernod and a beer chaser for Ganet.

'Food here very good, yes?' Ganet said with an encouraging smile as he watched Jack tuck in.

'Very good, yes.'

After a long pause, the Frenchman said, 'My wife, she look okay?'

Jack looked up to see anguish in the man's eyes. 'She looks tired,' he said carefully, 'but she's fine, I think. She's back home now – you should go to her. I can meet you tomorrow, if you like.'

Ganet shook his head emphatically and took a long drink. 'I must have more courage before I face her. Very angry with me, she is. Very angry.' With shaking fingers, he fumbled with a cigarette packet and offered one to Jack, who shook his head. Lighting the smoke, he said, 'I have a new boat.'

'Yes, your son was —'

'I call the boat *Marie*, for my wife, but she does not like the sea. I say, "We live by the sea, why not have a boat?" She say, "Only the future of the children is important." I say, "Children who live in Nice should learn to sail on the sea."'

A long drag on the cigarette was washed down by the last of his drink and he waved for another. 'It was only good chance I photograph the Aretino tragedy, you know? Like winning the lotto. If you win the lotto, you can provide for family, yes, sure, but you can also have some good times, no? My wife, she does not believe in good times.'

Jack felt uncomfortable in the role of counsellor. 'I'm sure you'll work something out.'

'No! Because already I must have money for fixing the boat.'

'How much money do you need?'

Ganet shook his head sadly. 'I have nothing to sell you.'

'What about the film of the Aretino jet?'

'No, no, there is no film. Only one photo.'

'You bought your lovely yacht for the price of one photograph?' The logic seemed to astonish Ganet, whose mouth fell open.

'Look,' Jack said, 'I know for a fact you've given private viewings of the film to discreet people for a reasonable fee. I don't want to publish the footage, just see if I can learn anything from watching it a few times. Of course, I'd pay extra to take a copy with me.'

'Okay, okay,' Ganet said, grinning crookedly, 'you catch me out. It is true, I make a film. But it is sold already, exclusive rights. I cannot sell it again.'

'Who bought it?'

'I cannot say. A friend to the Aretino family.'

'How can you be so sure?'

'He show me photos, him with Count Carlo Aretino and his brother, wearing the same, how you say, uniform. He tells me he is very close to the family. Old, old friends.'

'Photos can easily be faked.'

'This is my profession. The photos were genuine.'

'Nothing else you can tell me about him?'

'Nothing.'

Ganet's tone was emphatic, so Jack paused to dip his last chip in the salty, delicious soup at the bottom of his bowl. 'I'd really like to take a look at your yacht,' he said. 'I've done a bit of sailing in my day, mostly around Sydney Harbour. Perhaps you could give me a tour tomorrow.'

'She is very beautiful,' Ganet mumbled, steadying himself by gripping hard on the table. 'But tomorrow I must go to Cannes all day. Big wedding, good job.'

'In the evening, then? You could show me what needs to be done on the boat, and if you brought along a copy of the film, I could take a look and give you something towards the upgrades. I can bring my computer, so you just need to bring the footage.'

'I show you my boat,' Ganet slurred. 'She is very beautiful.'

'Yeah, you mentioned.' Jack was tempted to give the guy a gentle slap on the face to get his attention back. 'What about the film – will you bring it along?'

'Very beautiful.'

'Marcel? Are you listening? What about the film?'

But Marcel Ganet was beyond answering.

7

A little before noon the next day, Prinz Gerhard Wilhelm Otto von Hirschberg und Mindelheim was sitting behind the wheel of his pride and joy, a metallic grey Bentley Continental GT. With an emotion akin to genuine affection, he stroked the armrest crafted from the finest hand-tooled wood and leather. Of all the things he could no longer afford, this was his favourite. Well, this and his luxury cruising yacht. He'd given up everything else, including his business, his home and his family, but there was nothing to compare to the feeling of slipping behind the wheel of this beauty.

In his mirrors, he watched for the arrival of the man who was helping reverse the downward spiral of his life. Kurt Bauer was the only good thing to come from his association with the Eastern European scum who'd cheated him out of his company. Soon he would buy back his family lands and regain control of his business. Soon he'd be able to pay cash for new, even more outrageous and luxurious toys.

The powerful car was parked in a suburban street to the north of Milan and the area was quiet, now that schools were back in session. A navy BMW M5 pulled in behind the Bentley. The driver's door opened and a lean, bearded man in his early thirties exited and walked immediately to the passenger side of the Bentley. Once in the car, he closed the heavy door with a deep thud and all external noise was blocked. The two men did not shake hands but there was an air of familiar ease between them.

'Are you ready for Paris?' the prince asked in German. 'This could be our last chance.'

The blonde man nodded and answered in the same language. 'Yes, I'm ready. But if you still insist it has to be done cleanly . . .'

'It must be done, one way or the other. The cleaner, the better.'

'And Friday? Did you talk to your partner about that? I'm still not comfortable.'

The prince shook his head. 'He's insisting it's critical to our success. It gets done or we don't proceed.'

'I still don't understand the reasoning. It seems like such a high risk.'

'It's not your job to understand the reasoning. You said it was the best time to do it.'

'From a practical perspective, yes. Doesn't mean it's the smart thing to do.'

'Can you handle it or not?'

Bauer cracked the knuckles of his left hand. 'Yes, I'll take care of it. But I'll want a double fee for that one.'

'No problem,' the prince said, casually, 'but you know all these fees of yours will be nothing compared to your share.'

'Only if we're successful.'

'That's up to us, isn't it?'

'Which is why we shouldn't take any stupid risks. There's too much at stake.'

Prinz Gerhard thumped the steering room angrily. 'You don't have to tell me what's at stake.'

'Take it easy,' Bauer said. 'I said I'd take care of it.'

'All right, all right.' The prince took two deep breaths. 'I'm tense. I can't wait for the next week to be over.'

Bauer shook his head irritably. 'Think about what I've got to do in the next ten days. The hard part's over for you, isn't it? Don't you have the box already?'

'Yes, but we still have to get it out of Europe.'

'Have you looked inside?'

'You know I can't. It's secure and masked against X-rays. It can't be opened until we get it to America.'

'You're very trusting. Maybe that's what's worrying you,' Bauer said.

'Goddammit, it's not that. I saw a selection, and I saw the coffins. Now, when are you going to Andorra?'

'Sunday.'

'No pre-planning?' the prince asked.

'It's done.'

'So you have some time.'

'What do you need?'

The prince smiled. 'Remember that photographer in France, the one who filmed your handiwork?'

'What about him?'

'I have an arrangement with his wife. She calls me with the details of anyone asking about the film and I give her a few euros for her trouble.'

'Generous soul, aren't you? When it's not coming out of your own pocket.'

The prince ignored the barb. 'She hasn't called me for months, and every other time it's been about journalists or photo agencies.'

'Do they get anywhere with their cheque books?'

'No. So far Ganet's been reliable and, according to his wife, he still claims he gave me every copy. But she doesn't sound sure to me and someone new is stiffing around. This guy's not buying the story about the still and he claims he doesn't want to publish. According to his business card, he's a management consultant. Why would a guy like that want the film, and why would he want it right now, at such a critical time?'

'Sounds fishy.'

'His name is Jack Rogers and he's staying at the Four Points Hotel in Nice. His business address is in New York.'

'An American? I wonder what his interest is?'

'I don't know and I don't really care. All I know is, we can't risk attracting unnecessary attention.'

'I can be in Nice in three or four hours. You want me to take care of him?'

The prince put his hands on the steering wheel and savoured the feeling of quality under his fingers. 'If it can be done without attracting attention,' he said, 'I think both of them should go away.'

8

The warmth of the midday sun was tempered by a light breeze coming over the water. Under his towel, rounded stones pushed into Jack's back and he quickly understood why many of the wealthier tourists paid for a padded day bed in one of the roped-off sections of the beach. Nice was a very un-Australian seaside experience but he tried to relax and enjoy the heat on his skin.

He'd allowed himself a sleep-in that morning. Though he was willing to bet his hangover wasn't even close to Marcel Ganet's, it was enough to warrant two Advil, three bottles of minibar water and a few extra hours of bed time. A run along the great sweep of the Promenade des Anglais had woken him up while leaching the last of the alcohol from his system. When he reached a point along the bay where the reclaimed land of Nice's airport came into clear view, he'd stopped to contemplate the spot in the sky where the last Count and Countess Aretino had died, along with their heir and their staff. And while staring out across a sea that seemed impossibly blue, he sensed a presence closing up on him from behind.

'The jet came down there,' a familiar voice said, 'half in the water and half on the ground. The wreckage could be seen for days after the bombing and stuff was floating up on the beach for a long time after.'

Jack spun around. 'Louis! What are you doing here?'

Louis Ganet was sitting on a bicycle, one foot on the pavement. 'My school is just over there,' he said, gesturing with a thumb over one shoulder.

Glancing at his watch, Jack said, 'Running a bit late?'

'Double English this morning. The teacher prefers it when I don't come, because he hates it when I correct him.'

Jack smiled and looked back out to the airport. The view was strangely moving. Knowing a little more about the people who'd perished that day made it feel more real. 'What do the locals say about it?' he asked Louis. 'Are there any good theories?'

'Everybody in town has a theory. Al-Qaeda, Red Brigade, a rival company or Formula One team. A family feud, maybe. Who knows?'

'You've been following the story?'

'Sure I have. It changed our lives completely. Soon we'll moving out of our apartment and into a new air-conditioned place, and all of a sudden my mother wants me to go to university, maybe in Paris, even.'

'And you have a yacht,' Jack said, with raised eyebrows.

'Right,' Louis replied dourly. 'For the moment, anyway. And all because seven strangers were blown to pieces while my father captured it on film. It's pretty fucked up, isn't it?'

'You know anything about the guy who bought the film?'

Louis shook his head. 'I only know the cheque cleared. And my parents have been fighting ever since.'

'Give them a bit of time.'

'I will. And thank you for getting my father home safely last night.'

'No worries. I had to stop him from taking a swing at some Spanish guys.'

Louis smiled. 'It was good to see him at the breakfast table this morning rather than at the police.'

'He agreed to show me around the yacht after dinner tonight. You think he remembers that?'

'Yeah, he mentioned it this morning. He'll be there from about eight. I'll remind him if he forgets.'

'Thanks, I appreciate it.'

'That's okay,' Louis said, straightening up his bike. 'You want my suggestion for what you should do next?'

'Sure,' Jack said. 'A tip from a local is always welcome.'

'Get some sun,' Louis said, with a cheeky smirk. 'You look like a tourist.'

Offensive, perhaps, but Jack had decided it was good advice nonetheless. After buying a swimsuit from a boutique close to the waterfront, he'd found this spot on the pebbles and laid out a towel borrowed from the hotel. Overlooked by the wedding-cake Victorian architecture along the front, and surrounded by couples and flirting teenagers, it was difficult to ignore the romance in the air. His thoughts turned to Stella. He wondered what she was doing now.

Stop it, he told himself angrily, fixing his eyes on a passing bikini-clad bottom to derail his train of thought. It didn't work. It annoyed him that he still couldn't break the nexus between every sensuous notion and his business partner. Would he spend the rest of his life comparing women to Stella? How long would it take to think of her in a purely professional capacity?

Despite his best efforts, and not for the first time, he found himself reviewing a grim litany of wrong moves over the last twelve months. The first had come very soon after he'd hooked up with Stella. Her marriage of a dozen years had just come to a tragic end. His relationship of nearly eight was self-destructing. The circumstances were intense. They'd formed an instant bond, on both a business and intimately personal level. He needed a place to live. She invited him to stay with her. Wrong move number one.

He'd been smart enough to realise it was too much too soon for Stella. Once they'd decided to launch their new firm, her single-minded focus on making it a success had clashed with his desire for domestic bliss. He moved out to a rented apartment across town. The Stack Partnership won its first job and Stella was delighted. And although she often expressed concern about mixing business with pleasure, he never took it too seriously. It certainly wasn't an issue for him. The first job went well and it led to another. Then they had a break and he surprised her with the trip to Paris. He'd sensed her initial reluctance, but managed to convince her the paperwork and marketing could wait. She relented and they'd shared a blissful week in the city of lovers. And while there, he'd concluded that the only barrier to continuing that bliss in New York was real estate. He had to get her out of the apartment she'd shared with her husband.

In his mind's eye, he was suddenly back on Greene Street, in downtown Manhattan, standing outside the elegantly columned, five-storey cast-iron facade of number 103. Stella was next to him, a bemused look on her face. He pointed out the cool features of the street, from the chic clothing and interior-design boutiques to the cosy, quiet ambience and the tightly packed cobblestone paving of the roadway.

Now he was upstairs, in the spacious, open-plan condominium on the top floor that had been renovated to the peak of sophistication. He was drawing Stella's attention to the four-metre ceilings and the abundant natural light but her face was still not showing any of the pleasure or delight he was hoping for.

'Are you suggesting this could be the head office of the Stack Partnership?' she said. 'It's beautiful, but it's a little large, don't you think? We're just two people.'

'No,' he said, his mouth dry. 'Actually, I thought it would be a nice place to live.'

At once, he could see this was not the answer she was hoping for. 'You mean for us to live in together?'

'Yes.'

She turned away and her tone was a degree cooler. 'Didn't you think it might have been wise to talk to me about it first?'

'I thought if you saw the place, you'd love it just as much as I do. I had to act quickly – these places don't come up very often.'

'How much is the rent?'

'See?' he said. 'This is why I didn't discuss it with you first. You can rationalise any idea away. The cost isn't the issue; we can afford it.'

'How much is the rent?' she repeated.

'It's not for rent.'

'You want to buy it?' Her astonishment hit him in the gut and his eyes gave him away. 'Oh shit, Jack, don't tell me you bought it already.'

Now he was feeling a little nauseous. This was not how it was supposed to go.

Without his wanting it to, his tone turned defensive. 'The amount isn't important. It's a good price for a place like this in this location.'

Her eyes narrowed, as if she were seeing him for the very first time. 'And you're sure our business is going to be successful enough to support a gargantuan mortgage like that?'

'Oh, there's no mortgage,' he said, cheered by the fact that her concerns seemed to centre on the money. 'I paid cash.'

'You paid cash,' she repeated, as though he'd just confessed to a mortal sin.

'That's right.'

She turned away to lean exhaustedly against the granite top of the island bench in the stunning kitchen. 'I thought we agreed to take things slowly.'

'I want to live with you, Stella,' Jack said. 'Partners in business and partners in life. Isn't that what you want too?'

There was a long, painful pause. 'I'm not sure,' she said, and he felt the bottom fall out of his stomach. 'I thought I did, some time in the future maybe, but I'm not sure I know you well enough yet. And until the business is established, it's out of the question. You're going to have to take a step back, Jack. Can you do that, or should we call it quits?'

Jack opened his eyes to bright sunlight bouncing over the rocky beach. He heard gentle sounds from every direction: diminutive waves lapping on the shore; the laughter of children and the happy conversations of their parents; seagulls begging for food. Taking a step back hadn't been easy but a three-month assignment to evaluate a concrete company in Ohio had helped. They'd worked hard, impressed their client and stayed in separate hotel rooms. He'd salved his bruised ego by paying more notice to the women who regularly preened for his benefit and concentrated on impressing Stella by exceeding her expectations as a salesman and analyst.

He rolled onto his right side to change the angle of the sun's attack and found that his view had changed. A young woman in a purple bikini was lying barely a metre away, a novel open on the towel in front of her. Her dark-toned body was lean but shapely, and her eyes were sparkling as they ran up and down his form. Jack smiled and pushed his sunglasses up to his forehead. Being single wasn't all bad.

'Hello,' he said, 'my name's Jack. What's yours?'

Jack woke to feel a hand exploring his nakedness under the sheet.

'I want you inside me again,' she whispered into his ear, before teasing it with her tongue. Her Spanish accent made it sound extra sexy.

He shifted in the bed to reach for her perfectly shaped thigh and noticed the sky outside the window was already dark. 'Bloody hell,' he said, sleepily. 'What time is it?'

She whispered sensuously, 'I don't care.'

Her hand was achieving the desired result but he was now reaching for his watch on the nightstand. 'Damn it. I have to get going.'

'No, please,' the woman said urgently. 'We can be quick.'

'Sorry, Maria, I don't mean to be rude but —'

A scratching noise at the door made him freeze, halfway out of the bed. Somebody was trying to get into his room, ignoring the Do Not Disturb sign. His eyes flew across the floor, looking amongst the scattered clothing for a pair of shorts or something else. But it was too late. The door flew open and a shadow filled the space.

9

'Jesus, Jack! What the hell are you still doing here?'

She was backlit by the bright lights of the hallway and for an instant, Jack didn't recognise her. 'Shit, Stella,' he said, 'you scared the shit out of me!'

She stepped into the room and immediately flicked on the lights. Her gaze moved from his nakedness to the bed, where a wide-eyed Maria was holding the sheet to her chest. A momentary flash of pain crossed her face and Jack felt a mixture of guilt and satisfaction. But then it was gone and she locked her eyes to his.

'Your message said you were meeting Ganet at eight,' she said coldly.

'It was more casual than that,' Jack said, pulling up his boxers. 'Anytime after eight, he said. He'll be on his boat for a couple of hours. What are you doing here?'

'I did try to call.'

'I didn't hear it.'

'I wonder why.' She glanced across at the terror-struck figure sitting in his bed. 'It's okay,' she said, 'I'm not his wife.'

Maria looked relieved and she smiled meekly before wrapping herself in the sheet, gathering up her clothes and scurrying into the bathroom.

'How old is she?' Stella asked stiffly when the door had closed.

'Twenty-four,' Jack said. 'Very energetic.'

'Spare me the details. You want to put on some clothes, please?'

'What are you doing here?' he repeated, taking a pair of jeans from the back of a chair.

'Working, which is what I thought you were doing.'

'You don't think I can get Ganet to show me the film?'

'On the contrary, I had every faith in your success,' she said evenly. 'Which is why I thought it would be good to join you. Four eyes are better than two, if we're looking for small details. But the traffic was terrible, so I thought I'd missed the meeting, and when I crossed the border my mobile stopped working for some reason, so I decided to come to your hotel and call you from here.'

'You drove?'

'Yeah, I hired a car for the week. I thought it'd be handy for getting around Milan and for our trip on Saturday. And, if you add waiting time, it's quicker to drive to Nice than to fly.'

Jack made an ironic gesture to his own reflection in the window as he pulled on a polo shirt. Of course she would know that. 'Great,' he said, 'we can drive back together. Maybe we can pop down into Monaco so I can zip around the F1 circuit a couple of times. I've always wanted to do that. Or would that be considered too frivolous?'

She was still standing by the door, looking impatient. 'I'm sure we can call it research. At the rate Giorgio's team are coughing up information, we should have plenty of time.'

'It didn't go so well today?'

'I've exhausted all the useful data on their system. Now they're poring through the archives in Padua to see what else they can dig up. I think our best chance is to make a good impression with Count Aretino on Friday. We can show Giorgio how simple it would be to build a relationship with his client.'

'Sure,' Jack said, unable to suppress a smile at the thought of the Grand Prix.

Stella raised an eyebrow. 'We're not going to the race to watch the pretty cars go round. We're going there to gather as much intel as we can, and to build a relationship with the family.'

'But surely some interest in the racing will be appropriate, if only to maintain our cover and build rapport.'

She granted him a smile. 'You're incorrigible, Jack.'

As if to underline the point, Maria appeared from the bathroom, wearing a lightweight dress over her bikini. She slipped on gold sandals and picked up her beach bag, then walked over to Jack and kissed him quickly on the lips while stuffing a piece of paper into his hand. With a sheepish smile in Stella's direction, she muttered polite goodbyes and slid out of the door.

Jack moved to the desk to pack up his laptop, as if nothing unusual had happened. 'How did you get a key to my room?'

'It wasn't too hard,' Stella said. 'Knowing a lot about you helped.'

'Were you planning to stay with me?'

'I hadn't thought about it. Depending on what we find out tonight, I thought we might want to head straight back to Milan. I'm sure I can get another room, if necessary.'

'It's okay,' he said. 'We can share. I can handle it.'

She regarded the dishevelled bed with a dubious expression. 'No, thanks.'

It was already close to nine, so Jack asked the doorman to hail a cab. They were driven along the full curve of the Promenade des Anglais as it climbed to the dramatic point at its eastern end. At the base of the bluff was an immense war memorial carved into the rock itself, which came into view as the cab rounded the point and descended towards the old port.

Rows of yachts and cruisers and other watercraft – ranging from the modest to the gaudy – were tied up to long finger jetties extending into the rectangular harbour. Jack told the driver he wanted marina C, on the far side of the port, where a wide cobbled band of road and footpath separated the water from the buildings. The area appeared to be largely deserted. Parked cars, shuttered windows and closed businesses were the only things visible on the landward side as the taxi pulled away.

A breeze from the water made Stella shiver. 'Not so romantic here, is it?'

'It's eerie when you're used to the crowds around the hotels. Come on.'

He led the way down some stone steps to a metal gate marked with a large letter 'C'. The gate was propped open by a rock. This particular jetty was clearly not the first choice for the most moneyed owners. The yachts they passed, tied two or three abreast in places, were unexceptional examples of ten to fifteen metres. Some looked decidedly neglected and worn.

'He said it's on the right, towards the end,' Jack said, as he followed Stella's careful progress along the planks. The forest of aluminium masts around them was hardly stirring and the gentle lapping of water beneath their feet was the only sound apart from their own footsteps.

As they neared the end of the quay, Jack pointed to the stern of a white-hulled yacht. '*Marie*,' he said. 'You can see where he painted over the old name.'

The yacht was longer and more impressive than most at the jetty. The deck was deserted. 'There's a light on in the cabin,' Jack said, as he leapt onto the vessel. He held out a hand to steady Stella as she came aboard and then added in a low voice, 'He's probably drinking and he can get a bit boisterous.'

Towards the middle of the boat, a steep staircase led to a closed door of polished teak. Jack ducked his head as he descended to knock on the door. 'Marcel? It's Jack Rogers. Okay if we come in?'

There was no answer, so Jack turned the heavy brass handle and pushed the door open. Stella was right behind him as he looked around a surprisingly spacious room, with a neat galley and a sitting area complete with an entertainment unit. A single wall light provided weak illumination.

'Nobody here,' Jack said, his head slightly bowed under the low ceiling.

Stella nodded towards the door in the centre of the far wall. 'What's through there?'

'Sleeping quarters, probably.'

'Maybe he's taking a nap.'

Jack moved to the door and knocked. 'Marcel?'

No reply – just the hollow echo of the yacht bumping against the wharf. Jack turned the handle and pushed. It wouldn't budge.

'Try pulling it,' Stella suggested.

Jack grinned at himself when the door opened at the first tug. He leaned in, searching the wall for a light switch. When he found it, he flicked it on and heard Stella gasp. Both hands went to her mouth, as if suppressing a scream, and her eyes were wide and staring.

He looked into the room and his mouth, too, fell open. On the unmade double mattress against the far wall a man was slumped, with feet on the floor and torso flat on its back. From the shoulders down he might be mistaken for a sleeping drunk, but the head was merging with a deep-crimson pool of blood that was soaking into the bed.

Jack's first reaction was to turn off the light and step back into the salon. 'Fucking hell,' he said. His hands were trembling.

'Who is it?' Stella asked, hugging herself tightly with crossed bare arms.

'I'm pretty sure it's Ganet. The build and clothes look like his.'

'What the hell happened here?'

'I don't know.'

'I need some water,' Stella said, her face pale. 'I'll be in the galley.'

Willing himself forward, Jack flicked the light switch again and approached the bed. He locked his eyes to a clean spot on the mattress close to the body and took quick glances at the victim, trying to suppress his urge to get as far away from the body as possible. 'It's Marcel, all right,' he called out. 'I can't see any gun.'

Being in the room was getting to him. He clapped one hand to his mouth and backed away quickly, turning off the light and closing the door. 'We have to call the police,' he said, his voice thick with confusion. 'And I don't think we should touch anything. God, I hope the family's okay. I'd better check on them.' He moved towards the exit.

'What *is* this?'

He turned back to see Stella peering into the cupboards under the hotplates on the galley bench. Taking a step closer, he saw a small gas bottle in the cupboard. 'What am I looking at?'

'This stuff wrapped around the bottle.'

'Just some packaging, isn't it? Come on, let's get out of here.' He leaned in and saw two thick, brightly coloured strands encircling the gas bottle. 'Hang on, that's . . .'

'What?'

'A detonator cord; they use it in demolition.' Reaching out with one hand, he gently turned the gas bottle around.

'What's that?' Stella asked, her voice rising. 'Is that a timer?'

'It's a fucking bomb!' Jack said, already pushing her towards the door. 'We've only got a few seconds. Run like hell!'

10

They scrambled to the narrow staircase. Stella's foot slipped half-way up but Jack caught her and thrust her upwards and they both stumbled into the warm night air. Jack skidded across the teak deck and leapt to the jetty. He held out a hand to Stella and she grabbed it as she tripped over her loose sandals. He was already pulling her forward, but they'd only taken two clumsy strides when night turned to day as the port was lit up by a brilliant yellow flash, accompanied by an astonishing roar. In the same instant, the shock wave from the blast flattened them, face-downwards on the worn wooden slats of the dock.

Pieces of the yacht *Marie* flew in every direction and began to shower down around them. A fiery lump of wood fell between Stella's legs, burning ragged holes through her skirt. A strip of red-hot metal landed on her upper forearm and she yelped with shock as she frantically brushed it away.

Jack was first to his feet. He stamped on Stella's smouldering dress before dragging her upright and pulling her along the wharf. When he finally felt the heat on his back diminish, he stopped and turned to look at the burning wreckage of Ganet's yacht. It was thoroughly ablaze.

Stella was still catching her breath. 'What the fuck is going on, Jack?' she panted. 'That bomb was meant to destroy the evidence. If you'd been on time tonight, you'd probably be lying next to Marcel.'

He was brushing a smouldering ember from his jeans and shaking his head in disbelief. 'Why would anyone want to kill me? Nobody but the Ganets knew about our appointment.'

'Marcel must have told someone. Maybe he contacted the people he sold the film to.'

'Why the hell would he do that? And why would they kill him now, after all this time? Maybe it's got nothing to do with the film at all. I hardly know him. He might have had all sorts of enemies.'

'You really believe that?'

'No,' he said, looking across the port in the direction of the photographer's residence. 'We have to get to the Ganets' place. We can call the police from there.'

Stella grabbed his arm. 'Whoever did this could already be there.'

'I know, but I have to go. You want to wait here for the cops?'

'No! I'm coming with you.'

'Then run.'

Once off the jetty and onto the smooth cobblestones, Stella slipped off her flimsy sandals to run in bare feet. It was her only chance of keeping up with Jack as he sprinted around the straight sides of the port. The cataclysm behind them was already attracting attention. There were faces at the windows where shutters had been opened up. A few cars and pedestrians were moving towards the fire but Jack and Stella ignored them.

In Rue Cassini, the yellow sign above Ganet's studio was the only splash of colour in a grey streetscape. Jack rushed to the apartment entrance and pushed on the intercom button for a long two seconds.

There was no reply, and he tried again, with greater pressure. Eventually a loud click sounded and he pushed on the door. It opened and a light came on inside the vestibule.

'Louis?,' he called out, 'Is that you? Madame Ganet?'

There was no reply and Jack felt a shiver of trepidation.

Stella arrived on the doorstep. 'Don't go up there,' she said, breathlessly. 'Wait for the police.'

'I can't just leave them hanging out to dry. I'm not sure how, but I think I'm responsible for this.'

He started climbing the stairs and Stella followed behind, still barefoot. The sound of Jack's shoes on the treads seemed ominously loud in the stairwell. The door to the Ganet's apartment was hanging open about ten centimetres. He stopped completely just outside the door.

'Did you bring your phone?' he whispered.

Stella reached into the pocket of her ruined sundress. 'Yes.'

'Stay here.' He looked at her with stern eyes. 'Call the police and get them here now.'

She nodded quickly but opened her mouth to say something. He touched a finger to her lips. 'Better still, go back downstairs and call them. I don't want you to be hurt.'

Before she could respond, he turned away and pushed open the door to the apartment.

Stella felt paralysed by fear and uncertainty. She had been trying to tell him her phone wasn't working. Should she run down four flights of stairs onto a dark and empty street in a town where she didn't speak the language and search for help? By then it would be too late. Should she bang on a neighbour's door and try to convince them to call the police? That would be too noisy.

She took a deep breath to suppress her fear and moved slowly towards the door. Christ, she thought, we've been on this job only two days. How can it be that people are trying to kill us already? What the hell did we do?

Her total focus was now on the interior of the shabby French apartment, where a distant insipid light source was casting long shadows down the entrance hall. A rustic hallstand just inside the door was piled high with coats and hats, all dark in the gloom. Next to that, a bulky golf bag was propped against the wall, incongruous among the accumulated collection of mundane family possessions – shoes and children's toys on the floor and colourful beach towels slung over the back of a simple wooden chair. A door to the left was closed. The hallway ahead led towards a living room. She could just make out the end of a worn upholstered sofa backed against the far wall of the flat. To the left of that an arched opening led, she guessed, to the kitchen.

The lights were on in the kitchen, casting an arched-shaped pool of pale yellow on the threadbare carpet. Small flutters in that light told Stella that this was where the people were. How many people, she could not guess. Once more, the helpless feeling welled up in her gut and her hand flew to her mouth to stifle a scream.

Now she could hear voices, male voices in strangely calm conversation. Jack was trying his favourite approach – applying logic and common sense to talk his way out of trouble – but it didn't sound as if the usual magic was working on the other person, who spoke crisp, accurate English with a German accent. There was a brutal logic to his words, and the brittle edge in Jack's voice told Stella he was not as calm as he sounded. He was buying time, thinking the police would soon be arriving on the scene, and she almost turned to flee, realising that she'd been stupid not to go for help.

She was about to take another step towards the kitchen when Jack's shadow, and then Jack himself, backed slowly into the pool of light, his empty hands held out in a gesture of supplication.

'You don't have to do this,' he was saying.

'I have no choice,' the other voice said. 'If you cannot give me what I need, you are of no further use to me.'

'What you're looking for doesn't exist,' Jack said. 'The family knows nothing about it. At least leave them be.'

'Not possible. They are part of the story.'

Jack's tone turned angry. 'You're a heartless bastard.'

'A useful condition in my profession, I think.'

Jack continued to back slowly into the small living room. A hand firmly gripping a blackened metal handgun fitted with a silencer came into view. It was tracking Jack's movements. Stella's breath froze in her throat. Another step or two and the man holding that gun couldn't fail to notice the woman sneaking up the cluttered hallway. I'm a fucking business consultant, she thought. What the hell do I do now?

To her horror, the gunman did not wait for her to find an answer. Without further comment, he pulled the trigger. There was a soft noise and his target immediately crumpled to the floor.

Holy shit, Stella thought, he's killed Jack!

11

A searing pain swamped Jack's nervous system and he collapsed to the floor. He lay there, wondering whether he was dying. How had things gone so wrong so quickly?

Once he'd got inside the flat, he'd let his eyes adjust to the gloom near the cluttered hallstand. He thought of taking a driver from the new-looking set of golf clubs – presumably another of Ganet's recent purchases – but realised such an obvious weapon wouldn't help.

Taking a deep breath, he'd walked along the rest of the short corridor and stepped into the archway separating the lounge room from the kitchen. Louis and his mother were sitting at the table, their faces ashen. Marie Ganet's eyes were filled with terror and she had one of her son's hands clasped in both of hers, as if squeezing it might bring a solution to their predicament. Louis's defiant eyes settled only briefly on Jack before flicking back to stare angrily at the man standing by the sink.

The man was shorter than Jack and thinner, with brown, closely cropped hair and a neatly trimmed beard. His short-sleeved shirt revealed wiry, well-muscled arms. The left was heavily tattooed from elbow to wrist and in the same hand the man held a gun. It was pointed at Jack's chest.

Keeping his face composed, Jack ignored the weapon and looked over at Louis. 'Are you all right?'

The teenager nodded but his mother had tears running down her face. 'My husband,' she said, in accented English, 'he is dead?'

Jack's expression gave away the terrible truth and Marie's eyes flashed with unbridled anger. The gunman waved his pistol in her direction to remind her where things stood. 'You must be Jack Rogers,' he said.

Jack registered a soft Germanic or Scandinavian accent. 'That's right. And you are?'

'I was hoping we would connect tonight.'

'It's always nice to meet a fan,' Jack said nonchalantly, trying to project an air of calm by putting a hand in the pocket of his jeans.

'Keep your hands where I can see them,' the bearded man said with sudden menace.

'Of course. I should tell you I'm a business consultant. I don't carry a weapon.'

'I know what you are.'

'Then you'll also know I have no interest in whatever your business is.'

'You wanted to see the Aretino film. Why?'

Jack shrugged. 'I'm doing a project for a company that insures aircraft. It was silly, really, but I wanted the footage to demonstrate an extreme example. It was meant to make my presentation more, uh, riveting.'

The thin skin on the gunman's brow furrowed. It was obvious he wasn't buying it.

'The point is,' Jack said, 'I've never seen the footage. Just like these people. Whatever information you're trying to protect, none of us know anything about it. If you leave now, we have nothing that can hurt you.'

The gunman shook his head grimly. 'Ganet had a copy of the film. If you or these people,' he made a casual gesture with his gun, 'cannot provide me with that copy, then I will be forced to terminate our short association.'

Jack was now clutching at straws. 'If it exists at all, it's probably downstairs in the shop.'

'Possibly,' the gunman said, but he raised the pistol and pointed it at Jack's face.

Jack stepped backwards, towards the lounge room. 'You don't have to do this,' he said.

'I have no choice,' the gunman said, with no apparent emotion. 'If you cannot give me what I need, you are of no further use to me.'

'What you're looking for doesn't exist,' Jack said, desperation creeping into his voice. 'The family knows nothing about it. At least leave them be.'

'Not possible. They are part of the story.'

'You're a heartless bastard.'

'A useful condition in my profession, I think.'

He took two further steps back into the lounge room. His eyes, flicking around for an escape route, registered movement to his left. Stella! She was in the hallway, creeping forward as if there were something she could do to stop what was coming. He fixed his eyes back on the gun to mask her presence for another moment, and suddenly, he'd been shot.

But he still wasn't dead. Stunned, he concentrated hard to get his brain working. He could feel that the pain was localised – where? Left arm, his nerves replied, and when he tried to move he felt the burn across his triceps. The gunman's accuracy was astonishing. If he decided he wanted you dead, that would be it.

'That was your last chance,' the bearded man said with a supercil-
ious smile. The gun was now pointing at Jack's head. 'Do you have
the film, Jack?'

Slowly, Jack started to push himself up from the floor, noting
with relief that Stella had disappeared back up the shadowy hallway.

'Stay where you are. Answer the question.'

He fell back on his butt and held out his hands in a gesture of
helplessness. A hot trail of blood was now flowing down his arm.
'What can I say? Ganet never showed me a single second of film.
I don't know that a copy even exists. I am no threat to you and neither
are the Ganets. Please, just leave us alone.'

The gunman raised the weapon. 'So,' he said, with sarcastic civil-
ity, 'it was nice meeting you.'

Jack closed his eyes.

Thwack!

The iron head of a golf club came down hard on the gunman's
bony wrist. The gun clattered to the floor but the man recovered
quickly and was already turning on his attacker. Stella, who'd been
hoping to knock the weapon further away, swung the club again and
connected briefly with the barrel, spinning it across the floor. But by
then a sinewy arm was pushing her against the wall while the other
searched for her throat.

'Let her go!' Jack roared, grabbing the fallen gun and aiming it
squarely at the gunman. Suddenly Stella was flying in Jack's direction
and he instinctively reached out to stop her falling. As she collapsed
in his arms, gasping and clutching at her neck, he heard a sound
coming from the stairwell. The gunman was gone.

'Thank Christ you hung around,' Jack said quietly, as he helped
Stella to her feet and tentatively placed the gun on the floor. 'You
saved my life.'

'And you saved ours,' Louis said, emerging from the kitchen.

Marie Ganet was behind him, crying and mumbling. 'My mother says it's all her fault. She called the German and told him about you. He pays her for the details of people asking about the film, but nothing like this ever happened before.'

'The German? This guy with the beard? He's the one who bought the film?'

'No,' Louis said, 'another German. With a different voice and better French.'

'Does she know his name?' Stella asked.

'No, but she has a telephone number.'

'Get it for me,' Jack ordered. 'And call the police.'

His arm was still bleeding. Marie Ganet found a roll of bandage and handed it to Stella with trembling hands. As Jack's adrenaline ebbed, the pain became sharp. Louis returned with the number on a piece of paper.

'But what happened to my father? How did he die?' The teenager's voice trembled.

'It was quick,' Jack said, 'but the yacht's gone too, I'm afraid. It was blown up.'

A silence fell, until Louis spoke again. 'We're going to have to leave Nice. That man will come back to finish us off.'

'That's probably wise, at least until he's caught.'

'Who?' Louis demanded, his eyes wide. 'Who do you think will catch him, Jack? The local cops? No way. That man will be long gone before they even work out who he is.'

Jack said nothing. The boy was almost certainly right. He gritted his teeth as Stella wrapped his arm.

'What were you planning to do with the film, Jack, if my father let you have it? That story about the insurance company was bullshit, right?'

'Yeah. We're investigating the Aretino business empire. Obviously we'd like to see the film but I'm more interested in knowing who paid to take it out of circulation.'

Louis nodded his head. 'Whoever paid for the film also blew up the plane. The same German who sent that tattooed man.'

'That's what we —'

Jack's words were cut short by the shrill clang of a high-pitched bell cutting through the entire building.

'That's the fire alarm in the shop!' Louis said. He ran to the front door and opened it to find the stairwell already filling with smoke. Neighbours were hustling down the stairs.

Jack stepped out onto the landing and looked down. 'I'm a fucking idiot,' he said angrily. 'I should have known he'd go after the studio. I virtually suggested it to him.'

'Too late to worry about that now,' Stella said. 'We need to get these people out of here.'

Marie took the baby while Jack carried the three-year-old, who was so oblivious to the danger that she put her head on his shoulder and went straight back to sleep. As they made their way down the stairs, the smoke was thick but bearable. On the street, a man in uniform ushered them to one side, away from the furiously crackling photo studio. As Jack held the sleeping toddler, he glanced down the hill towards the port. He couldn't make out any smoke or flame, but flashing lights were reflecting off the dark water.

A fire engine arrived outside the studio and was soon pouring water through the shattered windows of the shopfront, but the damage had been done. Jack shook his head, depressed that their last chance to see the deadly footage was literally melting away. With the downturn in his mood came a sudden tiredness, and his arm began to throb and ache under the weight of the child.

Then he felt someone touch his arm. He looked around to see Louis pulling him back from the growing crowd of residents and stickybeaks. When they were deep in the shadows, the teenager reached into the backpack he'd carried down from the apartment. Jack caught a glimpse of something square and fluorescent – a CD case. Adrenaline pumped back into his system and the injured arm was instantly forgotten. 'Bloody hell, Louis, is that what I think it is?'

'Yes,' the unsmiling boy said. 'I made a copy for myself. My father didn't know about it. If you promise to find out who sent that guy to kill him, you can have it.'

12

It was nearly dawn when Jack and Stella were returned to the Four Points in the back of a police car. A solicitous doorman asked if everything was all right; the spacious lobby was otherwise deserted. In the elevator, Stella leaned against the wall and took a few deep breaths. 'I have a feeling I'll never forget Nice.'

Jack glanced at her. 'You could say it's been memorable.'

She was examining the bandage on her forearm. 'At least they patched us up. How does your arm feel?'

'Just a dull ache, unless I flex it.'

'For a while there, I didn't think they were going to let us go tonight at all.'

'We have the wounds and the witnesses to back up our story. But I think the local constabulary are out of their league on this one.'

'At least they have our description of the gunman, even if they weren't impressed by our theory. The phone number we gave them was a dead end and they seem determined to prove Ganet was killed in some drug deal gone wrong.'

Jack stepped back to allow her to exit the elevator first. 'It's an easy answer – a new boat on the Riviera, a big lump of undocumented cash . . .'

'Maybe they're right,' she said, as they padded silently down the carpeted hallway. 'We have no idea why the Aretino jet was blown up. It could be drugs.' She rubbed her reddened eyes. 'I'm exhausted. I'm going to need some sleep before the drive back to Milan.'

At the door to his room, Jack froze for a moment.

'What?' Stella asked. 'You think he might be inside? Not too likely, is it?'

He shrugged and pushed against the door, but couldn't resist glancing into the corners of the room.

Stella ignored him and plodded across the carpet to flop face-down across the bed, which had been remade by housekeeping. 'Just a couple of hours of kip,' she said into the quilt. 'We can still be in Milan by lunchtime.'

Despite his fatigue, Jack started to unpack his computer. 'I think I have something that might wake you up.'

Stella turned her head and looked at him through her tousled tresses. 'Don't tell me you got it? How the hell?'

'Louis kept a secret copy. I didn't want to mention it at the police station, especially since they think the film had nothing to do with it. Besides, Louis reckons the cops were given a copy months ago, just after the attack.'

'Then it can't be any help in identifying the culprits or they would have done something.'

'Not necessarily. Incompetence, corruption, politics – I'm sure the French police force is no less susceptible than any other. They might even have legitimate reasons to keep it quiet. Let's see if it tells us anything.'

He inserted the disk and waited impatiently for it to load. At last, the software geared up and, for a second or two, the screen filled with a jerky image of blue sea, spotted with a few vessels, then the camera jolted upwards and settled on a steadier shot of the pale-blue sky. A tiny dot in the centre of the image bobbed about as it grew larger. Eventually the outline of a sleek aircraft emerged, flying directly towards the camera. As it approached and descended, an idyllic panorama of the Nice foreshore drifted across the background. It was easy to imagine the passengers peering down at the azure water and the grand hotels, anticipating glamorous days ahead at the Monaco Grand Prix. Then the back of the plane exploded with a sudden ferocity that made Stella jump, though she knew it was coming.

The angry orange fireball captured in the still shot appeared briefly as the aircraft was cut in two. The camera vaguely followed the tail section down towards the water but then the perspective suddenly shifted almost ninety degrees, causing Jack and Stella to tilt their heads in unison. For a few moments the Mediterranean was back in the frame, with Nice's beachfront running vertically across the screen. Then the image jerked back and moved to the burning wreckage and emergency workers on the airport runway. It went on for several minutes, then stopped.

'Bloody hell,' Stella said. 'Those poor people.'

Jack was trying not to think about the victims. 'We're going to have to watch it again. Frame by frame.'

'You're right. There must be something in here that was worth Marcel's life and half a million euros.'

After a few more viewings, the footage wasn't quite so stomach-churning and they were able to take in some of the surrounding details.

'Can we just look at the frames that show boats on the water?' Stella said. 'If the bomb was triggered by remote control . . .'

'There are people and vehicles all along the shore. The operator could have been anywhere.'

'Indulge me.'

Soon, a moment was frozen on the screen. It was the instant Ganet had first started to record, when the camera was pointing east along the coast but at a downward angle. The rocky edge of the airport runway was just in the picture at the bottom left, but the shot was predominantly water. The sea was slightly choppy and disturbed by the downdraft from the chopper and the wakes of powerboats. Nearly a dozen craft could be seen in the snapshot – ranging from jet skis and dinghies to luxury cruisers – but many of them were too distant to make out. The vessel closest to the camera was in the pricey category. It was about twenty-five metres of sleek, ocean-going fibreglass with raked lines and dark tinted windows in the enclosed bridge and portholes. Even stationary, it looked fast.

'Every other vessel is moving,' Stella observed, 'but that one's just sitting there.'

'Fishing, perhaps?'

'Can't see any rods.'

Jack leaned closer. On the screen, the boat was only seven centimetres long, but he could see there was no disturbance in the water behind it. It was indeed just sitting there, stern to the shore. The back quarter of the cruiser was an open deck sheltered by a deep overhanging roof. Several figures were gathered at the far rail.

'They're looking up and away to the east,' he said, 'watching the planes come in.'

Stella's eyes narrowed. 'Go forward.'

There were only a few frames showing the boats, with no discernible variation between them. Jack moved to the second sequence of water, taken after the plane had exploded. These images were severely tilted. 'Let me see if I can rotate the image,' he said, moving the cursor to the top of the screen.

Stella reached out and tipped the laptop on its side so that it was propped open like a birthday card. 'That'll do,' she said. 'Look, the boat's bigger in this shot.'

'Zoom lens,' Jack said, his eyes exploring the vessel. 'Those blokes are all on this side now, looking up at the explosion. I guess you would, wouldn't you?'

'They are all men, aren't they? Fully dressed, too. Not your typical tourist cruise, is it? Can you make it any bigger?'

Jack managed to isolate the boat and create a new, larger image. It was possible to make out some extra details, but pixelation limited the definition. He put a finger up to the screen. 'I thought that was one big man, but it's actually two, hugging. What do you reckon, shock or celebration?'

'Celebration,' she said, and with a neatly trimmed fingernail she pointed out a third man standing apart, his hands on the rail as he leaned out into the sun and looked towards the devastation. 'Left arm.'

Jack could just make out a dark smudge on the man's forearm. 'Tattoo? You think that's the bearded fucker? It's such a fuzzy image. Maybe we're just seeing him because we want to.'

But Stella had already moved on. 'The waves cover up most of the name. I can see "e-t-t-a". Maybe Giulietta or Violetta or something.'

'Bit of a girly name for such a macho cruiser,' he said, and he scrolled through the following frames to see if more of the black letters on the white hull might be revealed. But in the few seconds of real time covered by the footage, the stern did not emerge any further from the swell.

'We need to enhance this picture,' she said. 'If we were back in New York, we'd know somebody who could do it for us.'

'I'll look for some better software when we get back to Milan. We should be able to do better than this.'

'Maybe you could change the colours. Even in black and white you might get better definition.'

'Can't hurt, I guess. Why don't you have a nap while I play around with it?'

'Thanks,' she said. 'I was hoping you'd say that.'

She crawled onto the bed and put her head on a pillow. Through the bronze-tinted glass of the windows she could see the sky at the horizon beginning its progression from insipid, pale dawn to summer-blue daylight. But before she could conjure a daydream of floating on the clear water, she was fast asleep.

13

'What's that you're humming, Father?'

Fra Patrice Albert de Montresson smiled at the middle-aged woman sitting opposite. 'It's from *Carmen*,' he said. 'I'm going to the opera tonight.'

His fellow passenger adopted a scandalised expression. 'Isn't *Carmen* a little racy for a man of the cloth?'

He laughed softly. 'Love. Passion. These are at the heart of God's message, madame.'

'And murder?'

'It is pointless to pretend that sin does not exist. Besides, the music is so beautiful. It must meet with God's approval.'

'Paris, Gard du Nord,' a female voice announced over the loud-speaker. 'Last stop.'

Fra Patrice looked out the window as another train passed their slowing carriage. The afternoon sunlight was glinting off the jumble of tracks and he felt slightly intimidated by the density and size of the capital. He rarely left the hospital in Amiens, where he was both chief administrator and spiritual leader, and it was almost a decade since he'd visited Paris. It was even longer since he'd last indulged his one private passion, the opera. He'd told himself it was one of the pleasures to be forgone when he took holy orders and devoted himself to the sick, just like the luxury and privileges to which his birth entitled him. He'd still be in his spartan office at the hospital right now if the invitation to opening night at the Paris Opera had not come from Cardinal Hinault himself.

From the station, he took a taxi to the glamorous eighth arrondissement, just a few blocks from the Champs-Elysées. The family's city apartment was on the second floor of an elegant, Hausmann-era building, and as soon as he stepped inside he felt a strange mixture of familiarity and alienation. The rich timber parquetry and ancient rugs he'd crawled over as a child were such a stark contrast to the worn grey linoleum of his tiny bedroom in the hospital. As he was reminded of the gilded furniture, crystal chandeliers and expensive objets d'art, he thought only of all the hospital beds it could pay for.

The apartment had been recently cleaned, though it was rarely used these days. His three married sisters all lived in other parts of France. He flicked on the lights in the main reception rooms and took his bag to the simplest of the bedrooms. His best cassock and cleanest collar were soon laid out on the bed. He wanted to look his best for the Cardinal. The Cartier clock on the mantelpiece in the sitting room had recently chimed six o'clock. He had time for a shower and a shave.

He was opening shutters at the front of the apartment to let in some fresh air when the harsh clang of a telephone bell echoed through the silent rooms. It was his oldest sister and self-appointed mother substitute, Caroline. 'Did you get there all right?'

'Obviously. You're talking to me.'

'Everything look as it should?'

'What do you mean?'

'In the apartment. Nothing missing?'

He looked around the room. 'Not sure I'd know if it was, but it still seems to be stuffed to the brim with unnecessary trinkets. Why do you ask?'

'I was talking to Odette today. She can't find her keys to the apartment and she's convinced they were stolen.'

'Well, nobody appears to have moved in. It wouldn't matter if they had, anyway. I only need one room for the night.'

'Don't be silly, Patrice. Now, have you hung out your cassock? Have you got a clean collar?'

'I am nearly forty-five,' the priest said. 'I think I can look after myself.'

'Now you're snapping at me? Just because I care about how you look?'

'Thank you for caring, my darling, but I'm pretty sure I can dress myself and get all the way to the opera house without coaching.'

'The last time you met a cardinal, you had soup stains on your cassock. You were photographed with him, looking like that.'

Fra Patrice sighed. 'It wasn't my soup, Caroline. A patient threw it at me. I think the Cardinal understood.'

'But there will be photographers there tonight, too.'

'That's true,' he said. 'No soup, then.'

'And no ice-cream!'

'Goodbye, Caroline. Love to the family.'

He was smiling as he replaced the handset. For all her meddling, he did appreciate the security of Caroline's protective cocoon. Bizet's overture was back in his head and he began to hum along. Now he was here in Paris, with the worries of the hospital far away, he felt more excited than he expected to. The night promised to be memorable.

There was a spring in his step as he hurried back to his room to get undressed. Wrapping a towel around his narrow waist, he carried his shaving kit to the bathroom at the end of the hall. With his spare hand, he conducted an imaginary orchestra.

The bathroom cabinets had been renovated in the seventies but the plumbing was much older. He stood at a gilt-framed mirror at the sink to shave, his hum turning to a whistle as he pursed his lips for the blade. Then he turned his attention to the rickety pipes over the bath.

The single faucet was fed by two taps that squeaked reluctantly as he turned them. The sound of rushing water filled the room and echoed off the tiled walls. When the temperature felt right, he pulled on the toggle that would divert the flow to the shower, but nothing happened. Bending closer to examine the mechanism, he could see it was bent out of shape and would not engage. Caroline could have told me that, he thought. She was here only two weeks ago. A bath will take longer. With a sigh of frustration, he bent down to insert the plug in the drain.

He rewrapped his nakedness with a towel while he waited for the bath to fill. He'd always been modest, even in his own company. There were three tall cupboards next to the sink with slatted doors. Maybe he would find a tool in there to fix the shower mechanism, but when he opened the double doors on the right he found only shelves filled with neatly folded towels. When he pulled on the third door, it appeared to be stuck fast. There was no obvious locking mechanism, but a strong tug would not budge it. By then, there was almost enough water in the deep bathtub to cover his frame, so he abandoned his handyman efforts and watched patiently as the warm water climbed up the white enamel sides of the bath.

When he turned off the taps, the roaring noise was replaced by an eerie silence broken only by a few echoing drips. He dropped the towel and pushed back the shower curtain as he tested the water with a toe. It felt hot but inviting. He put one hand on the rim and stepped into the bath. There was a moment of indulgent pleasure as he felt the heat radiate through his feet and into his legs. He'd forgotten about baths. This was going to be good. He allowed himself a groan of anticipation.

A loud bang and a sudden movement came from his left. The cupboard with the sticking door burst open and a black shape emerged. Before he could react, a gloved hand was clapped over his eyes. Another was fixed to the back of his head. Relaxation was replaced with pain and terror. The hands on his head were pressing together with incredible strength. It felt as though his eyeballs would burst.

'Who are you?' he squealed. 'What do you want?'

The hands began to apply downward pressure. 'Sit down!' a deep voice commanded in accented French.

He resisted. 'I am a man of God. I have no need for the trinkets and baubles out there. Take them with my blessing.'

The hands clamped to his head pushed down harder. 'I said, sit down!'

The attacker's strength was overwhelming. Fra Patrice grunted in panic as his knees buckled and he flailed his arms in defence. But when he gripped his assailant's arms, they felt like two branches of immovable oak. 'What is it you want?' he pleaded, as he blindly extended an arm to the side of the bath to prevent an uncontrolled fall.

Bang! The vicelike hands smashed his head back against the side of the tub and his body went limp. The gruesome sound echoed off the tiles. He was just on the edge of consciousness as the hands, pressing more gently now, eased his head below the surface. His eyes rolled up and saw a smear of bright-red blood running from the edge of the bath to the surface of the water. He felt the last of his living breath drain from his lungs as his body convulsed in a final act of defiance. Then he was gone.

14

'Look out!' Jack cried, but the driver didn't deviate and the powerful Mercedes surged forward from the lights, missing the beggar by milli- metres. The raggedly dressed woman was holding a filthy baby and as her face passed his window, Jack saw a look of unmitigated hatred.

'Romani,' the chauffeur muttered in a disgusted tone. 'Gypsies.'

Jack twisted his neck to look back. It couldn't be, but he was convinced for a moment they'd nearly collected Marie Ganet and her baby. He glanced at the faces in the back seat. Giorgio Borboli was smiling benignly but Stella was staring at him with a worried expression. He turned to face the front and wiped the fine sheen of perspiration from his brow.

Stella started talking business again and he had no desire to listen to her – questioning, analysing and explaining. His rational mind was hungry for the answers she would certainly find, but the rest of him found the talk pointless. Not even the prospect of a day at the Italian Grand Prix could overcome the sense of unease he'd been fighting since the drive back to Milan yesterday.

He'd spent the entire trip pretending to sleep, fearing that if he spoke to Stella, she'd realise he wasn't coping. The half bottle of gin he'd consumed before finally passing out on the couch had not been conducive to a restful sleep and now, on his way to Monza and a Formula One experience he'd long fantasised about, he still felt on edge.

He told himself it was just a normal reaction to the stress of being shot. Post-traumatic stress disorder; he'd seen it feature in plenty of television dramas. But what was the trick? Did he just have to acknowledge how bad he was feeling? Did he have to relive the terrifying few seconds when he was sure he was about to die? If he replayed the scene over and over in his head, would that make it more bearable?'

Whatever the solution, it seemed well out of his reach. Stella had nonchalantly saved his life with a golf club and simply moved on to the next task, apparently undaunted. Meanwhile here he sat, about ready to punch his fist through the window.

He forced himself to take in the sights. Every now and then he saw evidence of the Grand Prix circus – a Ferrari flag or chequered bunting decorating a café or shopfront – but most people appeared to be preoccupied with less glamorous activities.

On the raised motorway skirting the city, he gripped the door handle as the big Merc fired down the fast lane at such a clip it made slower vehicles appear stationary. That was wrong. Usually he loved going fast, but he felt a rush of relief when they hit the traffic snarl around the chic suburb of Monza.

The journey from the car to the select 'paddock' area behind the pits was a blur of sights, sounds and smells. There were green leafy trees around the track and throngs of fans in bright clothing, dominated by the red, yellow and black of the Ferrari team. Jack caught the aroma of good food and the stink of cigarette smoke rising above the crowds chatting behind giant grandstands along the home straight. He vaguely registered fine Art Deco architecture abutting functional modern design while they were being hustled through a series of security checkpoints and into a tunnel under the track. Nearing their exclusive destination, he sensed more space and fewer cheap T-shirts. The Paddock Pass around his neck was examined one final time and suddenly he was where he'd always wanted to be: in that glamorous avenue behind the pit garages known as Motorhome Alley. At last, he began to feel better.

The alley was formed by the teams' mobile headquarters on one side – more like portable high-tech offices than traditional motorhomes – and massive, glossily painted transporters on the other. The trucks were parked side by side, two per team, with their cabins facing out and their rears tucked under the dramatic, wing-shaped structure of steel and sweeping glass that was Monza's new pit complex. The area was populated by officials and team personnel wearing uniforms plastered with sponsors' logos, hurrying around A-listers, journalists and curious nobodies.

Jack realised that he was meant to be walking with the others. He looked around for Stella and Giorgio and spotted them a few metres ahead. By virtue of its low ranking, the Aretino team was located at the far end of the pit complex. Jack was glad of the lengthy walk. There was a lot to take in and it would give him time to gather his thoughts before entering social chitchat mode. As he closed in on his client, he heard Stella giving her opinion. 'It's not hard to see where all the money goes,' she was saying, as she took in the shiny, bespoke team facilities. 'I had no idea of the scale.'

Jack's attempt at a riposte was drowned out by a high-pitched and almost painfully loud shriek. It was coming from the nearby Jaguar garage. 'What the hell is that?' Stella shouted.

The noise stopped after a few seconds and Jack explained. 'They're testing an engine. Isn't it an amazing sound?'

'Haven't they ever heard of mufflers?' she said, but Jack just laughed. It's going to be all right, he said to himself, as he observed the Williams driver, Juan Pablo Montoya, striding from the garage complex towards his motorhome with a TV crew in pursuit.

A little further along, another group of reporters was following F1 supremo Bernie Ecclestone as he escorted some VIP guest on a tour. A separate gaggle of photographers was more interested in two supermodels – Jack recognised Naomi Campbell, but couldn't name the other one – who were strutting their stuff on the way to join a big-name team for the day. Vicky Cavendish was hovering there too. When she caught sight of him, he waved and she looked delighted. With remarkable speed, she trotted towards him on tall stilettos.

'Is that her?' she hissed, jerking her thumb towards Stella, who'd kept walking.

Jack nodded and leaned down to allow Vicky to deliver two air kisses that came nowhere near his cheeks. 'Don't want to fuck up the make-up,' she said, returning her gaze to Stella. 'She's beautiful, Jack, but she looks a bit serious.'

'She's working.'

'I'd better get back to it too. I'm hoping to blag my way into the Ferrari party by pretending I'm with Naomi. Remember, call me if you see Laura Aretino, or any other celebs for that matter. You still got my number?'

'Yes, but I'm not dishing the dirt on my clients or their guests. That's not how it works, I'm afraid.'

'Call me anyway. Ciao.'

She blew him a kiss and clattered away on her ridiculous shoes. Jack watched her for a few seconds and smiled. Vicky was quite a piece of work.

The Aretino team motorhome looked more like a traditional Winnebago than most. It was a two-level vehicle painted deep red and gold, with hospitality and press areas located in attached canvas marquees. There was no activity out front.

'At Monza,' Giorgio explained, gesturing towards the pit building, 'the Aretinos don't use the motorhome to entertain guests – it's a little too modest. They take one of the hospitality suites up there. Follow me.'

As he led them inside, Stella moved close to Jack. 'Are you okay?' she said in a low voice. 'You seem a bit . . .'

'I'll be fine,' he murmured, resolving to pull himself together.

He caught a tantalising glimpse of a Formula One monocoque perched on jacks in a spotless garage, before Giorgio directed them upstairs, where a long passage led to a string of hospitality suites. A pretty woman with a wide smile checked their passes before inviting them inside the suite at the end, directly above the Aretino garages. Jack saw a waitress offering drinks and tables laden with antipasti but it was the far end of the room that drew his eye. It was all sloping glass, promising spectacular views of not only the track but also the packed grandstands opposite and the pit lane below.

The spacious suite was filled with men and women dressed with casual elegance. The fifth-richest man in Europe was standing to one side, greeting guests with an affable expression. His hair was a touch greyer than it was in the paparazzi photos but he was still looking good for his age – tall and trim, with a strong jaw and an aquiline nose. He was dressed in a team shirt festooned with logos, over a pair of dark trousers. An exquisite Rolex sparkled on his wrist. After being introduced to Stella, he turned to face Jack.

'And this is Jack Rogers,' Giorgio said, 'also an Australian living in New York.'

Jack smiled. 'I'm very pleased to meet you, Count Aretino. Thank you so much for having us here today.'

'Please, call me Charles. We like to be informal here.' The Count's

English revealed no trace of his nationality. He took the proffered hand and said, 'Giorgio tells me you're a true Formula One fan, Jack.'

'Used to be. It hasn't been easy keeping up with it since I moved to America.'

'Ah, yes, the Americans. It has proved to be a difficult market to crack. We'll be racing there in two weeks, at Indianapolis. I hope we get a larger turnout than usual.'

'How do you fancy your chances this weekend?'

The Count shook his head. 'Not good. I love this circuit but it is one of the most problematic for us. We just don't have the top speed required to compete on such fast straights.'

'I'm looking forward to watching the team do their stuff.'

'So am I. I'm still learning, though I have some wonderful experts in the team to call upon.'

Jack smiled sympathetically. 'It must have been tough, adjusting to the loss. You've done very well to keep the team going.'

'Thank you. This was always my brother's dream. Now I want it to succeed in his memory.'

'I'd love to talk more about it with you. The inner workings of an F1 team have always fascinated me.'

'I'd like that,' the Count said politely, 'but I'm afraid you won't see much of me today until the qualifying session is over. The next practice session is about to start and we'll need to get the cars set up for their fast laps this afternoon. If you want to talk about the business side of it, I suggest you pick Alex's brains.'

He gestured to a man wearing Armani jeans and a tight-fitting polo shirt, who broke away from his conversation with two starry-eyed model types. Alessandro Aretino was a taller, slightly fairer facsimile of his father, with the same strong jawline and regal nose. His hair was a tangle of soft brown curls and his eyes were pale blue. When he smiled, deep dimples in his cheeks gave him a mischievous look.

'Alex,' the Count said, 'this is Stella and Jack, two Australian business consultants. They are here with Giorgio Borboli. Make them welcome while I pretend to understand what the engineers and mechanics are talking about.'

Alex shook Jack's hand quickly but held Stella's for longer. 'Make yourselves comfortable. Take off your jacket if you like, Jack. Are you followers of Formula One?'

'He is,' Stella said. 'I'm just getting my head around it.'

'As am I,' Alex said, giving her the benefit of his dimples. 'I'm still not sure I understand the point.'

'Pity,' she said, smiling back, 'I was hoping you could explain it to me.'

'Your father said you were an expert,' Jack said.

'I am the chief financial officer for the group,' Alex said, the American tinge to his English clear. 'You'd be amazed at the expense of running a complex operation like this. I have no choice but to understand all aspects of the business, if only to keep a lid on costs.'

'You sound like a man I should get to know,' Stella said.

Jack raised an eyebrow. He was distracted by the sound of racing engines coming from the many flat-screen monitors around the suite. A blue and yellow missile flew by on the track beyond the glass. It was one of the Renaults. 'Can't we hear the cars from in here?' he asked, incredulous.

'No,' Alex said, sounding smug. 'This space is soundproof. If you want the full experience, there is a block of reserved seating on the roof above.'

Jack shook his head. Why would you buy such a superb piece of real estate at the Grand Prix if you didn't want to hear the bloody cars? The noise was half the fun. Alex had moved away towards the windows, inviting them to follow. Stella hung back and looked hard into Jack's eyes.

'This is the man we need to get close to,' she said urgently, 'and Giorgio is watching.'

Jack glanced to his left and saw their client standing with a group of men of similar vintage. He was, indeed, watching. 'I'm not quite myself today. Why don't you talk to Alex?'

'Okay,' she said, leaning in closer. 'In that case, why don't you go look for his brother?'

That's right, he said to himself, as he watched her glide across the room towards Alex Aretino. You take the playboy and I get the priest.

15

The air was split by the high-pitched shriek of engines and the enthusiastic roar of the crowd. The two Ferraris had taken to the track. As the sound rippled through him, Jack pushed his way into a gap by the clear glass balustrade in front of the shaded rooftop seating. Behind him, a group of Aretino team guests in the banked seats were cheering along with the rest. No doubt he might find a few company executives among them he should be schmoozing, maybe even Giacomo Aretino himself. But what the hell would he talk to a priest about?

The action in front of him was much more compelling. The grandstand opposite was a throbbing sea of colour. His view of the track extended all the way from the famous Parabolica corner to the finish line and, looking down, he had a bird's eye view of pit crews in action. If he didn't move from this spot all day, he'd be perfectly content. Michael Schumacher's scarlet Ferrari swept onto the straight and powered towards the line to begin a fast lap. The grandstands rose up and roared and Jack found himself joining in.

The practice session lasted sixty minutes. To the delight of the masses, the Ferraris finished top of the timesheets, though Bar-richello rather than Schumacher was quickest of the twenty drivers. The Aretino cars finished eighteenth and last, respectively. It would be two hours before the F1 cars would be back, and Jack was already counting the seconds.

Reluctantly, he turned away from the railing and moved towards the stairs. His enthusiasm for hobnobbing was at an all-time low today, but he had a job to do and doing it well was his best chance of living up to the promise he'd made to Louis Ganet. He took a deep breath and headed downstairs.

The Aretino suite was busier than before, as guests and hosts alike returned to the free food and beverages. As Jack entered the room, he saw Stella standing beside Alex Aretino and wondered how she was going. Her relaxed smile implied she was at least enjoying herself and he experienced a burst of jealousy that he quickly buried.

'I think I know you.'

He turned sharply to find a man about his own age and height looking at him with dark-brown eyes. He had high cheekbones, lustrous black hair and an easy smile. Dressed in a short-sleeved Aretino team shirt, he held out a hand in greeting.

'I'm Jimmy Aretino,' he said in a British accent.

'Oh, right,' Jack said. He'd been expecting a black suit and a dog collar.

'Your name is Rogers, isn't it?'

'Yes, Jack Rogers.'

While they shook hands, Jack racked his brain for the connec-tion. 'You worked in the City, didn't you? Years ago.'

'You remember me too?' Jimmy looked pleased. 'I can't imagine why. You were the whiz-kid everybody was talking about. I was just a workaday analyst, and not a very good one at that.'

'I'm good with faces,' Jack lied. 'Schroders, wasn't it?'

'Wow, you are good. I was there four years.'

'And where are you now?'

'Rome. You?'

'New York. Nine years now. I was with Sutton Brothers on the Street for eight of those but now I have my own consulting firm.' He extracted a business card from his wallet and passed it across.

'The Stack Partnership,' Jimmy read aloud.

'It's a combination of my business partner's first name and my own. Stella and Jack.'

'Is that the pretty lady I saw my brother flirting with?'

'That would be her.'

'And what brings you to Milan?'

'We're working with the Banco Borboli. When Giorgio heard what a Formula One fan I am, he kindly invited us to join him today.'

'He's a sweet man. I've known him all my life.'

'What about you? Are you still in the markets?'

Jimmy smiled. 'No. I gave up my business aspirations after my time in London. In fact, I gave up worldly possessions altogether.'

'Oh, right,' Jack said. 'Then by Rome, you mean the Vatican?'

'That's where the ultimate boss lives, yes.'

A waiter approached with a tray of drinks. Jack took a beer and Jimmy a red wine. 'I don't mean to pry,' Jack said, 'but do you normally wear casual clothes when you're not, uh, working?'

'The Holy Father would prefer us to wear our cassocks, or at least a suit, but I've given myself a weekend off for the race.' He winked. 'I'll confess to my vanity next week, but I wanted to wear the team shirt.'

'Unlike your brother.'

'Pah! My grandmother's more interested in Formula One than Alex is, and she's been dead five years. I love it, though. I was glad when my uncle and father bought the team. Luckily, my boss is an Englishman and a motorsport fan. He gives me time off for the Italian GP.'

'The loss of your uncle must have been difficult for the team.'

'Of course,' Jimmy said, a slight crinkle forming at the corners of his eyes. 'It was a difficult time for all of us, but for my father in particular. Not only did he inherit the title and his brother's charity obligations, he's also had to learn more than just the money side of Formula One. Still, it's better than being dead.'

'You think your father was the real target? Sorry, that's probably a bit forward. If you don't want to talk about it . . .'

'It's okay, Jack. I've had time and a thousand questions like yours to get used to it. And I have no doubt my father was the true target of the bomb. That plane was scheduled to take him to Nice to meet a potential sponsor but the meeting was cancelled at the last minute. My uncle decided to use the jet to take his family to the race in Monaco. Turned out to be the worst decision he ever made, and he made a few ordinary calls in his time.'

'Who would want your father dead?'

Jimmy shook his head. 'I have no idea, but he's one of the most high-profile businessmen in Italy. Anti-capitalist feelings still run deep around here.'

'I thought the Red Brigade days were over,' Jack said. 'And nobody claimed responsibility, did they?'

'The names change,' Jimmy said, with a more serious tone, 'but the ideas don't go away. And there's a good reason they didn't claim the credit – they got the wrong Aretino. Instead of the greedy businessman, they blew up the harmless playboy turned philanthropist. In his later years, my uncle devoted much of his time to the Order's good works. Claiming responsibility for his death would only blacken the name of any terrorist group.'

'The Order? What's that?'

'The Order I belong to,' Jimmy said, with a hint of pride. 'The Sovereign Military Hospitaller Order of St John of Jerusalem of Rhodes and of Malta, now usually called the Sovereign Military Order of Malta. There have been Aretino knights in the Order for most of its 900-year history.'

Jack was impressed. 'It must be amazing to know what individual members of your family were doing so long ago.'

'Until recently, the Order needed to know every detail of your family history because the rules required strict, untainted aristocratic lineage on both sides. These days it's a bit more relaxed. We even have knights who haven't taken holy orders, like my uncle and my father. In the past, only priests of noble birth could be knights.'

'And what do you all do, if you don't mind my asking?'

'We are still hospitallers, as we were during the Crusades. Our Order is dedicated to healing the sick and protecting the defence-less. We run hospitals and clinics and do other charitable works.'

'And the military role is . . . ?'

'Largely symbolic these days, though our properties in Rome are regarded as sovereign territory, so we must be prepared to defend them just as we defended western Europe from the spread of Islam for centuries.'

'Fascinating,' Jack said with sincerity. 'Australians have such a short view of history. I'm not even sure where my grandparents were born.'

'I'm sure that has its advantages,' Jimmy said. 'When you're born into a family like mine, your career options are limited. Provider, playboy, philanthropist or priest.'

Jack smiled sympathetically. 'And your brother is the provider of your generation?'

Jimmy nodded. 'He was deemed to be a better businessman than me. He's taken on many of my father's responsibilities with the group companies since May.'

Stella's instincts were on the mark as usual, Jack thought wryly. She'd picked the right Aretino. 'And your cousin Stefano?'

'Playboy,' Jimmy said. 'His father's son, but we all miss him. No doubt he would have grown into a great charity worker, like Count Federico.'

'Is your sister here?'

'No.' For the first time, Jack detected a tone of sensitivity. 'She won't be coming to the race this year.'

Jack decided to change direction. He gestured to the room with his glass. 'Do you know all the people here?'

'Many of them, as you would too if you were Italian. There are leaders of business, minor celebrities – like that woman over there, who presents a daytime TV program – and politicians, of course.'

'Politicians?'

'Our family actively supports Lega Nord, the Northern League. They're part of the governing coalition at the moment, propping up that fool Berlusconi, though I don't know how they think that's going to advance the agenda.'

'Which is?'

'Independent autonomy for the northern provinces, basically. When it comes down to it, they just don't like sharing their wealth with those pauper southerners.'

'Seriously? They want to cut Italy in two?'

Jimmy made a dismissive gesture. 'It'll never happen. It's a cause that attracts votes and brings together a bunch of bickering conservative politicians under one banner, that's all. So they can be a force in the parliament, I suppose.' He nodded towards the group that included Stella and Alex. 'If you want to know more, that fat guy over there is Eduardo Moretti, party chairman and current Minister of Culture in the national government.'

Jack looked at the large gentleman standing opposite Stella. His jowls were wobbling as he reacted to some humorous comment. Next to him, a portly middle-aged woman laughed along.

'Now,' Jimmy said, 'shall we get some lunch?'

Stella checked her hair in the mirror. Though hardly a strand was out of place, she took her time – a break from the incessant chatter was welcome. The Minister of Culture and his wife had taken quite a shine to her, which in turn attracted other politicians to the circle. They'd turned out to be some of the worst gossips she'd ever encountered, but had nothing useful to reveal about the Aretino family or business. Alex was attentive and charming, but too much in demand to give her the opportunity for useful intelligence gathering. She would have to manufacture some quality time with him later. It wasn't such an unappealing task.

With a guilty, sexy smile at her own reflection, she turned away and exited the bathroom. The corridor echoed with the noise of happy revellers in the hospitality suites, but she opted for the stairs going down to the ground level. The outside air was warm and humid and tinged with the sharp, sweet smell of racing fuel. She took out her small notebook and a pen. In the shade of an Aretino transport truck painted in team colours and sponsors' brand names, she made a few notes.

Looking up at the massive semitrailer next to her, she wondered at its value. It was clearly customised to meet very specific needs. A set of metal stairs that folded out from a slot above the trailer's front wheel led up to a flush-fitting door. She trotted up quickly and poked her head inside to see a fully equipped workshop and a huge storage space complete with racks for containers and cars. No people, though. She was hoping to do a little informal employee research, but the crew was flat out preparing for qualifying.

She found a guy in team uniform standing by the second

transporter, but he wasn't much use. He'd only been hired the week before as a contract security guard and he wouldn't let her look inside, no matter how coquettish her smile. The only item of interest noted in her little book was the fact that one truck was guarded and the other wasn't.

Next, she headed for the team motorhome. It, too, was painted in glossy burgundy paint with gold highlights, the team colours borrowed from the old Venetian flag. Stepping inside the mobile office complex, she discovered a surprisingly spacious and well-appointed reception area. A sign on the table directed guests to the hospitality suite in the pit complex. There were two closed doors beyond the lounge and as she moved closer, she detected movement inside. Maybe here she'd find a few workers on a break, whose experience with the team she could explore in the course of a friendly conversation. She knocked lightly on the first door and pushed.

A semi-naked woman lay on her back across a table, her head rolling in ecstasy, real or fake. Standing between her flailing legs, a slim Asian man was pumping his hips back and forth. His fireproof racing suit and underwear were gathered at his ankles. It was the Japanese driver for the Aretino team. He looked around and appraised Stella without missing a beat. Then he grinned and gestured for her to come closer. She tried to look nonchalant as she closed the door, murmuring apologies in Italian.

With an embarrassed grin, she retreated to the other end of the vehicle. She saw a narrow winding staircase leading up to a second floor. She climbed it boldly, keeping up the front of a curious, entitled guest. This level was all offices, apparently. Some open doors revealed working spaces complete with desks, computers and telephones. Another stood ajar, and as she moved closer she could just make out a coffee machine and a refrigerator. She was about to push the door open when an argument in Italian erupted inside.

'That stinks!' one gruff male voice said angrily. 'Why should you get nearly twice what I got?'

The second voice sounded younger. 'Relax, I'll buy you a drink when we knock off.'

'But why the hell should you get more than me? I'm senior to you. If anyone should be getting more —'

'I worked extra hours, okay? I'm not supposed to talk about it. I didn't get more for doing the same hours, you arsehole!'

'Extra hours? You got an extra shift? That should have been offered to me first. When was this?'

'They only needed one lorry and the boss knew you'd be busy. You've been going on about Claudia's birthday party for weeks.'

'Last Saturday? But I was only busy in the afternoon, I could have —'

'It was an all-day job.'

'All day? Where did you go?'

'I told you, I'm not supposed to talk about it. Take my word for it, you wouldn't have made it back in time.'

'Is that why they've got that goon guarding your truck now?'

'Vito, please! I told you, I can't say anything.'

'What are you now, some lap-dog to the bosses?'

'I am not!' the younger man said, clearly offended. 'If it was anything interesting, you know I'd tell you. But it was boring. Take the truck, leave the truck, drive the truck back to headquarters, except with a security guy on board. I didn't see what they put in the back.'

'Come on. Where was it, the wind tunnel? Some secret supplier? What have they got up their sleeves now? Is it worth having a few euros on the team next round? Come on, Ugo, I can always go and look it up on your sat nav.'

'Okay, okay. It was Mira. Are you satisfied?'

'Mira?' the gruff voice said. 'What the fuck is in Mira?'

Good question, Stella thought, noting it in her book. But as she wrote, she was startled when a door opened at the end of the narrow passageway. A tall man with broad shoulders and a thick waist stepped out, a sheaf of papers in one hand. When he saw her, he stopped short and took off his spectacles.

'Can I help you?'

16

I should be enjoying this, Jack told himself as they toured the garages after lunch. I've always wanted to do this. So why do I wish I was alone in a dark bar somewhere?

The easy vibe already evident between Stella and Alex Aretino wasn't helping. The annoyingly self-assured aristocrat was lightly touching her arm now, as he leaned close to her ear to answer a question over the noise of nearby engines. Jack was well used to watching men fawn over his partner but, for some reason, he was finding it particularly annoying today. He looked away, his eyes gliding over an extraordinary display of racing and computer technology as he took in the frantic, highly rehearsed activity around the two gleaming cars.

The crew was disconnecting cables from the chassis of one machine, like taking a patient off life support. Electric-powered warming blankets were removed from the tyres. The car was dropped from its jacks onto the spotless painted-concrete floor and the driver opened up the throttle. The sound was almost painful and Jack inserted a finger in each ear. Sticky rubber rolled forward sharply and the racer turned right into the pit lane.

Once the second car had taken off to begin its run, many of the crew came to the back of the garages, where there was a seating area and a refreshment station. I should be talking to these people, Jack told himself. Interviewing employees was an important step in their methodology. But he just didn't feel like it. The fuel-laden air in the busy garage suddenly felt suffocating.

'Would you like to see the telemetry on the computers?'

He snapped back to attention to find Alex standing beside him, gesturing towards the bank of monitors on the rear wall of the double garages. 'No, thanks,' he said dismissively, but regretted it at once. He really did want to see the live data coming in from the cars.

Alex looked surprised, and Stella even more so. 'I'm going to head back to the roof,' he said quickly. 'I like watching the cars on the track. Thanks for the tour, Alex.'

As he stomped up the stairs, frustration chewed at his insides as he chastised himself. Claustrophobia now? Pull your shit together, Jack. But then he sensed that he was being followed. The bearded man with the tattoo was right behind him. On the landing he spun around, ready to throw himself on his attacker. But the kid following him had no tattoos, just a team shirt with multicoloured sleeves. The look on Jack's face was enough to make him scurry away in terror.

Pushing his way back to the spot by the railing where he'd been earlier, Jack drank in the hot air like a deep-sea diver returning to the surface, and focused his attention on the track. The Aretinos had organised a regular waiter service and he spotted a man approaching with a fully laden tray. Warm sunshine, fast cars, cold beer. This was more like it.

'Who's fastest?' he asked, as Jimmy appeared at his elbow.

'The usual suspects. Montoya's doing well but Schumacher looks the winner to me.'

'And your boys?'

Jimmy frowned. 'No good. Bottom two, so far.'

Stick to the cars, Jack advised himself. Don't think too much.

'Does the name Mira mean anything to you?' Stella asked quietly.

'What?' Jack said.

The action on the track was over for the day and they were back in the hospitality suite. 'Mira,' she said. 'It rings a bell with me and I can't think why.'

Jack was feeling slightly woozy after a succession of drinks in the sun. 'The family has a villa there,' he said, recalling his notes with satisfaction. 'Vicky mentioned it.'

'That's it, thanks. It's been bugging me all afternoon. Listen, about tonight . . .'

'What about it?'

But before she could say any more, Alex reappeared and gestured for her to join him in a discussion with Giorgio Borboli. As Stella moved away, his new mate Jimmy took her place, fresh beers in hand. 'Talk to me, please, or I'm going to be stuck with the politicians.'

Jack manufactured a smile and took a beer. 'You don't like politicians?'

'They're not so bad in small doses, but I have to spend the entire evening with this lot.'

'Oh?'

'Yeah, there's a charity ball tonight for the Order's African relief fund. My father's now the patron. In truth, it's just an opportunity for our Northern League friends to demonstrate compassion while pursuing a policy of turning away every desperate dark-skinned refugee who manages to reach Italian soil.'

'Here's to the hypocrites,' Jack said, and they clinked their beers together.

The arrival of Count Charles in the suite prompted a round of meagre applause. He said a few words in Italian that sounded to Jack like a man trying to put a positive spin on a bad situation. Then he moved to join the huddle around Stella and Giorgio.

What are they talking about? Jack wondered. It looks serious. As he sauntered over, Jimmy in tow, her heard Stella apologising. 'I want you to know, Charles, it was never our intention to take advantage of your generous hospitality.'

'What's going on?' Jimmy said, sounding a little inebriated.

Stella looked at Jack. 'Giorgio and I came clean with Alex.'

The Count looked cranky. 'A report?' he said. 'On our group?'

Jimmy laughed and dug his elbow into Jack's ribs. 'Sneaky fellow, you're a spy!'

'Not at all,' Jack said coolly. 'I'm a professional who respects my client's desire for discretion.' He looked to the Count. 'And I think it's a mark of the importance the bank places on your relationship that Giorgio didn't want to offend you by being more open about his concerns.'

Stella stepped closer to the Count. 'As Giorgio and I were explaining to Alex, it's not about your creditworthiness. We are simply trying to fill gaps in the information that any well-run financial institution should have about its largest and most critical client relationship.'

'A relationship that has worked perfectly well for many, many years now,' the Count said haughtily.

'Sure,' Jack said, 'but this is 2003 and circumstances have changed. Part of our job is to determine if some group or individual is gunning for the Aretino Group. Somebody blew up your plane, after all.'

Stella hid a smile. 'I think the point Jack's trying to make,' she said quickly, 'is that what's good for the Aretino Group is also good for the Borboli Bank. The primary objective of our work is to protect our client's interests, which means protecting your interests. Ideally, we'd like to achieve that objective with your goodwill and assistance.'

Count Charles did not look convinced. He turned his head to Alex and said, 'What do you think?'

Alex's brow was furrowed in thought. 'I'm open to talking about it. Stella can brief me on their approach tonight. Then we can decide whether to cooperate with their analysis.'

'Tonight?' Jack asked.

'Tonight?' the Count repeated.

'Yes,' Alex said to his father. 'I've invited Stella to be my guest at the ball tonight. I suggest we talk over dinner and make a decision then.'

'Whoops,' Jimmy said into Jack's ear, 'some starlet expecting a big night out is going to be crying into her pillow soon. My baby brother has a hot new target in his sights.' He cackled with delight and earned a stony-faced rebuke from his father.

'You'd better stop drinking now, Jimmy. You need to be on your best behaviour this evening.'

'Oh dear, Jack,' the sozzled priest said, 'I think I'm in trouble now.'

Jack was chewing his lip, imagining Stella on a glamorous date with Alex. Trouble, he thought? No kidding.

'What time are you going out?' Jack asked.

'Seven-thirty,' Stella said, her tone neutral. She used a key to open the gate on Via Ravizza.

Jack looked at his watch. 'What are you going to wear? It'll be black tie, won't it? You don't have anything appropriate.'

Stella shut the door of the wrought-iron elevator with a loud clang and pressed the button. 'Alex has a contact at Armani. He's arranging for an outfit to be sent over.'

Jack's jaw tightened. 'How nice of him.'

When they got to the front door of the apartment, Stella inserted her key, only to find it already unlocked. 'I'm sure I locked that when we went out,' she said.

'I can hear music,' Jack said, putting his ear close to the heavy wooden door. 'Sounds like heavy metal.'

Stella relaxed at once. 'That will be Sandy,' she said cheerfully.

'Sandy?'

'My cousin, Alessandra.'

'I thought we were visiting your cousins tomorrow.'

Stella pushed open the door. 'Yeah, but Sandy won't be there. I forgot to mention that she was coming to Milan for a concert tomorrow night. She said she might stay here for a night or two.'

'Thanks for telling me.'

'I forgot. You take my bedroom – I'll sleep on the couch.'

'Why can't she sleep on the couch?'

'Because she's here with her boyfriend.'

Jack looked up and rolled his eyes. 'Brilliant.'

17

In his time, Alex Aretino had escorted scores of beautiful women to some of the hottest events on the social calendar. Nonetheless, he seemed genuinely impressed when he saw Stella shimmering in pale-gold silk. The dress hugged every curve that it covered but, with a plunging neckline and no back at all, there was plenty of honey-brown skin to appreciate, too. Those looks and her undoubted intelligence were a rare and exhilarating combination, and he did not hesitate to tell her as much during the short drive to the venue for the charity ball.

'Thank you,' she said. 'You look very nice too.' In truth, she felt close to naked on the cool leather of the limo and wished she'd thought to bring a wrap or shawl. 'I feel a bit guilty about this amazing outfit,' she said, 'after our deception today. I'd like to apologise for that.'

'It's not your fault,' Alex said. 'I realise Giorgio asked you to conceal your real agenda. My father and I were surprised by the bank's concerns, and that they felt unable to talk to us about it themselves.'

'I felt sure you wouldn't object. Unfortunately, I think the bank feels a little restricted by its long history with your family.'

Alex nodded thoughtfully. 'I must admit we've probably come to take the relationship for granted over the years. Perhaps it's time we put things on a more professional footing.'

'Does that mean you've decided to work with us on this?'

'It's entirely up to my father,' he said, 'but that will be my recommendation. I had someone look you up. You've been involved with some major companies and some impressive deals.'

Stella smiled. 'I like a man who does his research.'

Alex smiled too. 'I thought you would.'

After fifteen minutes, the car rolled into the curved driveway at the entrance to the very grand Hotel Principe Di Savoia and under the long modern awning that had been added to protect visitors from the weather. A uniformed attendant opened the back door and Alex exited first before holding out his hand for Stella. With the ever-present fear of tearing the thin fabric of her dress, she was grateful for the assistance, but when she stood up she found herself momentarily confused by a cavalcade of bright flashes. A sizeable group of photographers was gathered together behind a red rope and every lens was pointing in their direction.

'Alex! Alex! Over here,' they called out as Stella steadied herself and ensured her tiny clutch was safe in her right hand. Alex took her left and started walking slowly up the red carpet towards the entrance.

'Alessandro, who's your date?' she heard someone call out in rough Italian. 'She's beautiful, bring her closer.'

There was no point trying to see who was shouting at them because the constant flashes were blinding.

'Alex, look this way, stop for a second.'

'Stella! Over here, Stella!'

Stella froze and looked over at the reporters. How did they know her name? Alex took it as a sign that she was enjoying the limelight. He smiled and stood close to her and the flashing lights went berserk.

'Good girl, Stella, now smile.'

It was same female voice, shouting in English. Automatically, Stella did as she was told and the photographers oohed and aahed appreciatively. Alex gently tugged on her hand and they walked on and up into the meticulously appointed nineteenth-century interior of the hotel. The photographers were already calling out the names of the next guests on the red carpet, a footballer and his tiny wife.

The ballroom sparkled with crystal and gold and the guests were almost as luminous. Impeccably dressed men in black tie escorted women draped in Milan's finest couture, their necks and ears dripping with diamonds and other precious gems. There were celebrities there from all fields – sportsmen, models, actors and politicians. The stars of Formula One were the main focus of attention, including drivers, team principals and wealthy owners, but Stella hardly recognised any of them.

Alex presented her with a flute of champagne and introduced her to a cross-section of the rich and powerful. Small talk, humorous anecdotes and mutual admiration were exchanged in an atmosphere of comfortable formality. Not once did she hear anyone mention the health crisis of the African poor. Even the priests, of whom there were several to be seen, seemed perfectly at home in this vortex of wealth and privilege.

When the guests were directed to the large circular tables, she found herself sitting between Alex and his father. The Count seemed distant as he introduced her to the Countess Anna, and Stella sensed that he had yet to forgive her. Her primary mission that night, she decided, was to bring him around, because without the family's cooperation it would be almost impossible for her to do her job.

Also at their central table were the Minister of Culture, Eduardo Moretti, and his wife, Lia; and the CEO of the Venetian insurance company sponsoring the racing team, whose wife reminded Stella of the actress Judi Dench. The male–female seating arrangement was upset by the two priests at the table. Jimmy Aretino was dressed in a simple black suit and a white dog-collar, a pale shadow of the colourful character she'd met at the track. The other man wore a fancier outfit of deep royal-blue velvet topped off with a short cloak sporting a white eight-pointed star. Stella was informed that this was the Prior of Milan, top dog of the local branch of the Order of Malta.

One corner of the ballroom was occupied by a dance floor and a small orchestra playing background music while the guests ate delicate morsels from gold-edged plates. At the first opportunity, Stella restarted her campaign with the Count. 'Can I say again how sorry I am for not being completely honest with you today. It wasn't worthy of the gracious welcome you extended to us.'

Count Charles gave her a long look. 'I'm assured your professional credentials are impeccable, Stella, so I don't doubt your intentions.' A small smile played around his mouth. 'Actually, from the moment Giorgio walked in with you this morning, I could tell he was hiding something. I've known him too long.'

'I feel confident that if we all work together, Jack and I can find information useful to the Aretino Group as well as the bank. Think of it as an opportunity to get some first-rate analysis at someone else's expense.'

The Count took a sip from his wineglass. 'I have no problem sharing financial data with you. I'll even give you access to the consulting advice we've already paid a great deal for. However, I'm not sure I approve of this wider investigation your partner talked about. For example, I don't think it would be appropriate for you to investigate the bombing of our corporate jet.'

'The authorities don't seem to have made much progress on that front.'

'And you think you can do better?'

'I think we have a knack for looking at things from a different perspective,' Stella said confidently. 'If the people responsible were motivated by ideology, we probably won't have any special insights. But if their objectives were business-related – to undermine the F1 team or decapitate the Aretino Group's leadership, or whatever – we stand a good chance of seeing things the police will miss.'

She leaned slightly closer. 'I've seen enough to know how powerful pure greed can be as a motivation for criminal activity in the business world. Your family and your company may be an irresistible target for some rival or thug who wants what you've got. We might be able to identify who that is.'

'I've received no personal threats or demands,' Count Charles said quietly. 'Not like the other times in our history when people from what you would call the Mafia tried to take advantage of us. People like that make their demands first and try to punish you if you don't comply. And I can't imagine any of our competitors sinking to the level of mass murder.'

'Is it true you were meant to be on the flight?'

'Yes,' he said, his face tightening with emotion. 'I was called back at the last minute for an urgent but unexpected meeting here in Milan. My only brother and my nephew and all those other fine people were killed for no good reason.'

'There must have been a reason,' Stella said with determination, 'and I'd like to know what it was.'

The Count gave her a sad and patronising smile. 'Your enthusiasm knows no bounds, my dear, but you should stick to what you know. I'll tell Alex to arrange for a set of reports and company accounts to be compiled for your perusal. Perhaps he could have it ready for you by Sunday.'

'Sunday?'

'Aren't you joining us for race day?'

'Well, I'd love to but I don't know . . .'

'Oh dear, have I spoilt the surprise?' He looked delighted. 'Alex said he was going to invite you.'

Stella turned towards her escort but Alex was entertaining the Morettis with a joke. Looking back to the Count, she said, 'Do you think Jack could come too? It would be good for both of us to understand the operations of the Formula One team better.'

'It's all business with you, isn't it?'

'Actually,' Stella confided, 'you'd be doing me a big favour. Jack wouldn't be happy if I got to enjoy the whole Grand Prix experience at Monza and he didn't.'

The Count laughed. 'Of course he's welcome to join us. Alex already suggested it.'

'You're too kind.'

'Not at all. Now tell me about your family connections in the Veneto. I understand you have relatives in Monselice. Did you know that at one time the Aretino family owned most of the land in that area? Your great-grandfather probably worked the fields for mine!'

Once the main-course plates had been cleared, the orchestra upped both its tempo and its volume and guests began to move around, some heading for the dance floor while others hobnobbed. Alex was quick to ask Stella for the first dance and proved to be a nimble and practised lead as they waltzed in a slow circle.

'So,' she said, 'I believe there's something you want to ask me?'

He gave her suggestive look. 'There are plenty of things I'd like to ask you, but all in good time.'

She was suddenly very conscious of his hand gently resting on her bare lower back. 'I meant Sunday – something about a Grand Prix race?'

Alex groaned. 'My father told you, didn't he? I was going to ask you later tonight.'

How much later tonight? she wondered.

'So, are you able to join us?' he said.

'Of course.'

He smiled broadly and pulled her closer. She relaxed into his embrace, a warm glow forming deep in her belly. Closing her eyes, she allowed him to glide her gracefully across the dance floor. One fact about Alex Aretino was already indisputable. He was a great dancer.

18

As the night wore on, there was no shortage of partners hoping for a slot on Stella's dance card. Eduardo Moretti, the rotund minister, demanded his turn but thankfully had little stamina, even at the pace of a chamber orchestra. He regaled her with tales of his fight to halt the looting of Italy's cultural heritage. Apparently he'd recently enjoyed national acclaim for preventing the sale of a rare collection of Roman artefacts, put up for international auction by a private citizen in Turin. Stella flattered his ego as required and returned him beaming to his long-suffering wife.

Jimmy also wanted a whirl but didn't have the finesse of his brother, though he had certainly sobered up since the afternoon. It felt odd being held by a priest in a dog-collar, but his informality and sense of humour provided for the most relaxed dance of her evening. He expressed delight at the news of their return to the Grand Prix on Sunday.

'I've got a great idea,' he said. 'Why don't you join us for mass in the morning and go to the track with us in the helicopter? My stepmother likes me to conduct a service in the family chapel when

I'm home, but it would be nice to have more than just the family in the congregation.'

'I can't imagine Jack at mass,' she said, 'but if you're sure . . .'

'Excellent! I'll make sure there's room on the chopper. Expect a car to pick you up at eight. I'll need to get your address. And tell Jack not to worry, I don't take the religious stuff too seriously.'

At the next break in the music, Alex was back to reassert his monopoly on her company. 'It's a pity you're busy tomorrow,' he said, drawing her close as the orchestra played again. 'I enjoyed my day at the track much more than I usually do. It won't be as much fun without you.'

'That would have been nice,' she said, resisting the urge to rest her cheek on his chest and listen to his heart beating. 'As soon as my relatives knew I was coming to Italy, they insisted on setting a date for a family get-together.'

'Where do you have to go?'

'Monselice. You know it?'

'Of course. In fact, my family —'

'I know, I know,' she said. 'Your grandfather owned my grandfather.'

He smiled and pulled his head back to look her in the eyes. 'I wasn't going to put it quite like that.'

His dimples were infectious and she smiled too. 'It's not far from Mira, is it?'

'Not far at all. Twenty minutes in a car. Why? Are you thinking of visiting the Villa Aretino?'

'Could we do that?'

'Sure, it's open on the weekends. If we open it to the public, we get a grant from the local government to help maintain it.'

'Is it worth a visit?'

Alex looked unsure. 'I rarely get there these days. When it was built, it was a retreat from the summer heat of Venice, but our centre of gravity has since shifted to Milan.'

'Are you telling me you've got a whole villa sitting there that never gets used?'

'It gets used for company meetings and charity events, sometimes. We had a few holidays there when I was a kid but it hasn't been a residence for a long time. It's one of those obligations that families like mine must live with.'

'You can't ever sell it?'

'If we do, then you'll know the family is in serious trouble. It is home to the Hall of Heroes.'

'The Hall of Heroes?'

'A ballroom decorated with giant murals depicting glorious episodes in Aretino history. It would be a crime if the place got turned into a conference centre or something. Actually, when I think about it, a visit to the villa is probably worth it for that room alone, even if the rest of the place is looking a bit shabby. It's a room with a secret, too.'

'What was that?'

'You heard me.'

His eyes were sparkling as he swept her sideways in time with the beat. His hips were now locked against hers. As the music came to a climax, she felt slightly breathless and her cheeks were flushed. The imperious voice of Count Charles, amplified by loudspeakers, brought her back down to earth.

'Please take your seats, ladies and gentlemen. Dessert is about to be served and we'll be starting the charity auction shortly, so have your chequebooks and credit cards ready.'

On the way back to the table, Stella was intercepted by Lia Moretti, the wife of the party chairman and minister. 'You look wonderful tonight, Stella. That dress is truly stunning.'

'Thank you, Lia. It's rather more revealing than I would normally wear.'

'Did the photographers catch you on the way in? If they did, you'll be all over the social pages tomorrow.'

Stella was horrified. 'Surely not. Nobody knows me.'

Lia's round cheeks bulged as she smiled. 'A stunning woman arriving on the arm of the most eligible bachelor in Milan. Believe me, that's going to make the papers.'

'That's ridiculous,' Stella said, with a dismissive laugh. 'I'm no Laura Aretino.'

Mrs Moretti visibly blanched. 'No,' she said, 'well, I should hope not!'

'You don't like Laura?'

The minister's wife made a sour face. 'I don't like the effect she has on some men,' she said, and moved towards her seat.

A series of speeches followed the delicious panna cotta, and for a brief while the city's elite were required to contemplate the miserable fate of AIDS- and malaria-stricken communities on the African continent. Count Aretino made a short presentation, as did the Prior of Milan. But the real money was raised when the co-presenters of the highest-rating morning show on local TV conducted the auction. Without intending to, Stella drew attention and approbation again when she paid €25,000 for a weekend at the Hotel Cipriani in Venice and re-donated the prize so it could be auctioned again. Her example was met with enthusiastic applause.

The Aretino family was certainly impressed, Alex in particular. When the fundraising was done, he held her closer than ever as they took a last whirl on the dance floor. He even resisted a call back to the table, where Eduardo Moretti had arranged for bottles of his favourite grappa to be served. But the heavyweight politician demanded the presence of the entire table before he raised his glass to toast the success of the Aretino racing team and, despite his wife's obvious discomfort, would not proceed until Stella, in particular, was by his side.

Oh good, Stella's inner voice said sarcastically as she acceded to the politician's petulance. At least the drunken fool has identified the most important issue of the night. The grappa, served in shot glasses, was aromatic, smooth and seriously strong. Stella silently toasted the AIDS victims of Africa and bolted her measure. Alex seemed to sense her cynicism and quickly steered her back to dance floor.

'It's not Moretti's fault that he's such a pig,' he whispered in her ear as he pulled her tight to his body and swayed to the rhythm. 'He was born that way.'

She smiled and relaxed into his embrace. His hand on her back felt good. She closed her eyes once more and felt the tension drift out of her body on waves of delicate music. And when he kissed her, she responded without inhibition, her nerves tingling with delight.

'I want you to stay with me tonight,' he said, in a low, sensual murmur.

She opened her eyes and found herself staring directly into his. In that moment, nothing seemed to matter except the ardour in those blue-grey orbs. 'Okay', she heard herself say, and then she felt his lips again and his tongue, testing her resolve.

Alex quickly decided it was time to leave, but soon found they were part of a general exodus for the door. Many guests at the ball had another two full days of social engagements to get through before the weekend was over. All the F1 drivers and most of the team members were long gone. The social butterflies and their mates were ready to move on to beds, foreign or familiar.

The whole of Stella's table decided to leave together and the Aretino family exercised practised discretion when they registered the electricity flowing between their favourite son and the new object of his passion. They'd seen it all before. The chitchat was light, meaningless and cheerful as the group made its way to the entrance of the hotel, satisfied at a successful evening that should attract only positive reviews.

Under the long awning over the driveway, a number of paparazzi had stuck it out. Many had been defeated by the deadline for the next day's publications but the bottom feeders remained, hoping for a drunken brawl, an embarrassing stumble or a revealing clothing mishap. There was a wait for limousines and drivers, and the air was thick with smoke from the cigarettes many had been too self-conscious to smoke inside.

When the cool midnight air first touched Stella's hot cheeks, she was already pulsing with self-doubt. Her mind was racing with rational arguments that proved she was about to make a terrible mistake. But a large part of her was longing to indulge in the spontaneous tryst that was on offer. The image of Jack flashed briefly into her mind, and she pushed it out again.

A shiver ran down her bare back. Then Alex squeezed her hand tighter and leant down to quickly nip her earlobe. The shiver turned to a shudder of erotic pleasure that radiated through her nervous system, and she knew the last bit of resistance was gone. She searched the line of cars slowly edging towards the red carpet and found herself anticipating the moment when she was alone with Alex in the back seat and he would take her in his arms and push those full lips against hers again. But their limo was only just inching into the driveway and it would be a few agonising minutes before they would have the privacy to indulge her fantasy.

Eduardo Moretti pulled her away from Alex to tell her how much he'd enjoyed meeting her. His wife looked apologetic as Stella tried to gently remove his fat fingers from her arm. But the minister was determined to complete the bond, launching into an inarticulate rant about the strong fraternal links between Italy and Australia.

Stella struggled to understand him over the high-pitched roar of an approaching motorcycle. She turned her head to see a figure on a powerful red bike weaving between the cars lining up at the hotel entrance. The rider was dressed entirely in tight black leather, the visor of his helmet dark and impenetrable. Suddenly, her perception shifted to slow motion as she registered the shiny metal of a gun strapped to the biker's left leg. She felt sure there was plenty of time to react but for some reason her body wouldn't move. The bike slid to a halt with an angry screech of tyres and the pistol was raised from its holster, pointing, it seemed, directly at her. A loud shot was quickly followed by two more, and she felt a great force knock her sideways. Then she was on the ground, her face pushed against the carpet.

With a piercing roar the motorcycle raced away. As the scream of its engine faded, Stella fought to get to her feet but her left leg refused to move. Then she looked down. Something about her golden Armani had changed. It had been neatly bisected by a dark, sticky spray of arterial blood. And when she looked to her left, she was confronted by the bloated body and lifeless eyes of Eduardo Moretti.

19

The room swirled with smoke, forming an impenetrable cloud that eerily stopped at the level of Jack's waist. He pushed towards the arch but the smoke clung to his legs, holding him back. Something terrifying was behind him. He had to move forward. He pushed harder and managed a single step. But then he looked up and realised the danger was in front of him now. The gun was there, seeking him out. The shape behind the gun was indistinct but coldly menacing. He racked his brain for the words that would stop what was about to happen but could only conjure up a jumble of platitudes. The gun had found him now. There was nothing he could do. He kicked his legs into the smoke and tensed his muscles for the terrible sound that was about to come.

The crystal shattered on the floor with a jarring crash. Ice cubes skidded across the polished wood on a spray of gin and tonic. Jack bolted upright on the couch. 'Shit!' he muttered to the empty room as he realised the nightmare had caused him to kick his drink off the coffee table.

His eyes shot to the clock. He'd been asleep barely fifty minutes.

Was Stella home yet? He rose from the couch and carefully tiptoed around the broken glass. Her bedroom remained dark and empty. The charity ball must have wound up by now, so where the hell was she?

There was no point trying to call her – the tiny handbag she'd borrowed from her aunt's wardrobe was barely large enough for her lipstick and keys. Maybe she got lucky, he mused as he plodded to the kitchen find a cleaning cloth and a container for the glass shards. But if she's going to be with another man, I'd prefer not to know. When he was done with the clean-up, he rearranged the sheets on the couch and switched off the lights in the lounge room. Curling up in the foetal position on the long sofa, he rested his head on a cushion and stared at the illuminated clock on the VCR.

At three-twenty, the front door to the apartment opened. Jack heard Stella's heels on the terrazzo. When the overhead light in the lounge room came on, he rolled over slowly and feigned emerging from a dream. But when he saw her standing by the door, he sat up straight. She was wearing a simple white oversized T-shirt and a pair of sweat pants. 'Where's the dress?' he said, conscious it sounded like an accusation. 'Did he want it back?'

She responded with an exasperated shake of her head. 'The police have it.'

'The police? Fuck, what happened?' He leapt from the couch and came over to her.

'Can it wait?' she asked, her face drawn. 'I need a shower.'

'But what the hell happened to your clothes?'

'Nothing,' she said wearily. 'There was a shooting. The dress was covered in blood and the police took it as evidence.'

Jack's mouth fell open. He took Stella's hand lightly in his and led her to the master bedroom, where she sat down on the edge of the bed with an exhausted sigh.

'Can I get you anything?' he asked.

'A cup of tea would be nice.'

'You got it.'

When he returned with a steaming mug, she was sitting exactly where he'd left her. She took the tea with both hands. Then he sat down next to her. 'Tell me,' he said quietly. 'Tell me all about it.'

She'd already repeated the tale to the authorities more than once, so her delivery was perfunctory. Jack sat incredulous by her side as she described the assassination and the chaos that followed it.

'The Minister of Culture?' he said. 'So it was political?'

'I suppose so. I haven't had time to think about it.'

'Bloody hell,' he exclaimed, as the implications slowly sank in. 'Do you think there's a link to the Aretino bombing? Maybe the plane was blown up because of the Count's association with the Northern League. Isn't he one of the party's biggest contributors?'

'Yes, he is. But so what? I bet there are plenty of connections between the Count and the minister. This is Italy, after all. But every one of them might be irrelevant.'

'You don't think the shooter was our man from Nice, do you?'

She shook her head. 'No way of knowing. He had a similar build, I suppose, but he was wearing head-to-toe leather.'

'Two people assassinated in a few days and you happen to be in both places? That's some screwed-up luck.'

She closed tired eyes and rolled her head to stretch her neck. 'Well, if there's a link between them, I guess we'll have to find it.'

They sat in silent contemplation for a minute and then she pushed herself up onto unsteady legs. 'I have to get cleaned up and out of these revolting clothes.'

By the time he brought her a glass of water in bed, the time was four-fifteen.

'Stay with me awhile,' Stella said in a fragile little-girl voice.

He sat beside her in silence, listening to her breathing.

'I'm glad you're here, Jack,' she said.

He smiled at her voice. It didn't pay to let his mind stray into thoughts of what had been, what could have been.

'I think I'll still have to go to Monselice in the morning,' she said sleepily. 'They're all expecting me. And to be frank, I wouldn't mind getting out of Milan for a while.'

'That's okay,' he said, struggling to keep his own eyes open. 'This time it's your turn to sleep while I drive.' And as he moved his hand gently across her shoulder blades, he silently added the earnest wish that she would cope with the trauma of the evening better than he had dealt with his own recent experiences.

An hour later, when Milan was at its quietest, a dented green van pulled into a rough, narrow laneway in a forested area on the edge of the city. Slowly, it inched forward into a small clearing just about large enough to turn the van around without reversing. The hand-brake was engaged with a metallic clunk and the driver's side door opened. A short, strongly built man climbed down and moved to the rear doors of the van, which opened with a rusty squawk. Quickly, he set up a ramp from the van to the ground. When he emerged from inside, he was wearing gardening gloves.

He switched on a powerful torch and pointed it at the trees and undergrowth surrounding the clearing. A full sweep of the beam did not pick out any break in the thick wall of foliage. Muttering curse words to himself, he started at one edge of the circle and moved around its circumference, stabbing the brush with his torchlight. Still he couldn't find what he was looking for.

With a pained plea to the starry heavens above, he stomped back to the van and used his torch to re-examine the hand-drawn map sitting on the front seat. This was the right place, he was sure of it.

He turned back to the trees and squared his shoulders. The sooner he found it, the sooner he could go home.

He began a methodical search of the leafy circle, pushing his body into the first layer of growth while poking further in with his torch. On his fourth go, he caught a flash of red paint. He started pulling at the branches, amazed at the thoroughness of the camouflage job.

Three minutes later, he was puffing hard as he pushed the red motorcycle up the ramp into his van. When it was secured, he returned to the hiding spot and collected the black helmet and the handgun in plastic garbage bags. Satisfied that the task was complete, he closed up the van and climbed behind the wheel. Before switching off the torch, he pointed it at his wristwatch. With a bit of luck, he'd be home in time for breakfast.

'*Madonna mia*, cousin!' Sandy said. 'What the hell did you get up to last night?'

She and her boyfriend were sitting at the small kitchen table when Stella appeared at the doorway, drawn in by the smell of fresh coffee. 'Look, look, you're famous,' Sandy cried. 'We went out to get some pastries for breakfast and look what we found. Your face is all over the newsstand.'

As she approached the table, Stella could see it was covered in glossy magazines. In fact, there were multiple copies of three magazines, including a 'Special Grand Prix Edition' of Vicky Cavendish's rag, *Peek!* There were also newspapers, none of which were open because Stella was on the front page of all of them. Some of the more tenacious photographers at the ball had captured the moment when Eduardo Moretti had collapsed on top of her. Stella was in the foreground of the pictures, the minister's blood already splattered across her torso. The expression on her face was oddly calm as she stared up at the assassin, who was out of shot.

Moretti Assassinated! one headline read. Another had a caption under the photo that read, *Minister Moretti collapses on model girl-friend of Alex Aretino.*

'This is awful,' she said vaguely, struggling to take it in. 'This is terrible.'

Jack came into the kitchen, attracted by Sandy's excited voice. One look at Stella and he knew she was battling her emotions. He looked down at the table for the source of her distress. His eye was drawn to the colourful magazines, already open to the relevant pages. He saw a picture of Stella in that sheath of a dress. And as his eyes moved across the table, he saw another picture and then another. Stella and Alex, actually, holding hands. Stella smiling. Stella walking the red carpet. Stella looking happy.

The headlines were in simple Italian even he could understand: *Alex finds new love! Alessandro Aretino does it again! Who is this girl? Turn to page 6.* But only *Peek!* had the full scoop. Alex and Stella were featured on the cover of the special edition and the headline read: *Alex Aretino's Aussie Babe – Love at First Sight? Only* Peek! *knows her name!*

He picked it up, but Stella took it out of his hands and opened it to the double-page spread. It had obviously been finalised before the assassination. 'This is Vicky Cavendish's magazine, isn't it? How did she know my name?'

The stress in her voice was worrying. 'Vicky saw us together at the Grand Prix,' he said.

'But you must have told her my name. What else did you tell her about me?' Her eyes were scanning the words interspersed among the photos. 'Stella Sartori,' she read, 'comes from good Venetian stock. Tragically, she was widowed only a year ago but she has not let tragedy stop her from pursuing a successful career in the high-powered business world of Wall Street.'

'Not very good writing, is it?' Jack said.

'Are you trying to ruin us?' she demanded. 'How can we build a business based on discreet advice when my name is splashed all over the press?'

Jack gave her a cool glance. 'I told her your name. The rest she must have dug up on the web. How could I know you'd make yourself interesting to Vicky?'

'Make myself . . .' she repeated, her brow furrowing. 'Are you suggesting I wanted this?' She waved her hand at the kitchen table, but her enthusiasm for an argument was ebbing, to be replaced by pure fatigue. Jack saw her swaying unsteadily, like a boxer recovering from a sharp jab, and he reached out to support her.

'Please,' she said, tears welling in her eyes, 'get me out of here.'

20

Stella sucked in long draughts of warm fresh air. The crunch of gravel underfoot was soothing somehow, a distraction from bitter self-recrimination. Getting people to see past the surface and treat her as a serious professional had taken years of discipline and hard work. Now those damned photos would be all over the net and she'd be fending off ogling fantasists once more. She'd given in to the lure of glamorous self-indulgence for one lousy night and the newspapers had chosen to describe her as a model, interesting only for her looks and the man on her arm. Put it behind you, she told herself. Prove to the bastards that you're more than just a pretty face, all over again.

It had been a rocky start to the day, and got worse before it got better. It took three hours for Stella and Jack to drive to her relatives' place in Monselice. When they'd finally arrived, they were greeted at the gate with enlarged pics of the glamour shots from her night out with Alex, under a makeshift banner that said *Welcome Superstar!* It had proved too much for Stella. She'd told Jack to keep driving and he'd checked a map before bringing them here, to the Aretino villa in the tiny riverside town of Mira. Her relatives would forgive her – and if they didn't, well, she didn't really care.

The tree-lined path from the street led to a two-storey white stucco facade complete with columned portico and baroque plaster-work around the windows. Compared to many of the neighbouring estates, the building and grounds were on a tastefully modest scale. There was no sign to entice passing tourists inside, so it was strangely quiet. Beyond French doors at the entrance, Stella and Jack found a young woman sitting behind a small table talking into her mobile phone. When she saw them she looked startled and stood up quickly, disconnecting her call and speaking briefly to them in Italian.

'She wants us to know the house is being renovated,' Stella trans-lated. 'She thinks we won't find it very interesting without all the furniture, but I'll tell her we'd still like to look around.'

There was another brief exchange.

'She's agreed to give us the tour.'

'Not very tourist-friendly, is it?' Jack said.

'Apparently they have to open up the house to get some sort of grant from the local tourist board, but very few visitors come here.'

'I'm not surprised.'

The young woman stood next to a second set of glass doors leading to the main entrance hall of the villa, and formally introduced herself as Gina. Then she launched into a prepared talk about the house.

Stella translated the highlights. 'Built in the first half of the eight-eenth century in the rococo style by Count Francesco Aretino of Venice and Padua. Apparently they knocked down an older Aretino palazzo to build it here.'

Gina pointed out some architectural features on the exterior facade before inviting them inside. They followed her into the main hall, where the lack of furniture and floor coverings gave it a ghostly feel. Only the elaborate Murano glass chandelier in the centre of the ceiling hinted at the lost richness of the interior. Jack's eyes moved around the walls, panelled in wood painted pale green, and noticed rectangular shapes of darker paint where paintings had once hung. There was some furniture in the corner, but it was hidden beneath large white dust sheets.

Gina showed them a dining room lined with worn blue wallpaper, and several smaller empty rooms. There was little to afford any insight into the Aretino family. At the top of a carved and gilded staircase, she made a sweeping gesture with her arm and started speaking her lines with greater gusto. They had come out on a gallery that looked down into a grand room at the rear of the villa. An ornate white rail ran around the gallery but it was the ceiling that caught Jack's eye. It was divided into large panels by fancy plasterwork, and each panel was filled with biblical scenes. In the centre of the ceiling there was a large moulded representation of the Aretino coat of arms. Latin words in raised uppercase letters circled the heraldry.

Looking down into the ballroom below, he could see a threadbare tapestry rug covering a marquetry floor. At the far end of the hall, tall windows and glass doors looked out to the garden. The other three walls were completely covered in dramatic murals of battle scenes.

Stella listened to Gina's talk and told Jack the hall had been added to the villa in 1800 by the grandson of the man who'd laid the foundations. 'This is the Hall of Heroes Alex told me about. He said it was a room with a secret.'

'Really? What did he mean by that?'

'Who knows?'

It's probably where he lost his virginity to one of the servant girls, Jack said to himself, as they returned to the staircase.

The room was even more imposing from ground level. The high ceiling framed by the gallery was an eyeful, but the depictions of

medieval conflicts on the three interior walls were even more remarkable. About six metres high and in some places nearly fifteen metres
across, the paintings all featured epic clashes between Christian and
Islamic forces at different times in history.

Stella, translating Gina's words, said the first one depicted the
battle for Jerusalem during the First Crusade. There were stone
battlements filled with vicious-looking Turks, and rolling hills covered
with armoured knights and foot soldiers waving flags bearing the red
cross of the Crusaders and the distinctive eight-pointed white cross
of the Hospitaller Order.

'The Order had already been in Jerusalem fifty years before the
Pope sent this lot to take it back from the Muslims in 1098,' Stella
explained, pointing to a series of out-of-scale buildings drawn inside
the city walls. 'Gina says this is one of their hospitals. It was only
after the fighting started that they added military duties to the task
of preaching and healing Christian pilgrims.'

Gina indicated an almost life-sized figure of a mounted knight
holding the Order's banner in one hand and, in the other, a sword
pointing down and away from his horse.

'That's an Aretino, apparently,' Stella said, 'although Gina says
they've never been able to prove beyond question that the family
was in the Order from the very beginning.'

They followed their guide as she walked to the opposite wall of
the room, still reciting from her memorised lines. 'This is 300 years
later,' Stella said, 'after the Holy Land was lost and the Knights of St
John had moved to the island of Rhodes, just off the Turkish coast.'

The second mural was dominated by depictions of dramatic naval
battles in which all the victorious vessels appeared to sail under the
Order's eight-pointed cross, while Islamic ships and their unfortunate crews were burning, sinking or fleeing in terror. As with the
first mural, a single knight stood out from the rest. He was shown

standing on the deck of the largest of the ships, one arm thrust out to point at some unseen enemy.

'Don't tell me,' Jack said, 'he's an Aretino, right?'

'This one is documented, apparently,' Stella said, keeping one ear on the unstoppable Gina. 'The knights held Rhodes for two centuries, holding a dagger to the belly of the Ottoman Empire and becoming the dominant naval power in the Mediterranean. Eventually they got kicked out.'

'Which is when they moved to Malta,' Jack said, indicating the third, smaller mural on the end wall.

Stella waited for Gina to catch up before saying, 'That's right. After seven years in limbo, they were granted the islands of Malta and Gozo by the Emperor Charles V. That's him standing off to one side next to the Pope.'

'And this would be the Aretino.' He pointed up to a prominent and handsome figure in knightly robes who seemed to be pointing straight back at him.

'Yes, standing next to Grand Master Jean de la Vallete, who won the Great Siege of 1565 which is depicted here. But interestingly, it's not the Aretino who was at the siege. It's a portrait of the one who built this room after the Order lost the island two hundred years later.'

'That's ego for you,' Jack observed drily as he looked more closely at Jimmy's ancestor. 'These Aretinos all like to point, don't they?'

'They really do,' Stella said slowly.

A curious tone to her words prompted Jack to look over and observe her staring at the ceiling. 'What is it?'

Instead of replying, Stella turned towards Gina, who was waiting patiently a few metres away. Her question caused the young guide to look up towards the coat of arms directly overhead before proffering an answer.

'I thought so,' she said to Jack. 'The Latin inscription up there says "Our ancestors point the way."'

Jack's eyes flicked to the Malta mural. 'You mean literally?'

'Well, if you look at all three Aretino boys, they seem to be pointing at the same thing.'

Turning to look at the long murals, Jack could see she was right. The knights were all pointing down from their respective poses towards a spot at the far end of the room. 'You think that's part of the secret?'

She shrugged. 'I haven't the slightest idea. I'm just spitballing, as our American friends would say. Come on, Gina wants to show us the kitchens and the garden.'

'You go on,' he said. 'Tell her I'm a history buff and want more time with the amazing murals. I'll catch up with you in the garden.'

She frowned. 'What do you think you're going to find?'

'I don't know. Nothing, probably. But you've roused my curiosity, and if I've learned anything in the last year, it's to never ignore your instincts. I just want to check it out. It'll only take a minute.'

Gina's reluctance to leave a guest unsupervised was quickly overwhelmed by Stella's charm and ease with the local Veneto dialect. Two minutes later, Jack was walking backwards over the massive rug, lining his feet up with the notional extension of each knight's right arm. He decided on a spot about two metres in from each edge of the carpet, at the window end of the hall. With a guilty look over his shoulder, he gripped the corner of the enormous rug with two hands and pulled it back on itself, revealing a large area of intricately worked marquetry.

The polished veneers, protected from the sunlight, glowed as they must have done two centuries earlier. The complex pattern featured cartouches containing the ubiquitous Maltese cross at regular intervals. He looked closer, seeing nothing except exquisite craftsmanship. But as he moved laterally, the angle of light from the windows changed and a subtle shape caught his attention. Faint footprints in fine dust. They stopped at the rug's edge, swept away by a cleaner who hadn't bothered to check underneath. He traced the prints backwards but soon lost them. Then he looked back and realised they disappeared at the same spot pointed out by the knights.

Dropping to his knees on the folded rug, he ran his hand slowly over the smooth timber. On his third sweep, the tip of a finger detected the slightest ridge between two carved elements within one of the cartouches. The Maltese cross motif was sitting proud by the width of a few hairs. He could see no way to lift the piece out of the floor without damaging it, so he gave its centre a push. It didn't move. Adjusting the angle of light again revealed fine lines running across opposing tips of the eight-pointed cross, forming two shapes each as small as an American dime. He pressed down on both spots simultaneously and smiled with surprise and satisfaction when the cross popped up a few millimetres.

The thrill of discovery was matched by the fear of being caught in the act, and his heart began to thump as he lifted up the piece of floor to reveal an inset brass handle. There was a gap to insert a finger under the rectangular latch and, with a final furtive look for any sign of Gina, Jack gave it a firm tug.

Amazingly, a trapdoor had been set into the floor with such precision that it was impossible to see in the patterned wood until it was lifted. A little wider than a man's shoulders, the panel was about two metres long and a few centimetres thick. Solid and weighty, it took both of Jack's hands to raise it up to shoulder height, revealing the top few flights of a wooden staircase descending into complete darkness.

Under the trapdoor he found a hinged metal arm, which he pulled free to insert into a slot at the top of the stairs. Without hesitation, he put his foot on the top step, ducked under the door and felt for the second step with his foot. He began to descend but the steepness of the stairs was disconcerting, especially as his feet were quickly swallowed by the dark shadow of the hidden cellar.

A noise from somewhere deeper in the villa startled him and his left foot slipped off the step. Instinctively, he threw out his arms to prevent a fall but it was too late. His butt landed painfully on the sharp corner of a wooden tread and the air was pushed from his lungs. As he bounced down into the gloom, a final fling with his hand connected sharply with the rod supporting the trapdoor, knocking it free of its housing. With a loud crash the heavy trapdoor slammed down and by the time Jack had hit the cellar's floor he was enveloped by an impenetrable blackness.

Disoriented and nursing several painful spots, he clambered to his feet and thrust out his hands, grazing his knuckles on a stone wall. 'Shit!'

He dug in the front pocket of his jeans for his Nokia and activated the keypad. As it came to life, the glow emanating from its little screen only penetrated a metre into the gloom but he could make out the wall that had claimed some of his skin. Then he turned around to try to locate the stairs but instead glimpsed an object that brought his breathing to a sudden halt. Moving closer, the unmistakable shape revealed itself and he could see that there was actually a pile of three ominous boxes.

'Fuck me,' he said out loud, 'coffins!'

21

Damn fool, Kurt Bauer thought, as he observed Prinz Gerhard looking for him in the middle of the restaurant. He lowered his eyes to the electronics magazine on the table in front of him. He wasn't about to draw attention to himself.

The trattoria was populated by a relaxed Saturday crowd, comprised of both the local glitterati and foreigners in town for the racing. Eventually, the prince came over Bauer's table.

'I didn't recognise you,' he said in a quiet voice as he sat down.

'That's the idea.'

'You shaved off your beard. And those glasses, and that shirt! You look like a kindergarten teacher.'

Bauer calmly took a sip of his coffee. 'I used to be a teacher, you know.'

'That's, er, hard to imagine.'

'I've ordered some pasta. You want something?'

'No, I have to get back quickly before I'm missed.'

'Did Schumy get the pole?'

The prince nodded. 'Only just. Montoya's very fast too. Should be a good race.' He reached inside his jacket and Bauer lifted up his magazine slightly. The prince glanced at the cover as he slipped a thick envelope under it. 'Thinking of building a remote-controlled car?'

'Something like that. Speaking of remote control, how did the clean-up go?'

'All taken care of.'

Bauer shook his head doubtfully. 'I don't like relying on other people to —'

'I know,' the prince said sardonically, 'you're not much of a team player. By the way, I saw a French newspaper this morning. They're pushing for a government campaign warning people about the dangers of slipping in the bath.'

Bauer allowed himself a slight smirk. 'Sounds like a sensible idea.'

Gesturing vaguely towards the magazine, the prince said, 'I included a bonus for the photographer.'

'You're very generous with your partner's money, aren't you?'

The prince ignored the gibe. 'If you do a good job, you deserve to be rewarded.'

Bauer's eyes narrowed a fraction. 'It wasn't as clean as I would have liked.'

'What do you mean?'

'Jack Rogers, the American. He saw my face. And there was a woman. Bitch nearly broke my wrist. I think I saw her last night, too.'

A waiter came to the table and deposited a plate of fettuccine on the table. Prinz Gerhard licked his lips and Bauer noticed.

'You sure you don't want a bowl?' Bauer asked.

'I've already eaten.'

'I see.'

The prince sat up straighter and pulled in his stomach. 'He's Australian, by the way. Jack Rogers. The woman is too. I don't think we need to worry too much about them.'

'What makes you so sure? You know more now?'

'A little. They're business consultants, preparing a report for Giorgio Borboli's bank.'

'Rogers gave me some other bullshit in Nice.'

The prince was looking at the pasta on Bauer's fork. 'Let them worry about the numbers. In a week it will be too late for them to interfere, anyway.'

'They can do a lot of damage in a week. Why were they chasing down the film if they're just analysts?'

'I don't know, but they didn't get it, did they?'

'I can't be absolutely certain of that.'

The prince tapped a fingernail on the table nervously. 'That could be a problem. We both know where a detailed analysis of that footage could lead. It would be nice to know for sure. But you said yourself it's a stupid time to take unnecessary risks. They've ingratiated themselves with the Aretinos. It's too close.'

Bauer added parmesan to his bowl and chewed a mouthful while he thought. 'All the more reason to be careful. Can you find out where they're staying?'

'That shouldn't be a problem. What are you planning to do?'

'Nothing that will come back to you.'

The prince looked nervous. 'My partner will want to know.'

Bauer gave him a withering look. 'Take it from me, he doesn't want to know details.'

'No, you're probably right,' the prince said, smiling. 'That's what I like about you, Kurt,' he added, 'you're such a professional.'

22

Where the hell is he? Stella looked at her watch and then back to the villa. She was starting to run out of questions about the garden and sensed Gina was itching to wrap up the tour.

'We should go and look for your husband.'

'He's not my husband,' Stella said quickly. Why were people so determined to link her to a man? 'What are those buildings behind the trees?' she said, moving further along the path bisecting formal lawns and empty flowerbeds.

'Garages and workshops at the front. We live at the rear.'

'You live here?'

'Yes. My family has worked for the Aretinos for generations.'

'What's the town like?'

'Mira?' Gina made a sour face. 'Boring. It's tiny, but at least it's close to Padua and Venice.'

'Are there any factories around here, or large warehouses?'

'There's a guy who makes shoes. Not sure you'd call it a factory.'

'Nothing to do with motor racing? I don't suppose there's a wind tunnel or a carbon-fibre workshop?'

'A what?'

'Things they use in Formula One.'

'No idea about that, but we did have a truck from the Aretino team here last weekend.'

'Here, at the estate? What was it doing?'

'No idea. They didn't open up for tourists so I was given the day off.'

'Those transporters are huge, aren't they? Where did they park it?'

'Over there,' Gina said, pointing towards the garages. 'They had a lot of trouble backing it in.'

Stella casually altered direction towards the driveway at the side of the villa. 'But you didn't see what they were doing?'

'Loading or unloading something, I imagine.' Her tone was wary.

'From the house or the garages?'

'I don't know. Why do you ask?'

'I was at the Grand Prix yesterday,' Stella said, 'as a guest of the Aretinos. I'm going to be there again —'

'I knew it!' Gina said, pumping a clenched fist. 'You're that woman who was with Alessandro at the ball last night. I saw your picture on the news. I thought it was you but when I saw you with that other guy . . .'

'He's my business partner.'

'Oh, right.' For some reason, Gina seemed relieved.

'My name's Stella.'

She held out her hand and the younger woman seemed delighted by the gesture. 'I'm Gina.'

'Yes, I know.'

Stella found the sudden flustered excitement amusing. Perhaps this celebrity thing had an upside. She was still leading the way towards the concrete apron where the truck had been parked. When they passed through the line of trees, she saw three wooden garage doors. One was open, revealing an interior largely empty but for some rusty tools and machinery. In front of the middle door a tired green van was parked.

With renewed boldness, she went up to the open door and looked inside the garage. There was nothing in there less than forty years old. 'The transporter was parked here?'

'Right there, where my uncle's van is,' Gina said. 'He looks after the gardens.'

Stella walked behind the green van, trying to imagine the huge Aretino team truck sitting in that spot. What were they doing here? she wondered. Some research so secret it couldn't be done at the team's factory? A splash of bright red caught her eye. A sudden flashback rocked her – a screaming red bike, and a man with a gun. It almost made her knees buckle and she put one hand on the van to support herself as she looked for the source of the colour.

Through a small window on the battered rear door of the van, a ray of sunlight was reflecting on some shiny red metal inside. She put her face to the thick glass but it was dirt-encrusted and she couldn't make out anything other than the patch of red metal. She tried the door but it was locked.

'What does your uncle keep in his van?' she asked Gina. 'Does he have a red machine of some sort?'

'Yes, he has a new ride-on mower. He moves it around in that van.'

Stella took a deep breath to calm her racing pulse. Jesus, she thought, I hope that doesn't happen every time I see something red. She smiled at Gina, who was looking at her with a concerned, curious expression. 'I'm sorry,' she said. 'My questions must seem bizarre. I'm having dinner with Alex tonight and I'm hoping to impress him with my knowledge of the Formula One operations.'

Gina made a face that said, I don't care, as long as you're talking to me. 'There was only one guy here last weekend I recognised,' she said helpfully, 'but I don't think he has anything to do with the team. I'm pretty sure he's a historian or professor. He's been here a few times in the last two or three years, mostly in the Hall of Heroes.'

'Do you know his name?'

'No, but the family should know it. I think he has some connection to the Order.'

'And he was here with the truck?'

'I don't know about that. But he was here at the same time. I saw him in the villa when I was going out.'

'On his own, or with a member of the family?'

'Alone,' Gina said. 'Personally, I haven't seen any Aretinos here since before the loss of Count Federico and his family back in May.'

Well, Stella thought, all that tells me precisely nothing. She moved away from the van and was relieved to see Jack coming through the trees to the driveway. He appeared to be brushing dirt from his jeans. 'We need to get going,' she said. 'Thanks for the tour, Gina. I really enjoyed talking to you.'

The young woman beamed but seemed sorry to see her new celebrity pal go. Stella joined Jack and they walked down the driveway together. 'Where the hell have you been?' she asked. 'Did you find something?'

He was examining his grazed knuckles in the sunlight. 'A tomb,' he said. 'Under the floor.'

'A tomb?' she repeated, incredulously. 'You mean a family crypt?'

'No, not really. There were no sculptures or inscriptions. Just a dark, narrow space large enough for nine wooden coffins, stacked in threes. The light was bad but I'm pretty sure they all date from a similar time. They were certainly of a consistent size and shape, but they weren't fancy. I'd describe them as simple pine boxes, though they probably weren't pine. Definitely very old.'

'Sounds a bit downmarket for this family.'

He shook his shirt and released a cloud of fine dust. 'They say every family has a skeleton or two in the closet. In the case of the Aretinos, it's the literal truth.'

She smiled at the joke. 'I guess a hidden tomb qualifies it as a room with a secret.'

'Are you going to tell Alex we worked it out?'

'I don't think so. He may not have intended for us to actually work *out* the secret. I don't want to embarrass him.'

'We wouldn't want that, would we?' Jack said, with a sly grin.

'Don't start. I don't suppose you took a look inside those coffins?'

'No. I was alone in the dark with them – you might appreciate why I didn't feel like opening them.'

'I guess you're right.'

'I did bang on a couple and they sounded pretty hollow, but they would, wouldn't they? It was pretty creepy down in that pit. I almost got stuck there.'

He glanced her way, expecting a response, but her attention was elsewhere. Her eyes were fixed and her brow wrinkled in a frown. He followed her gaze to the front lawn of the estate and saw a small, stocky man cutting the grass. He was riding a bright red lawnmower.

'You're going on another date with him tonight?'

'Why call it a date?' Stella said. 'Alex is effectively running the Aretino Group while his father is distracted with the team.'

Jack pulled the Alfa up next to the attendant. 'Well,' he said drily, 'if it's a business meeting with our most important contact, I'm happy to come along and take notes, if you like.'

'I'm sure I can handle it, thanks.' She opened her door and climbed out of the car.

Jack acknowledged the smiling lad waiting to park the car and followed Stella as she hurried up the ramp to the street. 'I wish you'd told me earlier,' he said. 'I might have arranged to go out myself.'

'Who with?'

'Oh, I'm sure I could rustle up some company.'

She gave him a sardonic look. 'I imagine you could, but I was hoping you'd play around with that film footage a bit more. If they're willing to kill to keep it out of circulation, there must be something incriminating in it.'

'The only lead I can think of is identifying the owner of that cruising yacht, but nothing I've tried so far has revealed any details.'

'Maybe you could get some better software. Think about it. If we can find a link between that boat and one of the Count's business or political rivals, we'll look like superstars.'

'Yeah, well, I suppose I could do that while you're fending off Alex's advances.'

Fending them off? Stella thought as they walked the wide pavements of the Via Ravizza. I'm not so sure. A shiver of anticipation snaked through her body.

Waiters from the restaurants along the street were preparing outdoor tables for the Saturday-night rush, including the blue and white marquee outside The Dolphin, a few doors down from their apartment building. It wasn't until they'd passed by the freshly set tables that they noticed the dark-blue car pulled up to the entrance gate of number twelve. Down the side of the car, large white letters spelled out the word: *Carabinieri*. Next to the car stood a tall, slim man wearing an impressive navy-blue uniform with red piping, complete with tall peaked cap. His chin was out-thrust and one hand sat on his hip, casually propped on the covered leather holster of a large pistol.

'Oh no,' Stella said, 'maybe the cops want to ask me some more questions.'

'Why wouldn't they call you? Didn't you give them your number?'

'I switched my mobile to silent,' she said. 'I knew I'd get a bunch of calls and messages from my cousins.'

Instead of looking at her phone, she spoke to the uniformed man. He looked down his nose at them and told her they should go upstairs.

'He reckons there are more of them in the apartment,' she said.

'Inside?' Jack said, already moving to the interior lobby. 'What the hell?'

The cage elevator was on another floor, so he began jogging up the stairs, with Stella close behind. On the third level, the door to their apartment was sitting ajar and Stella pushed past him to enter first. In the entrance hall she saw another uniformed officer writing in a notebook. He was looking at a spot on the floor a few metres inside the door and her eyes swivelled down to see a coagulating pool of blood on the olive-green terrazzo.

'Oh my God!' she said. 'Where's Sandy?'

23

'Is she okay?' Jack demanded, frustrated by an exchange of rapid Italian that he couldn't follow. Stella seemed to be asking as many questions as the officer was. 'Stella!' he said, touching her arm. 'Is Sandy okay?'

She switched to English and her anxiety was obvious. 'She was knocked unconscious but she's going to be okay. She's at the hospital.'

'An accident?'

She shook her head grimly. 'No. Apparently she came back to the apartment and surprised a man just inside the door.'

'He was already inside?' Jack asked.

'Yes, but he hit her immediately so she didn't register much more than a dark shape and a hand in black leather. She woke up on the floor and made it to the phone. She called the police and they took her to the hospital.'

'Thank Christ for that,' Jack said.

Stella nodded her agreement. 'She managed to tell the cops about me and my connection to the assassination last night, so the carabinieri have taken over. The captain who questioned me last night is on his way over now.'

'When did it happen?'

'About ninety minutes ago.'

'What about the boyfriend, what's-his-name?'

'Arno. He was out with some mates. They tracked him down and took him to the hospital.'

'Do you want me to drive you over there?'

'Yes, but this guy says we can't leave until the captain says so. He wants us to look around to check if anything's been taken.'

Jack, for one, hadn't forgotten about Stella's seven o'clock appointment. 'What about Alex?'

'Oh shit,' she said, reaching into her bag. 'I'd better call him off.' She went into the kitchen with her mobile to her ear.

Jack gave Stella her privacy and walked slowly into the lounge room, looking around for anything missing or out of place. On the low glass table, their computers and neatly piled stacks of papers appeared to be just as they'd been left. Both laptops were switched off and cool to the touch, as he would expect. Stella's relatives' possessions also appeared untouched, from the expensive television and sound system to the collectibles and crystal in the illuminated arched niches in the wall above the dining table.

A scan of the rest of the apartment revealed no signs of theft. By the time his survey was complete, the captain had arrived, already armed with a theory. They sat on the long brown couch while Stella listened to his hypothesis. When he was done, she turned to Jack. 'He thinks it was probably a journalist or photographer. They've been taking calls from hacks all day, apparently, trying to get more information about me.'

Jack opened his mouth to express the view that the captain's theory was absolute crap but he detected a tiny shake of her head, backed up by a look that said to keep quiet.

'They're going to keep a patrol on the street downstairs for a while,' she said. 'Until the fuss dies down.'

'Okay,' he said. 'That's good, I guess.'

'Sandy distinctly remembers the leather glove, so they're not going to dirty the place with fingerprint powder. They're canvassing the area for witnesses but don't expect much to come of it. The locks were picked very professionally. Apparently some of the paparazzi are pretty experienced with breaking and entering.'

Jack shook his head. Breaking in, maybe, but he couldn't imagine a paparazzo knocking someone out cold. This felt much more sinister than gossip mongering.

Stella wanted to visit Sandy at the hospital but eschewed the captain's offer of a ride or an escort. Soon the carabinieri politely took their leave and left them alone in the apartment.

'Talk about the gentle touch,' Jack said. 'They're treating you like a celebrity after a few lousy photos in the paper.'

'They think we move in powerful circles,' Stella said.

'Yeah, right. How powerful do you feel right now?'

She responded with a glum shake of the head. Jack followed her as she went to find a bucket and a mop. 'What's your theory behind all this?' he asked.

'It's just a minor assault, right? At least as far as the police are concerned.'

'But it wasn't, was it?' His tone was sharper. 'We both know it was no reporter or overzealous shutterbug. Why didn't you tell him about what happened in Nice?'

'Because I didn't tell him about Nice when he interviewed me last night. It was all too complicated and I had nothing more than speculation to offer. The same applies today. For all we know, it was a reporter or something, just like he says.'

'Do you really believe that, Stella?'

She stopped pushing the mop across the floor. 'No, I don't.'

Once the blood had been cleared up, Stella put the mop away and reached for her handbag. 'We'd better get to the hospital,' she said.

Jack grabbed the keys and headed for the door. 'Do you know how to get there?'

'We can ask the cops downstairs,' she said as he opened the door for her.

'Ask them what?' said the man in the dark-grey suit on the landing. His hand was raised as if he'd been about to knock on the door.

'Who are you?' Jack asked.

The man raised his other hand to show them the photo ID in his wallet. 'My name is Bruno Mancini.' His English was good but strongly accented. 'I am a deputy inspector attached to Europol.' He nodded to the younger man standing behind him. 'This is Sergeant Tolano.'

'Europol?' Stella said. 'Is that part of Interpol?'

'No, it's an agency that facilitates information sharing between police forces in the European Union. May I come in?'

Jack pulled the door back and made way for their visitors. Mancini looked to be in his late thirties. He was slightly shorter than Jack and wore chic designer spectacles, complementing a receding hairline that he made no effort to disguise.

'Why do you have carabinieri outside your apartment building?' he asked, once they were inside.

'You don't know?' Stella said, surprised.

Mancini shook his head. 'I'm here to talk to you about an incident in Nice last Wednesday night. I've been asked to show you some head shots of possible suspects who match the description you gave. Has something else happened?'

Jack briefly outlined the recent events, from Stella's near miss at the Moretti assassination to the break-in and assault on Sandy. 'The carabinieri think it was a reporter trying to get the scoop on Stella's background, but we think it's more likely to be connected to the guy we encountered in Nice.'

Jack held out a hand, inviting the Europol cop to step into the lounge room, but Mancini didn't move. 'You say nothing was taken from the apartment during the break-in?'

'That's right,' Jack said, his arm still extended.

'I need you to come back to my office,' Mancini said, his voice more serious.

'We're going to the hospital,' Stella said defiantly. 'I need to see my cousin.'

Mancini fixed her with a determined glare. 'It won't take long, Dottoressa Sartori. Please, come this way.'

He opened the front door and made a gesture to his junior partner, indicating that he should stay on the landing. Stella bristled and looked prepared to resist but Jack took her by the elbow and steered her in the direction of the elevator. There was something about Mancini's manner that gave him confidence. 'We were heading out anyway,' he said.

The old lift was still on their floor. As they shuffled inside the tiny box, Mancini was already speaking Italian into his phone. Stella couldn't help but eavesdrop and her eyes widened. 'He's asking for a surveillance technician to come to this address,' she said to Jack. 'Do you think that means —'

'If the man you encountered in Nice is the same man I think it is,' Mancini said, snapping his phone shut, 'there are only a few reasons why he'd break into an empty apartment. Either he was mapping the layout for some future attack, stealing some critical item or piece of information, or —'

'Installing a bugging device,' Jack said.

Mancini nodded, as if impressed. 'Quite possibly. I thought it was not a good idea for us to talk inside the apartment until we have made sure that it is safe. My office will send over someone to run a quick sweep. In the meantime, can you recommend a good bar?'

24

'He's not here,' Jack said, his voice thick with disappointment.

Mancini looked at Stella. 'Do you agree?'

She nodded her head slowly. 'Yes.'

'Relax,' the inspector said. 'There are more.'

He placed another sheet of photographs on top of the first. Eight more male faces, most snapped in the process of being arrested. Immediately, two index fingers landed on the bearded face in the bottom row. 'That's him,' Jack and Stella said in chorus.

Mancini looked satisfied and took a drink from his Japanese lager. 'This is what we thought also.' He produced another photograph from his portfolio. It showed a lean left arm decorated with an intricately drawn octopus, the tentacles of which curled towards the wrist.

'That's definitely the tattoo,' Jack said, swallowing an unwelcome memory. 'I'll never forget it. Who is he?'

The Inspector reached for another file but was interrupted by a phone call. 'The technicians have arrived,' he said. 'Tolano will let them in, if that's okay?'

Stella nodded her approval, her eyes fixed on the folder in Mancini's hand. The inspector barked instructions into the phone and flicked it shut. 'His name is Kurt Bauer,' he said, opening the file to look inside.

'Kurt Bauer,' Jack repeated.

Mancini nodded. 'Unfortunately, we don't know a great deal about him. He's very good at staying out of sight. He was born in Rostock, in former East Germany, and studied electrical engineering during a stint in the navy. He even taught for a while at a technical college. Then he lost that job and disappeared for a few years. There are rumours he was a mercenary in Africa.'

He paused to take another drink. 'The only time he was ever arrested was in Munich six years ago, when he was identified by two witnesses in connection with the death of a mother and her two children in an apparently staged swimming pool accident.'

'How revolting,' Stella said.

'It gets worse,' Mancini said. 'With a spotless record, he was released on bail.'

'Don't tell me,' Jack said. 'The witnesses turned up dead?'

Mancini nodded. 'One fell in front of a train and the other disappeared completely. Later, the husband of the dead woman admitted paying Bauer to kill his family for the insurance, but the next day he was found hanging in his police cell. The German authorities still don't know how Bauer achieved that.'

'Bloody hell!' Stella said. 'He's a ruthless bastard.'

'That is a good description,' Mancini said approvingly. 'His involvement with a number of unexplained deaths is suspected but impossible to prove. We know he operates around the Mediterranean these days, providing security – and no doubt other services – to the rich and powerful, including a number of known organised-crime figures. He specialises in high-end yachts and cruisers, because he has the skills to be both skipper and security chief.'

Jack and Stella exchanged a look.

'What?' Mancini said.

'The thing in Nice,' Stella said cautiously. 'You know it was all about the footage Marcel Ganet took of the Aretino plane?'

'I know that's one theory.'

'There was one thing we didn't mention to the French police . . .'

'I didn't mention it,' Jack said, 'because I understood the authorities already had a copy of Ganet's footage.'

'The footage?' Mancini said. 'You mean you have a copy of the footage Bauer was looking for?'

'Yes,' Stella said. 'And it shows a luxury yacht in the water when the plane blew up. We think you can see Bauer there, but the image gets a bit fuzzy when you enlarge it.'

Mancini was looking at them with new eyes. 'I'll need to see that footage – send me a copy. Looks like you two are going to be very important if we ever catch up with this guy.'

'You mean he's going to want us dead,' Jack stated flatly.

The inspector's expression didn't exactly inspire confidence. 'I'm certainly glad you have somebody watching your apartment. This guy specialises in accidents.'

Jack drained his glass, wishing it contained something stronger than beer, and glanced around the room. The Japanese pub was slowly filling with pre-dinner drinkers but he felt no connection to the carefree ambience. Death and violence seemed to be stalking him and Stella. They were bouncing from one bloody event to another without the slightest idea why or of how to stop it. He jumped slightly when Sergeant Tolano appeared at Mancini's elbow.

He watched Stella's face as she listened to their conversation, and it was soon apparent that she found the news extraordinary.

'They found bugs in the lounge, the kitchen and both bedrooms,' she said breathlessly. 'The latest technology, apparently; very expensive. Wireless devices linked to a nearby transmitter, which then uploads the signals to either the mobile phone network or the internet.'

'Jesus!' Jack said. 'Are they sure they got rid of all of them?'

She shook her head. 'I don't think they've removed any of them.'

'What?'

Mancini started speaking in English again. 'It's your decision, but I suggest we leave the listening devices alone for the moment. It's actually a good sign that he wants to listen to you rather than, uh . . .'

'Silence us permanently,' Jack suggested.

Mancini nodded. 'If they are removed, there's a good chance Bauer will see you as an immediate threat and feel obliged to take lethal action. He is trying to find out what you know and what your intentions are.'

'If we're careful,' Stella said thoughtfully, 'we should be able to reassure him enough to lessen his concerns.'

'Maybe even flush him out,' Jack said.

'Don't be reckless,' Mancini said earnestly. 'I've already explained how dangerous this man is. We'll be doing our best to track him down.' He gave each of them a business card. 'Send me an email with the film footage and the images of the boat you talked about. I'll see what we can do to improve the resolution. Just remember not to say anything about it while you're in the apartment. If Bauer knew you had the film he was prepared to kill for in Nice, he wouldn't be bothering with electronic bugging.'

'We'd already be dead,' Stella observed.

'Exactly. Keep that in mind whenever you're in the apartment, and if you ever feel something has changed or you have made even a small mistake, get out of there fast. Go somewhere random, where nobody knows you, and call me or the carabinieri.'

Stella was nodding her agreement when her mobile phone started to ring. She didn't recognise the number, though she could tell it was local. Reluctantly, she took the call and was soon looking happier.

'It's Arno,' she said to Jack. 'Sandy's already been discharged and she wants him to drive her home to Monselice.'

She kept talking to Arno and Inspector Mancini leaned closer to Jack. 'This is good news, in my opinion,' he said. 'You will be able to control what is said in the apartment better if there are only two of you. Be sure to repeat this news when you return inside, so that Bauer does not wonder what happened to the cousin and her boyfriend.'

'Of course,' Jack said. 'And we'll make it clear we don't think he's a suspect.'

'Be subtle,' Mancini warned. 'If you make it too obvious, he will realise you know about the devices.'

'I get the message,' Jack said. 'We might have to make a few disparaging remarks about Inspector Mancini of Europol, though, because he'll be wondering what we learned from you.'

Mancini smiled graciously. 'You are welcome to call me an idiot, if you find it necessary.'

'Oh no,' Jack said, with a grin, 'I'm sure we can do better than that.'

Getting caught up in a conspiracy they didn't understand was bad enough. Knowing an experienced assassin was on their trail made it even more chilling. But not being able to talk about it was the lowest blow of all. With every word potentially picked up by the listening devices, casual conversation was a clumsy affair and it seemed easier to cite tiredness as the reason for the lack of talking.

They'd brought home a pizza from Novecento across the street. As Stella finished her final slice, she said, 'I'm going to hit the sack early. Will you be okay sorting out Sandy's stuff in your room?'

'I'll take care of it,' Jack said. 'How do we get it back to Monselice?'

'One of the cousins will collect it. There's no hurry, apparently.'

'That paparazzo owes her the price of two concert tickets.'

'That's right. I'd better send her something. It's my fault she got caught up in this mess.'

'You couldn't know the Italian press would be so aggressive.'

'It's such an useless distraction,' she said, standing up. 'I just want to get on with our work for the bank. After all this fuss and our run-in with that crazy dude in Nice, I can't wait to get the report finalised and get back to New York.'

'The Europol schmuck is obviously buying the French cops' theory. The only mug shots he showed us were all drug dealers.'

'Well, we have no evidence to support any other hypothesis, do we?'

Jack sighed deeply. 'No, not a sausage.'

Stella smiled at the thought of Bauer struggling with the expression, but she hadn't been lying when she'd said she was exhausted. She felt a strong desire to curl up in her bed and hide from the world. Her self-doubt had reached an all-time high. Not only had her cool, professional, controlled existence been turned upside down, but she'd also managed to drag her innocent relatives into the mire. If the destruction of her image by a wash of unwanted celebrity wasn't enough, she now had one cousin recovering from a vicious assault and an uncle who would soon return with his family from their holiday in the Maldives to find his apartment under guard.

Thinking about the job they had to do for the bank didn't help. In fact, it churned her stomach almost more than the thought of Kurt Bauer hunting them down. The Stack Partnership had been her dream, and her ambitious vision for the business seemed to be drifting away. How could they produce an amazing outcome for their client when their lives were at risk and they had no idea who was behind it? As she shuffled off to bed, she was already dreading the blood-red nightmares that lay ahead of her.

As he watched her go, Jack gave himself a pep talk. When your partner's down, you have to be stronger. That's how it works. One supports the other. That's what she was doing when you were feeling weak yesterday. Now it's your turn.

He opened his laptop and sent the video file to the address Inspector Mancini had provided. Then he opened the file and paused it at the appropriate spot once more, pondering the options for making the name of the boat appear magically from behind the waves.

Suddenly conscious of the suspicions that might arise from the sound of tapping on the keyboard, he transferred the computer to his room and lay on the bed. With any luck, Bauer would assume he was surfing for porn. He was actually surfing for images of high-end cruising yachts, hoping to at least identify the model or maker – or, if he was really lucky, a picture of this particular vessel. But it was a pointless exercise. All he learned was that there were many more luxury toys on the water than he would ever have thought possible. Rebuffed by the overwhelming amount of useless information on the net, he went back to the original footage, but every attempt to improve the image or expose some unique identifier proved fruitless. Come on, you prick of a thing, he said silently to the computer screen, as he watched the jet explode for the umpteenth time. Give up your secret.

25

The Milan residence of the Aretino family was just a few blocks from the historic heart of the city. From the street, its facade was plain but imperiously substantial. Rendered in a yellowy-beige colour, three storeys of symmetrically spaced windows rose above a high central porte-cochere sealed with heavy wooden doors. The ground-floor windows were barred and surrounded with plaster scrollwork, while every second opening of the upper levels featured a wrought-iron Juliet balcony fronting tall French doors.

The big Mercedes bringing Stella and Jack to Sunday mass was admitted through the porte-cochere and into the expansive paved courtyard in the centre of the villa, where it pulled up next to a row of parked vehicles proclaiming the family's wealth. A silver Porsche Carrera 911 sat between a metallic-blue BMW 7 Series and a black Jaguar saloon.

They were met by Alex Aretino, who rushed forward to open the door on Stella's side. He kissed her on both cheeks. 'How are you? Is your cousin all right?'

Jack opened his door and climbed out, looking around the

generous courtyard to see a central fountain carved in marble and a Palladian colonnade decorated with potted topiary. Above the arches were more rows of symmetrically spaced windows. His pricey loft on Greene Street was a shoebox by comparison.

Size isn't everything, he mused to himself as he followed Stella and Alex to tall double doors leading inside. At the threshold, Alex stopped to shake him by the hand. 'It's good to see you again, Jack,' he said, with a sincere smile.

'Thanks for the invitation. You have some amazing homes.'

'Ah, yes, Stella told me about your visit to the villa in Mira. I'm afraid we don't get the opportunity to spend much time there these days.'

He led them inside an expansive double-height entrance hall. The gilded plaster ceilings, fine antique furniture and highly polished floors suggested the existence of a small army of retainers. A massive stone staircase was the centrepiece, climbing to a wide landing before splitting in two and continuing up to a grand balcony on the first floor. Large, dark portraits of unsmiling men and women looked down from the walls, projecting Aretino power over countless generations.

Stella looked suitably awestruck. 'It's very impressive, Alex,' she said.

'A little austere for my taste,' their host said. 'Some of these portraits used to hang in Mira, actually. The most important pieces from our Veneto estates are here now.'

A middle-aged attendant in a black suit appeared at one the doors opening onto the hall. Alex said, 'We should get to the chapel, the service will be starting soon. Please come this way.'

They passed through a plush reception room with a deep red colour scheme and then into another themed in dark green. Alex gently led Stella with a hand on her elbow. He was pointing out highlights but his words were too soft for Jack to hear.

The third room was more masculine, its walls lined with dark wood and hung with portraits of long-dead Aretino men, many wearing the robes of the Order of Malta or finely worked knightly armour. Examples of their weaponry hung over the fireplace. What a tedious place to grow up, Jack told himself, but he couldn't be sure it wasn't green-eyed envy talking. Not when country estates, Venetian palaces, luxury cars and attentive servants were taken into account.

'What's this?'

Alex and Stella stopped and turned back. Jack was standing by a glass display cabinet containing two sheets of parchment illuminated by hidden spotlights.

'That's known as the Pact of 1798,' Alex said, 'though it's just a small part of the complete document. The page there on the right includes the signatures of eight knights of the Order of Malta, including my great-great-great uncle.'

Stella looked where he was pointing and read, 'Fra Antonio Paolo d'Aretino. Didn't he have something to do with the villa in Mira?'

Alex looked pleased. 'You're right, Stella. He was responsible for the Hall of Heroes. That's why my great-grandfather bought these pages when they came up for auction, though it's the date that makes them especially rare. You see, 8 July 1798? Eight days after Napoleon and his fleet invaded Malta and kicked the Order out. Not only does this document prove my ancestor was there for that momentous event, but it is also possibly the last official document of the Order's time as a truly sovereign power.'

'Incredible,' Stella said. 'What were they agreeing to?'

'Nobody knows, for certain. The other page is a detailed inventory of treasury items, just one page of many, the experts say. It could be a list of valuables in the Order's possession at the time. Alternatively, it's an accounting of the treasure stolen by the French troops during the invasion. But most historians discount both theories, because the

Order was in poor financial shape by 1798. They think it's more likely to be a list of items once owned by the knights but lost much earlier.'

'The rest of the pages were destroyed?' Jack asked, finding it impossible not to be impressed by the depth of history behind the family.

'Sadly, yes. Pity, isn't it? One expert estimated that the present-day value of the items on that page alone would be close to one billion euros. There were probably about ten pages like that.' He seemed to take delight from the shock on their faces and laughed easily. 'Don't get your hopes up. If it hasn't turned up in the last two centuries, it's not going to now. That's Fra Antonio's sword over the fireplace, by the way.'

Stella scanned the artefacts in the room with new interest. The collection seemed more accessible than a normal museum display – she could imagine real people holding them. 'With such an amazing heritage,' she said, 'you must keep a bunch of historians on the payroll.'

'One or two, I believe.'

Before she could probe any more, the butler returned and spoke a few quiet words in his master's ear. 'My parents want to say hello to you before the service starts,' Alex said to Stella. 'We should keep moving.'

The Count and Countess d'Aretino were waiting by the entrance to the family chapel at the rear of the villa, and they greeted Stella with easy familiarity.

'How are you, dear?' the Countess asked. 'I hope the authorities treated you with respect after the horrible incident the other evening?'

'Everybody was very kind, thank you.'

Jack cleared his throat to be noticed.

'Oh yes,' Alex said. 'Mother, I don't think you've met Stella's business partner, Jack Rogers.'

'How do you do?' Jack said, immediately conscious of his attire – designer jeans, though they were – as he shook the Countess's hand. 'I'm sorry, I feel a little underdressed.'

'Not at all,' Count Charles said. 'We'll be changing before we go to the track.' His attention immediately shifted back to Stella. 'You've become rather famous, my dear,' he said, smiling congenially. 'Our friends in the press have been badgering us for more information about you.'

'I hope you haven't encouraged them,' she said. 'That sort of attention is not what I'm looking for.'

'How very un-Italian of you,' he said, approvingly. 'Don't worry, I've given instructions to my staff to say nothing without your say-so.'

'In my experience,' Alex interjected, 'giving them nothing only makes things worse. A bit of mystery stirs up the sharks like nothing else and they'll do anything to get a scoop. If they're not fed some facts, they embellish every rumour going around or simply make something up.'

'What do you suggest?' Stella said. 'I'm not holding a press conference.'

'Perhaps we could get some pertinent information to one of the more respectable newspapers,' Count Charles suggested. 'We might be able to arrange an interview with the right sort of journalist. Do you think there'll be someone we can rely on at the GP today, Alex?'

'Jack knows Victoria Cavendish from *Peek!* magazine,' Stella said, and three sets of aristocratic eyes turned to look at Jack with expressions ranging from suspicion to outright disdain.

'Not that woman!' the Countess said acerbically. 'She's one of the worst. The things she's written about Laura . . .'

'We'll talk about it later,' the Count said looking at his watch. 'We mustn't be late to the race, so we'd better get this over with.'

He held his arms wide to usher Stella and the Countess through the double doors. Alex and Jack followed closely.

The chapel was about half the width and twice the height of the reception rooms they'd crossed to get there. Eight carved wooden pews, in two blocks of four, were separated by an aisle leading to a raised altar backlit by stained-glass windows. The familiar Maltese cross motif was much in evidence, from the coloured glass in the windows to the flags and banners suspended above the pews.

Jack took a seat next to Stella, who was beside Alex. The agonised figure of Jesus Christ bleeding on the cross stared down at him from above the altar with disturbingly realistic eyes, and he shuddered at the thought of the unfamiliar religious ritual to come. The Count and his wife were in the pew right in front of them and the Countess already had her head lowered in prayer. Jack looked over his shoulder to see a handful of household servants shuffle in to take their place in the back row.

The sooner it starts, the sooner it's over, he thought, but there was no swelling organ music or priestly procession to mark the beginning of proceedings. Instead, a serious-faced man in blue velvet vestments with oversized white crosses stepped out of a side door and walked solemnly to the space in front of the altar. It took a moment for Jack to recognise Jimmy Aretino.

Jimmy opened his mouth to speak but at that moment the chapel doors opened again. Jack glanced around and immediately recognised the rather sad but beautiful face of the elusive Laura Aretino. As she shuffled up the aisle, her parents did not turn around and Jimmy gave her a brief disapproving look before looking back to the Bible in his hands and beginning to speak. Jack, however, could not tear his eyes away. He nudged Stella gently. Now he understood why Vicky Cavendish hadn't seen Laura at the hot spots lately. She had to be about eight months pregnant.

26

The body was at Prinz Gerhard's feet, the screwdriver still lodged firmly in its neck. He nudged it with his foot, to be sure, but the twitching had definitely stopped and the gut-wrenching gurgling had also petered out. 'Traitorous cunt,' he spat. 'You deserved it.'

Suddenly aware of his surroundings, he turned and climbed the short metal ladder to the workshop, careful to use only his left hand. On the upper level he opened one of the fitted cabinets, where he knew he would find a roll of absorbent paper. While he wiped the blood from his hand, he moved to the door and took two deep breaths before opening it to take a look outside.

It was still early. There was hardly a soul to be seen, especially at this end of the alley. He closed the door quickly and locked it tight. So far, so good. He reached for his mobile phone and called up the number identified by a single capital letter B.

'Why the hell are you calling me?' Bauer said. 'I thought we agreed —'

'I have a problem,' the prince said, and his tone was enough to get Bauer's attention.

'You know I'm in Andorra. How can I do anything from here?'

'The security guard I hired to guard the truck; I found him trying to open the container.'

'Sneaky swine. And?'

'I took care of it,' the prince said.

'You took care of it?' Bauer paused to release the anger and control his voice. 'Look, I don't need to know any of this.'

'I was hoping you might advise me on the best way to clean this up.'

Bauer sighed. 'If you've made a mess,' he said patronisingly, 'then you know what to do. You must be able to find a suitable place to dispose of the trash.'

'The trash,' the prince repeated. 'You don't have any other advice?'

'Yes,' Bauer said, with a steely voice. 'Make sure you do a proper job of it. If you screw this up, it will be over for all of us. No payday, no restoration of your family's honour. Do you understand what I'm saying?'

'Of course,' the prince said. 'Clean it up. Yes, I'm sure I can do that.'

'And one more thing,' Bauer added.

'What's that?'

'You're going to need a new security guard.'

27

Thank Christ that's over, Jack thought, before glancing guiltily at the glaring crucifix looming overhead. For him, the last hour had been a meaningless procession of standing, sitting and kneeling, interspersed with prayers for the lost – from the former count, and those who had died with him, to the minister assassinated so recently – and he'd mentally added Marcel Ganet to the list. It couldn't do any harm.

When the final benediction had been delivered, the servants shuffled out of the chapel unnoticed. Jimmy took a position by the exit to share a personal moment with each remaining member of the small congregation as they filed past. When he got to Jack, he smiled and shook his hand. 'Thank you for coming. I hope it wasn't too boring for you.'

'Not at all,' Jack replied, hoping he sounded sincere. 'Thanks for explaining the eight-pointed cross; that was very interesting.'

'It was a lazy choice,' Jimmy said dismissively. 'I used your presence as an excuse to talk about the Order and its symbols. I'm not so good with the religious parables and pious sermons.'

Jack smiled. 'I thought they went with the territory.'

'Mother Church is a vast and complex organisation, Jack. Even priests have to specialise.'

'And your speciality is?'

'Economics, mostly, plus a bit of diplomacy. You'll be glad to know I haven't wasted my qualifications or experience in the markets. The Order is like a mini-country, and I'm part of the mini-bureaucracy that runs it.'

Jack liked the analogy. 'Most civil servants don't get to wear such impressive robes.'

'Nice, aren't they? Another hand-me-down from an illustrious forebear. But they're stinking hot. I can't wait to get back into my team shirt for the day. I'll meet you at the chopper.'

He turned and walked back up the aisle, stopping for a quiet word with his sister, who was just struggling to her feet after some private prayer time. Jack held the door for her as she waddled out to the hall and she rewarded him with a distant half smile. Stella was talking with Alex and the Count and she stepped back to allow Laura to pass. Father and brother both murmured friendly words, wearing expressions that could be read as either sympathy or regret.

'Congratulations, Charles,' Stella said, refusing to ignore the obvious. 'I see you're about to become a grandfather.'

The Count's smile was philosophical. 'Thank you, Stella. It wasn't quite how we'd hoped it would happen, but I am looking forward to meeting the child.'

'I trust Laura's been well.'

Alex shook his head. 'From party machine to baby incubator overnight. It's been a hell of an adjustment for her.'

'I think she's done very well under the circumstances,' the Count said protectively.

Alex snorted. 'She's spent most of the last eight months in bed!'

The Count forced a laugh. 'She must be getting out of the house sometime,' he said. 'Her personal expenses have gone through the roof. I don't know how you girls do it.'

Stella was irritated enough to respond. 'A lot of new equipment and clothes would be called for, I'm sure. For both Laura and the baby.'

'Yes, you're right, of course. Now, before we leave for the track, Alex and I want to show you the information we've pulled together to help with your analysis. Follow me, please.'

He led Stella and Jack back the way they'd come and then up the broad central staircase to the first floor. A long corridor followed – with more old-master paintings on the wall, most of them landscapes – before Alex opened a door to one of the front rooms. Inside was an elegantly decorated study, the walls covered with bookshelves groaning under the weight of leather-bound volumes. In front of the French windows, a heavily carved mahogany desk was neatly arranged with masculine accoutrements, a Mac and, in the centre, a pile of documents topped by several computer disks in plastic cases.

Indicating the pile with one hand, the Count said, 'Copies of the latest audited accounts for the group's separate business, with soft copies of all the financial and administrative data. We've included our own consultant's report on group strategy and outlook for the next five years. It's going to be a busy week for Alex and me, especially with the funeral for Eduardo to attend, but you'll find contact information for our advisers at Ernst & Young here in Milan. Tomorrow I will instruct the partners there to answer any questions you put to them.'

He raised his head and looked Stella straight in the eye. 'Do you think that will be sufficient for your purposes?'

'Thank you, Charles, we really appreciate your openness. This will make our work much easier.'

'Good,' the Count said, sounding satisfied. 'Then you can allow yourself a day to relax and enjoy the Grand Prix experience. You've certainly earned it. We'll get someone to box this up for you and you can pick it up later. Now, we really must get going.' He opened his arms to shepherd them towards the door and chuckled self-deprecatingly. 'Can't imagine how the team is getting on without me.'

Jack's mood was improving, and it received an extra boost when they were led up a narrow staircase to a small room under the eaves. Through a door inset with glass he saw a walkway leading out across slate tiles towards a platform constructed in heavy steel. A sleek, futuristic helicopter sat there, its rotor blades sagging and bouncing in the breeze.

Alex indicated a row of chairs upholstered in red velvet along one wall. 'If you'll just wait here, I'll be back shortly.'

When he was gone, Jack went over to the door and took a long look at their means of transport. 'These Aretinos certainly know how to live, don't they?'

'Not all of them,' Jimmy said cheerfully, as he appeared in the stairwell. 'Some of us lead more frugal lives.'

He had changed into his Aretino racing team shirt, with a pair of black trousers that might have been borrowed from a suit. He joined Jack by the door and looked out. 'I think my father built it as an escape route – you know, "last days of Saigon" style. If the world turns against us and the revolutionaries are in the streets, this will be the family's way to escape retribution.'

Without waiting for a response, he turned to Stella and said, 'It's good to see you looking so well after that horrifying experience on Friday. You must be one tough cookie.'

'I'm not sure it's sunk in completely,' Stella replied. 'It's so strange to think that one minute, we were all drinking Minister Moretti's favourite grappa and the next, he was dead.'

Jack decided Jimmy could cope with some straight questions. 'Who would want the minister dead? From what Stella told me, the gunman was clearly seeking him out.'

Jimmy nodded. 'I have no doubt he was the target. The problem is narrowing down the list of people glad to see him gone.'

'He had a lot of enemies?'

'Like that guy trying to sell the Roman artefacts,' Stella suggested. 'Moretti told me himself that collection was worth millions.'

Jimmy shook his head. 'The motive is more likely to be politics or business. He was involved with a number of dodgy property deals, quite apart from his official duties.'

'You're not too good with conflict of interest in this country, are you?' Jack said.

Jimmy smiled sardonically. 'Well, our Prime Minister sets such a good example.'

'What about the political angle?' Stella asked. 'Who benefits from his, um, sudden departure?'

With a gesture of surrender, Jimmy threw up his hands. 'Do you have any idea how complicated politics is in Italy? The government is a shaky coalition of bickering parties, and each of those parties is a shaky coalition of bickering factions. The slightest shift in the balance can upset the entire apple cart. Eduardo Moretti was the chairman of a major coalition party that happens to be struggling with internal division. To calculate the possible permutations would require a supercomputer and an entire team of analysts.'

'There must be a short list,' Jack said.

'Not a very helpful one,' Jimmy said seriously. 'My father would be on that list, for a start.'

'What?' Stella said. 'I thought he was the party's biggest contributor.'

'He supports the party, yes, but Moretti wasn't his man. The leadership fight could lead to a major shift in factional power. Some would argue our family stands to gain a great deal of additional political influence.'

They stopped at the sound of footsteps on the stairs. Alex appeared, sporting a subtly Aretino-branded polo shirt under a linen jacket on his slim body. This season's coolest sunglasses were propped on his head, holding back a jumble of curls. Jack bristled and turned to look out at the helicopter pilot going through his pre-flight checks.

'Looking forward to a big day out?' Alex was looking at Stella, his dimples fully engaged.

She seemed flustered and the atmosphere in the room suddenly changed. Jack felt the shift and looked at Jimmy, who returned the gaze with raised eyebrows and an amused grin. 'We were talking about the assassination,' Jack said. 'It could put a dampener on the mood at the race.'

Alex dismissed the suggestion with a casual wave. 'Nobody's going to miss that fool,' he said, 'apart from his even bigger fool of a wife. He was an unfortunate example of a man whose excesses knew no bounds.' He sat down next to Stella, his grin undiminished. 'I'm certainly not going to let it spoil my day.'

Arsehole, Jack thought, unimpressed by Stella's coquettish reaction to the charm offensive. But as long as Alex is being blunt, I might as well be the same. 'You boys looking forward to becoming uncles?' he said. 'Who's the father?'

The brothers exchanged a look and Jimmy's eyes narrowed a fraction. Alex, though, would not allow his good mood to be tarnished. 'I have no idea,' he said, as if it didn't matter. 'She's not telling.' He looked up at Jimmy. 'Not me, anyway.'

Jimmy's frown deepened. 'The secrets of the confessional are sacrosanct,' he said, 'even in this family.'

Alex grinned and gave Stella a look. 'You don't have to worry about me,' he said suggestively, 'I never feel obliged to confess my sins.'

She decided to take advantage of his flirtatious mood. 'I wanted to ask you a favour.'

'Anything within my power,' Alex replied.

'My younger brother has an honours degree in history.'

That's a bit of a fib, Jack thought. Stella's younger brother was a dentist.

'But he has struggled to find work in the field,' she continued. 'I reckon he'd benefit from talking to your historians about their experience and any extra study they might suggest. Do you think you could get me some contact details for one or two?'

'I'm sure that's possible,' Alex said, 'though I don't know any names off the top of my head. What about you, Jimmy?'

'I doubt he'll learn much from their experience,' Jimmy said. 'Most have been priests or brothers over the years. History for us usually involves the Order.'

'What about the guy who did that study of the Hall of Heroes for Uncle Federico?' Alex said. 'He was an academic historian, wasn't he?'

Jimmy's brow wrinkled in thought. 'Yeah. Vincent, wasn't it? I want to say Vincent Franco, but it's a guess.'

'Not to worry,' Alex said. 'I'll get my secretary to dig out some contact details for your brother during the week.'

'Thanks,' Stella said. 'He sounds ideal. You mentioned the Hall of —'

She fell silent when the Count appeared at the top the stairs. He strode directly to the door and pulled it open. 'Come along, everyone,' he said. 'We have a race to run.'

28

From the air, Monza's famous circuit was a truly spectacular sight. The racetrack snaked its way through leafy trees and passed grandstands packed with tiny people in bright clothing. Along the finish straight, the great wing of the pit complex shimmered under a cloudless sky. The neat rows of transporters and team headquarters reeked of money and glamour and intense competition.

As the chopper descended, expectant faces could be seen turning in its direction. Here's another load of fodder for your celebrity mill, Jack thought ruefully, as he saw distant zoom lenses swing towards them. In another few seconds, they were hovering above the grass in a clearing to the east of the track, where a number of other helicopters were already parked. Gently, they touched down and the pilot soon gave the okay to disembark.

Two large men in Aretino team uniform were waiting to provide security for the Count and his sons. The group progressed slowly to the northern entrance of Motorhome Alley. The heavies ensured a path was cleared, but their presence alone was enough to turn every face and every second camera in their direction. Alex was playing security for Stella, his arm gently pulling her to his side when the crowd got close. Jack watched him flutter around her, a wry smile playing on his lips.

Once the Aretino party been admitted to the paddock, the crowd thinned. There were still more than ninety minutes to go before the main race got underway, but the activity around the team motorhomes made Friday's session seem positively tame. There wasn't much for the technicians and mechanics to do except wait for the off, but for the media this was go time. Television, radio and press reporters jostled for elbow room as drivers, owners and racing identities faced down gaggles of microphones and questions shouted in a variety of languages.

Their group soon became a target. The assassination had added an extra frisson to the lowly Aretino team and the Count was soon answering questions about both the racing and the violence that had touched his team during an extraordinary year. For the glamour photographers, Alex and Stella together again was the must-have shot of the day.

The look on Jack's face was mirrored by the serious F1 aficionados along the alley, who saw the paparazzi scrum as nothing more than an obstacle to team efficiency. Jimmy extricated himself and came to walk beside Jack. 'You can't blame the photographers,' he said. 'Stella's going to need a publicist soon.'

Jack raised an eyebrow. 'No way. She hates all this attention.'

'They all say that at the beginning,' Jimmy said, smiling automatically when he saw a camera pointing in his direction.

'You don't know Stella.'

Jimmy laughed good-naturedly. 'And you don't know the lure of fame.'

Jack shook his head and resolved to concentrate on the once-in-a-lifetime opportunity of spending race day at the heart of the F1 circus. Stella wasn't the only pretty girl in the paddock, not by a long shot. In every direction he saw attractive young women, many of them wearing skimpy tops and skirts or hotpants in team colours. More elegant were the bejewelled beauties on the arms of business moguls and elder statesmen, for whom grey hair, wrinkled faces and sagging bellies seemed no deterrent when coupled with wealth and power.

There were famous faces too, strolling the alley or sipping champagne in and around the motorhomes. Jimmy pointed out Italian pop stars and TV personalities while Jack focused on spotting drivers – some current and some retired – whose faces he'd only previously seen on the small screen. As they passed behind the Jaguar garage, they crossed paths with the only Australian F1 star, Mark Webber. Jack called out a friendly, 'Good luck today, Mark.'

Webber responded with a smile. 'Thanks, mate.'

The picture-snappers eventually peeled away from their group, responding like seagulls to rumours of a tasty morsel elsewhere. By the time the group had reached the Aretino transporters at the end of the pit lane, a measure of privacy had returned.

The Count peeled away towards the garages and Alex conducted Stella up to the hospitality suite to avoid any more press attention. Jimmy invited Jack to meet the Aretino drivers, who were relaxing in the shade of the marquees attached to their burgundy motorhome. The older of the two was a slightly built Spaniard called Felix, whose tight racing suit was unzipped to the waist and folded back to keep him cool. He had a friendly smile and was happy to field a few questions about the car and the track, though his English was limited. The younger driver, a Japanese kid with no English at all, was sitting on a chair in the shade of the marquee, getting his shoulders massaged by a leggy blonde.

'Excuse me, Jack,' Jimmy said. 'I've just spotted two senior knights of the Order. I'd better go and make them feel welcome. I'll see you upstairs, okay?' He hurried away in the direction of two grey-haired gentlemen in sober business suits.

Just like any other big business, Jack mused, as he watched Jimmy go. A good operator never misses a chance to impress the top dogs. He nodded his thanks to the drivers and wished them luck in the race but he dawdled as he left them, in no hurry to get to the hospitality suite. Where he really wanted to be was by the front rail on top of the pit complex, watching the preparations for the main event. But he knew he had social and professional obligations to fulfil first, including another mealtime full of vacuous small talk and bonhomie. The warmth of the sun hit him as he left the shade and his mouth watered in anticipation of a cold beer. He was halfway to the glass doors leading inside when he heard his name being called.

'Jack! All right, darling?' Vicky Cavendish was poured into a tight crimson minidress that maximised her assets. She was remarkably nimble on her high heels as she approached with arms open for an embrace.

As they air-kissed, Jack realised he was pleased to see her. 'G'day, Vicky. You're looking lovely.'

She wiggled her hips provocatively. 'Why, thank you. Not looking so bad yourself. *Much* more handsome than that Alex Aretino.'

Jack laughed. 'I don't know about that. And don't forget, Vicky, villas and private helicopters count for more than looks sometimes.'

'Give me looks every time,' she replied, grinning cheekily. 'You know if you ever need a bit of uncomplicated affection, you should call me. You have my number, right?'

He raised an eyebrow. 'Are you hitting on me, Vicky Cavendish?'

'Damn right, I am. If it's good enough for the aristos, it's good enough for me!'

'I'm flattered,' he said.

'And I'm available,' she countered.

They laughed easily and only then did Jack notice the two men standing a few metres away, cameras and lenses hanging around their necks. 'This is just a friendly chat, right? Anything I say is off the record. I'm not looking to be quoted; Stella's already pissed off with both of us.'

'That's ridiculous. How could you know she'd end up as Alex Aretino's date at the glamour event of the weekend?'

'That's what I said.'

'Tell her to grow up,' Vicky said dismissively. 'There's plenty of info about Stella on the web. My competition just didn't have time to do the research before their deadlines. Their next editions will have more than her name and business background, you can be sure of it.'

'She's not going to like that.'

Vicky chortled. 'She should've thought about that before looking gorgeous on the arm of the country's hottest bachelor and then standing next to a government minister during the course of a political assassination. This story's got legs to last a while yet. Didn't you see the photographers around her as she came in? Believe me, Jack, life in Italy's never going to be the same for that girl.'

29

Seven hundred kilometres south-west of Monza, Jose Cristobal handed his son an ice-cream. 'Don't tell your mother about this or I'll get in trouble for spoiling your lunch.'

Twelve-year-old Alfonse licked his lips in anticipation as he swapped his tennis racquet for the frozen treat. 'You mean you'll be in trouble for breaking your diet.'

His father took a spoonful of his own chocolate and pistachio combination and grinned with delight. 'Nobody likes a smartypants, Alfonse. Besides, we're on holiday. Will you be all right on the drive? You know how twisty the road is. I don't want you throwing up in the car.'

'I'll be okay,' the boy said. 'You can try to set a fast time if you like.'

'I don't know what you're talking about,' Jose said, but he winked. The quiet road that cut across the Pyrenean valleys between the mountain-top towns of Canillo and Ordino was the perfect piece of tarmac to test out his new Audi. Tight curves, long straights, perilous drops and dramatic scenery: it was an experience almost as spiritual as prayer.

They walked slowly towards the car while finishing their ice-creams.

'Will we get back before the start of the race?' Alfonse asked, walking the kerb like it was a narrow log bridge.

'We have plenty of time, but don't forget you need to do an hour or two of study before class.'

'I'll do it while we watch the race.'

His father gently tapped his backside with the covered head of the tennis racquet. 'Holding a Bible while watching the TV is not going to impress Father Yebra, Al.'

'I don't need to impress him. He's already impressed because you're my dad.'

Jose smiled self-indulgently. 'The final exam will be assessed by the archbishop back home in Madrid. Being my son won't be enough to satisfy him.'

The youngster made a petulant face. 'But we're on holiday, you said so yourself.'

'God does not take holidays, son.'

A plump, matronly woman ran up to them, puffing and wheezing. 'Excuse me, sir? Aren't you Don Jose Cristobal?'

'Yes I am, madam. Please, calm yourself.'

'I love your writing,' she said, between shallow breaths. 'Can I get your autograph?' She was hunting in her large handbag for a piece of paper. 'Every home should have a copy of *God in the Family*.'

'You're very kind. If you step over to my car, I'll gladly sign a copy for you.'

She almost swooned with delight. 'How lovely. May I ask, what are you doing here in Andorra?'

'We like to vacation in the mountains during the summer. My son comes to Canillo for tennis coaching with Pedro Olmaro.'

'Oh, yes, he's very good. Your son must be talented.'

'I believe he is, yes.' Jose opened the Audi's trunk and placed Alfonse's racquet next to the boxes containing copies of his three published works on the role of the Church in Spanish politics and society. Before long, his fan was proudly holding an autographed copy of each.

Young Alfonse had seen it all before. He let himself in to the passenger side, after carefully wiping his hands with a paper napkin. Within a few minutes, they were out of the town and the V8 engine was growling deeply as Jose accelerated through a wide corner and into a stretch of straight road hugging the ridge. The valley to their right dropped away sharply and the peaks in the distance glistened under a bright-blue sky spotted with fluffy clouds.

'Hold on,' Jose said, as he braked late into a tight bend.

The Audi hugged the road and Alfonse gripped his seatbelt with both hands to stop his small frame from sliding off the leather seat. We're going to smash the record, he thought, but as they pulled out of the corner a loud thumping made him shout and the vehicle weaved alarmingly. His father hit the brakes hard and managed to keep the wheels straight as they slowed. When they slithered to a final stop, both father and son were breathing hard.

There was no shoulder to pull onto, so Jose checked the mirrors before getting out. When he saw the shredded tyre on the front right wheel, he frowned. His immaculate cream shirt and matching trousers were about to be ruined. He opened his son's door. 'Alfonse, walk back to the last corner and make a waving motion to any vehicles coming up behind, okay? I'm going to have to change the wheel right here.'

As he climbed out, Alfonse found he was separated from a mesmerising vertical drop by a concrete wall that hardly reached his knees. He put one hand on the car for balance. The winding road continued all the way down to the valley floor. He looked back the way they'd come and saw another vehicle approaching. His father was removing boxes of books from the boot to get to the spare, so he started running up the hill while waving his arms.

Fortunately, the small red van wasn't moving fast and pulled up easily. Jose turned and looked, first at the van and then to the sky with a thankful expression. 'God has smiled on us,' he called to his son. 'It's a mechanic. You keep going up to the corner to flag other cars down. There's even less room to stop now.'

While Alfonse ran up the road, Jose walked over to the van, where the driver's window was being wound down. The side panels advertised an automotive repair business in a small town on the other side of the nearby border with France. 'Do you speak Spanish?'

'A little,' the van's driver said. 'You have problem?'

'Tyre blowout,' Jose said, pointing to the offending wheel. 'Can you help?'

'I no work today,' the driver said gruffly. 'Is Sunday.'

Jose reached for his wallet. 'I can pay you. It shouldn't take long for an expert.'

'How much?'

'Fifty euros?'

The mechanic didn't look impressed.

'One hundred?'

The van's diesel engine spluttered and died. Its hazard lights started to blink. Jose smiled with relief. 'Thank you, señor.'

The door opened and a slightly built man wearing dirty jeans and a long-sleeved denim shirt clambered out. On his head was a sweat-soaked yellow Renault F1 baseball cap. The mechanic ignored Jose's extended hand. 'You go to your son,' he said. 'I no want to be hit by car.'

A little stung, Jose moved to show the Frenchman the Audi's trunk but it was quickly evident no assistance was required. Halfway to the corner, where Alfonse was signalling a warning to a group of cyclists, he looked back and saw the spare tyre had already been extracted.

From a spot 120 metres up the mountainside, he kept one eye on the mechanic's progress and the other on the traffic – which, being a Sunday, was sparse and more likely to be two-wheeled rather than four. At one point, he looked down the hill and saw only the mechanic's boots. The rest of his body was underneath the jacked-up Audi. A few minutes later, the mechanic called him back. 'Come on, Alfonse,' he said. 'A fast time is out the window but we can still make the start of the Grand Prix.'

They trotted down the asphalt together, Alfonse's easy skipping making his father feel old. 'What were you doing under the car?' Jose asked as they approached the mechanic, who was wiping grease-stained hands on a towel.

'Pieces of tyre,' he said, indicating a pile of shredded rubber on the edge of the road. 'I pull from under floor.'

'Thank you so much,' Don Jose said, quickly handing over two fifty-euro notes. Then, noticing the Audi's trunk had been thoroughly repacked, he added an extra twenty. 'You were sent from above, my friend.'

The mechanic took the tip as if it was expected. 'Spare tyre is thin. Do not drive more than eighty kilometres per hour.'

The thought of what could have been was enough to moderate Jose's driving style, but the temporary wheel was a good excuse. As father and son continued their descent into the valley, the mechanic stayed twenty metres behind them, apparently content with the relaxed pace.

'The coach says your backhand is coming along nicely,' Jose said to his bored son.

'He says I have the best serve in my age group,' Alfonse said proudly. 'Do you think I could get a new racquet for Christmas?'

'What? You've only had that one six —'

'Papa! The man said you shouldn't go over eighty!'

They were on a long straight descending to a sharp turn. Jose looked at the speedometer. 105. But he wasn't pressing the accelerator. How could that be? He moved his foot to the brake pedal and pushed. Nothing. He felt the engine revving. Not possible. 115. He pumped both feet on the brake. 125. He pulled on the handbrake. A cloud of grey smoke flew out behind the car but the speed was unaffected. The powerful engine was still accelerating. He reached for the ignition but it was already too late. 135. The bend was looming closer, only empty space and death beyond the low wall. 142. The turn was impossible. He put out an arm to protect his son, but he knew it was futile. 155. He pulled hard on the wheel.

Alfonse screamed as the Audi hit the low wall side-on and was tossed off the cliff, rolling and spinning in the air like a child's toy top kicked off its axis. Far below, the rocky earth was ready to receive them.

30

Stella locked herself in a stall, closed the lid over the toilet and sat down with a sigh of relief. How long could I stay here, she wondered, before they come looking for me? If I have to answer one more question about the shooting or the damned party, I'll go crazy.

The most disturbing encounters were with those who'd idolised the former Northern League party leader. They didn't seem to realise that every query or comment elicited memories she would rather suppress.

Alex was solicitous and sweet, but he was too used to the cult of celebrity to appreciate its impact on her. She was appalled to find her sudden fame hadn't faded overnight as she'd hoped, but had intensified instead. And after today's outing to this hotbed of the glamour-obsessed, it could only get worse.

She longed for a good old-fashioned day of work. Strategies, research, reports. Big wins for her clients. A successful, highly respected business. These were her goals in life. Not being hailed as someone's new girlfriend, some dress's perfect dummy or some assassin's beautiful bystander. Where the hell had her life gone?

Thinking about the pile of data awaiting her analysis was reassuring. She just had to get through this day and collect the box of reports waiting in Milan. Then she could get her teeth into the work, preferably alone.

What do we need to do today? she asked herself. This could be our last direct contact with the F1 team. The mystery of the Aretino transporter was one that wouldn't be solved by looking at the numbers. She couldn't imagine how it could matter, but understanding what the team's truck was doing in Mira last weekend was a mission that might give this day meaning. And it would help her deflect some of the bullshit.

She stood up, waiting for two women to leave before coming out of her stall. She straightened her clothes and checked her face in the mirror, her mind already focusing on the problem. What I need, she decided, is that big guy who caught me snooping around the motorhome on Friday. Where would I find him?

'Stella's become quite the star, hasn't she?' Jimmy said to Jack as they ate lunch together. 'In two days she's gone from potential notch on Alex's bedpost to potential sister-in-law.'

'What are you talking about?' Jack said.

'Ours is the first generation in history that can even consider marrying someone without a noble bloodline,' Jimmy explained. 'And if my parents were ever going to accept a commoner into the family, Stella would be a strong candidate. Her family is from the Veneto, she's beautiful and accomplished and, most importantly, she already has the perfect media image. She's going to get talked about as a future Countess d'Aretino, you'll see.'

'You must be kidding,' Jack said. 'They only met two days ago.'

Jimmy nodded his head knowingly. 'These things soon take on a life of their own, Jack. You might be looking for a new business partner before long.'

Jack knew Jimmy was exaggerating but a part of him couldn't help but wonder if there was any truth in it. A moment's jealousy passed through him at the thought of Stella and Alex, but he pushed it to the back of his mind. She'd never give up the business.

'Jimmy,' he said, 'I was thinking: after your father, surely you'd be the next count. Aren't you older than Alex?'

Jimmy waved his fork dismissively. 'My father's taken care of that. He had his lawyers draw up a deed that effectively excludes me from the inheritance and passes the title and the control to Alex. They need the future count to produce heirs.'

'You weren't a bit offended by that?'

'I might have been once, but I've had a long time to get used to the way my father sees his two sons. Besides, until recently Alex and I never had any expectations about the title because my cousin Stefano was next in line. It only became an issue when he and my uncle were killed.'

'But if Charles had been on the plane as expected, wouldn't you have been tempted to take over the reins yourself?'

Jimmy deliberated for a moment. 'I'm confident I would have respected the family's wishes. Like I said, the count needs to be a breeder. That's why Alex's choice of a wife has become such a big deal, especially as he's already rejected all the eligible candidates from the noble families.'

Countess Stella, Jack thought. What a bizarre concept.

Stella spotted her target at the buffet table. He was taller and broader than most people in the room. She picked up a plate and eased in next to him. Reaching for a piece of bread, she brushed his arm and he looked around.

'Oh,' he said, smiling down at her, 'it's the spy.'

His English was clipped. She smiled too. 'I told you, I wasn't spying. I was just curious.'

He added an extra slice of prosciutto to the pile on his plate. 'But it's more than that, isn't it? The boss tells me you're doing some sort of risk analysis.'

'That's right. I wasn't able to mention it when we met on Friday. Did the Count say anything else?'

'He said I should give you every assistance.'0

'Well, I would like to ask you some questions. Shall we eat together?'

He hesitated. 'I don't have a great deal of time. We'll begin packing up as soon as the race starts and I need to brief —'

'It won't take any longer than you need to empty that.'

He looked down at his heavily laden plate. 'All right, then. Why don't you finish getting lunch while I find us a spot?'

Stella glanced around the busy suite. 'The quieter, the better.'

When she'd filled her plate, she found him at one end of the curved granite-topped bar where waiters were opening bottles of wine and champagne. 'This is the calmest spot I could find,' he said, 'if you don't mind standing.'

'It's perfect,' she said, putting her plate down and keeping her back to the curious glances and gossipy whispers of the other guests. 'My name is —'

'Stella,' he said, indicating to the barkeep that they'd like something to drink. 'You're pretty famous around here already. My name is Willy.'

'And you're the logistics manager. Did I remember that right?'

'You did. What would you like?' he added as a waitress approached.

'Champagne, please.'

'Mineral water for me.' His fork stabbed an artichoke heart. 'I love the Italian Grand Prix. Best food of the whole championship.'

'It must be an amazing life,' Stella said, 'travelling the world with this circus.'

Willy nodded and said, 'It sure is, but it's also the most challenging thing I've ever done. Every two weeks we have to move more than sixty tonnes of equipment across Europe, and then we have to deal with all the flyaway races. We travel more than 160 000 kilometres in a year. My team also has to organise hotel rooms, food and transport for up to a hundred people and make sure every piece of computer equipment has all the right connections and power.'

'And the cars, too,' Stella said, with a hint of humour.

Willy chuckled. 'Yes, of course, the cars too, but thank God I don't have to know much about them. The engineers and mechanics deal with all that but, believe me, if their data links don't work, they can be difficult customers.'

'Where do you go next?'

'Indianapolis, Indiana,' Willy said. 'I don't much like the food there.'

'Do you take those huge trucks to the overseas races?'

'No, no. We'll take about twenty-five tonnes of gear to the US Grand Prix but the big transports stay behind.'

Stella took a sip of champagne and said, 'How do you pack it all?'

'Custom-built containers designed to fit neatly in the belly of an aircraft. All the tools, spare parts and so on are packed in cabinets and chests like those in the garages. The boxes slot inside the containers. The cars also have containers that are constructed around them, to protect them.'

'And the transporters are designed to accommodate all these special containers?'

'That's right.'

'What a massive operation. It must represent a large slice of the team's budget.'

Willy nodded. 'Without logistics, there would be no Formula One.'

'I'd love to see how those special containers fit into the trucks.'

'Perhaps at the end of the day, if you're prepared to wait around. The transports are empty right now.'

'They can't both be empty,' Stella said, innocently. 'There's a security guard on one of them. I'm sure you're not paying him to protect an empty vehicle.'

He seemed surprised. 'You don't miss much, do you?'

'That's what I get paid for.'

'There is a container in that truck,' he said, 'but I can't tell you what's in it, because I don't know myself.'

'You don't know? But you're the logistics manager. Surely —'

'I mean I don't know the specifics. There's a lot of secrecy in Formula One, Stella. You'll have to get used to that if you want to understand it. When success is based on fractions of a second per lap, every new bit of technology is fiercely guarded.'

'That's what the guy downstairs is protecting?'

'So I'm told. Some new aero parts and other secret bits and pieces that they're planning to test at the last two races. I guess they figure there's no point trying to salvage a result this year, so it's all eyes on 2004.'

She raised her glass in a toast. 'Here's to the Aretino team winning next year.'

Willy laughed. 'Winning? That's not too likely.'

She shook her head. 'I don't mean to be rude,' she said, with an apologetic smile, 'but what's the point, then? How can you chew through so much money with no expectation of success?'

'When you're up against teams that can outspend you by three to one, success is not always about beating every other car on the track. Sometimes it's about incremental improvement and the pursuit of a design breakthrough no other team has thought of. Anything that gets more airtime for our sponsors. That's where we are right now. Next year, hopefully, we can be more ambitious and score a few points.'

He was a fast eater and his plate emptied quickly. 'Half an hour to the race,' he said. 'I'd better get moving, if you have no more questions.'

'I'd really like to see that container in the truck,' she said. 'If I walk down with you now, it would only take a minute or so.'

He wiped his mouth with a napkin. 'As I said, it's confidential —'

'I don't need to see inside, not that car parts would mean anything to me anyway. But a real example of how you address day-to-day logistical problems with tailored solutions to achieve maximum efficiency would be a big help. I'm sure the Count would be pleased to hear how helpful you've been.'

She held his gaze, hoping he'd fall for the management speak. She wasn't entirely sure herself why she wanted to see inside that truck so badly. The mysterious visit to the villa in Mira and the overheard conversation between the drivers were mildly intriguing, but her gut said it was more than that. Also, it was a perfect excuse to get away from the mob. Once the race was underway, they'd hopefully leave her alone.

Willy took his time to weigh the pros and cons. Then he emptied his water glass and said, 'You're pretty used to getting what you want, aren't you, Stella?'

She smiled enigmatically. 'The trick is not asking for anything unreasonable.'

31

The Formula One cars were already on the grid, surrounded by swarming crew members in colourful uniforms. Standing next to each car was a young woman wearing very little and holding an umbrella to shade the driver already belted into his cockpit. A television crew was moving among the cars, broadcasting close-up shots to the huge screens around the circuit as a commentator introduced each driver. The favourites were greeted with cheers from the packed grandstands on the other side of the track.

'It's an amazing buzz, isn't it?' Jimmy said as he joined Jack on the rail. 'Would you like a beer? I've arranged for a fellow to keep them coming.'

'You're quite the company asset, Jimmy. I've been watching you schmooze the guests. You have them eating out of your hand.'

'Hey, it's what I do. If I'd picked stocks as well as I schmoozed back in the London days, I might have had your career.'

'Take it from me, it gets boring after a while. That's why I moved into consulting.'

Jimmy nodded. 'Actually, the Order is pretty good, as far as variety goes. I like the work.'

'Just to be clear,' Jack said cheekily, 'I only gave up the trading desk. I'm not recommending giving up sex as well.'

Jimmy laughed easily. 'It's not as hard as you think, if you'll pardon the pun. It's a mental thing.'

'You certainly would have disappointed a few women out there, I'm sure.'

'That's not fair, reminding a priest of what he's missing out on. But remember, I had the wild days of my youth.' He tapped his temple with an index finger. 'I have some memories in here that would shock even you.'

Jack's laugh was drowned out by a burst of engine noise.

'Well, there it is,' Willy said, making a sweeping gesture with one hand.

It was a metal container with a strange, asymmetric shape. Stella guessed it was about two metres wide, five metres long and a little over a metre tall. The top looked flat but the bottom sloped up at the sides. There were doors on the side, meeting in the middle at a solid-looking latch with a keypad lock.

'It must be heavy,' she said. 'It's obviously not full of carbon-fibre components.'

'What makes you say that?'

They were standing in the workshop area at the front of the long trailer, looking into the vast storage space at the rear.

'As we came past,' she said, 'I noticed this truck is sitting much lower on its axle than the other one.'

The logistics manager shook his head as if amused. 'You're right, Stella. There must be an engine or two in there as well. But as I told you, it's not for us to know.'

'Have you any idea how much a container like that costs?'

'No, but I'm sure we can get that figure for you. They're built to specifications provided by DHL. They do all the international shipping for Formula One. Now, I'm sorry, but I should get moving. So should you, if you want to see the start of the race.' He turned back towards the door.

'What's that?' Stella was pointing down to the dimpled metal floor of the trailer below the container. 'All of your gear and garages are so spotlessly clean,' she said, 'except for that.'

Willy returned to the edge and looked down. There was an indistinct reddish mark on the metal floor. 'Somebody must have spilled some paint. I'll get it cleaned up tonight.'

'Looks like blood to me,' Stella said.

'Not possible. If there'd been an accident, I would've heard about it. Please, I really do have to get going and I can't leave you here.'

Reluctantly, she came away. She felt no wiser but her gut was sending stronger messages than ever. As she walked down the stairs outside, she caught the security guard leering at her legs and realised there'd been a shift change. Nothing odd about that, but for some reason an unpleasant shiver ran down her spine.

'How's it going?' Stella asked, when she found Jack on the roof, beer in hand.

Jack didn't take his eyes off the grid. 'Oh, it's the Countess,' he said, his tone playful. 'Where did you get to? Alex has been looking for you.'

'What did you call me?'

'Shush,' he said, putting a finger to his lips. 'They're about to play the national anthem.'

A brass band stood on the finish line about 100 metres away. When they launched into the anthem, the people in the seats stood in respectful silence. As the last rousing chord echoed between the stands it was greeted with a happy roar. The start was only minutes away.

'What did you call me?' Stella repeated tersely.

'Chill out,' he said, amused by her discomfort. 'It's just the latest rumour around the paddock. You're the new frontrunner in the race to become the next Countess Aretino.'

She almost laughed out loud. 'Don't be ridiculous, Jack.'

He chuckled. 'I don't know. I can imagine you in a tiara, being presented to the Queen.' He took a sip of his beer and nodded his head towards the starting grid. 'You want to talk work? Because this really isn't the best time.'

'That's why we're here, isn't it? I managed to talk my way into that truck . . .'

He shook his head with a smile. 'We get paid for financial analysis and strategic business advice, Stella, not for dreaming up crazy fantasies about unexplained truck journeys. Personally, I'm taking the day off, and so should you. It's been a stressful week, and I say we've earned it.'

'Without a doubt. But I don't think we can afford it.' She leaned a little closer. 'Look, I realise it might not seem like there's an obvious link between the truck, the villa and the bombing of the jet, but my instincts say something's not right. And now we're caught in the middle of the whole thing. Our apartment is bugged. We have Europol inspectors on our doorstep. It's not strictly business any more – it's personal too.'

'Maybe I'm not as invested in the Aretino family as you are,' he said, tearing his eyes reluctantly from the track. 'But I do care about Louis and his family, and I care about our place being bugged. I just don't think the answers are going to be found here.'

'You usually trust my instincts,' she said.

He shook his head, like a disappointed coach whose star gymnast has fallen off the balance beam. 'You're off your game. Maybe it's all the attention.'

Stella's expression didn't change but something unreadable crossed her face.

'Well?' he said. 'What did you find in the truck? A secret cache of contraband? Nine skeletons, perhaps, to match the coffins in the secret room under the floor? No? What was it then, a box of spare parts? A package of new secret components for the car? The sort of thing you'd find in half the bloody transporters out there?'

His attention returned to the cars and Stella twigged at last to his unusual reluctance to engage. 'You just want to watch the race,' she observed.

He gave her an exasperated look. 'Well, it's only a once-in-a-lifetime opportunity. We can talk all you like after the race, okay?'

The scream of twenty Formula One engines leaving for their parade lap cut through her response as she backed away.

The first light over the start line came on. Then the next. Three, four, five bright-red circles. Then all five went dark and an extraordinary howl split the air as the most advanced driving machines on the planet launched forward for 300 kilometres of intense racing.

There was an excited roar from the crowd as Michael Schumacher and Juan Pablo Montoya fought aggressively for the front position at the Rettifilo, but Schumacher dived ahead and his scarlet Ferrari shot away to consolidate a lead. With incredible precision, the drivers flew their vehicles around the track and every ninety seconds or so, when Schumacher swept onto the straight, the crowd went wild.

For the first twenty laps Jack concentrated on the racing, but once the cars had settled into a consistent pattern he felt a twinge of regret for dismissing Stella's brainstorming so bluntly. Maybe she had a point – or maybe she didn't. She was like a terrier with a bone when her instincts were onto something. But she obviously wasn't coping well with the stress of the shooting or her newfound celebrity – she seemed on edge. Hell, he felt the same way. What had started out as a straightforward job was fast becoming a complex, dangerous mess. And he couldn't extricate himself now – they were both involved, and he owed it to Louis to find out who was behind his father's death. However, as far as his gut was concerned, the answer was to be found in that damned footage, not in the back of a truck.

With almost two-thirds of the race completed he felt a tap on his shoulder and glanced back to see Stella and Alex, the latter wincing at the noise that was the heartbeat of Formula One. Stella leaned in to shout in his ear. 'I'm going to have that dinner with Alex tonight.'

He nodded, not surprised by Alex's persistence.

'The thing is,' she went on, 'he wants to take me to a favourite restaurant in Como.'

Despite his best efforts, Jack's head filled with an image of the romantic lakeside town on the Swiss border. 'Nice.'

'From here it's not so far,' she said, 'so he's getting a car brought up to the track. We're going to go on directly from here, so you'll have to go back on the helicopter without us, okay?'

'Fine. You'll be working hard, I imagine?' Jack couldn't help himself.

'I've asked him to tell the driver to bring those financial reports with the car, so Alex can take me through them.'

Right, Jack thought, now she's going to tell me it's all business. 'See you back in Milan,' he said, keeping his voice even.

When she was gone, Jimmy pushed himself into the gap next to Jack. 'Enjoying the race?' he shouted.

Jack grinned to cover up the pain as the gunshot wound on his left arm was bumped. 'Loving it.'

'Where are Stella and Alex going? Are they going to watch it inside?'

'Yeah. Then they're going straight on to dinner in Como.'

'Woohoo,' Jimmy said loudly. 'I told you she was special. He only takes the special ones to Como.'

'Oh? What's in Como?'

'A sunset dinner and then up to a suite in the most romantic hotel on the lake. He has an arrangement with the management. Alex is irresistible in Como.'

32

As the race unfolded it became apparent that Michael Schumacher was on course to cover the distance in less time than any driver in history. He wasn't only setting a record for the Monza circuit, but also a record for the fastest Grand Prix anywhere in the world. And though he led from start to finish, fans of every team remained entranced by his incredible consistent pace.

Unfortunately, the fate of the Aretino racing team was wholly consistent with its performance throughout the season. The Spanish driver was forced out after twenty-seven laps when his engine collapsed under the pressure. The young Japanese guy in the second car was still circulating but ended up two laps behind the leaders.

A mere seventy-five minutes after spinning his wheels off the start line, Schumacher crossed the finish line to take the win. The Ferrari-obsessed fans were delirious with joy. Their man had extended his narrow lead in the championship over Montoya, who was a mere five seconds behind him. Jack's beer-fuelled mood was buoyed by the general air of exuberance, and the creditable seventh place achieved by his countryman, Mark Webber. Jimmy shared the moment with him as the winners completed their victory lap and made their way up the pit lane.

The spectacle below came to a colourful climax when people poured out of the stands and onto the circuit, rushing towards the area below the dais where the top three drivers would be awarded their trophies. Some VIP guests couldn't resist hurrying down to join the throng of Ferrari-flag wavers but Jack and Jimmy stayed in place and watched the presentation ceremony on the big TV screen, the latter singing along to the Italian anthem with gusto.

'You look a little sunburnt,' Jimmy said, when it was all over and they were moving with the crowd towards the exits.

Jack put a hand to his face and felt the heat radiating from his skin. 'Bugger. Oh well, now I look like a true Australian,' he said.

Back in the Aretino hospitality suite, many of the remaining guests were cheerfully downing cool drinks to soothe throats hoarse from cheering and shouting. Jack glanced around to see if Stella was still there, but it was soon apparent that she and Alex had already gone, presumably to avoid the worst of the traffic.

After one more beer at the Aretinos' expense, Jack began to feel oppressed by the genteel formality and the sea of polite smiles. He told Jimmy he would make his own way back to Milan and asked him to pass on his thanks to the Count.

The only priest he'd ever befriended made a sad face. 'Why so soon?'

'Business calls,' Jack replied. 'Can't let Stella steal a march on me, can I?'

'Is that what you call it?' Jimmy said, smiling. 'Well, for me it's back to black robes and the serious business of the Order tomorrow. I fly to Rome early in the morning.'

'Your boss, the English GP fan,' Jack asked. 'Will he be disappointed by today's result?'

'Probably. He's a Williams supporter.'

'What do you call him, exactly? Is he a cardinal or a bishop or another sort of priest? How does it work?'

Jimmy smiled indulgently. 'My boss,' he said proudly, 'beats just about everybody on the totem pole. I work for the Grand Master himself.'

Jack made an appreciative face. 'Kudos, Jimmy. If you've caught the eye of the CEO, you're on your way.'

'Don't be too impressed; the Aretino name carries a lot of weight.' He extended his hand. 'I'll be back in Milan later in the week. Will you still be here?'

Jack took the hand and shook it firmly. 'Probably. We haven't made much progress yet.'

'If you have time for a meal, give me a call.' He pulled a card from his pocket. It was simply embossed with his name and a mobile telephone number.

'I'd like that,' Jack said warmly.

He went in search of his jacket and slung it over his shoulder as he made a discreet exit from the suite. Descending the stairs of the pit complex for the last time, he saw Count Charles coming in the other direction, looking tired and distracted. Only when Jack spoke did he look up.

'Thanks for a great day, Charles.'

The Count stopped midstep. 'Oh, Jack, hello there. Yes, I'm glad you enjoyed it. Are you not coming back with us?'

'Thanks, but no. I'm sure I can find my way back to the city.' He needed a break from the Aretinos and their expensive toys.

'Very good. I imagine I will see you again.'

They shook hands but as Jack was turning away the Count stopped him. 'Just remember what I said about sticking to what you know, all right? And look after Stella, she's a very special girl.'

'Yes, she is,' Jack said, but something sounded odd about Charles's words. Did he have something to hide after all?

He returned to Motorhome Alley to be greeted by scenes reminiscent of a travelling circus. The reporters and celebrities were pushed aside, replaced by the hundreds of stagehands who made the whole outrageous show possible. Despite all the frenetic activity, Jack felt lethargic and alone – as much as he didn't want to admit it.

He dawdled around the paddock, knowing he wasn't likely to have this kind of access again. For him the thrill had always been about the machinery and the athletes, never the glamour and celebrity. And watching Stella get sucked into the paparazzi machine had turned indifference into contempt. When he briefly toyed with the idea of calling Vicky Cavendish to see if she wanted a drink somewhere, he couldn't help thinking she was tainted by association. He tucked his phone back in his pants.

But his mood didn't improve. He was in a foreign country, surrounded by strangers. He could go back to the empty, bugged apartment and drive himself nuts with repeated viewings of Ganet's footage. Or he could move with the crowd to the local bars and eateries and see how long it took for some local girl to invite him to join her table. What were the chances of finding some socialite with a sports car who'd suggest a romantic drive around Lake Como?

The sun was beginning to edge towards the horizon as his slow walk brought him to the other end of the alley, where the party at Ferrari was still in full swing. The glow of winning seemed to radiate from the scarlet motorhome complex, highlighted by the vivid flashes from countless photographers. Jack decided to take a wide berth around the fans and press, but then he felt a presence trotting up beside him. He turned to look.

'Hey there, Vicky,' he said. 'Still working?'

'Just wrapping things up,' she said, putting one hand on his arm to balance on a single stiletto while she readjusted the strap on her other shoe. 'Had enough of the A-listers? Want to go get a drink?'

He wasn't sure. 'Don't you need to hang around here? What if some supermodel throws her phone or something?'

She smiled. 'My boys are on the case with their cameras. Besides, it's too well covered to hope for an exclusive.' Her hand was still on his arm. 'Go on, have a drink with me. I don't bite. Do you have a better offer?'

No, Jack thought, I really don't.

33

The sky took on a golden glow, fading to pink as the sun dropped towards the awesome mountains. The sparkling lake, ruffled by a light breeze, reflected and enhanced the light show while friendly waiters brought delicious platters of food, including an eggplant and mint ravioli in an unctuous sage and butter sauce that was to die for.

They were eating early at Alex's suggestion. He'd promised her the combination of food and sunset would be spectacular, and he hadn't lied. Only a few tables on the waterside terrace were occupied, and the whole establishment reeked of discretion and class. No annoying photographers or curious gawkers here. Stella felt more relaxed than she had in days.

The drive from Monza had been lovely, the convertible Porsche affording sweeping views of blue water, quaint towns and majestic lakeside villas, all against a backdrop of snow-capped peaks. The hotel was on the north side of the lake, well away from the sprawl of Como itself. Alex had continued to treat Stella perfectly, as he had all day. Attentive but not pushy; flirtatious but not smarmy; intimate but not crowding. And he liked to talk business.

'I'm impressed with your knowledge of the team's operations,' she said, as she contemplated a newly arrived course of grilled fish in a delicate sauce. 'Are you on top of all the other group companies as well?'

'I've been paying particular attention to the team,' he said, 'because it's such a money pit, but don't be fooled by my comfort with the numbers. I might know how much it costs for an hour in the wind tunnel, but I still don't know why they have to spend so much time in there.'

She shrugged. 'Recognising what you don't know is just as important.'

He smiled at the oblique praise. 'Does this mean you'll be telling Giorgio you believe the Aretinos are still a good risk?'

'Let's not get ahead of ourselves,' she said with a grin. 'My initial analysis tells me you must be facing some serious cash-flow issues.'

'But you haven't even looked at the data.'

'It's not hard to figure out, especially if you factor in the drain that is the Formula One team. I suggest you sell off the detergents business. I'm guessing it's going to need a big capital injection and I reckon you'd get a decent price from one of the big players, or maybe the Chinese, because of your Italian market share.'

He looked somewhat taken aback. 'Are you sure you haven't had access to those reports?'

'They're still locked in the boot of the Porsche. Why?'

'Because we just paid half a million bucks for a six-month study that reached exactly the same conclusion.'

'I could have saved you a lot of time,' she said, with a mischievous tone to her voice, 'but I probably would've charged you something similar.'

'Cheeky,' he said, raising his wineglass to her.

'The value of advice is not always measured by how long it takes to come up with it, Alex.'

He contemplated her for a while. 'Maybe there's some more pressing advice you might be able to offer.' The playful note in his voice was gone.

'What's that?'

'Without even looking at our reports, you've taken the measure of the Aretino Group. You're very good at what you do. Have you picked up any sense of whether somebody might be trying to bring down the group? An explanation as to why our jet was bombed?'

Stella looked into Alex's eyes and saw the fear there. 'Nothing much, Alex, otherwise you would have known about it already. I'm following up a few hunches, but let me see where they take me. If there is some sort of systematic attack on the Aretino Group underway . . .'

'That means my father would be next,' he said. 'Ever since he missed that flight to Nice, I've been worried. I can't talk to him about it, though – he dismisses any suggestion of a coordinated attack or sabotage as nonsense.'

'I don't think it's nonsense,' Stella said, 'and I don't think you should be complacent, either. You're already earning a reputation as an effective leader in the business community. If your father is a target because someone is trying to bring down the Aretino Group, then you are too.'

He flashed a confident smile. 'I won't give in to fear.'

'Of course,' she said, returning the smile, 'but don't be reckless either. I, for one, would be very unhappy if something happened to you before I've had a chance to work it all out.'

That hadn't come out quite right, and she reached for her wineglass. He took her hand. 'Are you worried about me or your ability to solve the puzzle?'

Her cheeks flushed slightly. 'Both. But obviously I'd hate anything bad happening to you, in any circumstances.'

'I'm glad,' he said, softly. His skin was smooth and dry and his nails were expertly manicured. His fingers played suggestively with hers. 'I've been on fire since that kiss on Friday,' he said, leaning closer. 'The horrible thing that happened afterwards wasn't enough to spoil the memory.'

She allowed him to keep her hand. 'Yes,' she said, 'until then, it was a perfect evening.'

His fingers pressed more firmly. 'So, do you think we can pick up where we left off?'

She ran a fingernail along his palm like a fortune teller and he visibly shivered with delight. 'Let's see what you've ordered for dessert,' she said, seductively. 'The right sweet goes a long way with me.'

The windows of Alex's second-floor suite looked out over the lake. A small commuter ferry was chugging across the water, its lights reflecting on the silvery surface. Stella heard the pop of a cork and soon sensed Alex behind her. He reached around with one hand to offer her a crystal flute. As she took a sip of the tingling bubbles, he moved closer and she could feel his breath wash the back of her neck.

'Peaceful, isn't it?' he said, looking out over her shoulder.

'Very,' she said, allowing her body to drift backwards until she was leaning against his chest.

He nuzzled his face in her hair, drinking in her scent. His hand moved to her hip, pulling her closer. She could feel his hardness pressing against her. The hand moved over her belly, exploring her form through the fine linen of her dress. She closed her eyes. Lips brushed her right ear and his tongue teased her lobe, sending a delicious shiver through her body. A light nip with his teeth made her groan. His mouth moved down to her exposed neck and she put down her glass before she dropped it.

The hand now grasped the opposite hip and pulled her around to face him. His lips found hers and his tongue gently moved inside her mouth. His hands were exploring her back, tickling and tempting. She gasped when he found the zip of her dress and began to tug it open. The material peeled away from her body easily and suddenly the dress had slipped over her hips and was on the floor. He reached for her bra strap.

To slow things down, she pushed him back gently and tugged at his shirt. His blues eyes gazed into hers as he quickly tore the polo off. She wrapped her arms around his bare torso and they kissed again. His skin was evenly tanned and his body fit.

She found herself objectively comparing his body to Jack's. Why the hell am I doing that? she thought. Alex's experienced fingers soon undid her bra but he took his time to remove it, slowly revealing her breasts. Gentle cupping became more forceful as his ardour increased, and he used the tip of his tongue to get his first taste of each erect nipple. She sighed and held his head to her breast, her fingers lost in a forest of loose curls. His hair is beautiful, she thought, as her breathing quickened. More beautiful than Jack's.

His mouth stayed on her breasts but his hands moved down across ticklish ribs and a narrow waist to the hips that held up her G-string. He hooked his fingers under one side of the thong but wasn't prepared to wait, pushing down into the panties and slipping his fingers inside her.

'Wait!' she said, breathlessly, pulling back. Her cheeks were flushed and the pulse in her neck throbbed in time with her racing heart.

'What's wrong?'

'I can't do this.'

'Why not?'

'I don't know. Yes – no. I do know. You're my client.'

'I don't care,' he said, reaching for her.

'I do.' She crossed her arms over her breasts, feeling suddenly modest, and looked around for her bra. 'I don't sleep with clients.'

'But really, I'm not a client.'

'No, you're even worse. You run the company I'm investigating. Talk about a conflict of interest.'

She grabbed her clothes and ran to the bathroom. When she looked at herself in the mirror, she shook her head in frustration. I've always been so good at keeping business and pleasure separate – and now here I am, one skimpy G-string away from committing professional suicide. What was I thinking?

You were thinking he's gorgeous and charming, a voice in her head replied, and she felt a surge of regret. Maybe you can come back here when the job is done, the same voice of temptation suggested, and she felt that tingle in her groin again. But she knew nothing planned would work. Spontaneity was vital, because she certainly didn't want to give the impression that she was angling to become a countess. Besides, after the unresolved confusion of her relationship with Jack, she'd promised herself a break from men for a while.

When she emerged from the bathroom, Alex was fully dressed and siting cross-legged in a padded armchair. She approached him with an apologetic smile. 'I'm so sorry,' she said. 'That was a mean thing to do. The truth is, your charm overwhelmed my good senses. I didn't mean to lead you on.'

'I'm sorry, too,' Alex said. 'I pushed too hard. I always knew you were a woman who deserved a gentler courtship. It was wrong of me to think of you as . . .'

'A good-time girl?' Stella suggested, and they both laughed easily.

'Maybe it's the threat that's hanging over me,' Alex said, offering up her untouched flute of champagne. 'The family's under attack and I'm behaving like there's no time left for proper romance.'

She thought of the assassin monitoring their apartment. The sense of dread was very real to her, too. And one fact was incontrovertible: sipping champagne on the shores of Lake Como wouldn't get her any closer to discovering who or what had them all living with fear.

She put down the glass and said, 'I need you to take me back to Milan.'

Stella was a little surprised, but mostly relieved, to find the apartment empty after Alex dropped her off in Via Ravizza. Jack had a knack of reading her like a book and she couldn't bear a sarcastic, albeit amusing, critique of her professional detachment. She hoped a long shower would wash away some of the self-recrimination and refocus her mind on the problem at hand, but as she soaped her body under the hot water, she found herself still aching for release. It felt good, being wanted, but why did it have to be so complicated?

As she towelled her hair, the post-it notes she'd stuck around the apartment warning against misspoken words reminded her there was plenty more at stake than male ego and sexual frustration. The carabinieri at the front entrance seemed relaxed, but they didn't know about the bugs. Assuming Bauer was the one listening, his only possible interest could be the film. He wanted to know if they'd come up with a copy and if they'd learned anything from it. But what did that have to do with the container in the Aretino team transporter? For some reason, she couldn't let go of the idea that there had to be a connection.

And even if Ganet's film was evidence that Bauer was responsible for the bombing, it didn't explain why he'd done it. Was he a paid minion of some megalomaniacal business rival, or part of some reactionary communist terrorist cell? Whatever his motivation, it wasn't just the Aretino Group in the firing line any more. The Stack Partnership was now invested, too. And if you fuck with us, she said to herself, then we'll fuck with you.

The clock read 10.45. After the day she'd had, it felt like it should be much later, but it was more than seven hours since she'd left Monza. Dressed in a T-shirt and loose pyjama pants, she settled onto the soft cushions of the sofa in the lounge and unpacked the material provided by Charles Aretino, which Alex had helpfully squeezed into two soft leather bags. Piling it up on the glass coffee table, she decided it would have to be treated with suspicion. Large lumps of information provided voluntarily had a tendency to be one-sided. Just because the Aretinos were so forthcoming didn't mean everything they provided was to be blindly believed.

But before she started on the pile, she opened her laptop. She wanted to know if Deputy Inspector Mancini had responded to Jack's email. When she saw that she'd been copied in on a reply from the Euro-cop, she was initially excited, but it proved to be disappointing. It said the French authorities hoped to process a warrant for Bauer's arrest on charges including murder and arson, once the courts opened for business on Monday. The video file Jack had sent through wouldn't be examined until Tuesday at the earliest, due to a backlog in the relevant department.

Bloody bureaucrats, she said to herself. The authorities clearly weren't going to be any help. Okay then, if the footage is a dead end for now, what about the transporter? Why was it at the villa in Mira and why was there a historian there at the same time? What was Jimmy's guess at the guy's name? She googled the name Vincent Franco but it produced no relevant results. Then she had another idea and reached for the pile of disks Alex had provided with the files. One of them was labelled *Consolidated Payroll Records 01/02*. She dug it out and loaded it into her computer. It contained dozens of spreadsheets stuffed with a phenomenal amount of data. A global search produced five Francos, none of whom were named Vincent and all of whom had job titles that were decidedly industrial.

She searched for anyone designated as a historian or something similar and eventually came up with a few names. One of them was a Victor Drago, who was listed as 'historical adviser' to the Aretino Family Trust. His location was recorded as Valletta, and an internet search produced an entry in the research section of the website for the National Library of Malta. Jimmy's guess hadn't been far off.

Valletta, she thought, capital of Malta. Valletta, spiritual home of the Order of St John that Jimmy had been going on about this morning. Hang on. She sat up straight. Valletta, a name that ends with e-t-t-a. Holy shit! She closed Mancini's email and loaded Jack's enlarged still of the boat sitting off the coast at Nice. The black lettering she could make out wasn't the cruiser's name at all, but its port of registration. The name should be on the stern above but it looked as if it had been painted out. Or had it? She played with the brightness and contrast settings on her screen and stared at the patch of white fibreglass from every angle. At last, she discerned a subtle edge and realised the cruiser's name was painted in pale-gold letters that had been masked by the sun's reflection on the original image.

Twice a Knight, she read silently. As in the Knights of St John, or was that just a coincidence? The Order of Malta was a big part of the Aretino family story, but could there be a link between the religious body and the bombing? Why would the knights of the Order assassinate Count Federico and possibly attempt to take out Charles too?

Not all of the knights, she reminded herself, just the one who bought the film. Who was presumably also the one in the photo Marcel Ganet was shown. A German knight who employed the services of a German assassin. And Ganet had told Jack that the men in the photo were all wearing the same clothes. Could that be the robes she'd seen on a number of men at the charity ball? Was this the mystery business mogul pulling the strings to bring the Aretino empire down – another high-powered aristocrat with big ambitions and small morals?

If they could identify him, it would be a real coup, and all paths seemed to be converging on Valletta. And when the unsettling presence of Bauer's listening devices was factored in, there was only one logical next step. The financial reports had to be analysed, but there was no obligation to do the work in Milan. They could start on the plane and finish at a nice hotel with a decent swimming pool. It would work wonders for their emotional health too, she was sure. Two near misses in less than a week had taken their toll.

With renewed energy, she returned to the internet to make flight and hotel bookings. Typing out a note for Jack to read when he came in, she couldn't help wondering where he might be. She could understand why he didn't want to sit at home alone, especially with Big Brother listening, but it was now after midnight and if he'd continued drinking from the time she'd last seen him at the track, he'd be in rotten shape tomorrow. Damn it, she thought, recalling her grandmother's standard advice before a night out. *I hope he's keeping himself nice.*

34

Jack woke up feeling slightly disconnected from his body. He was aware of the throbbing in his head and the dryness of his mouth, but that was about all. He moved a leg and registered a smooth sensation on his skin. He moved an arm and felt the same light touch. Two things were immediately apparent – he was lying on his side under a sheet, and he was naked.

His eyes snapped open and in the low light he saw a naked woman lying next to him. The memories flooded back. Leaving the track with Vicky, hitting a bar in Monza, finding her more interesting than he'd expected. Then being driven back to her modern apartment in a battered Fiat, drinking a lot of Scotch on the couch, and then . . .

Shit. Probably not the most professional move. The images in his head were coming back in searing clarity. He looked at Vicky to see if she was awake. In the warm air, she had thrown off her side of the sheet. Her hairdo was slightly tousled and her lipstick smeared but otherwise her body remained a testament to cosmetic enhancement and a meagre diet. It wasn't a wholly unpleasurable sight.

Her breathing was long and even but as he tried to exit the bed without disturbing her, she said, 'You okay, Jack?'

'Yes,' he said. 'Well, no. I've got a pretty fucking horrendous hangover.'

She turned on the overhead light with a switch by the bed and watched him wince as he searched for his clothes. 'I told you,' she said.

'Told me what?'

'That you'd regret it.'

Regret what? he thought. The booze? Or sleeping with you? He hadn't made a worse alcohol-induced decision since his university days, and never one with such uncomfortable professional consequences. Or maybe it wouldn't be such a big deal – after all, Vicky was hardly a paragon of professionalism herself.

'Your clothes are in the lounge room,' she said, as she sat up in the bed and put her feet on the floor.

By the time he'd located all the discarded items of clothing and footwear scattered over the rug in the compact living space, she'd donned a short silk housecoat. 'Would you like a coffee or something?'

'Water, please,' he said, pulling on a sock.

He drank three large glasses in quick succession then looked at his watch and saw that it was early morning. Stella might be home. Or maybe she wouldn't be. He wasn't sure if he was relieved at that thought or not. 'You're leaving, then,' Vicky said, with a touch of humour.

He gathered the last of his belongings and looked to the front door. 'Sorry to race off like this, Vicky. We've got a big week ahead of us and I shouldn't be playing up tonight. I mean, no offence . . .'

'I'll be all right, Jack. Don't you worry about me.'

He smiled gratefully. 'Where are we, exactly?'

'If you turn left as you go out of the building and walk a couple of blocks over, you'll find plenty of cabs. You should be back at your place in fifteen minutes or so.'

'Thanks,' he said. 'You've been very kind. I seem to remember you giving me lots of good advice.'

'Can I give you some more?' she said, as she followed him to the front door. 'Don't tell her. She doesn't need to know.'

A pang of guilt travelled up his spine, but he ignored it. There was no reason to feel guilty. 'She knows I'm no Boy Scout.'

Vicky shook her head as if she knew better. 'You claim to be no more than business partners now, but there's something between you still, I can feel it. And since you're in business together, keep your personal life your own, Jack. She doesn't need to know. It would only hurt her and won't get you any closer to winning her back.'

Jack looked Vicky in the eye. 'I no longer harbour that expectation.'

She reached up on her toes to kiss him quickly on the cheek. 'Liar.'

BE CAREFUL WHAT YOU SAY!

The advice, in Stella's handwriting, was posted on the wall just inside the front door. Jack stared at it, struck by its sudden profundity. His head was still woolly from the booze and he wasn't sure if Stella was home. The birds were beginning the dawn chorus outside and the light was on in the hallway, but it might have been like that when they left for Sunday mass. His bedroom was just inside the entrance. Stella's master suite was at the other end of the apartment, near the bathroom. He was in desperate need of a shower, which meant sneaking past her room.

He moved quietly into his room and stripped off his clothes. Wrapping a towel around his waist, he padded the length of the terrazzo hallway with senses as alert as he could manage. He didn't fancy doing the walk of shame past her if she popped out of the room all wholesome and refreshed. His own reflection in the hall mirror startled him. His face was pink from too much sun and his hair was mussed up. The bandage on his arm was seeping. His eyes looked puffy and red. 'Christ,' he muttered, without thinking, 'what a catch!'

'Jack, is that you?'

The open doorway to her bedroom lit up. He quickly straightened his hair before he stepped into view. She was in her uncle's large bed, her head propped up on a pillow. Her shoulders were bare.

'Hi there,' he said.

'Where have you been?' she asked, with interest. 'You must have had a good day at the race, coming in this late.'

'Yeah, I did,' he said, straining to keep a conversational tone. 'I caught up with Vicky Cavendish afterwards.'

'Oh!' she responded, taken aback. 'How was that?'

'Not such a good idea,' he said, tapping his temple. 'Too much to drink. She can really put it away.'

'Everything off the record, I hope?'

'Of course.' He was still standing in the doorway, trying to keep his face in the shadows. 'Though I can't promise you won't be in the magazine again this week.'

Stella shook her head with a look of resignation. 'Come in,' she said. 'I was reviewing the financial data last night and it got me thinking.'

'I really need to take a shower,' he said.

'I don't mind.' She patted the bed. 'I want to tell you about my initial take on the Aretino reports. I think there's scope for a lucrative spin-off of the detergents business.'

She gestured with her head and held out some papers that had been lying on the bed next to her. He hesitated. Then the penny dropped. She wasn't talking about detergents. 'Sure, I'll take a quick look now,' he said. 'Sounds interesting.'

He took the papers from her hand and sat on the edge of her bed.

Her notes were on top and as he read through her findings and her conclusions about the connections to Malta, he raised his eyebrows. Was she drawing too long a bow? Who cares? he decided. Getting out of this bugged box was an appealing option and, as far as he was concerned, the boat's home port was reason enough to pick Valletta.

'I was thinking we should do a SWOT analysis of the various businesses when we visit the bank tomorrow,' he said in a clear voice. 'This detergents idea could have application to other divisions, but I need to get my head around the opportunities and threats.'

'Good idea,' she said. 'But you should get a few hours' sleep. We've got a lot of work ahead of us.' She took a pen from the bedside table and leaned forward to write on the paper in Jack's hand. *Pack light,* she scribbled. *We're sharing a room so we only need one suitcase and one computer.*

Jack took the pen from her hand and wrote: *What about the cops? Do we tell Mancini?* He passed her the pen.

Not until we know more. They move too slowly.

He nodded his agreement but the close proximity of her bare shoulders was distracting. He did miss that beautiful skin, and he was suddenly conscious of his own state of undress.

Stella pulled the paper from his hand and turned it over for more writing space. *Go and have your shower,* she wrote. *You stink of whisky and sex!*

35

Air Malta's direct flight from Milan to Valletta departed just after ten-thirty on Monday morning. There were eight first-class seats at the front of the aircraft but only two were occupied. Through the windows, Jack watched the ground drop away until the view was swallowed by a cloudbank that had arrived over the city during the night. Sitting back, he stole a glance at Stella and saw her face still twisted in thought, her eyes focused on the open report on her lap. ·

'That was a nice piece of work with the footage,' he said, stifling a yawn. 'I couldn't get it to reveal anything.'

'You just weren't looking at the right spot on the stern,' she said without looking up. 'Once I knew it had to be there . . .'

'Good job digging out the name of the historian, too,' he said. 'Sorry I wasn't around to give you a hand.'

She glanced at him quickly. 'It's probably a good thing you weren't, with Bauer listening in. Long silences and scribbled notes would have made him suspicious.'

'Let's hope he wastes a lot of time waiting for us to show up again.'

'We can't stay out of sight too long,' Stella said seriously. 'I don't want him taking out his paranoia on my relatives when they get back from their vacation. But with any luck, after a day or two in Malta we'll know who he's working for, which might give us some insight into their motivation and intentions. That should give us a little more leverage. And more credibility with the cops.'

Jack shook his head. 'It's a dangerous game we're playing. The closer we get to the truth, the more unhinged they're going to become.'

She closed the report in her lap and turned her head towards him. 'I know,' she said, 'but what choice do we have? We're part of this thing now. We either expose the plot against the Aretinos or we go home. Do you want to quit?'

'No, of course not. I'm just saying, we need to stay on our toes.'

'Agreed. But look, they have no reason to suspect we've gone to Malta, so I figure we're at least as safe there as we would be in Milan. Safer, even.'

Yeah right, Jack thought. We'll see about that.

Barely an hour later the pilot began descending and Jack's eyes were drawn back to the windows. The cloud had been left behind long ago but the endless blue of the sea – only occasionally disturbed by the frothy wakes of tiny vessels – had not held his attention for long. Now there was more to see, as vague earthy spots in the distance grew into islands edged by high, rugged cliffs.

Apart from countless tiny white boats in countless tiny inlets around the coast, few other signs of human habitation were obvious from a distance. But as they flew lower over the land, he realised it was an illusion caused by the uniform beige hue of landscape and buildings alike. Straight roads bordered by dry stone walls criss-crossed the arid, treeless countryside, connecting small villages to larger towns. By the time they were approaching the runway, he'd concluded that the main island was actually quite densely populated.

Outside the terminal building Stella and Jack were enveloped by an intensely dry midday heat that almost stopped them both in their tracks. The taxi wasn't much better, so when they entered the air-conditioned lobby of the five-star Hotel Phoenicia it was with audible sighs of relief. They were given keys to a corner room on the second floor but, with only one rolling suitcase between them, they declined the offer of a porter.

When Stella saw the double bed, she visibly baulked. 'I asked for a twin-bed room.'

'We'll be all right,' Jack said, dropping a heavy bag stuffed with Aretino reports on a chair. 'Even I understand the boundaries by now.' He was peeved to see her still hesitating. 'What? You don't trust yourself?'

He was secretly pleased to detect her uncertainty but, a second later, it was gone.

'I'm sure I can control my lustful urges,' she said sarcastically.

The room was decorated in cool white, with sliding glass doors leading from the bedroom to two balconies, one facing east and the other south. Jack gratefully deposited the second shoulder bag full of Aretino reports on the desk, and raided the minibar for an overpriced Coke. Stella sat on the bed and picked up the phone, asking to be connected with directory information.

While she waited on the number for the National Library, Jack unpacked his few possessions and powered up his laptop. He heard her dialling and then asking to be connected to Victor Drago. There was a delay while she listened to a voicemail recording and then she said, 'Hello Victor, my name is Stella. I'm from Australia and I'm researching my family tree. I've discovered an ancestor from an Italian noble family with links to the Order of St John and I've been told you might be able to help with my research. I'm staying at the Hotel Phoenicia, room 211, or you can call my mobile.'

She recited the numbers and hung up the phone. Jack was looking at the map he'd picked up at the airport. The National Library and Archives building was only a short walk away, within the walled city of Valletta. This no doubt explained Stella's hotel selection. The Phoenicia sat on a high bluff just outside the old city gates and was some distance from the sea. It wouldn't be the destination of choice for the jetskiing crowd or family vacationers. It probably appealed more to those who wanted to immerse themselves in the history and culture of a piece of rock that had been at the crossroads of civilisation for millennia.

The map showed the tiny city thrusting out into the sea, strategically positioned to dominate the large harbours on both sides of the peninsula. Malta's craggy shoreline offered innumerable places to moor a boat. Jack turned the map around for Stella to see and said, 'Where do we start looking for a boat on an island that is one big marina?'

'I don't know,' she said, looking closer. 'Maybe there's a harbour master or a registry somewhere.'

'Grand Harbour,' Jack read, pointing to the body of water forming the eastern edge of Valletta. 'With a name like that, it's bound to be full of boats.'

Stella picked up the printed photograph of *Twice a Knight* from the desk. 'Hopefully not too many like this.'

'I wouldn't be so sure,' he said. 'You weren't looking out the window as we came in to land. There are hundreds of bays filled with thousands of boats around this island. Anyway, I suppose it's as good a place to start as any. I'm getting hungry; maybe we can stop at a café on the way?'

'Sounds good. Let's get going then.'

Stepping out of the hotel's front gate, they were immediately in the thick of things. Semi-antique orange buses were lined up in long rows that curved around a grand circular fountain in the centre of the plaza that separated the hotel from the city gates. Jack led the way between diesel-belching tourist icons to the wide pavement, which was dotted with trees and vans selling drinks, snacks and souvenirs.

The distractions did not diminish the awe generated by their first clear view of Valletta's walls. A deep cutting separated the bluff where the buses were gathered from the entrance to the city, and it was only as they crossed the bridge joining the two sides that they realised how deep the dry moat was. The cars parked at the bottom looked toy-sized. From that extraordinary depth, perfectly cut blocks of sandstone sloped back at first but then rose vertically to cast a dramatic silhouette against the sky.

Moving down the pedestrian-only main street packed with foreign visitors, they took in a streetscape that felt like a movie set. Whether restored or original, it was impossible to tell – the elegantly carved wood and stone architecture was convincingly sixteenth-century. They passed the ruins of the opera house – kept as a memorial to the terrible pounding the city received during the war – and found an outdoor café close to the walls of the cathedral, where they ordered sandwiches and coffee.

Their lunch was interrupted by a call on Stella's phone. The conversation was short. 'Victor Drago will meet me at four-thirty,' she said when she'd hung up. 'At the statue of Queen Victoria, which must be a little further down this street.'

'That was easy.'

'Turns out we have something in common. He's an Aussie too.'

'Small world,' Jack said, consulting his watch. 'That gives us two hours before you're due back here. You want to start with Grand Harbour?'

'Why not?'

They finished their meal quickly and walked further down Republic Street past the Grand Master's Palace, now a museum. At the next corner they turned right onto a street that appeared to lead directly to the Grand Harbour but it proved more complicated than the map implied. When they first caught sight of the water it was still a long way below them – an enormous jagged inlet of bright blue surrounded by towering forts and other stone buildings memorialising the rule of the knights.

Looking out over the impressive scene, Jack could see it primarily served large ships, like liners, cargo freighters and navy vessels. 'No pleasure craft down there,' he said. 'We should try the other side of the peninsula.'

'Fishing trawlers,' Stella said, pointing down. 'They ought to know about the boats in these waters, particularly the big ones.'

Four vessels were tied up almost directly below them and Jack could see small figures moving on and around them. 'I suppose it's worth a shot,' he said doubtfully, wiping sweat from his brow with the back of his hand.

After another fifteen minutes, descending hundreds of steps and traversing narrow laneways, they reached the harbour side. The sun bounced into their faces from the surface of the water, only adding to the sensation of being cooked in an airless oven.

The trawler crews didn't appear to be hard at work. As Stella and Jack moved along the stone wharf, the occasional wolf-whistle directed Stella's way grew into a competitive chorus. When Jack finally managed to speak to a few of the men, none seemed to grasp his questions. To Jack's ear, Maltese sounded like a cross between Italian and Arabic. Stella found a few Sicilians on the second trawler who understood her, but they shook their heads when they were shown the photograph of *Twice a Knight*.

'This might be harder than we thought,' she said.

The captain of the third vessel was on the quayside and he put an end to the whistles and bawdy suggestions of his men with a gruff command. He, too, shook his head when shown the image but he gestured to the last boat. 'The skipper speaks English,' he said in Italian.

The steel hull of the fourth trawler was painted a faded, rusty red. Its captain was nowhere to be seen, but there was a fresh gang of deeply tanned fishermen ready to show off for the pretty lady. Two young alpha males stepped forward, displaying their muscular torsos, but they turned away quickly. Jack looked over his shoulder to see what had put them off.

Two men were approaching from the direction of the dockside buildings. They were older than the men waiting by the boat and were dressed in shirts and canvas trousers rather than the shorts and optional singlets of the lower hands. The taller one was modestly built with a deeply lined face and dark curly hair greying at the temples, topped with a black cap. It was clear he was the captain when he barked orders and his men scurried aboard the vessel.

As he turned to Stella and Jack, he seemed to be evaluating them. He obviously reached a quick conclusion. 'You speak English?'

'Yes.'

'Let me guess,' he said. 'You open new restaurant and want exclusive supplier. But you must come to dawn market like everybody else.'

'We don't have a restaurant,' Jack said.

'My name is Stella, and this is Jack.' Stella held out her hand and the surprised skipper checked his own for cleanliness before taking hers.

He smiled, showing a set of crooked teeth with thick gold caps. 'My name is Petroni,' he said, touching his leather cap with a finger, 'and I am the captain of this beautiful vessel.'

Jack took his cue from Stella and extended his own hand. 'What do you catch?'

'*Lempuki*,' Petroni said. 'In English they are dolphin fish.'

'Been doing it long?' Stella asked.

'Thirty years, almost.'

'And this is your base?'

'No, we sail out of Marsaxlokk Harbour, on the eastern end of the island. We usually come here only to unload the fish. Today we come to get paid.'

His offsider was hovering a few metres away. Petroni turned in his direction and listened as the man muttered something in Maltese. 'My first mate wants to meet you, Stella. He thinks you are Italian movie star. Is this so?'

Stella laughed. 'No!'

The first mate stepped forward and put out his hand with a timid smile. 'Joseph,' he mumbled.

'Hello,' Stella said, 'and this is my husband, Jack.'

Jack quickly hid his surprise and stepped forward to offer his hand, which Joseph shook unenthusiastically.

'If you don't want fish,' the captain asked, 'why come here? It's not so good for tourists.'

Stella handed him the picture. 'This boat is called *Twice a Knight* and is registered in Valletta. Do you know it?'

The captain glanced at the photo then turned to look at his mate, who was making an unpleasant face.

'You know it,' Stella stated.

Petroni frowned. 'I have seen it, yes.'

'Do you know who owns it?'

'No.'

'Does the name Kurt Bauer mean anything to you?' Jack asked.

Petroni shook his head slowly.

'Where would you suggest we look for this boat?' Stella asked.

Petroni rubbed his chin with a calloused hand. 'Msida marina, I think.'

'How do we get there from here?'

'From the city gate, take any bus going to Sliema and tell the driver you want Msida.' He spelled it out for them. 'It's not far from Valletta. When you come down the hill and see yachts close to the road, then you get off. If she is in port, that is where you will find her.'

Stella smiled and held out her hand. 'Thank you, Captain,' she said, 'you've been very helpful.'

'Be careful,' Petroni said earnestly, holding onto her hand for an extra second or two.

'Why do you say that?'

He shook his head, as if the subject bothered him. 'In these waters, fast boats like that attract trouble.'

'Smuggling?' Jack suggested.

Petroni said nothing but his body language was telling.

'Drugs?'

The captain shrugged. 'Drugs, women, refugees; everything crosses the Mediterranean. I wish you good luck.'

'Thanks again,' Stella said.

As they made their way back along the quay, she walked with new purpose. 'Drug running!' she said triumphantly. 'I told you someone was using the F1 team as a cover for smuggling. I should have tried harder to get inside that container.'

Though he remained dubious, Jack wasn't about to say so. 'Drugs, hey?' he said. 'That makes the most sense. Maybe they use the boat to get the stuff from Africa to Europe and then it goes with the F1 team to God knows where.'

'Next week,' she said, 'it's going to America. Maybe Federico stumbled on the operation so they blew him out of the sky. By the way, thanks for not hesitating when I introduced you as my husband. That Joseph guy gave me the creeps. It was a defence mechanism, I guess.'

'Any time,' Jack said. 'He was a strange fish.'

Stella smiled, but then her face turned serious. 'Did you notice his startled look when you mentioned Kurt Bauer's name?'

'No, I was looking at the captain. You reckon he knows Bauer?'

'Can't be sure but, if he does, I'd say he's scared of him.'

'Yeah, well,' Jack said, as they began their ascent back into the city, 'I can't blame him for that.'

On the water below, Captain Petroni had just ordered the cast off and, from the wheelhouse of his trawler, he watched as a laughing youth pulled away the last rope and jumped easily onto the deck. He added revolutions to the engine and turned the wheel to starboard. Slowly, the old girl pulled away from the quay.

One deck down, his first mate Joseph was alone in the galley, turning around on the spot to find the best reception on the mobile phone pressed to his ear. 'Yes,' he was saying, in halting English, 'a man and a woman . . . Yes, very beautiful, Stella is her name. They ask about your boat. They ask about you. Yes, by name. You always said, if I could be useful, I should call. Yes . . . Yes . . . Of course, but I —'

He looked blankly at the phone in his hand, wondering if the call was cut short by a lost signal or the speaker's impatience. But he wasn't about to try calling back. He valued his life too much.

36

'You'll have to go on without me,' Stella said, as they walked through the city gate towards the bus terminus. 'There isn't enough time for me to go looking for the boat and get back to Queen Victoria by four-thirty. Besides, I need a shower after that climb.'

'A shower would be nice,' Jack said, pulling sweat-soaked cotton away from the skin on his back, 'or, better yet, a dip in that pool I saw behind the hotel.'

'No,' Stella said, with a hint of satisfaction. 'For you, a nice bumpy trip in a hot old bus. Find out who owns the cruiser and I'll meet you by the pool at sunset for a drink.'

'You come at sunset and I'll be on my third,' he said, but she had already turned away towards the hotel.

He contemplated the bewildering parade of pale-orange buses in front of him. His lost look prompted a friendly local to point him in the right direction. He boarded a fifties-era Leyland that had been lovingly maintained. A few holiday-makers were already seated, and by the time the driver arrived to collect the meagre fares, it was half-full. Jack's patience was fast dissolving as the bus grew stuffier, without any sign of movement. He was about to disembark and look for a cab when the driver started up the engine and closed the doors.

The route bounced them past monumental government buildings then down from the high bluff of Valletta and around the narrow bay separating it from the next peninsula, home to the tourist town of Sliema. Once the bus was running alongside the sea, Jack saw rows of masts extending from the shoreline. With relief he pushed his way towards the door.

The wide stone pavement between the road and the crowded marina doubled as a car park and there wasn't a single patch of shade. When the bus pulled away in a cloud of black exhaust, Jack was already rummaging in his backpack for sunscreen. Rubbing it into his forearms, he let his eyes explore the boats bobbing on the water. The finger wharves were similar to those in Nice, but these were longer and better organised. Pleasure craft of all kinds were neatly parked, sterns in to the dock, but there was nothing of the size and sophistication of *Twice a Knight*. He began walking, carefully checking each row of boats as it came into view, but a quick glance ahead revealed a forest of masts extending as far as the eye could see. Christ, he thought, this could take hours.

Stella arrived at the statue of Queen Victoria early and found a shady spot nearby to wait so her shower wasn't rendered pointless. Five minutes after the appointed time, a man in a white open-necked business shirt appeared and Stella watched from the shadows as he walked around the monument twice. He looked in her direction both times but apparently did not see her as a viable contact. He was about to leave when she stepped out into the sunshine. 'Victor?'

He stopped in his tracks. 'You're not Stella, are you?' he said. His accent was distinctly Australian, though he had the looks of an Egyptian soap star.

'Yes, I am,' she said, holding out her hand. 'Stella Sartori.'

'Victor,' he said, sounding slightly taken aback. 'Victor Drago.'

'Are you all right?'

'Sorry. I just didn't expect . . . I mean, I thought you'd be . . . I mean, most people interested in the knights aren't . . .'

'They're not what?'

'As young as you,' he said, flashing white teeth as he laughed. 'Where are you from?'

'Melbourne.'

'Really? Me too. What suburb?'

'I grew up in Fairfield.'

'Brunswick East,' he said, jamming a thumb into his own chest.

'Almost neighbours. Isn't it a small world?'

Drago shrugged. 'Well, you know the Maltese community. Half of them seemed to end up Down Under.'

'Actually, I'm not Maltese. My parents came from Italy.'

'Right, you said that in your message.'

'Yeah, I'm in Europe doing my family tree and I discovered my father's mother comes from a line that includes some knights of St John.'

'Fantastic!' Drago said, his grin broadening. 'Blue bloods in the lineage – lucky you. What was the name?'

'Aretino,' Stella said.

Drago's smile faded completely. 'Really?'

'Yes, why? You know the family?'

'No,' he said, quickly, 'not well.'

'Well, I do,' Stella said. 'I also know about your interest in the Villa Aretino in Mira.'

Drago looked at her for a long moment. Then he gestured towards the building behind him. 'You'd better come inside,' he said.

*

The area around the Msida marina was annoyingly quiet. The boats were all privately owned and the buildings opposite mostly apartments. Only the road separating the two was busy, with a steady stream of traffic in both directions. It was fifteen minutes before Jack found a shop that could sell him a bottle of water. He showed the guy behind the counter the picture of *Twice a Knight* but it prompted only a lacklustre shake of the head. With a long swig from the bottle, he stepped back out into the heat.

It took time to assess each row of watercraft. Motor cruisers were mixed in with yachts and the larger craft tended to be at the far end of the long wharves, so it was difficult to make out the details from a distance. The novelty of the task soon faded and Jack began to think there had to be an easier way. He could now see that the shoreline turned left up ahead and there were boats moored along most of its length for kilometres to come. It was a hopeless task.

At the point where the harbour wall turned, there was a gap in the marina and a shirtless man was sitting on a folding chair with a fishing rod resting on his round belly. He turned at the sound of Jack's footfall and nodded his head in greeting.

'Caught anything?' Jack asked.

'Not a bloody bite,' the man said, in a Welsh brogue. 'Still, I never have high hopes for this spot. I just like sitting in the sun.'

'Know the area well?'

'The wife and I retired here five years ago,' he said, holding up one hand to shade his eyes.

Jack took out the photograph. 'Sounds nice. By any chance, have you seen this boat?'

'Oh yes, isn't she beautiful? Our apartment looks out over the water down there.' He twisted in his seat and pointed left. 'See where the marina ends? After that's where the fancy cruisers berth, right up against the wall. I love watching them come and go.'

'I don't suppose you know who owns this one, do you?'

'No idea. There's a bar a little further along; it has a nautical theme, you can't miss it. That's where all the yachties hang out. Try in there.'

'I will, thanks. You ever see anyone aboard this vessel? Maybe a guy with a tightly trimmed beard?'

The Welshman's brow furrowed. 'Why? Are you a policeman?'

Jack laughed easily. 'No, I'm a tourist looking to organise a trip. I'm told this bearded fellow is a good skipper, with experience along the north African coast. I'm hoping I can hire him to take me and a few friends to Tangiers.'

'Oh I see, lovely. Well, truthfully, the wife and I rarely see anyone on board that boat. It comes and goes at odd times. We think they must be into night fishing or something.'

Night fishing? Jack thought. I doubt it. 'So just along there?'

'Couple of hundred yards, that's all. Look for the beer umbrellas on the pavement.'

Jack licked his lips. Beer. Now you're talking.

Before leading her to the administrative wing, Victor Drago took Stella on a short tour of the National Library and Archives building, pointing out a few highlights from the collection on display in the empty public areas. His office at the back of the building was at the other end of the glamour scale. One small window provided the only natural light, and the room was a cluttered conglomeration of books, papers and journals piled on every flat surface. There were two desks, but he explained that his colleague was attending a conference. His desk had a cleared central space for a computer that looked due for an upgrade.

'These papers don't look very old,' Stella observed.

'Oh, no,' Drago said. 'If we want to examine the originals we do so in a secure, environmentally controlled environment.' He patted his monitor. 'Most of my work is done on this these days. I scan the documents I'm working on.'

'Can you show me something with my family name on it?'

Drago's eyes shot to the computer. 'No,' he said quickly, 'I don't think I have anything like that at the moment. I can show you an interesting piece I was working on recently, if you like.' He pulled out a sliding shelf from under his desk, revealing a keyboard and a mouse. 'It's a record of the Grand Master's ball celebrating the 200th anniversary of the Great Siege. It includes the menu and everything.'

'Is that the Pact of 1798?' She was looking at a framed print on the wall behind his desk.

'Yes. You'll find the Aretino name up there, of course, but it's just a copy.'

'I've seen the original,' she said, with a hint of smugness. 'What's your theory about it? Do you believe the treasure exists?'

It was meant as playful banter, but she found his reaction odd. His eyes shot left and right. He smiled weakly. 'I wouldn't know any-thing about it. Most experts agree the pact can't be about treasure. You see, at the time, the Order was —'

'I know,' she said. 'The Order was crying poor by 1798.' He was obviously uncomfortable so she eased the pressure by turning back towards the computer. 'Where's that menu, then? I'd really like to see what they ate in the eighteenth century.'

He was smiling again, clearly relieved, as he reached for the computer mouse. Stella's eyes shot to the monitor, looking over his shoulder. The screen had activated and the cursor was quickly moving towards a folder named *Anniversary Ball 1765*. But before he could open it, Stella glimpsed another file on the desktop. It was tagged with a single word: *Aretino*.

*

Behind the Phoenicia were large gardens threaded with gravel paths leading to intimate nooks overlooking Valletta's ramparts. Jack hurried down the long central walkway with purposeful strides. When he came to a series of stairs, he descended at a vigorous trot and was pulling at his shirt even before he reached the bottom. He deposited his sunglasses, sandals and few items of clothing on the nearest unoccupied sunlounge and leapt headlong into the cool water. Powering down the full length of the pool, and ignoring the pain in his left arm as his biceps sliced through the cool water, he surfaced with a smile of happy relief and wiped the water from his face.

'You really don't have the complexion for this much sun, do you?'

'Stella!'

She was standing in the shallow end of the pool, elbows resting on the tiles behind her. 'What took you so long?'

He pushed back his wet hair with both hands, giving her a clear view of his flexing chest and abs before he turned to lean back against the tiles too. 'What happened with Victor Drago?'

'I did all right,' she said. 'Turns out he was born in Melbourne, so it was pretty relaxed. I would've liked more time with him but he had another appointment. How'd you get on?'

'Prinz Gerhard von Hirschberg,' Jack said, grinning. 'Knight of St John and smuggler. I found his boat, tied up and large as life. Took some pics with my phone.'

'Von Hirschberg,' she repeated. 'Why does that name ring a bell? Was there anyone on board?'

'No, and there were plenty of tight lips when I first found the bar where all the yachties hang out. That boat scares a lot of people. It cost me a bunch of beers and €200 to the bartender before I got anywhere. Want to know why it's called *Twice a Knight*?'

'Why?'

'Because Prinz Gerhard is a German knight from an old aristocratic family, and also a knight of the Order of Malta. He's the last in an old line, so he's inherited lots of silly titles.'

Stella was impressed. 'A German. He has to be the one who bought the film from Michel Ganet.'

'And had him killed.'

'Well done, you.'

'Thanks.' He couldn't help but watch as she moved away from the pool's edge to drop her head under the water. When she stood up in the shallows and lifted her arms to pull back her long hair, her taut, bikini-clad body was perfectly on show. He looked away with a wry smile. Anything he could do, she could do better.

The swimming pool was perched on a cliff overlooking the city walls, which were beginning to take on a golden glow in the late-afternoon sun. In the other direction, there was an unimpeded view over the bay where he'd been searching an hour ago. Blue water, warm air and a cloudless sky. It was the stuff of fantasy honeymoons – all the more reason to stick to work.

'You say Victor had another appointment?'

'So he said, but the man's a chronic liar.'

'Really?'

'Every time I mentioned the name Aretino, he started back-pedalling.'

'How did an Australian end up with that job, anyway?'

'I didn't get the full story but I gather his dad migrated to Melbourne after the war then moved back to Malta in his sixties, after his wife died. Victor got a degree in history from La Trobe Uni. Says his dad never stopped talking about the knights, so it was sort of inevitable that he ended up here.'

'And what's his deal with the Aretinos?'

'I don't know. He got very defensive every time I mentioned my distant cousins.'

Jack did a double-take. 'Your what? Stella, you didn't! What if he checks with the Count?'

'How can he, if he claims he doesn't know them very well?'

Jack shook his head. 'I guess it doesn't matter. Now that we know who owns the boat we should probably get back to Milan. Maybe Inspector Mancini knows this prince character.'

'Not yet,' she said. 'I still want to know what Drago was doing at the villa last weekend.'

'Why? The prince is the guy we should get to know better. He's probably Kurt Bauer's boss.'

'The prince is also a knight. And Victor Drago is an expert on the knights.'

'But the prince is probably also a smuggler,' Jack countered. 'If he's responsible for the bomb on the plane, it's going to be because of his criminal activity, not his aristocratic or religious pedigree.'

'Yes, I agree. But if he's using the Count or the Formula One team for his own crooked ends then he must have some influence over the family. Either it's somebody they trust or somebody who has a powerful hold over them.'

Jack pondered a moment before nodding his head. 'Okay,' he said, 'so what's the plan? I thought you said Drago was a brick wall.'

'Brick walls crumble, if you chip away at them long enough. He's taking me for a lunchtime drive tomorrow. He volunteered to show me the sights, after I suggested it to him.'

'Right. And what do I do?' Jack asked. 'I suppose I could visit the cathedral and the Grand Master's Palace. Can't hurt to get inside the history of the brotherhood, can it?'

'We can do that together in the morning,' she said. 'But while I'm picking Victor's brains over lunch, I've got a suggestion for you.'

'Oh? What's that?'

Her smile was slightly guilty, as if she knew she was about to ask him something she knew she shouldn't.

'All right, Stella,' he said heavily, 'what the hell do you want me to do this time?'

37

Victor Drago was sitting on the small balcony outside his shoebox apartment in St Julian's. His foot tapped nervously on the terracotta tiles and in his right hand he turned his mobile phone over and over, willing it to ring. His other hand gripped his third cigarette in thirty minutes. Modern residential blocks similar to his own dominated his view, but between the buildings he could see tourists frolicking in the water below. Jet skis barrelled across the laconic swell while, closer to the shore, kayakers and swimmers made the most of the late-afternoon sun.

At last the phone rang. With a quick glance at the screen he put it to his ear. 'Thanks for calling back,' he said.

'Are you all right, Victor? Your message sounded a bit stressed.'

'I'm fine. I just needed your advice because I think this is the critical week, isn't it?'

'Yes it is. Why? What's happened?'

'A woman contacted me today. She said she was doing some research on her family and wanted to get a briefing on the knights. I was bored, so I agreed to meet with her, but when I did she started asking a lot of questions about the Aretino family. She claims to be distantly related.'

'Was her name Stella?'

Drago breathed a sigh of relief. 'So you do know her. But she's no Aretino, is she?'

'No,' said the voice in his ear, 'she's no Aretino. She's very clever, though. How did they track you down so quickly?'

'They?'

'You didn't see a man with her? She has a partner by the name of Jack Rogers.'

'She didn't mention him.'

'Well, she might be there on her own. She's probably happy to be out of Italy for a while.'

'Why?'

'It's a long story. Let's just say she attracted some unwanted press attention over the weekend.'

Drago stubbed out his cigarette in a flowerpot already crowded with butts. 'What do you want me to do with her?'

'What did you tell her?'

'Nothing. I evaded her questions and pretended I had to leave early. But I'm meeting her for lunch tomorrow.'

'Excellent job, Victor. That's exactly what I need you to do. String her along. Tease her with bits of the story, if you must, but don't let her get too close. I want you to keep her in Malta for a few days, all right?'

'She strikes me as someone who won't be put off easily.'

'No, you're right, you'll have to keep your wits about you. But you can handle her, I'm sure. Have some fun with it. In another few days it won't matter, but timing is everything and at the moment I need you to play for time. Can you do that for me?'

'Yes, of course.'

'Good man.'

Drago stood up and looked out at the view. 'What about the prince?'

There was a thoughtful pause before the voice on the phone said, 'He doesn't need to know. It wouldn't help our cause if something happened to Stella and Jack.'

'Why would anything happen to them? Drago asked.

'Things are bound to get a little tense in the last week,' the voice said reasonably. 'I don't want anyone doing anything rash.'

'Anything rash? What do you mean by —'

'You've got a big payday coming up, Victor. Concentrate on that. Leave the rest to me.'

Drago pictured a different water view in his mind, on the other side of the world. 'I'm thinking of buying a place overlooking Sydney Harbour,' he said. 'I can't wait to get back home.'

'It won't be long now. Keep in touch.'

The connection died and Drago was left with his Australian day-dream. Malta had been fine but it was time to settle down with his new nest egg. He turned his mind to the next day. Lunch and a little play-acting with a beautiful girl from the home country would be a massive improvement on a standard day. And if she wants a bit of history, he said to himself, I can certainly provide.

Feeling happier, he lit another cigarette and went inside the apartment to get a beer from the fridge. On his way back to the balcony, his phone rang again and he smiled when he saw who was calling. He admired this guy, and he usually had the best grass on the island.

'G'day, Kurt,' he said, 'how are you?'

'I'm okay. You?'

'Great, thanks. Are you back in Malta?'

'I will be soon. Later tonight, I hope.'

'You're not sure?'

'I'm taking a roundabout route,' Bauer said.

Drago didn't push it. He knew Kurt had a few shady dealings. 'Staying on the yacht as usual?'

'Yes.'

'You want to catch up for a drink tomorrow?'

'Yes I do.'

'Anytime but lunchtime,' Drago said, cheerily. 'I have a date with a beautiful girl.'

'Is that so?' Bauer said. 'Tell me more.'

38

Stella was waiting under the hotel portico when Victor Drago pulled in to the semicircular drive. She'd pictured him driving something worn but chic and had to look twice to recognise him behind the wheel of a late-model, open-topped Mercedes. His face was a picture of masculine pride as he hopped out to open the passenger door for her.

'Nice car,' she said, knowing a compliment would be expected.
'Thanks.'

'You must be a hit with the ladies, cruising around in this thing.'
He looked smug as he walked around the car. 'I do okay.'

When he was back behind the wheel, she said, 'You're in great shape too, Victor. What do you do for exercise – swimming, I suppose?'

'Yeah, and martial arts.'

'Me, too,' she said. 'I love kickboxing.'

He slipped the convertible into gear. 'I'm more into jiujitsu.'

'Woah,' she said, hoping it sounded sincere, 'that's not just exercise, that's real fighting. Well, it's certainly working for you.'

A smile formed on his face as he accelerated the car into traffic.

Only then did Stella register that she was sitting on the right in a country that drove on the left. It felt odd to be facing the oncoming traffic without a steering wheel in front of her.

'I'm going to take you to the old capital,' Drago said, talking over the engine and the wind. 'Mdina is a walled city on high ground in the centre of the island. Some of the buildings there date back to Norman times.'

'Sounds great,' Stella said, as she searched her bag for a band to tie back her hair. 'I've got plenty of time.'

Jack was conscious of his pounding heart as he hovered around the public rooms in the library. He felt conspicuous without books or other study aids. There was a portrait of a former British governor in a corridor outside the main reading room and he spent a long time pretending to absorb every detail in the painting. It allowed him to occasionally glance down the hallway to the reception area at the end.

The young dark-haired woman sitting at the desk was tapping away at a keyboard and rarely looked up, but Jack had been hoping she wouldn't be there at all. The reception had been unmanned when Stella was here yesterday. As one o'clock approached he decided this would be his last chance. If she didn't take her lunch break on the hour, it was going to be too late. He moved to an adjacent room and kept an eye on his watch, gently bending his left arm. Yesterday's swim had irritated his flesh wound and it was aching again. At 1.03 he strolled back towards the corridor and almost knocked over the receptionist hurrying in the other direction, handbag under one arm.

She smiled apologetically and said, 'The library closes in fifteen minutes, sir.'

'It does?'

'Yes, it shuts early in the summer.'

'Lucky you,' Jack said.

'Not me,' she said, 'I'll be back in an hour.'

'Pity. Enjoy your break, then.'

She nodded and walked away towards the front exit. Jack waited for her to disappear then turned to head straight for her workstation. On the counter she'd placed a dog-eared cardboard sign that read, in both Maltese and English: *If reception is unattended please push the buzzer*. Behind her desk was a heavy wooden door. According to Stella, it shouldn't be locked – security for the library's back offices was token at best. With his heart in his mouth, he took hold of the doorhandle and turned. Pushing the door open, he stepped inside.

Victor Drago parked the Mercedes a good distance from the tourist coaches in the car park and led Stella into the fortified township of Mdina, taking her first to the ancient walls overlooking the rocky landscape sloping down towards the distant sea. In the narrow streets, he pointed out broad arches typical of Norman architecture and gave her an unsolicited summary of the waves of occupiers who had imposed themselves on the long-suffering Maltese people since the beginning of history.

His next stop on the tour was the cathedral. 'It's named for St Paul,' he said, 'who was shipwrecked off Malta two thousand years ago. They reckon this is where he met the Roman governor at the time.'

The interior was similar to the amazing cathedral in Valletta that Stella had visited with Jack during the morning. The walls and ceilings were a baroque feast but the floor was most compelling, because much of it was a mosaic of graves. Knights of St John were buried shoulder to shoulder under intricately designed, dramatically colourful marble grave markers. Heraldic motifs and gruesome, skeletal images of death surrounded Latin inscriptions spelling out lengthy aristocratic names.

Victor led the way towards a corner of the church where a tour group was receiving a lecture in Hungarian. As they moved away, Stella saw that they'd been looking at one of the chapels around the sides of the cathedral.

'This is the chapel of the Langue of Italy,' Drago said. 'The knights organised themselves by region and language.'

'It's stunning,' she said with sincerity. 'The craftsmanship is truly remarkable.'

Drago pointed to the floor by the chapel's entrance. 'Look here.'

Stella stepped forward and examined the inlaid floor. He was pointing at one of the ubiquitous graves but as her eyes explored it, she quickly saw what made it unique. 'Ludovico Aretino,' she read aloud, 'wow!'

'Died in 1626,' Drago said, obviously pleased with himself. 'Perhaps he was your great-uncle fifteen generations back. But then again,' he added with a new edge to his voice, 'for that to be the case, you'd have to be related to the Aretinos – and we both know that's not true, don't we?'

Jack could hear Stella's voice in his head. 'Along the corridor to the left until you see a stairwell on the right. Up the stairs one level, then turn left and go to the end of the hall before turning left again to start counting offices. The fourth door on the right is the one you want.'

Thank God for old buildings, Jack thought, as he walked quickly along the corridor. This would never be possible in an open-plan office. He had one close encounter along the route, when he had to hold back while a man in a pale-blue shirt walked ahead of him before turning into a doorway. When he slipped inside Victor Drago's office, he realised he'd been holding his breath the whole way.

The room was just as Stella had described, though smaller than he'd imagined. Less than a metre separated the two desks and much of the remaining floor space was dominated by steel filing cabinets and bookshelves. Immediately he noticed that the two sides of the office dealt with completely different aspects of Maltese history. All the books and papers piled on and around Drago's desk related to the knights, but his colleague's focus was more contemporary. In the centre of the second desk was an open report on the government's current application to join the European Union. And next to the report Jack saw something unexpected and alarming – a steaming mug of tea.

Drago found a café away from the tourists, with an outside table shaded by an umbrella.

'I'm sorry for lying to you,' Stella said as they sat down. 'I'm a consultant, trying to understand everything I can about Count Aretino and his business.'

'It's not me you should apologise to,' he said in a patronising tone. 'They seemed quite taken aback that you would claim to be a member of their family.'

Stella held his gaze. 'I'm confident the Count would understand I was acting in his best interests.'

Drago looked at her for a long time then slapped himself on the thigh as if he'd had a revelation. 'You did it on purpose, didn't you? You knew if I checked out your story . . .'

'It would prove you're a bigger liar than me,' she said.

'Now, hang on —'

'You said you hardly knew the family. Every time I mentioned the Aretinos you fed me bullshit. I don't think you have a right to be pissed off that I lied to you when it's all you've been doing since the moment we met.'

Drago's arrogance melted away. 'That's a bit unfair. My dealings with the Aretinos are none of your business.'

'Like the fact that you're on their payroll?'

'I beg your pardon?'

'You don't work for the Order, do you?'

'I don't see how that —'

'And you don't work for the library. They're more concerned about the records of the Maltese people, not the knights.'

'The two are closely related.'

'The Order has its own archives, I'm sure,' Stella said.

'Yes, but the Camilleri papers are held by the National Library.'

'The what?'

Drago looked surprised she didn't know. 'During the Second World War, Malta earned the dubious distinction of being the most bombed place on the planet. Professor Camilleri was chief archivist in those days. He was an old man so he kept working during the bombing raids, while all his younger colleagues went to serve in the defence of the island.'

Stella nodded, encouraging him to get to the point.

'My father was only a teenager then and he earned pocket money by helping out the professor, who had trouble getting around, particularly with all the rubble in the streets. Anyway, long story short, during a raid on Vittoriosa – which is the old town on the other side of Grand Harbour from Valletta – a bomb opened up a hole in the floor of a building that was once the hostel for the German knights of Malta.'

'Ironic,' Stella said.

'Hitler didn't care much for history,' Drago said, 'and he really hated Malta.'

'So, what did they find in the hole?'

'It was like a secret room or prison cell. The only way in was from above.'

'No doors?'

'No doors but there was a little window, I think. I know it was dark when they first went down there, because my dad was given the job of carrying a torch for the professor. They found some empty chests and a couple of skeletons.'

'People died in there?'

'Yeah, a man and a woman. You can look it up on the web, if you don't believe me.'

Stella cocked her head to one side. 'Why wouldn't I believe you?'

'No, I didn't mean . . . I mean, if you wanted to check the facts.'

'Why would I need to do that? Is this somehow relevant to my analysis of the Aretino Group?'

'No,' he said, uncertainly, 'but you were asking about the Camilleri papers.'

'And they were found in this hidden room?'

'That's right. They found one chest that wasn't empty. It was stuffed with papers relating to the knights, and Professor Camilleri was thrilled with the find. Unfortunately, just a few weeks later he was killed in another raid. The cache of documents was named in his honour and locked away for safekeeping with the National Archives. If it weren't for me, they'd still be gathering dust in the vaults.'

'Why you?'

'My dad was sixteen at the end of the war. He never knew what happened to the papers and two years later he emigrated to Australia. But as he got older, he kept talking about that day with the professor. After Mum died, he finally decided to come back and find out what had happened to the discovery. The Order claimed to know nothing about it. After a lot of digging around he located the papers in the National Library's collection, completely ignored. They don't have the language skills, see?'

'So he encouraged you to get involved.'

Drago waited while they were served two salads and mineral

water. 'I was a public servant in Melbourne by then, thinking my history degree had been wasted. My dad had decided to stay in Malta with his sister and he offered to fly me over. Because of his connection to the papers, he'd managed to get permission for me to catalogue them.'

'When was that?'

'Nearly five years ago.'

Stella took a mouthful and did some thinking while she chewed. 'Let me guess,' she said, 'the library had no funding to work with the Camilleri papers but they found you some office space.'

'That's right.'

'It must have been tough.'

'It was.'

'Until you found a sponsor.'

He said nothing, but there was tension in his eyes.

Stella tapped her plate with a fork. 'That Merc you drive is a continental import,' she said. 'It looks like a hand-me-down from the stable of some wealthy family. And I don't imagine you're still living with your rellies after five years. Where are you now, some fancy apartment in Sliema?'

'St Julian's,' Drago said, 'but it's not so fancy.'

'Ah, the new hotspot – I've read the brochures. I bet you even have a view of the sea.'

Drago tilted his head slightly. 'I'm not ashamed that my work has attracted a generous grant. It's not unusual for academics to rely on the support of patrons.'

'So you convinced the Count that cataloguing the Camilleri papers was important enough to underwrite a fancy lifestyle?'

'It's well beyond cataloguing now,' he said, haughtily. 'I'm making solid progress with the translation and interpretation of the collection.'

'With what objective?'

He smiled. 'Enlightenment, knowledge, elucidation, take your pick.'

'Nothing more tangible?'

'Like what?'

'I don't know. It just seems like quite an investment to make with no particular outcome in mind.'

'The study of history is often like that.'

'I suppose,' she said, but she sensed he was holding something back. 'By the way, have you ever heard of someone called Prinz Gerhard von Hirschberg?'

His nervous twitch was impossible to miss.

Jack pulled the keyboard shelf out from under the chipped laminate desk. When he moved the mouse, the blank screen of the monitor flickered and came to life. It was just as Stella had said: security precautions clearly weren't a high priority.

It didn't take long to find the folder named for the Aretino family. He squatted next to the hard drive on the floor under Drago's desk and inserted a flash memory stick. It seemed to take ages for the computer to recognise it, and when he instructed Windows to copy the entire Aretino folder, the dialogue box said it was going to take two minutes. His eyes shot to the door and then to the steaming mug on the adjacent desk. 'Come on, come on,' he muttered to the machine. 'How the hell do they get anything done with such crappy equipment?'

He straightened up, feeling tense as he stared at the screen. Microsoft's interpretation of a second seemed much longer than his. He followed the countdown in his head, somehow convinced that willing the next number to appear would speed things up. Suddenly, the door to the office opened and he recoiled with surprise. A stout middle-aged woman came in, her head down as she read from an open journal in her hands.

She looked up and stopped dead. She brusquely asked something in Maltese, which was almost certainly, 'Who the hell are you?' When she registered his blank, startled look, she switched to English. 'Who are you?'

'Isn't this Dr Spiteri's office?' he said, improvising.

The woman's forehead wrinkled in a suspicious frown. 'No, it is not. Which Dr Spiteri were you looking for?'

'There's more than one?' His eyes darted to Drago's monitor. Ten seconds to go.

'Why aren't you wearing a visitor's badge? Nobody should be back here without an escort.'

'Um,' he said, feeling like a kid caught shoplifting, 'I was working with Dr Spiteri in the library and he told me to come back to his office when it closed. There was nobody at the desk, so I —'

'He?' she said, accusingly. 'Both our Dr Spiteris are women. I'm going to have to call security.'

She stepped towards the phone. Jack ducked under Drago's desk and pulled the flash drive from the computer. Annoyingly, a distinctive tone sounded.

'What are you doing down there?' the woman said. 'What have you got in your hand?'

He closed his fist over the device and pushed past her to reach for the doorhandle.

'Stop right there!' she screamed, but he was already running down the corridor.

Drago's plate looked untouched and Stella's was almost empty – which was telling, given that she was doing most of the talking. He had the look of a suspect facing interrogation, labouring to keep his face calm despite the relentless probing.

'So a Von Hirschberg was also a signatory to the Pact of 1798?' she said.

'That's a matter of public record,' Drago said stiffly.

'Then why are you so sensitive about it?'

'I don't know what you mean.'

'And this Prinz Gerhard is a descendant of the guy who signed the pact?'

'I wouldn't know,' he said, but his response wasn't convincing in the slightest.

She leaned in for emphasis. 'You know him, don't you? Have you been on his boat? Sucked back some of his champagne?'

He said nothing, but couldn't meet her eyes.

'Victor,' she said, with a deliberate and serious tone, 'people have died. I believe this prince is responsible for the death of half the Aretino family.'

'No!' he said, sounding exasperated. 'Bloody hell, Stella, don't be ridiculous. That was terrorists. It had nothing to do with . . .'

'With what?'

'Nothing,' he said. 'I've already said too much.'

Jack was lying face up on the bed when Stella returned to the hotel room. He was stripped to his jocks, his hands behind his head on the pillow, cooling off under the air-conditioning vent. As she came in the door he got up quickly and grabbed a shirt.

'Did you manage to do it?' she asked, keeping her eyes on his face. When he turned around, his expression was pained. 'What's wrong?' she said, suddenly concerned. 'You didn't get caught in the act?'

He nodded, grim-faced. 'I was sprung by the woman who shares his office. Her conference must've finished.'

She sat down heavily on the bed. 'Shit! What happened? Did you talk your way out of it?'

'No,' he said, shaking his head, 'but I was able to get out of there before she could call security. She knows I stole something from Drago's computer. It won't be hard to work out what it was, and he'll obviously make the connection to you. I've already rung the airline; there's a flight to Milan at six-thirty. We need to get out of here before the police come knocking on the door.'

'So,' she said excitedly, 'you got the files?'

'Yes,' he said, 'I got the bloody file, not that it will do us any good.'

'Why not?'

He gestured angrily at the laptop on the desk. 'The fucking thing is password protected.'

39

Kurt Bauer stood on the deck of *Twice a Knight*, which his boys had kept spotless as promised. From his pocket he extracted one of his three mobile phones and pressed a speed dial button.

'I thought we were keeping contact to a minimum,' Prinz Gerhard said as soon as the call connected.

'Our Australian friends are in Malta,' Bauer replied.

'What? How can that be? I thought you were listening in.'

'They were playing me,' Bauer said.

There was a pause. 'Who *are* these people?'

'I'm starting to wonder the same thing. That Europol pig must have twigged, which probably means they've identified me too.'

'I can't afford to lose you,' the prince said nervously, 'not this week.'

'Don't worry about me. Worry about the Australians.'

'What do you suggest? You need to stay in Rome.'

'I'm already in Malta.'

'No! Why didn't you call me?'

'There was no time. They're looking for your boat, trying to find out who owns it. And they have a picture, presumably from Ganet's video.'

The prince's breathing was clearly audible. 'But you said they didn't have a copy. Christ, if they find out I own the boat . . .'

'It gets worse,' Bauer said. 'They've gone to work on the historian, too.'

'Shit! Where are they getting their information?'

'No idea, but clearly they know too much.' His tone dripped with meaning.

The Prince made a noncommittal noise. 'I'd need to talk to my partner about that.'

'It doesn't matter what your mysterious partner says,' Bauer said angrily. 'He's not here, on the front line.'

'Of course it matters. For a start – as you keep reminding me – I don't have the funds for a further, uh, investment.'

'It's a question of looking past the fees to the big prize. This job will be on the house. This is my home turf, I can control things here.'

'He still won't like it. He won't be happy you've left Rome at all.'

'Don't tell him,' Bauer suggested. 'The time has come for us to protect our own best interests.'

The prince took a moment to let that thought sink in. 'Be careful with the historian. They're pretty close.'

Bauer grunted his disapproval. 'Another one who knows too much.'

'We'll need him next week, for the authentication process.'

'We have the document, don't we?'

'Yes, my partner has the original, but history man will be useful for verification.'

'But not vital.'

'Maybe not. But any more, uh, mess won't be helpful.'

'Can't you move the stuff earlier?'

'No, it has to go with the rest of the gear. It's just a few more days.'

'Then I don't believe we have any choice. Do you agree?'

There was a long pause, filled only with the prince's strained breathing. 'You do what has to be done,' he said finally, 'and I'll pretend we never had this conversation.'

'Very good,' Bauer said, grim satisfaction turning up the edges of his mouth.

40

As they walked down Republic Street, Jack felt a creeping sense of paranoia. They were only a short distance from the National Library and he kept seeing Drago's colleague in the crowd, one minute dressed as a tourist and the next as a local lady with a scarf on her head. He stopped at a souvenir shop and purchased a baseball cap emblazoned with the Maltese flag. Pulling it down to shade eyes already masked by sunglasses, he stayed close to the other tourists as he caught up with Stella.

'Relax,' she said. 'You said you wanted to get out of the hotel.'

Their bags were packed and ready to go, but waiting in that room for a knock on the door was unbearable. Besides, they couldn't get the dial-up connection to work. 'There,' Jack said, pointing up to a sign advertising an internet café down the street to their left. 'I saw it earlier.'

They went down the hill two blocks then turned onto Old Bakery Street, which was comparatively quiet. Entering the café, Jack felt his tension ease but he checked the compact space for middle-aged women before buying some online time at the desk.

'The link between the Aretinos and this Von Hirschberg seems to be the Pact of 1798,' Stella said, as he sat down next to her. She was already typing in her search parameters.

'I thought we decided it was all about drug smuggling.'

She shook her head. 'We're still a long way from sorting it out. Maybe the pact brought the prince and the Count together, then the prince used the relationship to get access to the F1 team somehow. Here we go.'

A scanned image of the two pages they'd seen behind glass in Milan was on the screen. 'It's not easy to make out,' Jack said.

Stella was reading the commentary under the image. 'Just the usual stuff,' she said. 'Napoleon waltzes into Malta in 1798 and tells the few hundred knights remaining on the island to piss off. For some reason, these eight decide to draw up a pact in the week after the invasion. The author of this website reckons it was a mutual assistance pact. All of Europe was in chaos and these guys apparently decided to look out for each other in the difficult times ahead.'

'And what does it say about the catalogue of treasures?'

Stella pointed to a shaded box on one side of the screen. 'Their theory is the knights sold the listed items or melted them down to underwrite their future security. They even claim great family fortunes like the Aretinos' were founded on this stolen treasure. It's not a very flattering theory for our aristocrats.'

She tried another site and got a different hypothesis altogether. 'This guy reckons it was a list of treasures stolen from the Order during the invasion. They hoped to bring Napoleon to account for the theft. The eight knights, according to him, were the most honest and influential from each langue. They were tasked with recovering the items if possible.'

'Neither theory fits well with the supposed poverty of the Order at the time, do they?'

'Not really.'

'And it's an accepted fact that the French cleaned the place out, isn't it?'

'Yep. Even the official history suggests a pile of booty was taken aboard Nappy's flagship, *L'Orient*, but a lot of it came from the local Maltese churches.'

'And *L'Orient* was then sunk at the Battle of the Nile soon after,' Jack said, 'when Nelson kicked their butts in Egypt. I read about that yesterday. But, as I recall, they've explored the wreck without finding any treasure.'

'Maybe we're missing the point,' she said. 'Maybe it's not about the treasure but the people. We know two of the eight knights have living descendants. What about the others? Could there be a link?'

The signatures on the scanned parchment were almost impossible to decipher, but they found a typed list on one site. Stella sent the page to print and then asked Jack to spell out the names.

'You should start with Gerhard von Hirschberg,' he said, 'though his ancestor's name was Fra Maximilian Wilhelm Otto Ritter von Hirschberg und Mindelheim. Christ, what a mouthful!'

'"Fra" is like Brother,' she said, as she carefully typed out a Google search. 'The Order still uses the title to refer to its members. And "Ritter" is German for knight.'

'Well, well, who's been boning up on their history?' Jack said, waiting for the results to load.

Stella scrolled down the screen. 'Hmm, nothing much. Various relatives get a mention in genealogy tables for the Euro aristocracy, but I don't see anything about Gerhard.'

'I didn't think you would. If he's a drug runner, he's bound to keep a low profile, isn't he?'

'How do you do that if you're a prince?'

He shrugged dismissively. 'Every second German blue blood has a fancy title like that. Want to try the next one?'

'I guess so.'

'Okay, here we go. Fra Sebastian Albert Octavius de Montresson.'

'Spell it for me,' Stella said. While waiting for the search results to load, she tapped the desktop with a fingernail. 'Ooh, this is more like it.'

'What?' Jack said, leaning closer.

'A recent posting. Wait, it's just loading – it's on the Order of Malta's own website.'

'Another living descendant of the original eight,' Jack said. 'I wonder if he knows about the pact.'

'Not living,' Stella said.

'What?'

Her tone was grim. 'It's an obituary. Fra Patrice Albert de Montresson. Forty-four years old. Knight of the Order and hospital administrator. He died last week. He's survived by two sisters.'

Jack felt his skin prickle. 'How did he die?'

'An unfortunate accident at his family's apartment in Paris, it says.'

'When?'

'Thursday evening.'

'The day after our run-in with Bauer in Nice.'

Stella met Jack's eyes and saw what he was thinking. She shook her head. 'Not everything is connected. You said so yourself.'

'Yeah, right.' He looked to the list in his hand. 'Try another one.'

The next two names produced no hits other than the usual genealogical links. But when she typed the surname *Cristobal* a number of articles surfaced, including recent newspaper stories, about one Jose Alfonse Ferdinand Cristobal.

'One more dead knight,' Stella said bleakly. 'The only article in English I can find is another obituary on the Order's website. Apparently he was descended from a long and noble line and wrote books promoting Catholic values in Spanish politics.'

'How did he die?'

'Car accident, on a mountain road in Andorra where they were holidaying.'

'They?'

'His twelve-year-old son was killed too.'

'Oh hell. When?'

'Sunday.'

'While we were at the Grand Prix?' He fell back in his seat. 'You were right,' he added cheerlessly, 'these people do have something in common apart from being knights of the Order. They're dropping like flies. That's a lot of bad luck in a few months, if you include Federico Aretino and his family.'

'Too much,' she said, 'and things seem to be accelerating.'

'If only we knew why.'

After a contemplative silence, she said, 'My gut's telling me the answer is in that file you nicked. We need to crack the password.'

'Maybe Inspector Mancini could open it for us. Your A-list status in Italy might still be useful.'

She shook her head. 'I want to know what's in there before we involve the cops any further. We're still supposed to be working for the bank, remember.'

Jack made an ironic face. 'Discretion's a tricky thing when you're dealing with killers. By the way, Eduardo Moretti wasn't a descendant of the eight knights, was he? Is his assassination completely unconnected?'

Stella sighed, resting her head on her hands as she stared, unfocused, at the screen. 'Who the hell knows?'

'Drago, maybe? But I'm not breaking in to his office again.'

'He seemed keen to catch up with me again tomorrow,' she said, 'but there's no way he's going to cough up his password, even if he hasn't figured out we stole his files.'

Jack squared his shoulders. 'When we get back to Milan tonight, we'll try every possible password we can think of. We're smart; we'll work it out.'

She looked up and smiled at him, as if remembering why she'd suggested going into business together. 'You're right. If we just do what we do well, we *will* get to the answer.'

Jack smiled back. 'That's the spirit. Now, do you want to eat before —'

Her mobile phone rang shrilly. He gave her a questioning look and she read the display. 'I can't tell who it is.'

'Then don't —'

But she'd already accepted the call. 'Hello?'

'Stella? It's Victor Drago.'

She gave Jack a wide-eyed look. 'Oh, hi, Victor. Listen, thanks for lunch today. I really enjoyed the tour and the history lesson and I'm sorry if I got a little —'

'No need to apologise; you were just doing your job.'

'You're very understanding,' she said, hoping to deflect the underlying accusation. 'Did you get some useful work done this afternoon?'

'I didn't go back to the office,' he said, but his voice sounded strained. 'I've been thinking about everything you said. Are you really convinced there's a link between my work and the bomb on the Count's plane?'

'I think it's a real possibility,' she said, cautiously.

'I'd like to talk more about it,' he said, 'if you're willing to meet me tonight.'

'Tonight?' Her eyes were fixed on Jack's startled face. 'I'm not sure. You see, I need to get back to Milan. I'm not sure I can learn anything more here.'

'No,' Drago said, almost pleading. 'There's something I need to tell you – I'm certain you'll find it helpful, maybe even important.'

'Like what?' she said, more confidently.

'Not on the phone,' he said. 'We should meet face to face. The only problem is I can't do it 'til later tonight. It's my aunt's seventieth birthday and I've been given the job of ferrying people from the airport. Then we've got a family dinner. Would you be able to do it at ten-thirty? I thought we could meet at Hastings Gardens, just inside Valletta's walls – only five minutes' walk from your hotel and not far from my aunt's place.'

She held her hands out to Jack in a helpless gesture. 'I suppose I could do that.'

'Great,' Drago said, sounding happier. 'I'm not sure why, but I've been feeling guilty all afternoon. It feels like the right thing to do.'

'It is, Victor, believe me. And I promise to be discreet with anything you give me.'

'Okay, then. Gotta go. I'll see you tonight.'

'What the hell was that all about?' Jack demanded, when she'd hung up.

'I'm not sure,' she said, in a faraway voice, 'but we need to change our flights.'

He looked astonished. 'You're not planning to meet with him, are you? If we suspect a connection between him and Prinz von what's-his-name, then there's bound to be a link to Kurt Bauer.'

'But Bauer's in Milan,' she said with certainty, 'waiting for us to return home after a long day's work at the bank. And Victor said he didn't go back to the office.'

'That's a lie. Of course he went back to the bloody office. And as for Bauer, he could be anywhere. He must realise we didn't go back to the apartment last night, and I'm sure he has plenty of connections in Malta.'

'Jack, we can't ignore this opportunity.' She looked into his eyes. 'What if Victor's telling the truth? He sounded genuinely distressed about a possible connection to the plane bombing. If he can give us a motive for all these deaths, we'll be getting somewhere. Right now, we're absolutely nowhere.'

Jack's eyes were defiant. 'I still think it's dodgy.'

Stella's eyes sparkled in a way he hadn't seen in a while. 'Every situation can be controlled,' she said, 'you just have to be prepared.'

41

Stella walked close to Jack's side. His powerful six-foot frame would make an attacker think twice, and there was no denying the added sense of security his presence always gave her. 'It's dead, isn't it? The place is so crowded during the day.'

The square inside Valletta's formal gateway was dark and empty. A few lonely singles sat inside the Burger King, but Republic Street looked like an abandoned Errol Flynn movie set.

'There are no big hotels inside the walls,' Jack pointed out, 'so there isn't much nightlife.'

They took the first turn to the left and stopped in the shadows. Stella consulted her watch then glanced nervously up the gloomy street. 'Ten-thirty,' she said. 'I suppose I should get up there.'

Jack put his hand on her elbow. 'I don't think you should go.'

'I have to,' she said, but she squeezed his hand for courage. 'We've talked it through; it'll be okay. At the first sign of trouble, call the police. Have you got the number ready?'

'Yes, but can we trust them to be fast and honest?'

'We have to trust someone, Jack.'

Grudgingly he let her go. Six months ago he might have kissed her for luck — or just because he could.

With a last look back, she started climbing the steep slope of the street, looking for an entrance to the park that ran along the top of the fortifications. The streetlights were dim and widely spaced, casting bizarre shadows on the wall beside her. Then the wall ended and she could see trees and garden beds surrounded by knee-high hedges and metal railings. The fronds of tall palms rustled in the breeze as she tentatively followed a path between the gardens, leading her deeper into the darkness.

The rhythmic chirping of hidden insects seemed to synchronise with her racing heart. She saw a light in the distance and moved towards it. It was coming from a tall lamp next to a park bench that faced a gap in the sandstone battlements, a wide gunport for the knights' anti-siege cannons.

'Over here.' Victor Drago stepped into the light and waved her forward. 'Sorry for asking you to come out so late.'

She approached cautiously. 'That's okay,' she said, 'I appreciate you taking the time. How was your aunt's party?'

'Still going. I think it could be a big night.'

'I won't keep you then.'

'I have a few minutes.'

As she came into the weak puddle of light, he held out his hand and she shook it while trying to read his face. 'This place is a bit creepy at night,' he went on, 'but I wanted you to see the view.' He stepped toward the gunport. 'From here you can appreciate how formidable these defences were. The knights dug out this incredible moat to cut Valletta off from Floriana, where your hotel is. Look, you can see the swimming pool.'

'I'm not too good with heights,' she said, hanging back.

'We're nowhere near the edge,' Drago said. 'And the wall is four metres thick in any case.'

She inched forward and glanced at the view framed by the deep gunport. 'Very nice, Victor, but I'm not here for another tour.'

Drago's tone turned acerbic. 'In a hurry to get back to the file your partner stole from me, are you?'

She took two steps back, but her words weren't defensive. 'Look, Victor, I've already told you how serious I think this matter is. There's some link between your work and the attack on the Aretino family, I'm sure of it. Maybe the answer is in that file. And I really need to know what you were doing at the Villa Aretino last week, with that transporter from the F1 team.'

His mouth opened but it took a second for him to speak. 'My only interest in the villa is the murals in the —'

'Don't bother with the bullshit, Vic. You're such a lousy liar.'

'Yes, he is, isn't he?'

She spun around to face the new voice and saw a figure moving out of the shadows. It took a moment for her to recognise Kurt Bauer, who was dressed in a short dark coat that covered his distinctive tattoo. Without the beard he had a deceptively kind face and he wore round spectacles that deflected the steel in his eyes. She looked back at Victor. He didn't seem surprised.

'Nice look, Kurt,' she said boldly. 'Think it will fool the French authorities?'

'You know each other?' Drago said, his voice rising in surprise.

'We met briefly in Nice,' she said, 'just after he killed an innocent photographer and was about to murder an entire family. How's the wrist, Kurt?'

Bauer held her gaze, his hands thrust into the pockets of his jacket. Drago's response was a nervous laugh. 'Don't be silly,' he said, 'Kurt's no killer. He skippers a boat for . . . a mutual friend. He's just here to help me with this file business.'

'Was that your suggestion or his?'

'What's that go to do with —'

'You're a bloody fool, Victor.' She thrust an accusatory finger in Bauer's direction. 'This is the man who blew up the Aretino jet. I have the evidence on film.'

Drago shook his head disbelievingly.

'That's enough,' Bauer said. 'We're wasting time.'

Stella felt the first chill of fear at the menace in his voice, and wondered how long she needed to string things out before they would hear the sound of approaching sirens. 'So, you want me to erase the file from my computer?'

She was looking at Drago but Bauer replied, and his tone was eerily businesslike. 'We will require the whole computer, Ms Sartori. I want to know exactly what you did with the data while it's been in your possession.'

'I did nothing with it,' she said insistently. 'It's password protected. I don't even know what the file's about.'

'I will be the judge of that.'

'But there's all sorts of other confidential client material on that computer. Surely we could work something —'

Bauer withdrew his hands from his pockets. In his left was a handgun, already fitted with a silencer. Drago seemed more stunned by its appearance than Stella was. 'Kurt, there's no need for that,' he said. 'Stella will cooperate, won't you?'

'Of course,' she said, holding out her hands in a calming gesture. 'So, you want me to go to the hotel and get the flash drive and the computer, is that it?'

Bauer simply shook his head. 'You will wait here with us.'

'Oh? Then how —'

'Mr Rogers will get them for us.' He made a gesture with his free hand and nodded his head in the direction of the path behind him.

Stella peered into the gloom and detected three shapes moving towards her. Jack's arms were pinned back by two beefy men. As they brought him into the light, she could see a small cut on his cheek.

'Are you okay?' she said, her voice cracking. No help was coming.

'I'm just dandy, thanks,' he said, trying to sound flippant. 'Nice to see you again, Kurt. You look ten years younger. And you must be Victor Drago. Good to meet you.' He bowed his head in greeting until his minders roughly pulled him upright. 'Watch that arm. That's an injury your boss inflicted last week.'

Bauer stepped closer and made sure Jack could see the gun in his hand. 'If you do anything stupid or unexpected,' he said in a measured voice, 'I will kill Ms Sartori. Do you understand me, Mr Rogers?'

'Yes,' Jack said, exchanging a quick, fearful look with Stella, 'I understand.'

Stella racked her brain for a plan C. By now Jack was no doubt on his way back from the hotel with her computer. Bauer was annoyingly self-assured. There seemed only one possible point of weakness. 'What are you expecting to get out of this, Victor?' she demanded. 'How much money does it take to turn you into an accessory to murder?'

Drago was looking pale, but his sense of denial was still strong. 'You've got your wires crossed. That terrorist attack on the Aretino plane had nothing to do with my work.'

'You discovered something new, didn't you?' she said quickly, one eye on Bauer's gun hand. 'And you shared it with Prinz Gerhard. Something to do with the Pact of 1798. That's what's in your precious file.'

At last, his eyes met hers and she realised she'd hit the mark. 'Did you realise the male descendants of those knights have been dying off at an alarming rate lately, Victor? Montresson and Cristobal, do those names ring any bells? Both suddenly dead in the last week. I bet if you track Captain Kurt's movements at the time they died, you'll find a convenient overlap, just like his attempt to wipe out the Aretinos in one go.'

Drago was shaking his head, dazed. 'No,' he said, as if trying to convince himself, 'that can't possibly have anything to do with . . .'

'With what?'

Bauer took a menacing step in her direction. 'Be quiet, both of you. I won't ask you again.'

He tensed and looked down the path and Stella followed suit, but it was a while before she could make out Jack and his two minders approaching in the shadows. Jack walked over to stand by Stella and briefly touched her hand. One of the thugs was carrying a computer.

Bauer didn't take his eyes off them as he received a terse report in German, but he was nodding his head, satisfied. He barked something and the man holding the computer turned and quickly walked away. Stella groaned inwardly. She'd been hoping they'd just throw the computer into the moat.

'Who wants to poke through my private stuff,' she asked Bauer, 'you or your boss, the prince?'

He responded by waggling the pistol. 'Move back to the wall, please.'

Jack looked to his left and for the first time noticed the wide slot in the battlements. His head filled with a daytime image of the bastion. The drop to the moat had to be at least fifty metres.

'Wait a minute,' Drago said. 'We got what we came for, didn't we? The boss doesn't want them hurt.'

'You heard her,' Bauer said. 'She knows too much.'

Drago's naivety dissolved. 'Are you saying it's all true?'

'You'll be next, Victor,' Stella said. 'And whatever cut you think you're getting from the American deal, you won't live to spend it.'

That sealed it for Bauer. He raised the gun.

'No!' Drago lunged for Bauer's arm.

There was a soft crack and a puff of dirt flew up from the ground between Stella and the remaining thug. They both jumped but she recovered first, swinging her leg in a wide side kick that connected with the henchman's groin. He doubled over and Jack launched in with his knee, slamming it into the man's head with as much anger-fuelled force as he could muster. The man dropped to the ground, his hands clutching at a shattered, bloody nose.

Bauer and Drago were still wrestling. Drago had both hands around Bauer's pistol arm and was trying to topple his stronger opponent using what looked like a jiujitsu move. But he was having little effect. Bauer's feet were firmly planted, though the historian was hindering his aim.

'Run!' Drago screamed. 'Get the hell out of here!'

Jack grabbed Stella's hand and tugged. She resisted for a microsecond before allowing herself to be dragged away from the fight. She pulled her hand free and started running at full speed. 'That didn't go quite to plan,' she panted.

'No,' Jack said, slowing a fraction to keep pace with her, 'and it's not over yet. That goon has my hotel key.'

'Fuck! Should we tell the hotel staff? Maybe they'll —'

'There's not enough time. We need to get our stuff and get out of there. We can't waste a second on explanations.'

As they ran onto the bridge leading back to the bus depot, a piercing scream filled the air. They turned their heads to see a tumbling shape bouncing off the floodlit city walls, its shadow flitting down the dimpled sandstone surface as an anguished cry echoed around the moat. Then there was a dull, gut-churning thud and the scream was cut short. Victor Drago had hit rock bottom.

42

'Oh God, oh God, oh God!' Stella said as she slammed the door behind her. 'What the hell have we done?'

'No time for recriminations,' Jack said, leading her towards the suitcase on the bed. 'Just grab what you need. Come on, Stella! It won't take them long to regroup.'

He hurried to the bathroom and reached up to the rack next to the shower. Pushing his hand into the folds of a fluffy bath towel, he pulled out Stella's computer and took it back to the bedroom. 'Thank God neither of us is prepared to leave home without our computer.'

Stella was trying to jam her toilet bag and a change of underwear into a briefcase already packed with Aretino financial reports. 'These bloody things are so heavy, but we can't leave them behind.'

'Yeah, well,' he said, slipping the laptop into his own bag, 'we thought they might want the computer, but we didn't reckon on them getting it so easily.'

'We didn't reckon on a lot of things,' she said angrily. 'That's why we came away with nothing and Victor ended up dead.' She slid open the glass door to the eastern balcony, which looked down over the front entrance of the hotel. 'I'll keep watch,' she said, stepping outside.

Within a minute, the glass flew back with a bang. 'Fucking hell, Jack! They're here already. Bauer and the second guy are just going under the portico now. If they'd looked up they would've seen me.'

Jack's eyes flicked to the door with the security chain that suddenly looked decidedly flimsy. 'I'll call for hotel security,' he said.

'No, wait!' she said. 'I don't want to get anyone else killed. I have a better idea. Come here.'

Jack stepped out onto the balcony and looked left to where Stella was pointing. He saw only the two other balconies tacked to the end of the hotel wing. When he looked down, he registered a long drop to the bitumen driveway.

'What the hell are you suggesting, Stella?'

'It'd be better if Bauer got free access to our room. No chain, no security. He'll think we never came back here. After all, we wouldn't have, if we'd thought to move the important stuff first. It'll keep them guessing.'

'You don't think they'll look on the balcony?'

'The next balcony along is outside our bathroom but there's no door. The third one is outside the next room and look, the door's open. You can see the curtain flapping through the gap. They're not so far apart.'

'What if there's somebody in there?'

'No lights are on.'

'They could be in bed.'

'It's a chance we have to take.' She grabbed his hand. 'Jack, if this is going to work we have to do it now!'

He shook his head doubtfully but bolted into action, rapidly moving to the peephole in the front door. Their position at the end of the wing gave him a view down the full length of the hallway. He unclipped the security chain and let it fall. Then he had another glance through the peephole. 'Shit!' he said, 'they're coming.'

He grabbed his bag and slung the strap over his head so that it was secure against his chest. By the time he'd closed the curtains and the glass door behind him, Stella was already on the second balcony. 'Just don't look down,' she said. 'Pass me my bag.'

He leaned over to swing the weighty briefcase into her hands and immediately pulled himself up onto the metal railing, one hand on the wall of the building for balance. The metre gap to the next railing suddenly looked enormous.

'Put your bag on your chest,' Stella suggested. 'You want forward momentum.'

Clumsily, he pulled the strap of his bag until the weight of his case was over his stomach. Then, focusing all his attention on the rail of the next balcony, he took a wide step into midair. His front foot fell perfectly on the rail but his push-off had been too tentative. He found himself balanced between the two balconies, one trainer on each narrow rail. He looked up for Stella's help but she'd already dropped her bag and was leaping nimbly to the last balcony. When she looked back her eyes widened. 'What the fuck are you doing?'

'Get inside,' he hissed, his heart beating at an alarming rate.

There was movement in the room behind him. Adrenaline flooded his veins. Flexing his back leg, he thrust himself forward and brought his feet together on the same rounded rail. Throwing his arms out to tip his weight forward, he hopped down to the second balcony as gently as he could. Without pausing, he ran hard at the next rail. With one hand he scooped up Stella's bag, then leapt at the rail like a steeplechaser, pushing off with his left foot and sailing straight over the gap.

His landing was clumsy, hindered by the two bags, but Stella grabbed hold of his arm and pulled him inside before he fell over.

She slid the glass door shut and engaged the lock. As she pulled the curtains closed, he fell on the floor next to bed, breathing hard.

Suddenly the room lights came on and for a second they were frozen in place, like two mimes doing an impression of a prison escape. A heavy-set, bare-chested man was sitting up in the bed, his face a mixture of shock and anger.

'Sorry, mate, wrong room,' Jack said, already running to the door. He was fumbling with the chain when the big man started shouting in an unknown language while reaching for the phone by his bed.

Stella came up behind Jack. 'Bauer might come out any second,' she warned.

'We can't stay here. This bugger's going to wake up the whole wing.' He pulled open the door after a quick glance through the peephole. 'Come on.'

She followed him into the corridor but before they'd got very far he ducked to the right and pulled her by the wrist through a swinging door. They were in the housekeeping stores, surrounded by shelves filled with toilet paper, soap and towels. Jack pushed Stella behind him, flicked off the light and knelt by the door, easing it open just enough to peer out.

They could hear activity in the hallway. 'It's Bauer,' Jack whispered, trying to hear what was being said. He looked back into the shadowy storeroom for anything resembling a weapon, but the supplies were all so soft-looking. Then he heard running footsteps and glimpsed uniformed legs rushing past the crack in the door. 'Hotel staff,' he murmured. 'Our neighbour must have called downstairs.'

Someone speaking quiet German was approaching. Jack tensed, ready to fight for his life, but two dark shadows passed his slice of light, heading for the stairs. He held his breath until he was sure they were gone. 'Now we just have to worry about hotel security,' he muttered.

'And that's just getting out of the hotel,' Stella said despondently. 'Then we have to work out how to get off the island.'

'He's going to have the airport covered, isn't he?'

'We can't risk it, and I'm not sure who we should trust. Cabbies, cops, even the concierge.' She paused and he heard her take a deep breath. 'I just want to get off this bloody rock.'

His attention was still glued to the narrow slice of outside world and it took a few seconds for him to realise she was crying behind him, her shoulders silently convulsing with emotion. 'Jesus, Stella!' he said, standing up and turning away from the door. 'Don't blame yourself. Victor made his own choices. It's not your fault.'

He opened his arms as wide as the narrow storeroom would allow, but she baulked. Stepping forward, he folded her in a hug. He knew it was what she needed. She collapsed against him, a week's worth of anguish, stress and self-doubt washing over her like a tsunami. 'Everywhere I go,' she said between breathless sobs, 'people get killed. Victor had no idea what was going on around him, but he died saving our lives.'

'You can't blame yourself,' Jack said softly, holding her close. 'All week I've been racked with guilt for bringing Bauer down on Marcel and his family, but it wasn't me who pulled the trigger. The proper response is to make the bastards pay for what they've done.'

She took a few long, stuttering breaths. 'And how the hell are we going to do that? We have no evidence, no credible motive and no fucking idea. Would you like to explain it all to Mancini?'

'No,' he said, 'you're absolutely right. But we must be onto something, Stella, or they wouldn't be trying to kill us.'

43

When Jack was convinced the coast was clear, he led the way to the stairwell at the far end of the hall. They descended to the lowest level of the hotel and exited through the rear gardens, where they huddled in a quiet nook to kill some time. Coming back inside via a staircase on the other side of the building, they ducked out the front doors when the skeleton night crew was distracted. Sticking to the shadows, they stayed behind the wall where the driveway entered from the street. Jack scanned the piazza beyond.

Public transport had ceased for the day and the rows of empty buses in the giant roundabout offered a tempting route to approach Valletta surreptitiously. But they were also perfect cover for someone watching the hotel.

Eventually they crept along the street towards the buses, using the trees on the pavement to stay out of the moonlight. With racing hearts, they scurried into the gap between two rows of buses and moved slowly towards a point closer to the city gates. The open forecourt and wide bridge between them and Valletta looked frighteningly huge and featureless. They cringed at every sound coming from behind the buses, not knowing if they meant the worst.

Jack offered Stella his free hand, and she gripped it firmly as they peeked around the end of the last bus in the row and prepared to run.

'Wait,' Jack whispered, holding her back. 'Look at the walls.'

From their vantage point she couldn't see down into the dry moat but flickering lights were reflected on the sandstone blocks rising up to where Victor had fallen from.

'Police cars,' she said softly. 'They've found him.'

'They'll be here soon, too,' he said. 'We should wait.'

'I don't want to talk to the cops,' she said. 'Bauer will be expecting that and could easily be watching the police station. Remember Mancini's story about the guy in jail? If Bauer knows where we are, he'll find a way to kill us.'

'Yeah,' Jack said, 'but he certainly won't be hanging around here when the cops turn up. Trust me.'

Another long minute ticked by and sure enough, two police cars arrived from inland, flying up the hill with lights flashing but no sirens. One stopped on the bridge and two officers leapt out and went to look over the edge. The other kept driving through the gates and turned left towards Hastings Gardens. A surprising number of people emerged from the dark edges of the precinct, drawn to the commotion.

'Come on,' Jack said. 'Look like a tourist.'

Still holding hands, they stepped out from between the buses and trotted towards the bridge, like stickybeaks not wanting to miss a show. The two policemen were now waving people on and discouraging a group of drunken Englishmen from leaning over the railing. Jack slowed to a walk but continued to pull Stella forward, past the police car and towards the columns of the city gate. He didn't look back until they were through the gate and hurrying towards the shadows at the edge of the square. There was no obvious pursuer in sight, but his anxiety did not begin to ease until they were in a dark side street.

The internet café was supposed to close at two a.m. but the bored manager was trying to shut up shop thirty minutes early when Jack and Stella burst through his door. When they said they only needed a few minutes, he told them to go ahead. Meanwhile, Stella picked the computer furthest from the entrance and checked out their travel options.

'The airport's too small,' she said when Jack joined her, 'and too easy to watch. I think our best bet's going to be a boat.' She pointed at the screen. 'There's a ferry to Catania in Sicily at seven in the morning. We can fly back to Milan from there. It leaves from Grand Harbour, but on the other side from here.'

'Won't they watch the ferries too? It's the only logical alternative to flying and I can't imagine the ferry terminal is going to be any safer than the airport.'

'Do you have a better idea?'

'Nothing springs to mind.' He glanced to the front of the café. 'This guy's ready to close up. You want to try to find a hotel for the night?'

'No, Bauer's going to have his feelers out. We need to find a quiet place to wait out the next few hours. When the sun comes up and it gets busier, it will be safer to leave Valletta and get around to the ferry port.'

'Okay,' Jack said, 'I guess that's a plan.' He wasn't thrilled by the idea of spending the night like a vagrant but he could understand Stella's logic. And the night was warm, with floral scents carried on the Mediterranean breeze. There were certainly less pleasant places on earth to be stuck outdoors for the night.

The great star-shaped fort at the tip of the peninsula was eerily quiet, and the moon's reflection on the waters of the Mediterranean cast a ghostly hue over the medieval scene. Stella and Jack were still jittery, and every sudden noise made them jump and seek out the darker shadows as they followed the road in the direction of Grand Harbour. Eventually, as they were descending a long steep staircase leading down to the port, Stella stopped and said, 'This will do.'

The landing she'd chosen was hidden from the streets above and had a good view of the harbour below. In the corner formed by the smooth, sun-bleached stone, they deposited their bags and rearranged the contents so they could double as seats, albeit uncomfortable ones. Jack sat with his back in the right angle and Stella sat next to him.

She let her head flop against his shoulder. 'Sometimes I think the thing we're best at is getting into trouble,' she said.

'We do seem to have a knack for it.'

'We'll have to call the hotel, pay our bill and get them to send on the suitcase.'

'And the airline,' he said. 'We have flights to cancel.'

They contemplated the lights on the water for a minute and then Stella sighed. 'Victor's family deserves to know what happened to him. They're going to think he jumped or slipped.'

'Unless he's got a bullet in him.'

She shuddered. 'Either way, they should know the circumstances. When the time is right, we'll have to contact the authorities.'

After a contemplative silence, Jack said, 'So, you still think this is the best job the Stack Partnership's taken on so far?'

She laughed with soft irony. 'It hasn't quite worked out as we expected, has it? Is it too weird to say that part of me finds it all a bit . . .'

'Exciting?'

'Something like that. It's a terrible thing to say, when you consider the people who've been hurt or killed.'

'Maybe, but I know exactly what you mean. I guess there's nothing like a near-death experience to make you feel completely alive.'

'How do we build running for our lives into the business plan?'

Jack chuckled. 'We could add a tagline to our business cards, like: "Criminal conspiracies our speciality". Just be sure not to use one when our insurance broker comes to call.'

Stella smiled into the dark. She loved the way Jack always managed to raise her morale. It helped her believe there was a future worth looking forward to. And thinking about the future helped block out the present for a while.

After a few minutes she said, 'What did you end up doing with the Greene Street loft?'

It was the first time she'd mentioned the place since the disastrous viewing in April, and Jack took it as a positive sign. 'I leased it to a start-up public relations firm. Four twenty-somethings with big ambitions and a lousy business model. With the rent they're paying me, I give them six months, tops.'

'You think Stack could afford those rates?'

'I'm sure the landlord would gives us a good deal. Why?'

'Well, it's a beautiful place in a perfect location and we can't run a business like ours from our homes forever. If we have another year like this one, we're going to want to hire some help. You don't want to handle all the administration, do you?'

'Administration?' Jack asked. 'What's that?'

'Just as I thought.' She gave his thigh a gentle punch. 'The only thing I dislike about running our own business is the endless bloody paperwork. So, unless you want to do all the invoices or order the stationery or manage the filing or —'

He groaned. 'Okay, okay, I get the idea. That shit's more scary than escaping this tiny island.'

She returned to her musing. Jack told himself it was a good thing she was focusing on paperclips rather than dead historians. But he was all too aware that any grand ambition she had for the business would come to nothing if they didn't survive the next few days.

They said nothing for a long time, both lost in thought while their eyes drifted across the harbour to the tiny spots of light and colour on the far shore. A grey ship was moored in the heart of the narrow waterway, its deck lighting the brightest thing on the water.

Suddenly Stella sat upright. 'There's no way I can sleep. That mystery file is really bugging me. You want to have a crack at the password?'

Jack was already reaching for the computer. 'I guess it can't do any harm. Although we don't know anything about Victor to help us.'

'We know a little bit,' she said, digging for a pen and paper as he booted up the machine. 'No wife, kids or pets, and both parents are dead. Drove a Merc and lived in St Julian's; went to high school in East Brunswick and barracked for Collingwood in the AFL. And he was a historian, obsessed with the Order. We should be able to come up with a few ideas.'

Sure enough, they quickly produced a long list of possible passwords but as Jack methodically tried each one, only for each to be rejected, their optimism began to fade. After nearly an hour, Jack looked across at Stella's list and said, 'It could be a combination of any of these, or none of them. We haven't even thought about numbers. Birthdays, favourite holidays, important dates in history . . .'

'Do you remember the date on the Pact of 1798?' Stella asked. 'It was at the heart of his work and there was a print of it hanging over his desk.'

'July 8,' Jack said confidently. 'It was all over those websites we checked out this afternoon.' He tried the date in various formats but still the file refused to open.

'The pact was written in Latin,' she suggested, 'so the date was probably in Roman numerals.' She wrote it out in capitals on her pad and asked him to make sure she'd got it right.

'Looks okay to me,' he said, copying the string of letters into the dialogue box on the screen. Immediately, the box disappeared and he jerked with surprise and excitement. 'It's working! You did it!'

Tensely, they waited for the file to open. A folder appeared, containing two documents. The first was a scan of antique pages handwritten in Latin, and Jack screwed up his face. 'This isn't going to be much help.'

He closed the file and tried the second. It was immediately more promising, typed in English and bearing a tantalising title: *The Scribe's Testament*. Settling the computer on his knees, he turned it so they could both read the screen. The white glow of pixels seemed to form a protective bubble around them as they huddled closer in the shared hope that these few pages would somehow advance their search for understanding.

44

The following translation was prepared by Victor P. Drago, BA
(Hons), Senior Research Officer at the National Archives of Malta.
The original document was discovered among the Camilleri papers
by Victor Drago in October 2002. It is called *The Scribe's Testament*:

*The story of my life is not worth the price of this parchment and can
be summarised in a few lines. However, the story of my death is worthy
of God's good grace and forgiveness.*

*My name is Michel Moncoutier and I am the bastard son of the
Comte Guillaume de Montresson. His traditional lands lie deep in the
south of my beloved France, where the blood of martyrs to the terrible
revolution still soaks the earth. I was raised to take holy orders and
trained as a scribe at the Abbey of St Michel, for whom I am named.
The temptation of the flesh led to my dismissal from the abbey at the
age of twenty-four and I was taken by my father's brother, Fra Sebastian
de Montresson, to be his page and scribe.*

*As a noble knight of the Order of St John of Jerusalem, my lord trav-
elled extensively to the priories of the Order and the courts of Europe. It*

was my happy duty to play a small part in his important work. He is a great soldier, a great diplomat and a devout and pious man, and I wish him every blessing for the remainder of his life. I pray for the return of his family's fortune, taken without cause after the accursed revolution. In those terrible days we fled together across Europe, eventually coming to Malta in 1794. For a few short years we lived in relative peace and I found my beloved Annabella, a pure girl from a proud local family.

The story of my death begins on the night the shameful Grand Master von Hompesch gave Malta away to Napoleon without a fight, on the first day of July in 1798. He would not fire on fellow Christians, he said, but my lord named him coward. There followed many days of chaos on the island. An arrogant French army demanded food and the favours of local women. Those brave knights remaining were commanded to leave Malta within the week and it soon became clear Napoleon intended to strip both the nation and the Order of their riches.

My master was known to Napoleon's lieutenants and his life was in jeopardy from the moment of the surrender. But the great fortresses and halls of the knights afforded endless routes of escape and it proved simple enough to stay out of sight. After a few days of this shadowy exist- ence, my master asked if I would accompany him to a meeting with a select group of his brother knights. They had need of a scribe, he told me, but he added a dire warning – what I would hear that night was so secret that it may cost me my life. I knew at once that this was the mission for which God had prepared me.

My master and I dressed as ordinary soldiers before we ventured out to the streets of Valletta in defiance of the French curfew. It was a moonless night and the city was dark and quiet. The air was warmed by countless stars in the Lord's firmament. The French patrols were betrayed by their flickering torches but my master needed no illumina- tion to guide us safely through the streets and across the black waters of the Grand Harbour. Two loyal Maltese rowed us quietly to the docks of Vittoriosa and we crept quietly up the hill through silent laneways to a building I had not seen before.

My master led me through a side door to an interior as shadowy as the streets. Without speaking, we moved through several rooms to a large empty hall in the centre of the building. In the weak light of a few oil lamps I could discern a group of hooded knights, but their faces were indistinguishable, one from the other. My master greeted the men and they spoke in soft voices while I kept a discreet distance.

At last, my master bade me approach. The knights formed themselves in a circle around me and I kept my eyes downcast to cause no offence. Before his brethren, my master bade me swear an oath before God that I would give my life to protect the secrets of the Order. I gladly complied.

I was then conducted to one side of the chamber, where stood a great marble statue of Our Lord Jesus Christ healing a poor leper. Six of the cloaked knights gathered on one side of the statue and heaved in unison against its base. Slowly the great stone pediment moved along some hidden track, but no further than the length of a man's hand. This small movement revealed the edge of a flagstone in the floor about the size and shape of a matrimonial bed. Without hesitation, three of the knights stood together on the far end of the stone and the edge was raised up. My master and one of his brothers were ready to catch their fingers under the flagstone and pull it upright.

Once the stone was fully raised, my master called me forward. I confess I was filled with mortal terror when I looked down into the black void. I prayed for courage and for my soul as I followed my master down a ladder more than two times my height. When Fra Sebastian applied his flame to candles in the hidden chamber below, my foolish fear was replaced by curiosity, as this was my first glimpse of what was to become my tomb.

The room itself was unremarkable if one excluded the lack of a single doorway. It had facilities for sleep and for hygiene and for work – which is what the knights had in mind for me. The necessities of a scribe were *already installed, including parchment, quills, ink, blotters and candles. My master kindly bade me to sit at the table to make a record of his instructions. I prepared my equipment while he took his torch further into the chamber, and I observed a row of strong chests, each bearing a weighty lock. There were eight chests in all.*

Over the centuries, he told me, the Order had accumulated great wealth and suffered great losses. But from the time of the knights' exile from Rhodes in 1523 there had been a pact between the treasurers of each Langue to protect and preserve the Order's greatest treasures. Deliberately, these most precious of objects were allowed to pass from the written record and oral history of the knights. Each Langue was responsible for part of the collection but now the entirety was gathered together in this chamber and the eight knights were determined to keep it from the likes of Napoleon or Tsar Paul and thereby safeguard it for the Order's return to sovereign authority.

When my master opened one of the chests and held his torch close, my heart was fully stopped. Never in all my travels to the great estates and palaces of Europe have I seen treasure like this. The oldest pieces, my master told me, date from before the First Crusade. The most unique and mystical were once the property of the Knights Templar.

My task – and my master deemed it a noble and righteous one in the eyes of God – was to draw up the terms of the agreement between the knights and prepare a detailed inventory of their most prized possessions. One of their number was to be assigned the duty of securing the legacy until such time as the Order is again granted sovereignty over secure and defensible territories. My master and his brother knights feel sure that once the Holy Father is free of the influence of the militarist French, he will convince the Christian kingdoms to restore Malta to the knights or grant them new lands. In his wisdom, however, my master also knows it may take time, perhaps even generations, for God's will to be done.

The knight chosen as custodian was Fra Antonio Paolo d'Aretino.

He is regarded by his brothers as a most honourable man and his family has been joined with the Order since the earliest days. It will be the duty of Fra Antonio to fulfil the obligations of the pact and, if required, pass that burden on to his heirs. The terms I was commanded to write provide for the return of the artefacts to the Order as soon as it is restored to defensible sovereign territory. If two centuries pass without such a restoration, the eldest surviving male heir of each of the original signatories will be entitled to take a share of the treasure for the benefit of his own family or of the Order or of Mother Church. I pray to God that the knights are restored in the lifetime of my master and that these provisions are never relied upon. Surely even Napoleon cannot keep the Order under his heel for two hundred years.

It took me one day to pen two copies of the pact described by my master and a further two days to make lists of the treasure in each chest. While I worked, the chamber was closed from above and my only connection to the world of men was via two arrow slits in the outer wall. At the end of each day, I listened eagerly for the sound of the statue scraping on the floor overhead because my master would then appear to bring me food and wine and evaluate my progress.

When my work was complete, the knights transferred their exquisite and holy cache from the carved chests to plain coffins, nine in all, which they winched ingeniously to the hall above. I observed the last of them go with a large measure of sadness but then I saw a new chest being lowered to the hidden room. My master told me it contained maps and histories that would not survive the sea voyage he would soon undertake with Fra Antonio and the disguised treasure. I was handed the key and invited to indulge my thirst for knowledge while waiting for God to determine my fate – for he also told me the brothers had agreed in their wisdom that I could not be allowed to leave this place with the secret I possessed. I was soon resigned to this end, knowing in my heart I could not withstand the attention of Napoleon's torturers.

On the day my master was to depart Malta, he visited me one last time. He and Fra Antonio delivered a large barrel of salted fish and a barrel of wine. My master took my confession and blessed me, then he called out to the floor above and a vision appeared at the top of the ladder – my Annabella. My master told me he had explained my circumstances to her and she had demanded to share my tomb. With tears on my cheeks, I begged her to run home but she could not be stopped from climbing down to my arms.

There is little chance anyone will return to open the chamber, I told her. It is known only to the knights, who would soon flee to their homelands. We have food and water for near half a year, she said. Imagine what a time we will have together, away from the troubles of the world.

It was an honour beyond measure to be married by Fra Sebastian de Montresson, my master and my friend. It was his final favour to me, and most full and satisfactory compensation for any small service I have done for him. My wife was by my side as the stone lock was closed above our heads for the last time. At my request, the ladder was removed – to avoid a temptation that could lead only to madness. Annabella was brave and her presence fuelled my own courage. We will have a life together as full of love as many a longer journey. When the time comes, I pray God will forgive us the sin of choosing to leave this earthly prison in a manner of our own choosing. For surely the obligations I have fulfilled for the Order, culminating in the sacrifice of my own life and that of my young wife, are deserving of God's forgiveness and the grace of Our Lord Jesus Christ.

Pray it be so,
Michel Moncoutier
Vittoriosa, Malta
25 August 1798

45

Stella's wide green eyes glowed in the light of the screen. 'Oh my . . .'

'God,' Jack said.

'The most valuable treasures in the Order's possession – that's what was hidden in that secret room under the Hall of Heroes?'

'Nine coffins stuffed with centuries-old, individually catalogued artefacts. It would have to be worth millions.'

'Billions,' Stella countered. 'You remember what Alex said.'

'Alex also told you the hall had a secret. Does that mean he knew about the treasure?'

She shook her head. 'Maybe he knew there were coffins down there, but I refuse to believe he knew about the treasure.'

'Treasure that now might be sitting in a container disguised as Formula One equipment, about to be shipped to America.'

'That would explain why the container was so heavy. Victor Drago must have supervised the transfer at the villa last weekend.'

'Somebody on the team has to be in on it.'

Stella's tired brain was struggling to filter out a confusing array of implications. 'So, the German prince must have commissioned

Bauer to knock off the other descendants. Clearly, he doesn't want to share.'

'He's still going to have to share with the Aretinos. He didn't get all of them on the jet.'

'Christ,' she said, 'you're right. Which means the Count and maybe even Alex are definitely still in his sights. Jimmy, too, when you think about it.'

'Or . . .' Jack said, his tone suggestive.

'Or what?'

'Well, think about it. The treasure was under the Aretinos' villa. If Alex knew about the room, other members of the family must have known too. Surely the Count knew what was inside the coffins. And it's the Aretino team that's being used to smuggle the treasure out of Europe. Do you reckon all that could happen without an Aretino knowing about it?'

She gave him a quizzical look. 'You reckon Charles is behind all this? But he was supposed to be on the plane.'

'Maybe missing the flight was no lucky accident.'

'Jesus!' she said. 'Are you suggesting he killed his own brother and nephew and all those other people because he wanted it all for himself?'

'Because he wasn't the oldest,' Jack said, shaking his head. 'The title carries all the control, all the power and prestige. Until May, Federico was listed as one of the richest men in Europe, now it's Charles.'

'But he's already wealthy, like you said . . .'

'Nobody's rich enough to ignore a few extra billion. The pact gives a share of the treasure to the senior male heir in each family. With half that lot, he'd be one of the richest men in the world.'

Stella fell back against the wall and was instantly aware of the stiffness in her muscles and the pain in her butt. 'I suppose it would be infuriating, doing all the work to grow the business empire when, legally, it all belongs to your older brother. But infuriating enough to drive someone to murder?'

'Or . . .' Jack said.

'What now?'

'Maybe Charles was supposed to be on the plane, as he claims. That would put Alex back in the frame.'

'Alex?' she said, sitting up straight. 'Why not Jimmy? He's the oldest.'

'Because his father made Jimmy sign away his right to inherit.'

'Before the bomb?'

'No, after. But he's a priest. He didn't seem bothered with Alex getting the title.'

She wrapped her arms around her knees defensively. 'I can't believe it could be Alex,' she said, but she sounded less certain. 'Why would he ask me to help protect his father?'

'And I can't believe it could be Charles,' Jack said, 'let alone Jimmy.'

Stella hugged her legs tighter. 'We need to know more about this prince character.'

'Or . . .' Jack said.

'What?' she said, hoping for a more palatable option.

'Maybe Moretti was the prince's partner. Maybe he found out about the treasure through his ministerial role. Maybe he was being paid off to look the other way while the artefacts were being snuck out of Italy and he asked for more money, or threatened to expose it.'

'Maybe,' she said, fighting off a yawn. 'Moretti had nothing to do with the F1 team, though.'

'As far as we know. Then again, it could have been Count Federico all along and the prince thought he was being doublecrossed. Or Federico and Moretti together.'

Exhaustion was beginning to overwhelm Stella. 'We're just clutching at straws. We don't know for sure the treasure's actually in that container.'

Jack shut down the computer and they were once again wrapped in dark shadows. 'We need to be careful what we say next, and who we say it to. The Aretinos are very powerful, and when it comes to the crunch Giorgio Borboli won't take kindly to any unsubstantiated allegations against them. I'm not sure we can even share these theories with the cops without sounding like crackpots.'

'I agree,' she said. 'We're still on our own until we can get some hard evidence. And the faster we get it, the better.'

'And how are we going to do that?'

'No idea,' she said, looking up at the moon and struggling to keep her eyelids open. 'We need to get out of Malta. Let's worry about that first. Is that shoulder of yours available for a quick nap?'

'Of course.'

Almost as soon as she relaxed against him, she was asleep. Jack put his throbbing left arm around her to hold her more securely and smiled to himself when she shifted closer to him in her sleep. He could feel his own head wobbling uncertainly, desperate for some rest, but he had one last task. Slowly, so as not to disturb her, he pulled his mobile phone from his pocket, flicked it open and started punching the keys.

As the first hint of dawn began to dull the starlight overhead, Jack gently nudged Stella awake. Opening her eyes, she lifted her head to look at the harbour. It was still dark, but there was movement near the fish market. Running lights on an approaching trawler were reflecting off the black water. Near the entrance to the harbour, another fishing boat was approaching, its outline discernible against the sea.

'What time is it?' she said, stretching her arms.

'Quarter to six. If we're going to get to the ferry terminal and buy tickets, we'd better get moving.'

She stood up clumsily and looked out over the harbour. The big catamaran they hoped would take them to Sicily was just visible on the far side. 'If we go around the edge of the harbour, it's going to take ages and we'll be out in the open. I wonder if there's a taxi service across the water.'

Jack bent down to repack the bags. 'I'm sure there is, but they'll no doubt come in to a single jetty. Don't you think Bauer will have a bottleneck like that covered?'

'Probably,' she said despondently. 'Just like the approach roads, the ticket office, the gangplank and God knows how many other exposed spots.'

'We've already agreed it's not an ideal plan, but it's the best we've got.'

Stella swung her arms vigorously to get the blood moving. 'It was just the best idea we could think of at the time.' She looked down.

He followed her eyes to the fishing boats, which were arriving to unload their catch at the market. 'Captain Petroni?'

'You never know,' she said. 'He had an honest face. But if he doesn't show maybe we'll find another honest face. Don't you think it's a better option than the ferry?'

'Slower,' he said, 'but safer. We'd better get going, then. If we strike out with the fishermen, we'll have to hustle to catch the ferry.'

The floodlit wharf was bustling with activity by the time they'd completed their descent. Tubs of fish were being off-loaded and the air was thick with the smell of the sea, attracting a happy flock of shrieking gulls. The men worked with quiet efficiency, eager to finish the long shift. When Stella and Jack walked along the wharf they attracted far less attention than they had on Monday.

'Hello.'

They looked left to see the slim figure of Petroni's first mate striding towards them. 'Good morning, Joseph,' Stella said, smiling to cover her unease.

'Good morning,' he replied. 'You come see fish?'

'Where is your boat?' she asked.

He gestured down the dock.

'I want to talk to Captain Petroni.'

His eyes narrowed a fraction but he indicated that they should follow him. 'Beware,' he said loudly, as they passed the unloading activity. Stella assumed he meant 'be careful' but she couldn't help taking his words as an ominous warning.

The rust-stained hull of Petroni's trawler was tied up alongside the stone wharf. The captain was standing on the deck, smoking a cigarette and watching like a hawk as the last of his load was being weighed. When he saw Stella and Jack, he took on a puzzled expression for a moment but then returned his attention to the off-loading.

Stella boldly stepped up the gangplank. Petroni was surprised. 'Be careful, please!' he said urgently.

The first mate and Jack followed her across the steel ramp. Petroni registered the grim look on her face and grudgingly gave up on the fish count. 'What are you doing here?' he said, his eyes moving to her overstuffed bag. 'Are you out late or up early?'

'A bit of both,' Jack said.

'We need your help,' Stella added.

Petroni frowned. 'I can help you with fish.'

'We have to get out of Malta quietly,' she said, glancing nervously at the first mate, who was standing too close. 'We'd like to charter your boat. We have money.'

'To go where?' Petroni said, shaking his head doubtfully.

'Sicily. Preferably some place with a decent airport.'

The captain stroked a stubbled cheek with his fingers. 'You are in trouble?'

'Yes, but not with the police,' she said. 'We are not criminals.'

Petroni showed his gold-capped teeth, apparently amused by the suggestion, but then looked serious again. 'The boat you were looking for, it is the cause of your trouble?'

'It's closely connected, yes.'

'And this man you asked about . . .'

'Kurt Bauer,' Jack said.

Petroni nodded. 'Yes, I know him.'

'But you said —'

'By reputation, I know him,' Petroni said, his eyes flashing angrily. 'I do not share such information with strangers.' He switched to Maltese and looked at his first mate.

Joseph seemed reluctant to depart, but orders were orders. When he was gone, the captain turned back to Stella and said, 'You must be careful who you talk to in Malta.'

'You don't trust Joseph?'

Petroni shrugged his shoulders but didn't answer. 'In this old tub, Catania is eleven hours away. We could make Siracusa in nine, maybe, but then you got to drive to the airport. Anyway, we just came in from a night's fishing. I need to top her up.'

'We'll pay for the fuel,' Jack said quickly.

'And cover you for any loss of fishing time,' Stella added.

The furrow in Petroni's brow deepened, then he glanced at his watch. 'We'd better get moving.'

46

The Mediterranean was choppy, its azure waters tipped with foam stirred up by a warm southerly. Captain Petroni's red trawler pushed its way methodically through the waves with the wind at its back. The sun was climbing into the sky and Malta's stony cliffs would soon disappear over the horizon.

Petroni stood at the helm, his callused fingers nervously tapping the wheel as he mentally urged his old girl forward. Looking down to the forward deck, he could see some of his crew sleeping on the hard steel – heads resting on ropes or nets – completely oblivious to the rise and fall of the boat.

'Captain!'

The call came from the stern and Petroni turned from the wheel to look out the rear window. The man on the watch was pointing directly aft. Grabbing a pair of binoculars, the captain raised them in the direction of a worrying cloud of spray. A sleek white hull was slicing through the sea directly towards his trawler. He could make out heavily tinted windows on the sloping bridge.

Twice a Knight was similar in size to Petroni's boat – about twenty-five metres from bow to stern – but that was where the similarities ended. The luxury cruiser had more than four times the horsepower and was designed to suit the time-sensitive. It would be on top of them quickly. Petroni's eyes shot to the throttle, but it was already at maximum. He opened the cabinet behind the wheel and pulled out a shotgun, checking it was loaded before leaning it against the wall just inside the hatch.

Pushing the door open, he stood on the landing at the top of the ladder. Calling the watch, he ordered the man to wake up the rest of the crew and make sure everything was secure below decks.

Fifteen minutes later, the million-dollar yacht was risking its perfect paintwork as it reduced speed to keep pace with the trawler. As it pulled close alongside, Petroni signalled his surrender by cutting the trawler's throttle and the faster craft reversed its monster engines to come to a halt.

The open deck at the rear of *Twice a Knight* was occupied by three lean men, two casually cradling assault rifles and the other sporting a bandage across his nose. As Petroni watched from outside his meagre wheelhouse, they were joined by a nondescript man wearing round glasses.

Kurt Bauer leaned on the teak handrail of the cruiser. 'You have something I need, Captain Petroni,' he called out in Maltese. 'Are you going to give me any trouble?'

Petroni cracked a gold-plated smile. 'I'm a poor fisherman, sir, and you are a wealthy man with powerful weapons. If I have anything you truly need, you're welcome to it.'

Bauer smiled blandly. 'Mind if I take a look around?'

Petroni chewed his lip. 'Do as you must, but I don't want any guns on my boat.'

The German spoke to his men and they deployed by the rails. He then made a show of removing a pistol from the pocket of his black jacket and passing it to the man with the plaster on his nose. With catlike grace, he leapt assuredly from one vessel to the other. The trawler crew took a wary step backwards and their captain called out some reassuring words.

Looking up to the wheelhouse, Bauer said, 'You are a respected skipper in these waters, Captain Petroni. I don't want to make an enemy of you.'

'Believe me,' the captain said sincerely, 'I don't want that either.'

'Will you bring them to me or are you going to make me search?'

'I don't know what you're talking about.'

Bauer's mouth tightened. 'Are you telling me there's nobody cowering in your cabin?'

Petroni shook his head grimly. 'I'm saying I don't know anything about it. If you find somebody in there, I'd be very happy if you took them off my boat and we all forgot it ever happened.' He turned and walked back inside the wheelhouse.

'You're a wise man, Captain,' Bauer said, staring down the trawler crew.

Cautiously, he moved to the hatch and stepped through to the cabin, his senses alert. The compact space was neatly arranged but otherwise empty. He quickly assessed the three doors available to him – pantry, storeroom and head. He chose the storeroom, turning the doorhandle and pulling back sharply. The door flew open but there was no sudden flurry of movement. The room was dark but he could hear breathing.

'Come out now!' he ordered, but there was no response.

Inching forward, he flicked the light switch. As the fluorescent bulb flickered to life it illuminated the terrified face of the first mate, Joseph, who was sitting on the floor, bound and gagged.

Bauer thumped the wall with the soft part of his fist. '*Scheiss!*'

*

Two hours later, the high-speed ferry service from Valletta was coasting into the picturesque and ancient Sicilian port of Catania. On the deck, Jack and Stella – and a happy crowd of holiday-makers – were taking in the view.

'I can't believe it's not even eleven o'clock,' Jack said. 'Only four hours. For a while there I thought we'd be on that stinky little trawler all day.'

'We were lucky Captain Petroni had enough sway to get us on board from the water.'

'And was prepared to act as a decoy. He's a very decent bloke.'

'He was well compensated. We'll have to get some more cash when we disembark.'

'I have a feeling he would have done it anyway. He knew Joseph was likely to betray us and he's obviously a man who doesn't take kindly to disloyalty.'

'Or junkies. Joseph's fishing career is finished, and Bauer's nice little sideline in dealing heroin has probably just lost a steady customer.'

Ahead, the looming mass of Mt Etna rose up behind Catania like a colossal black pyramid. The breeze played with Stella's hair, still straight and glossy despite the rough night. As the catamaran closed in on the shore, Jack's phone beeped and he pulled it from the pocket of his jeans. Stella looked at the screen as he read.

'Vicky Cavendish?' she said, her voice rising imperceptibly.

'Yeah,' Jack said, 'I sent her a text last night. I figured if anyone could find out something about a mysterious German aristocrat, it would be her.'

Stella looked him in the eyes for a second but then nodded her approval. 'And?'

'She's emailed me something,' he said. 'We need to get online.'

47

'His full name is Prinz Gerhard Wilhelm Otto von Hirschberg und Mindelheim,' Jack said, reading from the screen, 'but his father's name was also Prinz Gerhard, so most people know him as Wilhelm or Willy.'

'Willy?' Stella felt a disturbing knot forming in her stomach.

'Usually just Willy Mindelheim, apparently. He's had a pretty underwhelming career as a businessman and was forced to sell off his family estates in Bavaria to avoid bankruptcy. Vicky reckons he got caught in an old-fashioned gambling scam by some Russian mafia types. Now they control his former company.'

'Don't tell me it was a logistics business,' she said, as if dreading the answer.

'Vicky describes it as warehousing and transport, so I guess you could —'

'Bloody hell! Is there a picture of him?'

Jack moved his cursor to open the attachments. As soon as the first image opened Stella rocked back in her chair. 'Willy,' she said, with a long sigh.

Jack looked puzzled. 'Yeah, I said that already. You know this guy?'

'It's Willy,' she said, gesturing open-handed at the computer. 'He's the Aretino team's logistics manager.'

'Holy shit! This is the bloke who gave you the tour of the transporter? I guess that explains how he's been able to use the team.'

He opened another image and saw Willy in a group shot. The six men in the photo were dressed identically, in the robes of the Order of St John. 'I bet this is the picture he showed Marcel. Look, there's both Charles and Federico Aretino.'

Stella was reading the caption under the picture. 'According to this, Willy Mindelheim is the Aretinos' second cousin.'

'They're cousins?' He switched back to Vicky's notes and kept reading. 'She confirms it, listen. Willy lost his business three years ago and when his cousins bought the F1 team, they offered him the position of logistics manager. They were doing him a favour.'

'Which he returned by blowing half of them out of the sky,' Stella said bitterly. 'What a bastard.'

An announcement in Italian echoed through the lounge. 'They're calling our flight,' she said.

Jack was still staring at the screen. 'This means he could be acting alone. You saw Charles Aretino at the Grand Prix. He didn't seem to know what was going on half the time. It wouldn't be hard to keep him in the dark.'

'But they're cousins.'

'Blood's not so thick when it means sharing a prize worth billions.'

She was shaking her head, as if willing her brain to produce a solution. 'This makes things harder, if anything. Even if the Aretinos are blameless, we can't go slurring their cousin without proof.'

'We have the film. We have the image of his boat.'

'No,' she said, with determination. 'We need a clear motive. We need to lay our eyes on that treasure and prove the scribe's story is real.'

He looked at her as if she were crazy. 'And how the hell do you think we're going to do that?'

'I haven't the slightest idea,' she said, standing up to gather their few belongings together.

Willy paced around his office, wringing his hands as he practised the words in his head. If only he had Kurt's guts . . . but it was a long time since he'd felt truly in control. He tried to recall the awesome surge of power he'd experienced when he killed the security guard, but it was such a fleeting moment.

Eventually he summoned the courage to pick up the phone. He dialled the number, hoping it wouldn't be answered, and shuddered when it rang only twice.

'This had better be an emergency,' the voice at the other end said softly.

'Hello, partner,' Willy said quietly. 'Not an emergency, as such, but I thought you should know . . .'

'What?'

'Um, I've just been talking to Kurt —'

'I don't want names. I've never wanted names. Don't start now.'

'I'm so sorry, I didn't mean to —'

'Get to the point, and do it quickly.'

Willy licked his lips, still pacing. 'The Australian couple who were looking into —'

'What about them?'

'They turned up in Malta.'

'I know. So what?'

'Uh, well, my guy found out they were trying to identify the owner of *Twice a Knight*.'

'I don't care.'

Willy put a hand on his forehead and found it slick with sweat. 'But they also made contact with, um, the historian.'

'I know that too.' The voice was increasingly impatient. 'What's your point?'

'You know that?' Willy said, shocked. 'Did you also know they stole a copy of *The Scribe's Testament*?'

There was a pause. 'No, I didn't know that. They're a tenacious pair, aren't they?'

'Very,' Willy said, feeling slightly happier. 'My guy decided to get it back.'

'He did what?' The tone was enough to make Willy quiver again. 'You fucking idiot. What did you think they were going to do with it?'

'I don't know. But as it turned out, they couldn't read it anyway. They didn't know the password.'

'Exactly,' the dour voice said. 'And even if they cracked it, what would it really mean to them? What could they do with it in the time remaining? I hope your man didn't do anything rash.'

'Um,' Willy said.

'Mother of Mary, what did he do?'

'There was a confrontation. The historian tried to interfere . . .'

'Interfere in what?'

'What had to be done. My guy was only trying to clean up the mess —'

'My God! You told me you had access to a real professional, someone with discipline and control.'

'He is,' Willy said, almost pleading. 'He was just trying to protect our collective interests.'

There was a deep, frustrated exhalation on the other end of the line. 'My instructions were clear. Have you forgotten how important the Rome operation is? Your man should be in position now.'

'He's assured me there will be no interruption to the schedule.'

'There'd better not be. And the Australians?'

'Well, they seem to have escaped.'

'Good for them. The historian?'

Willy coughed nervously. 'He wasn't so lucky.'

There was a sharp intake of breath. 'I don't believe it. Without him, this whole project would not exist. If you have a future at all, Willy, it is thanks to him.'

'It'll still work, won't it?' Willy asked nervously. 'We'll still be able to prove —'

'Of course it will still work. The proof is in that container. You just have to get your boy back on the program.'

'Consider it done.'

'Good. Then don't bother me again until it is.'

'How much?' Jack looked at the shop attendant with an incredulous expression.

The woman repeated the price and Jack weighed the telephoto lens in his hands, as if valuing it by the gram. Milan's fancy Malpensa airport had an impressive range of shops but it clearly wasn't the place to find bargains. He put the lens down next to the digital camera already on the counter and picked up the binoculars, the most powerful pair sold in the shop. 'How much for the lot?'

He found Stella in a nearby store, buying a rolling suitcase into which they transferred the Aretino reports, her computer and their few personal possessions. 'I'm going to pay a cabbie to take this stuff back to the apartment,' she said. 'The building super will take care of it.'

'Good idea,' Jack said, packing their new surveillance equipment into his now empty leather shoulder bag. 'I like your new jeans, by the way. And I say that purely from a professional point of view.'

She shook her head, but she was smiling. 'There are a few menswear shops around the corner if you want to get some new gear. I'll meet you at the Hertz counter.'

'You really want to rent another car?'

'We should get there while it's still light if we can. It would take us two hours to retrieve the other one and get back to Saronno, and I don't think we can do this with a taxi, do you?'

'No.'

'We're sixty kilometres from Milan. The factory in Saronno is about halfway. If we get moving, we can be there in forty-five minutes.'

Jack pulled the bag onto his shoulder. 'Then we'd better get moving.'

Stella used the steering wheel of the hire car as a rest for the heavy binoculars. Despite their best efforts, the sun had set by the time they reached Saronno and she could just make out the lettering on the long, low building: *Aretino Racing Team*. Gently tilting the view downwards, she saw one of the glossy articulated transporters parked on the wide concrete apron in front of the factory. Powerful spotlights illuminated four large square openings sealed with metal shutters along the front of the building.

'The workers are leaving,' she said.

Jack was using the camera lens as a telescope. He could see men and women in Aretino team shirts streaming out of glass doors at the far corner of the building. They were in groups of two or three, cheerfully chatting as they moved to the parking lot on the northern side of the compound. Others walked down the road in the direction of the train tracks, presumably to a nearby station.

'They're working late,' he said, 'which might mean they'll be shipping the gear soon.'

'I know it has to go to a DHL facility in Munich first. It'll arrive in Indianapolis by Tuesday, so it will have to be shifted before this weekend. This could be our last chance.'

'There,' Jack said, suddenly tense, 'that must be Willy, right? You said he's a big guy.'

Stella focused her binoculars on the tall, beefy guy talking to two team members in front of the glass entrance. He was lighting a cigarette as he waved a farewell to the others. 'That's him,' she said. 'It's hard to believe he's the mastermind behind all these deaths, isn't it?'

Jack pressed the shutter on the camera a couple of times. 'Shit! He's looking right at us.' He could see Willy walking in their direction, between the transports and the factory.

'Don't worry,' she said, 'he's in the light and we're in the dark. He won't be able to see us.' They were parked under one of only a few trees along a street of large industrial plots. The warehouse next to them was unlit and seemingly unoccupied. 'See? He's going back inside.'

Willy tossed his half-smoked butt and went back through the glass doors.

'What do we do now?'

'We can't go in there if he's still around,' she said. 'I guess we wait.'

'I really need to pee,' Stella said, some time later.

Jack was struggling to keep his eyes open. 'This isn't much fun. Maybe he's already gone home, but went out a different door.'

'You said you didn't see any other exits as we drove in.'

'I didn't, but I've been known to be wrong.'

'Perish the thought,' she said. 'Anyway, the glass doors are still slightly askew. The place hasn't been locked up yet.'

'Maybe it's still full of people.'

'What do they all do in there, anyway?' she asked. 'They call it a factory, but what does that mean?'

'They build cars,' he said, 'but not like a Ford plant. They get engines from an outside supplier but they design and manufacture the chassis, the electronics and everything else here. They have big autoclave ovens to bake carbon fibre into parts, like the monocoque and the wings. It's all done by hand, which is why it's so expensive. I'll tell you something interesting —'

'Heads up!' she said, sliding down in her seat with eyes fixed to the rear-view mirror. 'A car's coming.'

'And there's Willy again,' he said, ducking his head down to the level of the dashboard. The big man was standing in front of the glass doors, puffing smoke into the light cast by the spots. 'He's looking this way again.'

'He's waiting for the car.'

At that moment a black Mercedes swept past them from behind, its powerful headlights cutting through the gloom. When it stopped in front of the glass doors, the rear door opened without waiting for the chauffeur.

'It's Count Charles,' Stella said, her eyes glued to the binoculars. 'They're hugging and kissing cheeks.'

Jack pressed the button on his camera. The Count and Willy were standing in a bright pool of light, their faces and actions clear through the long lens. 'They seem pleased to see each other, don't they?'

'We shouldn't read too much into it,' she cautioned. 'It's his team, after all, and they are cousins.'

'But why would the Count come out here at nine-thirty on a Wednesday night?'

Stella sighed. 'He could have any number of legitimate reasons.'

'They're going inside.'

'Inspecting the treasure container or innocently planning the trip to America? That's the big question.'

'Well, we can't go in there now, can we?'

'No,' she said, shifting her backside in the seat, 'we'll have to wait some more.'

Jack let his head fall back on the headrest. 'While we're waiting,' he said in tired voice, 'maybe you can explain how you think we're going to break into the place.'

Knights in shiny, spiky armour filled every inch of the walls, standing shoulder to shoulder. Were they covering the doors? Or were there no doors at all? He looked up. There was a coffin-shaped hole in the ceiling and hooded faces were gathered at the edge, looking down at him. He spun around to the windows and realised he was teetering on the edge of a cut-stone chasm. For some reason jumping seemed like the safest option and so, with complete serenity, he stepped forward and started falling, falling towards the parked cars way down at the bottom.

'Jack! Wake up.'

Jack's eyes jerked open to find his head resting on the car window, his neck twisted uncomfortably. Stella was prodding his thigh with her hand but her eyes were pressed to her binoculars. 'The Count's leaving,' she said. 'Get down.'

Folding himself forward, he tried to restart his brain as the Mercedes exited the car park and powered towards them, its high beams filling their small Fiat with harsh white light. 'Sorry,' he said, 'I haven't really had my full eight hours a night lately.'

'I know,' she said in a soft voice, her face bent close to his. 'That's why I let you sleep.'

'What did you see?'

'Nothing much, but it's clear they've got more security inside. Two guys came outside for a smoke and one of them was the guy watching the transporter on Sunday.'

'Then we're screwed.'

'Unless they leave with Willy.'

'I doubt he's going to leave at all,' Jack said in a resigned voice. 'If I were a bankrupt and ruthless person sitting on a box of treasure worth billions, I'd be spending the night. I wouldn't let it out of my sight.'

Stella exhaled her frustration. 'You're probably right.'

'We're going to have to call Inspector Mancini,' he said. 'Hopefully we can convince him without evidence – or at least enough to arrange a warrant or whatever.'

'There's no point,' she said emphatically. 'He'll never get a warrant without evidence and he's not likely to look too favourably on a 200-year-old testament we claim to have stolen from the computer of a dead man. It's just a computer file, for Christ's sake. We could've made the whole thing up. By the time they verify our story, the container will be long gone. Besides, what if we're wrong? If we start throwing unsubstantiated accusations around, we may as well shut up shop. Our business will be over.'

Jack wasn't entirely convinced but when he sat up, he realised the discussion was moot. 'Oh, fuck!' he said.

'What?' Stella raised her head and saw three men walking purposefully towards the Fiat. They were only metres away. Willy was in the middle, flanked by men who were shorter than him, but almost as broad.

'Start the fucking car,' Jack said, tersely.

But the men were almost upon them. 'I'm not running anyone down,' she said. 'We haven't done anything wrong.'

'Stella! It won't matter.'

But it was too late. One of Willy's henchmen ran forward to pull open the driver's door before Stella could reach for the central locking. Willy strode up to her side of the car, looking down at her with a look that could only be interpreted as malevolence. 'We don't get a lot of parked cars in this part of town,' he said condescendingly. 'Your extraordinary luck just ran out.'

48

'If it's any consolation,' Stella said, feeling her way along a cool steel wall, 'I now think we should have called the cops.'

Jack was on the opposite side of the small room, trying to detect a weak point, or just a light switch. 'No, you were right. They would have wanted long statements and hard evidence. The treasure would have been long gone by the time they got their shit together.'

'Bastard could have left the light on,' she said, wincing as her finger caught on a sharp rivet.

'I don't think he could bear to look at us. Did you see how he kept averting his eyes?'

'Not a good sign,' she said grimly. 'If we don't get out of here, we're dead.'

'I should have fought,' Jack said, clenching his fists.

'Against three big blokes? Even you would have been hard pressed.'

'I might have landed a few.'

'One thing's clear, though,' she said, giving up on the left-hand wall. 'Willy's not the decision-maker. He's out of his depth. There's no way he's running this show.'

'Then it must be the Count.'

'Maybe. The two Italian security guards certainly aren't in on the secret. Willy told them we're spies from another F1 team.'

'With our surveillance gear, that must be just how it looked.'

Jack was pushing at the wall, seeing if there was a seam or joint that might give way under pressure, but the empty storage room was solidly constructed. He moved to the back wall and almost tripped over Stella, who was sitting on the floor with her head in her hands. 'Are you okay?' he asked, sliding down the wall to sit next to her.

'Oh God, Jack,' she said. 'Everything's turning to crap. I don't know what I'm doing – I feel utterly incompetent. I haven't made a good decision since we arrived in this damn country.'

'That's simply not true,' he countered. 'Apart from anything else, you decided to come to Nice, and that saved my life. You decided to take us to Malta, which exposed what's driving these bastards forward. And your suspicions about the Aretino transporter – which I dismissed out of hand – were obviously spot on.'

'But where did it get us? Locked in a steel box, waiting for our executioner to arrive. We should have stuck to the financials. We should've done no more than Giorgio expected of us.'

'That was my fault,' Jack said. 'I went chasing after the footage without discussing it with you first.'

'I would've told you to go for it. You know I would.'

'Exactly. It's who we are. We want to run down every angle. And you can't blame yourself for anything that's happened since. We've just been trying to stay ahead of the game.'

She shook her head in the dark. 'Maybe my first bad idea was starting this business together. Out on our own, with no resources and nobody who even knows or cares where we are. We could've stayed in cushy bank jobs in Manhattan where our biggest worry would have been finishing up in time to get to a Broadway show.'

'*Boring*,' Jack said, with feeling. 'When we started the company, we both believed we could deal with any situation that might confront us. Okay, so we didn't anticipate anything like this, but we're doing our best. If you don't take risks, you don't reap the rewards. And neither of us like Broadway shows anyway.'

Stella sighed. 'Even so, what can we really do here? We're out of our depth, and there's a good chance that these fuckers are going to get away with it.'

'Then it's time they found out just who they're dealing with. What do you say?'

In the dim light coming through a vent at the bottom of the door, he saw her wipe her eyes and heard her draw a deep breath. Then he felt her hand squeeze his forearm. 'I can always rely on you to make me feel better,' she said gratefully. 'All right, then, no more doubts. If we go down, we're going to do it fighting.'

He put his hand on top of hers. 'Now you're talking.'

They contemplated their limited options for a moment, their gaze drawn to the only source of light. 'How big do you reckon that vent is?' she asked. 'If we got it off the door, you think I could squeeze through?'

Kurt Bauer accepted the call as soon as his phone rang. 'What?'

'Where are you?' Willy's voice was more strained than usual.

'I've just arrived in Milan. I'm following the trail of our Australian friends.'

'I've got them,' Willy said quickly.

'What? Where?'

'Saronno, at the Aretino factory. They were watching the place, probably hoping to get a look in the container.'

'Shit,' Bauer said. 'That means they somehow kept a copy of the file and managed to crack it open.'

'But I thought you said —'

'It doesn't matter. When you say you've got them, what do you mean?'

'They're my, uh, guests,' Willy said.

'Who else is there?'

'Nobody, now. I've sent my security guys home.'

'Good. And what do you want me to do?'

'Can you come here, please?' Willy said, his tone full of entreaty.

'Can't you take care of it?' Bauer said sharply. 'I thought you had a taste for it now.'

'No,' Willy said quickly, 'I don't have the, uh, tools and I think it needs a professional touch.'

Bauer thought for a moment. 'You're probably right. I can be there in forty minutes.'

'Thank you,' Willy said. 'Thank you.'

'What's your mysterious partner going to say about it?'

'I can't tell him,' Willy said, his voice shaking. 'He would never approve. But they've made the connection to me now; I have no choice.'

'Don't worry,' Bauer said confidently. 'I'll make it as clean as possible.'

'This isn't working,' Jack said, handing her the coin. 'It's too thick. We need something thinner, or something with a right angle.' He was lying on the concrete floor, attempting to turn one of six Phillips head screws securing the louvred metal vent to the door.

'Try this,' she said, pulling at her waist. 'I bought this belt with the jeans.'

The belt buckle was thin, gold-plated metal embossed with the Armani logo. Jack felt in the dark for a screw head and pushed the corner of the buckle into the slot. 'It fits,' he said cautiously, 'but will it be strong enough to turn the screw?'

He slowly twisted the buckle in his hand, easing the screw loose while being careful not to strip the head. Triumphantly, he dropped the fastener onto the floor. 'One down, five to go,' he said, 'though from down here it's hard to imagine even you could fit through this gap.'

'I'll get out there, even if I have to scrape away a few centimetres.' Her tone reflected new hope and determination. 'The lock sounded like a simple bolt, so it should be easy enough to let you out.'

She hovered impatiently while he worked each of the screws free, and when he was done she crouched next to him to help pull out the vent as quietly as possible. The rectangle of light they'd opened in the bottom third of the door revealed a partial view of polished concrete floor in the hallway outside. Without hesitation, Stella pushed her head through the hole and looked both ways. She saw a long passageway with a series of doors on one side. The ceiling was high and lit with long fluorescent tubes.

'It's clear,' she whispered, edging her body forward, but her shoulders would not fit and she pulled back to extend her arms overhead like a diver. Wriggling and writhing like a trapped snake, with Jack assisting and keeping her clothes from catching, she pushed herself slowly through the rectangle. Her hips caught for a moment and Jack pushed her butt while she grunted and pushed against the cool floor with her hands. Then she was through, collapsing on the concrete with her legs still inside their makeshift prison cell.

At that moment, a shout of alarm rang down the corridor. She looked to her right and saw Willy, looking massive from ground level as he started running towards her. Frantically, she pulled her legs free and leapt to her feet, sprinting away from her pursuer.

'Run!' Jack shouted, his head at the hole. As the thump of Willy's boots came closer, Jack reached out with his left hand and caught the big man's ankle, tripping him up. Willy cursed loudly as he crashed clumsily on the hard surface. When he'd struggled to his feet, he aimed a kick at the hole in door. Jack tried to grab the boot but managed only to receive a painful blow to his knuckles before the foot withdrew to run after Stella.

Desperately, Jack tried to push himself through the hole but it was impossibly small for a man of his size. Full of dread, he put his ear to the gap and listened hard, silently urging Stella to complete her escape.

'Come out, bitch!'

Willy's menacing voice bounced off the steel walls and into Stella's terrified brain. He backed up his words by whacking the upright of a tall shelving unit with the long bar in his hand. The metallic threat echoed around the room. 'You're trapped in here,' he called out. 'There's no way out except past me.'

She withdrew further into the shadows on the far side of the large workshop. He sounded completely unhinged and she was sure he'd beat her to death if he got the chance. She'd run the wrong way, taking her deeper into the labyrinthine complex and further from the exit. She'd passed glass-walled rooms that looked like science laboratories, and others filled with computers and wide tables covered with technical drawings. Every door she'd tried was either locked or led to a dead end. Eventually, she'd found herself in the central work area of the factory, where the Formula One cars were assembled. There were hoists and pits and tall stacks filled with parts and crates. A partially constructed racing machine sat in the middle of the space, its burgundy body glowing under a ring of lights.

Willy advanced into the room, swinging his weapon like a batter at home plate. Stella had a partial view of him between two boxes on the shelves that were her cover. She looked up. Should I climb? she asked herself. The storage unit rose up almost to the ceiling. But it just was another dead end. She glanced around for some sort of weapon but the only loose components close by were made of carbon fibre, too flimsy to defend against a powerful man with a metal bar.

Or was it? She recalled reading somewhere that carbon fibre was stronger than steel. It had to be better than nothing. She pulled out a flat wing component almost as tall as herself, but startlingly light. Willy was just a few metres away now and she instinctively backed away, moving behind the shelves as he strode into the circle of light around the car. If she could keep the two deep under-car pits between the two of them she might have a chance, because she was confident she could outrun him if the opportunity arose.

Bang! He pounded his weapon on a metal storage box and she jumped in surprise. The end of her long wing knocked a suspension bracket from the adjacent shelf and it clattered to the floor. Instantly, he ran in her direction and she let out an involuntarily gasp of fear as she ran around the shelves in the direction of the nearest pit. As she came out from cover he roared and lunged at her, and she knew there was no chance of making it to other side of the deep hole before he reached her.

She turned to face him, backing away and holding her carbon-fibre shield with a wide grip. He loomed over her, his face twisted in fury. He raised the bar. She tightened her hold. As he brought the bar down she extended her arms to block the blow. The power of his swing radiated through the wing and knocked her off her feet, but the carbon fibre held its shape. She was on her back now, pushing away from him with her feet as she kept the wing above her with outstretched arms. Then she stopped, realising she was about to push herself into the pit.

Willy seemed shocked by his failure to hurt her but recovered quickly. He lifted the bar high overhead, ready to crash down with greater force. She tried to position the long shield to protect as much of her body as she could. The bar swung down for a second time and smashed into the edge of the wing, which shattered as if it were made of glass. The blow was deflected into the floor but the bar was already rising up again and Willy's face looked triumphantly spiteful.

Stella's arms ached painfully but she realised the shattered piece of wing in her tingling right hand had become a vicious-looking weapon. She pulled her torso upright and lunged at Willy's leg with the jagged carbon fibre, stabbing with all her might. The razor-sharp edge cut easily through his trousers and he screamed in agony as it plunged into his quadriceps. Staggering backwards in horror, he dropped the metal bar and reached for the carbon fibre. A dark stain had quickly formed on his pants leg and when he saw the blood and the burgundy car part firmly lodged in his thigh, he reeled and mewled like a lost kitten.

Stella watched with fascination and revulsion. Willy's face paled and his eyes lost focus as he stumbled sideways, blood now gushing from the wound. His good leg smashed into a toolbox as he collapsed in a dead faint, tumbling head first into the two-metre-deep hole beside her. A distinct crack rose from the pit. When Stella crawled to the edge and looked down, she was sickened by the sight of Willy's body. He looked to have broken his neck.

'Holy fuck,' she whispered, with genuine horror. 'I've killed him!'

49

Damn it, Jack thought when he heard approaching footsteps. She didn't make it. But then Stella's legs appeared beyond his small window and she was sliding back the bolt. 'You little beauty,' he said enthusiastically as the door opened. He was ready to run, certain Willy must still be in pursuit, but then he saw her tortured face and trembling hands.

'What's wrong?' he asked. 'Where's Willy?'

'Dead.'

'Dead?' He searched her eyes. 'What do you mean, dead?'

'What do you think I mean?'

His head cocked in confusion. 'He had a heart attack?'

'No.'

'You didn't . . . ?'

She nodded.

'Jesus! How?'

'He came at me with an iron bar. I stabbed him in the leg with a piece of carbon fibre and he fell into a pit. Broke his neck.'

Jack's mouth hung open. 'No fucking way! My God, are you okay?' He held both her arms in his, looking hard into her eyes. 'It was self-defence,' he added, 'not your fault.'

'I know,' she said, fighting to keep her emotions in check. 'He was going to kill me, I'm sure. But that doesn't make it any better. We have to call the police.'

'I suppose,' he said.

'You're not sure?'

'No, I am sure. There's just going to be a lot of explaining. And the press coverage.'

She closed her eyes. 'I know. I can see the headlines now: *Alex's New Squeeze Kills German Prince.*'

He released her arms. 'We'll do it later,' he said decisively, 'when we're a long way from here. We'll call Mancini. After being kidnapped, I reckon we have every right to take off. What about those other security guards?'

'He must have sent them away. If they were still around, he would have called them to help find me.'

'You're telling me we have the run of the place?'

Her shaking had stopped and she looked him in the eyes. 'You want to go for the container?'

'We have to find our phones and the keys to the car anyway, otherwise we'll be stuck here. It couldn't hurt to have a quick look around, could it?'

'I think the offices are right above us,' she said. 'There's a staircase at the end of the hall.'

Upstairs they found a row of large glass-walled offices for the team's senior executives. The office of the logistics manager was positioned at the end, with toughened glass windows looking down into the huge loading bays. Their phones and wallets were sitting on Willy's desk but the camera, binoculars and car keys were nowhere to be found.

Jack went to the external windows and scanned the street outside. 'Shit,' he said, looking both ways, 'they've taken the bloody car.'

He turned back, curious as to why Stella had no comment. He saw her looking through the internal windows to the loading bays. 'Down there,' she said, pointing to a stack of aluminium containers ready to be loaded into the burgundy transporter parked in the dock. 'That's where the container will be.'

They cautiously made their way down to the dock through the empty, fluorescent-lit building, its corridors eerily quiet. They had just reached the containers when one word from Jack made Stella freeze.

'Bauer!'

'Where?'

'Willy's office,' Jack said, staring up at the windows overlooking the loading bay, 'but not any more. He's seen us. Move!'

'We can't go back to the main entrance. He'll be coming that way,' said Stella.

'Follow me.'

Jack was already dropping down to the lower level of the dock. He ran alongside the semitrailer to the exit sealed with a heavy shutter. He hit a green button on the wall, hoping it did what he thought it would, and was relieved when a loud clunk signalled the motors engaging. The tall shutter began rolling up slowly.

Stella threw herself to the ground and wriggled under the door as soon as the gap was wide enough. Jack followed suit and clambered quickly to his feet to chase after her as she ran across the spotlit forecourt towards the deep shadows beyond. He didn't dare glance back as they sprinted along the dark street to the intersection.

'The station must be this way,' she said, recalling the departing workers. 'There will be people there.'

'That might not help,' Jack said between long breaths. 'You didn't see the look on his face.'

*

324

Death had halted the bleeding but the broken piece of wing sticking out from Willy's leg was still a disconcerting sight. Bauer stood at the edge of the pit, staring down at his client with an expression of disgust. The fool had broken his neck. 'I bet you weren't even pushed,' he said in a disappointed tone.

He climbed down the access ladder and approached the body. Reaching carefully into the pocket of Willy's canvas trousers, he extracted a mobile phone and checked the call register. Choosing the right number was easy enough and he put the phone to his ear.

'I thought I told you not to contact me —'

'The prince is dead,' Bauer said.

There was silence on the line.

'Did you hear me?' Bauer said.

'Who is this?'

'I am the contractor you've had on your payroll for the past few months.'

There was a sharp intake of breath. 'Is that so? Where are you?'

'Saronno.'

Another long pause. 'Did you kill him?'

'No,' Bauer said flatly, 'it was the Australians. You know who I'm talking about?'

'Yes, but I can't imagine them being capable of that.'

'He fell,' Bauer said simply. 'It was probably unintended.'

'Can you make it disappear?'

Bauer permitted himself a small smile. 'Possibly. What do you have in mind?'

'How much do you know about my arrangement with the prince?'

'Enough.'

'Then you know he had a big payout coming his way.'

'Yes.'

'His full share is yours, if you keep the operation going.'

Bauer's smile widened. 'You mean Rome.'

'Yes. You've been preparing things there, haven't you?'

'Everything is ready to go, but what about the container?'

'Leave that to me. It's in the system and will go wherever the system takes it, which happens to be where we need it.'

Bauer felt a rush akin to winning the lottery. His reward had just multiplied a hundredfold, or more. 'The Australians escaped,' he said. 'They will probably call the police.'

'It won't matter,' the voice on the phone said confidently. 'If you fix things properly, they won't have any grounds to search the containers. Whatever happens, I need you in Rome tomorrow. That is the most important thing.'

'They are trouble,' Bauer advised. 'They need to be dealt with.'

'They're too late. The gear will be transported in the morning. Whatever accusations they throw around, it will be over by the time the authorities act on them.'

Bauer's smile narrowed. 'They can identify me.'

'Then get moving. Clean up the mess and get to Rome. If that operation doesn't proceed, there'll be nothing to share. Remember, my friend, you'll soon be rich enough to disappear without a trace.'

It was Bauer's turn to pause for thought.

'Do we have an agreement?' the voice said.

'Yes,' Bauer said. 'Yes, we do.'

'Good. Keep this phone with you.'

The connection died and Bauer stared at Willy's corpse with a measure of wry satisfaction. Cutting out the middleman has its compensations, he thought, but whatever his new boss might think, one thing was certain. Before going to Rome he would take care of the Australians, once and for all.

50

'Pull over and wait, please,' Stella said to the driver, who steered the taxi into a driveway without comment. He seemed unconcerned as long as the meter was running.

Via Ravizza was quiet as midnight approached. The last of the late diners were strolling to aid digestion, many heading in the direction of the popular gelaterias around the corner on the Via Marghera. The entrance to the apartment building seemed peaceful enough, but there were trees on the pavement – and parked cars and restaurant awnings and dark doorways, each one perfect cover for an attack.

'It looks okay,' Jack said, leaning forward on the back seat, 'and we made pretty good time.'

'Bauer will have his own transport,' she said, straining her eyes to analyse the shadows. 'I'd rather not take the risk until . . . okay, here we go.'

Blue flashing lights speckled across building facades on both sides of the street as a carabinieri car approached and pulled into the driveway of number 12. Two uniformed men climbed out and took up the familiar pose of handsome arrogance, their tall leather boots glistening under the lights.

'Right,' Stella said, counting out cash for the cabbie, 'I'll go give them the keys so they can check upstairs. Then we can tell them about the body in Saronno and, with any luck, they'll find the treasure.'

'We can stay here tonight, can't we?' Jack asked hopefully. 'If I don't get some decent sleep soon . . .'

'If the carabinieri agree to keep watch again it shouldn't be a problem. Bauer's not going to risk falling into their clutches. We can move to a hotel tomorrow, after we've met with Giorgio.'

'Assuming he's available,' Jack said. 'We don't even know he's in Milan. Maybe we should confront Count Charles first, preferably somewhere public. Try to get some confirmation of our theory that way. Or Alex, perhaps. Didn't he tell you he was worried about someone attacking the family?'

Stella was clearly conflicted. 'I can't be sure any more. Alex and his father work so closely together – it's hard to imagine one of them being behind this without the other one knowing. Maybe I'm being paranoid, but Alex might just have been trying to find out what I know.' God, I hope it's not true, she thought. Not after the feelings he stirred up in me.

Jack made a gesture of resignation with his hands. 'So we just have to hope Giorgio will know what to do,' he said. 'But I doubt he'll respond positively to any theory that puts the Aretinos at the centre of a conspiracy.'

Stella nodded. 'But he's our client,' she said. 'We can't ignore our responsibilities to him. Our report to the police tonight already has the potential to make things difficult for him and the bank. We have a duty to keep his best interests in mind.'

Jack opened his door to exit the cab. 'When the cops find Willy's body, it'll give them an excuse to search the place and find the treasure. Then nobody will be able to deny the truth. Giorgio might not like it, but he'll agree that we were right to expose the plot.'

She climbed out her side and looked up at her uncle's apartment. 'My first priority is going to be locating and destroying all those bugs. There's no point keeping up a pretence with Bauer any more.'

Jack's face looked pained. 'I have a feeling we left the diagram of their locations in the suitcase we abandoned in Malta. I guess we could ask Mancini for a copy.'

Stella slammed the cab door shut and tapped a finger to her temple. 'No need. It's fixed in my memory.'

An hour later, Bauer was walking calmly along the opposite side of the street, a black nylon holdall slung over his shoulder. There were cops on the footpath in front of the building and lights still burned in the third-floor apartment, but that was to be expected. As much as he would like to take care of matters face to face, he would have to follow a less direct course.

When he'd passed beyond the sight of the carabinieri, he pulled a notebook from the pocket of his jacket. He'd been watching when Jack and Stella had driven away from the hotel in Nice, so he had the make and registration of their rental car. Their bugged conversations may have been structured to fool him but they hadn't hidden the fact that the car was still in their possession and parked nearby, but where?

Both sides of the street were packed with vehicles parked bumper to bumper. More filled the spaces between the trees and the outdoor eateries on the wide footpaths. Tourists never got permits to park on the pavement, and street parking was generally impossible. He looked up and around at the signs on the buildings nearby and soon spotted the obvious solution for a well-heeled consultant – a large white P on a blue background. Shifting the heavy bag to a more comfortable position, he headed to the garage.

It was diagonally opposite the Sartoris' elegant stone building, about a hundred metres further down the street, squeezed behind postwar concrete apartment blocks. The entrance was a rectangular opening wide enough for two compact cars. As Bauer drew closer he could see through the passageway to a ramp leading to an upper floor. A second, steeper ramp on the right led down to another level of parking, and an arrow painted on the wall indicated that the office was down there too.

Late-model automobiles filled almost every available space. The upper ramp was constricted by a line of cars parked nose to tail. On the lower floor, capacity was maximised by parking the vehicles two and three deep. Behind a desk at the bottom of the ramp, keys hung on a large board. The attendant was also there, his feet up on the desk and a cigarette between his lips. He was listening to a small radio tuned to a sports channel, which he turned down when he saw the spectacled man approaching.

Bauer evaluated him quickly. Early sixties; prosperous working-class. 'You the manager?' he said in fluent Italian.

'Nope,' the taciturn man said, looking up at his suspiciously. 'I'm the owner. I wouldn't pay somebody to sit here and smoke on a Wednesday night. Do you need me to get your car? I don't remember you dropping it off.'

Bauer took a photograph from his pocket. 'Recognise these people?'

Retrieving a pair of glasses from the top pocket of his shirt, the little man examined the picture of Jack and Stella. 'Why do you ask?' he said, his brow furrowing.

The recognition in the man's eyes was all Bauer needed. 'Never mind,' he said, snatching back the photograph. His eyes quickly scanned the board of car keys and detected at least two with the large plastic key rings issued by hire companies. 'What time do you close?'

'Within the hour.'

Bauer nodded and turned to go as the owner took the cloth cap from his head and scratched his scalp. Strange guy, he thought, but his attention was soon back on the radio, where a panel was discussing transfer rumours at his favourite football club.

At the top of the ramp, Bauer looked back to see the owner lighting a fresh cigarette and repositioning his feet. Calmly, he moved into the shadows, checked the street for passers-by and ducked up the ramp to the top level. He headed to the darkest corner of the dimly lit concrete hangar and there he settled down to wait.

At two a.m. he heard the metallic grind of the motorised shutter closing over the street entrance and soon after, the faraway sound of a door slamming. After fifteen minutes of complete silence, he decided it was time to go to work. He opened his bag, pulled on a pair of close-fitting gloves and extracted a torch with a variable beam. With senses on full alert, he made his way through the rows of shiny status symbols and down the ramps to the so-called office.

He started with the keys hanging on hooks behind the desk. There were more than a hundred on the board but the beam of his torch only picked out three from rental companies. He quickly found a Hertz key with the right registration number. From its position on the board, he determined that the Alfa was parked on the lower level. He shone his torch into the shadowy void opposite the desk and saw about forty vehicles parked in neat rows. The silver Alfa had been garaged for a few days and had been shuffled to the end of the back row. Perfect.

Returning the torch to his bag, he retrieved a smaller light on an elastic strap, which he pulled over his head. He took out a polished wooden box from the bottom of the bag and opened it on the floor, selecting a tilt-activated detonator with a ten-minute delay. Then he moved into the gloom around the cars.

Every movement was calm and controlled and the routine thoroughly refined, from checking the fuel level in the Alfa's tank to positioning the charge to create a good burn without destroying everything around it. His new partner might forgive the unauthorised action against the Australians but would certainly not welcome the public outrage and police attention that would follow the death of some passing child or old lady.

When he was done, he checked his bag to account for every piece of equipment and replaced the key on the board. In a simple card file on the desk he found the only record of the Alfa and tucked it into his back pocket. He consulted his watch and was satisfied. The whole task had taken less than twenty minutes. As he surveyed the scene, he felt only one regret. He wouldn't be there to see them die.

Exhaustion had rendered Jack mute as he observed the vigorous Italian exchange between Stella and the policemen. A shower had recharged his batteries but its effects were quickly wearing off as the clock swept towards two-thirty in the morning.

Eventually, he had to ask, 'What the hell's going on?'

Stella shook her head as if she wasn't quite sure. 'They've heard from their colleagues in Saronno,' she said. 'They found the factory securely locked up and had to break in.'

'They don't seem very pleased.'

'They didn't find anything.'

'No body?'

'No body and not enough blood to be suspicious, as far as they're concerned. They seem to suspect I'm addicted to publicity and this is some sort of stunt.'

'Maybe he wasn't dead,' Jack said. 'Maybe he recovered and left with Bauer.'

'He was dead,' she said, with certainty. 'Take my word for it.'

'Then Bauer must have cleaned up.'

'That's what I said, but these gentlemen don't seem interested in our theories any more.'

'What about the container?'

'They didn't look for it. They're already worried about the consequences that will flow from pissing off the Count. The Aretinos are like royalty in this town.'

Jack sighed with frustration. 'At least you're off the hook,' he said. 'You can't face charges for a death they don't believe occurred.'

'No,' she said, 'but they're thinking of charging us both with wasting police time.'

'Jesus! What about the guys downstairs? Are they going to take them away?'

'I don't know,' she said uncertainly. 'I'll try to get them back on side.'

She turned on a conciliatory smile and switched languages again. Jack flopped back on the couch and let his hands fall open by his sides. Damn it, he thought. Every time we get close to sharing the burden of this with someone else, it gets screwed up somehow. When are we going to catch a break?

51

'If you're going to make serious accusations like that about a man as respected and influential as Count Aretino,' Inspector Mancini said sternly, 'you'd better have solid proof.'

'I'm not saying the Count's definitely involved,' Stella said, making a face to Jack as she spoke into the phone. 'I just want someone to stop the shipment of that container so it can be properly examined.'

'Because you think this Prinz Gerhard fellow, who can't be found, has stuffed it with priceless artefacts.'

'Actually, I'm pretty sure it was packed by a man called Victor Drago.'

'And where is he?'

'Dead,' she said miserably, 'in Malta. But I have the document he translated, like I told you.'

'You also told me this document suggests the Count has every right to share in this treasure, if it exists. You also claim the artefacts have been in the family's possession for more than 200 years. Do you even have the original of this so-called testament?'

'No.'

'Have you seen the original?'

'No.'

Mancini huffed into the phone. 'Then it's difficult to see a crime here.'

'People have died! You said yourself, Kurt Bauer is a known killer. Surely —'

'Proof,' Mancini interjected. 'Evidence. These are the things we need.'

'The proof is in that container.'

'Whatever is in the container, it won't prove murder, Ms Sartori.'

'It will establish the motive.'

There was a silence. 'Perhaps, if we can locate this prince . . .' the Inspector said.

'He's dead,' she said, with a resigned sigh.

'So you say. My colleagues in the carabinieri aren't so sure.'

'I'm not a crank,' she said tersely. 'I'm not making this shit up.'

'Even so, there's nothing I can do. I am a liaison between police forces. I do not have the resources or the authority to investigate a crime such as you allege. You need to convince the locals.'

'They're too frightened of the Count.'

'I would expect them to be cautious. Can you imagine the pressure a man in his position can bring to bear?'

Stella said nothing, feeling defeated.

'Look,' Mancini said, with a more conciliatory tone, 'if we locate Kurt Bauer, we have more than enough to arrest him, and now we can involve the Maltese police.'

'He was in Saronno last night,' she said angrily, 'and he was in Malta the night before. Clearly he's not finding it too bloody hard to move around. He's shaved his beard and is wearing a pair of John Lennon glasses.'

'That's helpful, thank you,' Mancini said. 'I will add that information to the file.'

Stella shook her head in the face of the bureaucratic brick wall. 'We've destroyed Bauer's bugs,' she said. 'We're moving from the apartment this morning.'

'That's a good idea. Some of the better hotels have floors with enhanced security. When you're settled, call me again and I'll tell you if there's any news.'

After terminating the call, Stella looked at Jack with serious eyes. 'Well, partner,' she said, 'it looks like we're on our own again.'

Despite the assurances of the carabinieri, the protection detail had obviously been withdrawn during the night. Jack stood at the tall metal gate for a long time, evaluating the street before venturing out. It seemed bizarrely normal. Didn't all these people going about their daily chores realise how violent and unpredictable the world could be?

He'd decided to go and get the car so they didn't have to lug their bags down the street in the open. Before they left the apartment, Stella had insisted on sweeping the floor. Her uncle and his family would return from their vacation in a few days and no international criminal conspiracy was worth earning a reputation as the cousin who didn't clean up after herself.

'We can check into a suite at the Park Hyatt,' he'd said. 'We still have a report to write.'

'And what are we supposed to say about the Count?' she asked derisively. 'Either he's being robbed of billions or is about to make billions thanks to a string of murders. Do we describe him as a victim or a criminal mastermind?'

'What else can we do?'

She stabbed at the floor with her broom. 'You won't like the only idea I've come up with.'

'Oh, Christ. You're not about to suggest we go back to the factory, are you?'

'Not inside,' she said, her face brightening, 'but if we follow the transporters when they leave, we might be able to intercept them in Switzerland or Germany.'

'You're absolutely right,' he said dryly. 'I don't like that idea. Our chances of stopping that transporter on our own are next to none. Can we agree it would be wise to brief Giorgio first?'

'Can you imagine Giorgio standing up to the Aretino empire if the carabinieri won't? He'll tell us to drop it.'

'We should give him the chance to surprise us. He is our client, after all. Honestly, Stella, if you sweep that bloody floor any more, you'll rub away the terrazzo. Let's go!'

She gave him a stubborn look but he wasn't moved. 'Hotel first,' he said, by way of compromise. 'Then we'll decide how crazy we want to get.'

'Fair enough,' she said, giving him a small smile.

Now he was standing in the doorway, carrying both his hand luggage and Stella's. He repositioned the bags before stepping out to walk quickly down the pavement. He found himself drawn to the trees and cars and other potential cover, and felt horribly exposed as he crossed the intersection. By the time he reached the entrance to the car park he was almost running, and exhaled in relief as he ducked inside.

Coming down the ramp, he was greeted with a cheerful smile by the guy in the cloth cap who seemed to be here most of the time. As he handed Jack the key to the Alfa, the attendant talked excitedly but Jack couldn't understand what he was going on about. If he knew the context, he could often follow Italian speech but this man seemed to be talking about a picture or a photograph, which didn't make sense. Nodding politely, he repeated the words 'si' and 'grazie' several times and tried to convey the fact that they were leaving today.

The guy had to shift two cars to allow the Alfa to exit. While he did that, Jack opened the boot and placed his two bags deep inside, leaving room for the big suitcase they'd bought at Malpensa. With a final wave of thanks, he climbed in behind the wheel and turned the key. Nothing happened. Then he remembered the brake had to be depressed for the engine to start. He turned the key again and the diesel coughed into life.

At the top of the ramp he had to make a left turn across the oncoming cars, and he waited for a delivery van to dawdle by before pulling into the street. Miraculously, a car pulled out from the kerb in front of the fancy bedding shop next door to number 12 and Jack pushed the Alfa's nose into the spot before anyone else could grab it. Once he'd straightened the car, he turned the engine off and popped the boot.

A minute later Stella appeared, pulling the suitcase over the paving stones. She stopped at the gate to say goodbye to the wizened caretaker, Signor Colonari, who'd emerged from his dark little office. Jack got out of the car and collected the suitcase, adding his own 'arrivederci' and 'grazie' to the sweet old man. He wheeled the bag back to the car and added it to the boot. By the time he was done, Stella was waving to the old man as she walked to the passenger side.

Back behind the wheel, Jack pulled out the road map supplied by Hertz and checked his route into the city. The Park Hyatt was close to La Scala opera house and the magnificent Galleria shopping arcade. He pulled on his seatbelt while Stella rummaged in her handbag. She pulled out her wallet and checked inside. 'I should get some more cash,' she said.

'In case we have to make another emergency escape?'

'Well, if history is anything to go by . . .'

'Do we need to do it right now?'

'I'll just be a minute,' she said, opening her door. 'My card doesn't work in every machine but I know it works in the one around the corner.'

Her door banged shut and Jack's eyes left the map and settled on the rear-view mirror. He didn't like hanging around here and he didn't like letting Stella out of his sight. His eyes followed her until the marquee of the neighbouring Dolphin restaurant blocked his view, then scanned the street for any possible threats. It still looked unforgivably ordinary. His attention returned to the map.

Turning the corner at the bank, Stella frowned when she saw a line of three people at the ATM. When she'd finally made her withdrawal, she came back around the corner and her eyes settled on the bar where they'd enjoyed delicious coffees over the past ten days. Maybe one for the road, she thought, looking to the car to see if Jack was watching his mirrors. They'd earned some normality. She waved her arms and gestured towards the bar but his head was down, so she moved closer.

Suddenly, the air was split by a flash of light. She watched the car disintegrate before her eyes, torn to pieces by a fiery orange monster. Furniture and glass from the nearby restaurant flew towards her, a chair missing her head by millimetres. Then the blast wave struck, knocking her backwards onto the footpath and pushing the breath from her lungs. A frightening roar followed and she covered her face with her hands as the air filled with dust and smoke.

After just a few seconds she was back on her feet, oblivious to the screams and cries of passers-by. The smoke was coalescing into a thick black column, boiling up from the burning fuel tank of the Alfa Romeo. Through the smoke she saw a body, its head bent forward more than ninety degrees, fire still licking at its back. Her knees gave way and she slumped forward onto the hard pavement, her mouth open in a soundless, agonising scream of anguish.

*

Something hard was pressing against the side of Jack's face. He tried pulling his head away but his neck wouldn't move. He opened his eyes but saw only a terrifying white fog so he closed them again and concentrated on his sense of touch. Why did his arms and legs feel so disconnected? He could barely move them but could detect no obvious injury, no sharp pain. It was as if he'd been wrapped in bandages. Panic reopened his eyes.

His vision was still a white blur but looking to the right added red splotches to the image. Flowers in the fog? He tried to focus but could make no sense of it. Even more disconcerting was the complete absence of sound. Where had the world gone? He opened his mouth and said, 'Hello?'

He heard the word croaking in his throat but the sound was all inside his head, as if his ears were blocked. Earplugs, he thought. Am I still at the Grand Prix? He forced his addled brain to concentrate. What's the last thing I can remember? The map. I was looking at a map. I was sitting in a car, looking at a map. What next? An aroma, or was it a taste? The memory was teasing him. The window. I opened the car window with my left hand and I smelled . . . coffee!

Sitting in a car, looking at a map, smelling coffee. Was that it? His brain grudgingly offered up the image of a bed – a double bed made up in white linen and pillows of black and gold. That's it, he thought. I got out of the car to get a coffee and I stopped to look in the window of the bedding shop.

Instantly the white fog lost all its terror. He wasn't blinded – he was wrapped in a feather quilt. The hard object against his face was the floor of the shop. The reason he couldn't move or feel the rest of his body was because he was lying face down across soft pillows, his legs constricted by twisted sheets. Somebody or something had thrown him through the shop window and across the bed on display.

With renewed confidence he wriggled vigorously and managed to roll onto his back. His neck felt instant relief but pain signals arrived from several other spots on his body. He quickly determined that the red pattern on the quilt cover was not floral decoration, but blood. One leg was pinned by the heavy mattress and the bed frame, but he managed to pull it free and used it to push himself upright while he thrust out his arms to extricate his head from the quilt.

His position on the floor gave him a view of the sky and the tops of the buildings opposite, framed by the shattered shop window. Black smoke was billowing upwards from an unseen fire, and the tree on the footpath outside the shop was partially alight.

Fucking hell, he thought, they blew up the bloody car!

Stella!

He struggled to his feet, indifferent to the cuts and bruises. The twisted body of the Alfa was still burning furiously. One of the rear doors had been blown off completely. The other was raised in a sick salute. Bizarrely, the cars parked on either side looked remarkably intact. He shook his head. Sounds were still muffled, but at least his eardrums appeared to be intact. Looking around the shop, he saw a chaotic jumble of items strewn about the floor but somehow the neat stacks of linen on the shelves were undisturbed, except for the settling dust.

A sudden movement startled him and a woman brushed his arm as she ran out to the street through the broken front door, her panicked shrieks barely audible to his ears. Stepping carefully out the front door, he forced his eyes away from the awful but mesmerising sight of the burning car and looked down the street to where Stella should have been. Smoke and dust still thickened the air but he could make out a line of people standing about ten metres away. Figures were running about on the far side of the bombed vehicle. He sensed rather than heard a person shouting at him. But he only wanted to see Stella.

The heat radiating from the fire forced him to raise his arms protectively as his shoes crunched through broken glass. Approaching the growing gaggle of spectators, he saw a smaller huddle to one side. Two people seemed to be comforting a third. One of them was the friendly manager of the bar where he'd been heading for coffee. He looked closer and saw Stella on her knees, hands pressed to her face as she sobbed uncontrollably. The bloke from the bar was patting her back while a sweet-faced elderly lady was muttering in her ear.

Her grief was unbearable to watch. He stunned the good Samaritans by reaching down to put a hand under each of her armpits. He pulled her upright like a rag doll and folded her into his arms. 'I'm here, Stella,' he said softly into her ear. 'I'm okay.'

It took a long second for her to understand, but then her arms stopped hanging loosely and wrapped themselves around his back. Her crying transformed into a loud wail of relief and joy. The concerned locals stared but Jack and Stella held their embrace, as if nothing else on the planet mattered.

52

The sound of approaching sirens triggered a return to reality, though it took longer for Jack to register them. 'I'm still a bit deaf,' he said loudly. 'Hopefully it will pass.'

'You're bleeding too,' she said, touching his ear. 'It doesn't look too bad but you've got blood all down your neck and shoulder.'

He did a quick physical inventory. 'My legs feel battered and my ankle's starting to hurt. I must've hit something hard when I went through the window.' He released her to turn towards the destruction. 'Still, it's a bloody good thing I got out of the car.'

Stella scanned the burning Alfa with fresh eyes, no longer so terrified of what she might see. Now the fire was diminishing, her mistake was clear. The body she'd imagined was just the twisted driver's seat, its headrest bent forward. 'We should get out of here,' she said, lifting her mouth towards Jack's ear. 'Bauer might be watching.'

He glanced dazedly in the direction of the apartment building but Stella tugged him in the opposite direction, away from the smoking car. 'We can't go back to the apartment. The carabinieri detail disappeared without notice. I'm not sure we can trust the authorities any more. They might be in the Count's pocket.'

His mind still foggy, Jack allowed himself to be led away. 'I'm going to take him to the pharmacy,' she said to the bar manager, who was hovering behind them. 'I'll get them to put a bandage on his ear and then we'll be back.'

The chemist was less than two blocks away and the boss himself was standing in front of his shop anxiously looking up the street when they arrived. He ushered them inside, pleased to be involved, and cleaned and bandaged Jack's ear before allowing him the use of a small bathroom out the back to clean up.

As the shock ebbed, the pain increased. Jack's right ankle was starting to swell and bruises were already emerging on his shins. A fresh graze on his chin complemented the healing cut he'd earned in Malta and the still-bandaged wound on his arm. This consulting lark leaves a few scars, he thought wryly as he looked at his battered reflection in the mirror.

Gritting his teeth, he pulled his jeans back on. A tap at the door was Stella, delivering a T-shirt purchased at the closest menswear store. He was going through clothes as if they were tissues.

The pharmacist asked a lot of questions, which Stella evaded as best she could. He sold them painkillers, fresh bandages and an elastic ankle brace, and advised Jack to be properly evaluated for concussion. They left his shop as if to return to the scene of destruction, but Stella pulled Jack down the first side street, supporting his arm as he hobbled towards the Wagner metro station on Via Michelangelo Buonarroti.

A fire engine and a police car wailed past as the already congested traffic became even more gridlocked. Nearby pedestrians were magnetically drawn to the commotion, but two short blocks further on, daily life continued in the usual way. Commuters scurried down the stairs to the trains. Cars queued impatiently at the traffic lights while the sidewalk cafes busily pumped out espressos and pastries amid a haze of cigarette smoke.

The only response drawn by Stella and Jack's plodding progress down the stairs was annoyed grunts from those caught behind them. When they reached the wide ticket concourse, Jack headed straight for the nearest concrete bench to adjust his shoe and make the ankle more comfortable.

'You should put your leg up,' Stella said, her face full of sympathy as she saw the swelling. 'Do you want a drink?'

'Grab me a Coke,' he said. 'I feel the need for some sugar.'

When she returned with drinks and chocolate bars, she sat down next to him. 'I'll try to put that elastic strapping on if you can bear it. We should've bought an icepack at the chemist.'

'We don't have time for icepacks,' he said, swallowing three pain-killers. 'I'll be okay when these kick in.'

As she carefully removed his shoe and sock, he clenched his teeth and tried to distract himself with a bite of Mars bar. 'What the hell are we going to do now?' he said through a mouthful of caramel. 'We've lost two Hertz cars in the last twenty-four hours. They might hesitate to rent us another one.'

They shared a short, manic laugh at the terrifying ridiculousness of their situation. 'And we can't fly anywhere,' he added. 'We don't have passports any more. All I've got is my phone and a few euros in my pocket.'

'And all I've got is my wallet,' she said. 'We're pretty screwed, aren't we?'

'Maybe it's time to call it quits,' he said. 'There must be an Australian consulate in Milan. They might be able to get us back to New York, even if we have to go via Australia.'

She gave him a quizzical look. 'You want to give up?'

'No, of course I don't want to give up. But we're out of our depth in a city where we can't be sure who to trust. If we've made an enemy of the Count, we don't stand a chance on his home turf.'

'We don't know for sure that it's the Count.'

'With Willy gone, he's the last man standing. That's good enough for me.'

Her face took on a distant, defiant expression.

'Look,' Jack said, an edge entering his voice, 'we know there has to be someone else pulling the strings, don't we? Willy died last night and Bauer still came after us. He must be taking instructions from someone.'

She chewed her bottom lip nervously, unwilling to admit defeat. 'He might have put the bomb in our car before Saronno,' she said, trying to stay rational. 'He might have done it when we went to Malta.'

'Stella!' He groaned with pain and frustration. 'You're missing the damn point. We nearly got blown to smithereens twenty minutes ago. I think it's safe to assume they want us dead. Is there any job worth dying for?'

'No,' she said, but the pause after her words spoke volumes. 'Now that the car's been blown up, they might think they've succeeded in getting rid of us – for a while at least. We have a window of opportunity.'

'To do what, exactly? I'm telling you now, we're not chasing down those fucking trucks.'

She stared up at the vaulted ceiling, as if searching for inspiration. 'The carabinieri would have to take us more seriously after this attack.'

'So what?' he said disdainfully. 'When it comes to the Aretino empire, they're going to do everything by the book, and our car blowing up doesn't prove any connection to the F1 container. Besides, any evidence we had is now a pile of charred scrap. No computer files, no financial reports, no nothing.'

'God, you're right. They weren't prepared to do anything with what we had; they're even less likely to help now. And explaining why somebody tried to kill us to a new crop of investigators could tie us up for days.'

Jack gripped the sides of the bench as he lowered his legs slowly to the station floor. 'So, no cops,' he said through clenched teeth. 'Unless you can come up with a better idea, I can only suggest we get out of this cockamamie country. Maybe we can intercept the container in the States.'

She shook her head. 'By the time we sort out passports and visas, the contents of that container will be in some auction house in New York or in the private collections of millionaires.'

'The only other choice is to confront the Count,' he said. 'I suppose you could argue there's a fifty-fifty chance he's not involved. Fancy taking those odds?'

'Not really,' she said, her brow wrinkling with a new thought. 'What we really need is someone whose influence and contacts might trump the Count's.'

'Ha!' he said, wincing as he added weight to his foot. 'Unless you've got Prime Minister Berlusconi's private number in your back pocket, good luck with that.'

'How about the one person with an unquestionable stake in keeping the treasure in Italy? Someone with lots of influence, I would imagine.' She stood up with renewed vigour and looked at her watch. 'Rome is about four hours away by train, I think.'

His head tilted to one side. 'Rome?'

'Yes, Rome,' she said, the sparkle back in her eyes.

53

The piazza in front of the Spanish Steps was thick with tourists, though the sun's warmth was beginning to wane. One of the most photographed scenes in Rome was at its picturesque best as fluffy clouds in a blue sky took on a pinkish hue. And after snapping each other on the steps with the church on the hill behind, lovers and friends alike were drawn like moths to the brightly lit windows of the adjacent Via dei Condotti. Cartier, Bulgari, Prada, Valentino – they were all represented along the paved street that was once the haunt of romantic poets and artists.

The narrow thoroughfare was more crowded than the shops were. The average tourist wasn't well dressed or well heeled enough to venture inside the exclusive boutiques, but they were enthusiastic window-shoppers. Among them, one man seemed more interested in the shop displays than most. He spent time at almost every window as he worked his way up and down both sides of the street, yet he did not have the look of a self-absorbed follower of fashion. A simple long-sleeved shirt hung loose over his trousers and a baseball cap was pulled low over his eyes, almost touching a pair of wire-framed spectacles.

Kurt Bauer was supremely unmoved by the frivolous trinkets, and felt no connection to the people around him. They were just cover for his surveillance, as ignorant as shrubbery. Not one among them realised that as they peered into the windows of the Hermès emporium, they were technically looking into a foreign country. The boutique was part of the Palazzo Malta, which occupied the corner where Via dei Condotti was crossed by the Via Bocca di Leone. Three storeys of beige stone filled almost a quarter of the entire block. While the ground floor was leased as high-end retail space, the rest of the building was the sovereign seat of government for the Order of St John. It was also where Bauer's final target would be tonight.

Between the boutiques, a vaulted archway was overhung by poles flying the red and white flags of the Order. It led to a courtyard paved with a large Maltese cross and decorated with a fountain and a plaque bearing the Order's insignia. As Bauer passed the gated entrance for the third time, he noted the same two undistinguished cars parked in the courtyard, but he knew the palace was more occupied than it looked.

Of greatest concern were the soldiers of the Order's token military force. Though most were trained as medics, all of them carried weapons. This week the Italian army was running manoeuvres in the south and most of the Order's men would be participating. Their absence made the job feasible, but by no means straightforward. He would still be required to test the limits of his skill, and even if the toy soldiers were in the field, this front entrance was not the way in.

A little after six p.m., a ripple in the crowd signalled the arrival he'd been waiting for. Two black limousines nosed slowly through the tourists towards the palace, where men in red and blue uniforms emerged to open the gate. The car windows were deeply tinted but Bauer knew who was inside. He didn't wait around – it was time to return to his listening post.

As he set off to circle the block, he pushed against the crowd flowing down the hill from the Piazza di Spagna. A taxi was holding up the traffic on the cross street, and his attention was drawn to the woman exiting on the near side of the cab. She had a body worthy of designer labels, but as his eyes travelled up from her hips to her face he experienced a sudden and unfamiliar shock. Instinctively, he dropped to his knee and pretended to tie his shoelace and then, keeping low, he turned and moved with the crowd back towards the palace.

Facing a window display of impossibly high-heeled shoes, he focused on the reflection in the glass, hoping he'd been mistaken. But no, there she was: Stella Sartori, very much alive, walking around with Jack Rogers, who was nursing an annoyingly mild limp. Rage boiled in his gut and his hand moved under his shirt to the grip of the pistol tucked into his belt. Real effort was required to resist the urge to finish them off right there in the street. How was this possible? Not only had they escaped incineration but they were in Rome. What the hell were they doing here? With any luck, his precious bugs would provide some answers.

'Another dead end,' Jack said with a sigh.

'Give them some time,' Stella said, taking a sip from her cup.

'It's been two hours already.'

'They're priests, Jack, not bankers. They don't rush things.'

'They're just too polite to kick us out on our arses.'

She raised an eyebrow. 'Tell you what, though, they make a lovely pot of tea.'

'Well, the current boss *is* an Englishman.'

'And they did a nice job with your ear.'

He acknowledged this with a nod. 'My ankle feels much better too, with this new strapping.'

'They're just simple hospitallers, after all.'

He huffed in frustration. They'd been given that line a dozen times already. 'They might be priests and doctors, but they talk like bureaucrats.'

'Think of the Grand Master as a CEO or government minister,' she suggested. 'His underlings won't facilitate a meeting unless they think it's both important *and* unlikely to embarrass him. If you were in their place and two strange foreigners turned up with a story like ours, what would you do?'

His face adopted a more conciliatory expression. 'I guess our appearance doesn't help.'

'I'm not so sure,' she said. 'If you didn't have your injuries, I doubt they would've believed we were the people targeted by the car bomb. Without that, we probably wouldn't have made it through the front door.'

Jack shook his head. 'I disagree,' he said. 'The only reason we got this far is your celebrity. Once they worked out you were the girl on the front page of the weekend newspapers —'

Their debate was cut short by the return of the middle-aged priest who called himself Fra Sebastian. He held the door open for a servant carrying a large tray with two steaming bowls and a bottle of mineral water. 'I thought you should eat something,' he said with a polite smile.

Stella stood up. 'Have you spoken to the Grand Master?'

'The Grand Master is hosting a dinner this evening,' Fra Sebastian said serenely. 'He won't be available until that is complete. Have you reconsidered your position?'

She shook her head. 'We can't give you details until we meet the Grand Master.'

Fra Sebastian frowned. 'I'm sorry, but I'm not sure an unsubstantiated accusation against an unnamed knight of the Order is enough to justify a meeting.'

'Your Order is about to lose one of the greatest collections of precious artefacts ever assembled,' Jack said forcefully.

'So you say, Mr Rogers, but where is your evidence?'

'Destroyed, as we've already told you, by the same people who have killed and lied and killed again to achieve their ends.'

'Yes, yes, and you claim the Pact of 1798 is at the heart of it, but the experts agree —'

Jack smacked the table with his palm, rattling the cutlery. 'Then the bloody experts are wrong.'

'Now there's no call for anger, Mr Rogers,' the priest said patronisingly. 'I suggest you have some food, it will make you feel better.' He then turned to Stella. 'If you are not prepared to go to the police as I advise, I can only suggest you talk to your friends, the Aretinos. From the media coverage I have seen, you must be close to them. As it happens, we can assist —'

'We can't talk to the Aretinos,' she said, grimly, 'not yet. Please don't tell Jimmy we're here.'

He narrowed his eyes. 'I hope you're not suggesting the Count has anything to do with it?'

A young brother in a simple cassock burst through the door, giving them all a start. 'Fra Sebastian,' he said breathlessly, 'you need to see this.'

He handed the older man a sheaf of photographs. 'After what you told us about this man Kurt Bauer, I checked with palace security. I found them reviewing the footage from our new CCTV system. This man, filmed on the Via dei Condotti this afternoon, attracted their attention. I think he matches the description you gave.'

Fra Sebastian placed the photographs on the table and Jack pulled them towards him. Stella sat down next to him and studied the grainy images blown up from the security footage. Even with the baseball cap and nondescript clothes, the now familiar build and jawline were unmistakeable.

'That's him!' Jack said, his voice rising in alarm. 'That's Kurt Bauer. He must have followed us to Rome.'

'No,' Stella said, pointing to the time stamp in the lower right corner of the images. 'These were taken before we arrived. He was already here.'

'Jesus,' Jack said, oblivious to the disapproval of the churchmen. 'Why would he be here?'

'I don't know,' Stella said, but she looked up at Fra Sebastian with new determination. 'But I think you'd better get us that meeting now.'

Kurt Bauer switched channels. Eight listening devices fed data to his tiny apartment on the other side of the block, but there'd been no hint of the Australians on any of them. After a while he allowed himself to hope they'd been turned away from the palace, but he was acutely aware of the many rooms in the building that he couldn't monitor.

He could, however, follow the progress of the Grand Master and most of his dinner guests. After a civil but rather sombre meal, there'd been some gentle conversation followed by polite goodnights, just as he'd been anticipating. But then there was some unexpected and distinctly unwelcome activity in the old man's office.

'It's an extraordinary tale,' he heard the Grand Master say in his public school English as he entered the room. 'You really believe I should meet with these people, Sebastian?'

'They seem very sincere, Your Highness,' a second voice said. 'And they may have highlighted a security issue for us.'

'Is that why you've put a man outside my door?'

'Yes, Your Highness.'

'And the woman is the one who was next to Moretti when he was shot, the one Alex Aretino . . .'

'That's correct.'

'What a small world,' the Grand Master said. 'We were talking about her earlier. All right, Sebastian. Bring them in to see me.'

Bauer's fist slammed down on the table. His incredible prize and idyllic future life were hanging by a thread. Never in a long career of dispassionate killing had he so wanted two people to be dead.

A minute later, he listened while formal introductions were made. 'His Most Eminent Highness Fra Anthony Robert Gerard Blanchard,' Fra Sebastian announced pompously, 'Prince and Grand Master of the Sovereign Military Hospitaller Order of St John of Jerusalem, of Rhodes and of Malta, Most Humble Guardian of the Poor of Jesus Christ.'

There was a pause and Bauer pictured Sebastian bowing formally before going on. 'I present Ms Stella Sartori and Mr Jack Rogers, residents of New York City.'

The Grand Master's tone was especially haughty. 'I'm pleased to meet you,' he said, 'but I understand from Fra Sebastian that you have some very grave accusations to make. Before we go any further, I will need a name.'

Bauer heard the voice of the Sartori woman, sounding more nervy than usual. 'Thank you for seeing us, sir. If I can just explain —'

'A name, please, Ms Sartori.'

'Prinz Gerhard von Hirschberg,' she said, 'and possibly Count Charles Aretino.'

The Grand Master reacted with an intake of breath loud enough for Bauer to overhear. 'Count Aretino?' he said. 'I'm sure you must be mistaken.'

'Sadly, no,' Sartori said. 'It's rather complicated but if you let me start at the —'

'Before you say anything else,' the Grand Master said imperiously, 'there is something you should know. The Count is my guest this evening. At this very moment, he and his sons are one floor above us, preparing for bed.'

Bauer's thin lips formed a smile, imagining the woman's face. She wouldn't have been expecting that.

54

'The Count is here?' Jack said, dismayed.

The Grand Master nodded. 'Fra Charles is an old friend and often stays with us when he has business in Rome. Sadly, on this occasion, he is here to attend the state funeral for Eduardo Moretti tomorrow morning.' He turned his head in Stella's direction. 'I'm surprised you didn't know that.'

'Alex is here too?' she asked, concentrating hard to keep her voice even.

'Yes, indeed, and he had some very complimentary things to say about you over dinner. That is why I find it so bizarre that you would come here with a story that casts such a stain on the family.'

She shook her head despondently. 'I take no pleasure in it.'

He held her gaze, as if evaluating her sincerity, then gestured to a gilded baroque lounge suite around an unlit fireplace. 'You'd better sit down. Have you eaten?'

'Yes, thank you,' Stella said. 'Fra Sebastian was kind enough to arrange something for us.'

As she sat down she was suddenly conscious of the stark contrast between her worn blue jeans and the embroidered damask upholstery of the couch. 'Please forgive our casual dress. The rest of our clothes were destroyed along with our car this morning.'

The Grand Master was dressed in a grey suit with a red tie. 'I saw the footage on the television; it's a miracle you escaped with your lives. But your subsequent disappearance has confused the authorities, I think. The evening news report said the police have worked out the car was rented but they're still describing the event as an explosion in an empty vehicle with an undetermined cause.'

Jack shivered at the memory, which seemed more distant than the ten hours that had actually passed. 'We're pretty sure the man responsible is very close by, even as we speak.'

'We are perfectly safe here,' the elder statesman said in a fatherly tone as he sat back in his chair. 'Now, you'd better tell me the whole story.'

'Well,' Stella began, 'our assignment for the bank seemed pretty straightforward at first . . .'

Moving to the window of the little apartment half a block away, Kurt Bauer checked the sky. It was dark and cloudy, perfect for his purposes. Returning to the listening equipment, he set the transmitter to forward the signal from the Grand Master's office to his earpiece. He'd already changed into dark overalls and a black beanie, and he now began the final check of his gear.

As he listened to the Australians tell their story, he found himself both appalled and impressed by the combination of good thinking and blind luck that had brought them this far. But it was also gratifying to hear that every piece of evidence supporting their theory was gone. If they tried hard, they might be able to make things sticky for his new partner, but they'd never be able to prove anything. And as long as they kept talking, they were providing the perfect diversion.

The nylon pack fitted snugly to his back. A silenced pistol slid into a long pocket on his left leg, so the grip was within easy reach. A syringe and an ampoule kit went into the long pocket on the right. Two fighting knives slid into hidden sheaths. It was time to move.

The route from his apartment to the Palazzo Malta had been scoped and prepared. He'd rehearsed the trip several times. He opened the window at the rear of the apartment block and checked the area. There were lights burning in some of the buildings nearby but most shutters were already closed for the night.

The flat roof of his apartment building was three metres above the window. Internal access to the roof garden was locked after dark and monitored with a security camera, so he'd installed a climbing line to his window. Even with the weight of the equipment on his back, he pulled himself up easily and was soon crouching in the shadows on the roof.

From here, he would have to make his way across the roofs of six adjacent buildings, each a different height and configuration. There were climbs and drops – some equipped with newly installed hand and footholds – and there were security devices, ranging from barbed wire to cameras. None of it would come as a surprise to him. In twenty minutes, he would be approaching the last hurdle, which would take him onto the palace itself.

As Stella finished the tale – all the way from Milan to Nice to the Grand Prix ball and on to Mira, Malta, Monza, Saronno and, finally, to the car bomb that morning – it seemed incredible, even to her, that so much had happened in little more than a week.

The Grand Master clearly found the tale astonishing and seemed impressed by her earnestness, but he was far from convinced. 'I find it impossible to imagine Charles Aretino ordering any killing, let alone that of his own brother and the other innocents on that plane.

Willy Mindelheim, of course, has had a troubled life, but I would have thought the conspiracy you describe was well beyond his capabilities. You say he was killed, but you weren't exactly clear on how that happened. Did he have a falling-out with this Bauer character?'

Stella turned pale. Jack leaned forward in his seat and said, 'He attacked Stella with a metal bar. He was trying to kill her. But he slipped and fell into a pit in the factory floor, breaking his neck. Bauer must have disposed of his body, because we called the police but they didn't find anything. They refused to search the factory for the container.'

The Grand Master formed a steeple with his fingers and brought them to his chin. 'The Pact of 1798 has generated any number of theories since it first surfaced. A quick search of the internet will produce half a dozen.'

'We've seen some of them,' Jack said. 'But this new document was discovered among the Camilleri papers, by the historian Victor Drago. He did the translation himself. And I saw the nine coffins under the Villa Aretino with my own eyes.'

The older man seemed unimpressed. 'Where is this document and why haven't I heard of it?'

Stella recovered her composure and blocked out the mental image of Willy. 'We don't know where the original is held,' she said. 'We assume it was with Willy or the, uh, his partner.'

'And our copy was lost this morning,' Jack added grimly.

'That's a pity,' the Grand Master said. 'How can we possibly determine if it's real, especially if poor Victor Drago is another victim, as you suggest?'

'The descendants of the knights who signed that pact have been dying off at a remarkable rate,' Stella said. 'I think that proves it's real enough.'

'Accidents,' the cleric said, with sad eyes. 'Fra Jose Cristobal and

Fra Patrice de Montresson were both good men who will be greatly missed. But their deaths were accidents.'

'Under the terms described by the scribe,' Jack said firmly, 'there are three men still alive who are entitled to share that treasure. All three of them share the name Aretino.'

'Isn't it worth protecting?' Stella asked, slightly mystified. 'Even if it were only the pieces described on the single known page of the pact, it must be priceless to the Order. This is your history, after all.'

'According to you,' the Grand Master said, after a thoughtful pause, 'even if the treasure exists, the passage of 200 years has ceded title to the heirs of the eight knights.'

'There must be a legal argument,' Jack said, as if advising a client. 'The scribe talked about the return of sovereign territory to the Order. Surely any good lawyer could mount some sort of case. And there are bound to be Italian or European laws protecting artefacts as unique as these.'

For the first time, their host showed signs that his patience was not limitless. 'Nobody would like to recover such treasures more than me, I can assure you, especially given our recent loss. But however genuine and well meaning I believe you to be, I can't possibly act on a theory that has no evidence to support it. The authorities will have to investigate – with your complete assistance, I trust – and if these artefacts surface, the Order will take appropriate action to recover —'

'People have died,' Jack said in a low growl. 'Including the innocent and naive. As a man of God, how can you possibly stand by and allow such travesties to go —'

'What loss?' Stella said, her gaze fixed on the Grand Master.

'I'm sorry?'

'You mentioned a recent loss, and the young priest we met earlier said your security camera system is new. Did you have a break-in?'

'Indeed we did,' the Grand Master said, his mouth tightening.

'Earlier this year. Our security was upgraded as a result. Unfortunately, with a building as old as this, the options are limited.'

'What was taken?' Stella demanded.

Jack was surprised by her brusqueness but also sensed her mind working through one of its trademark lateral connections. The Grand Master, too, seemed taken aback by her sudden intensity. He ran his hand uneasily through thick locks of white hair. 'A few of our oldest and most valuable pieces of church plate were stolen,' he said. 'They were kept in an antique safe that proved to be no barrier to the thieves. Given the small size of our collection, it was a devastating loss, and we still have no idea how it was done.'

Jack watched Stella carefully, wondering what insight this new information was giving her. She was concentrating hard, her green eyes fixed on the empty fireplace while she processed a complicated mental trail. At last, she looked across to the Grand Master and said, 'Could you please ask Alex Aretino to join us?'

Jack wasn't expecting that. 'Is that a good idea?' he said in a whisper. 'I thought we agreed that Alex would be in the frame if his father was cleared.'

Her face looked as if she'd just eaten something unpleasant. 'I'm beginning to suspect that we fell for the same scam as Willy and Kurt Bauer,' she said.

'Scam?' Jack said. 'What the hell are you talking about?'

Her fingers had moved to her mouth and were rubbing her bottom lip anxiously. 'The treasure we've been chasing . . .'

'What about it?'

Finally, her eyes met his. 'The treasure doesn't exist.'

55

'It's been bothering me all along,' she said. 'All the credible experts are so sure the Order had lost virtually all its wealth and treasures by 1798. But it's clear that Willy believed the big hoard was very real. He was prepared to kill for it, after all.'

'And the best way to convince him . . .' Jack said, the cogs of his own brain spinning.

'Would be to show him a sample or two, exactly. Back that up with a forged document that gives life to a cryptic pact everybody accepts as genuine, and you have all the motivation you need for a desperate descendant with underworld connections.'

The door to the Grand Master's office opened and Alex Aretino was ushered in by Fra Sebastian. He was wearing a business shirt without a tie. When he saw Stella and Jack, he stopped dead, his expression one of complete astonishment. 'What on earth are you doing here?' he said.

'It's a long story,' Stella said, standing up.

He appeared to recover from his surprise and stepped towards her. 'It's wonderful to see you, of course,' he said, giving her a kiss on each cheek. 'Have you come to Rome for Moretti's funeral? I don't think you should feel obliged to see him off.' Alex turned his dimpled smile to Jack. 'Nice to see you again. What happened to your ear?'

'Car bomb,' Jack said simply.

'What? No! That was your car? What the hell have you been up to?'

He's either a superb actor or completely out of the loop, Jack thought. 'We've been finding out who blew up your family jet,' he said.

'You have?' Alex turned to Stella for clarification, his smile replaced by an anxious frown.

'Please sit down,' she said. 'I just have a few questions.'

They all sat down together, the attention of the three men fixed on Stella. Alex, in particular, was staring at her with a tense look on his face.

'Do you remember telling me the Hall of Heroes was a room with a secret?'

Immediately, Alex looked uncomfortable. 'I shouldn't have told you that, I'm sorry. My father wouldn't want others to know about it.'

'What was the secret?'

'It's a private thing,' he said, cautiously, 'known only to the immediate family.'

'Does it have anything to do with treasure?'

'Treasure?' His lustrous curls shook with puzzlement. 'What treasure? You haven't fallen for some new theory about the pact, have you?'

'There are nine coffins under the floor,' Jack said, pointedly.

'You found the cellar? You went down there?' Surprise leapt into his voice. 'How the hell?'

'Stay calm, please,' the Grand Master said, with serene authority. 'Alex, I believe Ms Sartori is close to understanding who is ultimately responsible for the attack on your family. Why don't we hear her out?'

Alex crossed his arms defensively as he took a moment to think.

'One of my illustrious forebears – you don't need to know which one – returned from Malta with a secret family. He was a respected knight who'd taken holy orders, of course, but it seems he fathered six children with a young Maltese girl over the course of a decade. When he had to flee the island, he brought her, her parents and their children to live on the Mira estate. They are the people interred under the floor of the Hall of Heroes. I've known about it since I was a child.'

The Grand Master seemed most affected by the tale. It was easy to see he was regretting the entire conversation.

'Would Willy have known that?' Jack asked.

'Willy?'

'Prinz Gerhard von —'

'Willy Mindelheim?' Alex said, indifferently. 'No way. He's only a distant cousin. This secret was a big deal to the older generations of my family. Wait, why are you asking about Willy? Is he linked to the bomb on the plane?'

'Yes,' Stella said, 'but not on his own.'

Alex was instantly sceptical. 'Willy doesn't have the skills —'

'He's been paying a hit man by the name of Kurt Bauer,' Jack said.

'Paying him? With what? Willy's so in hock he sleeps at the factory in Saronno. He couldn't afford it.'

'Somebody else has been providing the cash,' Stella explained. 'The same person who convinced Willy he was entitled to share in a treasure trove worth billions, and got a man named Victor to fake the proof and pretend to fill an F1 container with the precious goodies.'

Alex's expression returned to complete confusion. 'Who?'

'Your brother,' Stella said.

'Jimmy?' Alex and Jack said together, their voices scratchy with disbelief.

'Jimmy?' the Grand Master repeated, similarly stunned.

She nodded. 'It can only be Jimmy. He's been very careful to keep things at arm's length, but I believe he wants to control the Aretino empire. He needed his uncle, cousin and father out of the way so it would all come to him, but his father missed the critical flight. He had to keep the myth of the treasure going. As part of that, he allowed Willy to commission the killing of the other descendants.'

'Jose Cristobal's twelve-year-old son died with him,' the Grand Master said, his mouth slack with shock.

'I know,' she said.

'Wait,' Alex said, pushing back. 'Jimmy has access to even less cash than Willy. His vow of poverty is taken very seriously by my father. He's completely cut off.'

Stella licked her lips tentatively. 'Well, I think you need to ask your sister about that.'

'Laura?' Alex raised his hand as if fending off an attack. 'What are you suggesting?'

'Count Charles said her trust fund expenses had been incredible recently. I think she's been giving Jimmy the cash.'

Alex shook his head dismissively. 'Don't be ridiculous. Why would she do that?'

Stella thought for a moment, as if picking the right path on a map. 'Do you know who might be the father of her child?'

'No,' Alex said irately, 'as I'm sure I told you. She's been completely tight-lipped, despite my parents' pleas. Unfortunately, she has quite a history of inappropriate relationships. There are a number of possible candidates.'

'You don't recall any unpleasantness involving Eduardo Moretti?'

Alex absorbed the question and then fell back in his seat. 'My God!' he said, raising his hand to his mouth. 'Back around Easter time, she went skiing with the Morettis at their chalet in Cortina.

I remember she came back early and seemed even more messed up than usual. You don't think . . .'

'I think it's almost certain that something unpleasant happened to her there,' Stella said apologetically. 'And as a result, Moretti is now dead. Of course, his death serves another purpose, too. It brings you all to Rome. Bauer is here, watching the palace. He must be planning to finish the job on your father.'

'I thought Jimmy had signed away his rights to the title and the money,' Jack said, his brow furrowed.

'He's supposed to,' Alex said, 'but I'm not sure he's actually done it. My father gave him the legal documents a couple of months ago, and he wanted time to read it all through.'

'Why Rome?' Stella asked Alex, determined not to be deflected. 'There must be a reason Jimmy wanted the Count to be here. Is there something in his schedule tomorrow that Bauer could take advantage of?'

Alex looked shell-shocked. 'I can't think of any. Security at the funeral will be watertight because the Prime Minister will be there. And we'll be travelling in the Order's own vehicles.'

'I'll make certain they're thoroughly checked,' the Grand Master said.

But Stella was shaking her head. 'I doubt it'll be another bomb or a public assassination. Bauer went to a lot of trouble to ensure the deaths of the other descendants didn't appear suspicious. I imagine he'll want to do the same with Charles.'

'What about his sleeping arrangements?' Jack suggested. 'Presumably he's on his own here, whereas in Milan he'd be with his wife, or . . .'

He stopped talking, realising he sounded crude. Fra Sebastian, who was standing discreetly by the Grand Master's desk, cleared his throat. 'If I may,' he said timidly.

'Yes, Sebastian?' the Grand Master asked.

'The Count's sleeping arrangements,' he said. 'I happen to know he specifically requested a bedroom with windows that can be opened. He likes the fresh air, you see, and we —'

'Holy shit!' Stella exclaimed, jumping to her feet. 'Bauer's going after him tonight!' She looked over to the Grand Master. 'Sir, you need to get some of your soldiers up to the Count's room immediately.' She grabbed Alex's hand and pulled him to his feet. 'Do you know the way?'

'Of course.'

He started striding to the door and Jack followed, his heart racing. As soon as they were in the hallway, any semblance of decorum was overwhelmed by Stella's sense of urgency. 'Can we hurry, please?' she said. 'I have a very bad feeling about this.'

They half-ran to a carpeted set of stairs and loped up one level. Alex led the way to a mahogany door among many in a long corridor. As they reached it, the thump of boots echoed from below. The soldiers weren't far behind. Alex hesitated, raising his fist to knock, but Stella grabbed the handle and pushed the door open.

The room was dark but she could make out antique furniture and rugs on an expansive polished timber floor. She saw a figure lying askew on a high double bed. The Count was wearing white pyjamas and wasn't moving. She rushed to his side but was distracted by a movement in the shadows. One of the sash windows was wide open and a dark shape suddenly moved towards it. Before she could react, a lean figure in black had ducked out of the window without making a sound.

'Bauer!' she screamed, but then the overhead light came on. Count Charles's face had a sickly grey pallor and his eyes were open and unseeing. A syringe lay beside him on the covers. She stood help-lessly beside him, calling his name, until the professionals arrived with both assault rifles and medical kits.

With Jack, she was pushed back into the corridor while the

medics went to work. They were soon joined by the Grand Master and Fra Sebastian. 'It doesn't look good,' she said despondently.

Jack was still reeling from Stella's deductions. His brain was struggling to process the world in real time. 'I can't believe Jimmy's behind all this.'

Stella nodded miserably. 'The worst thing is, unless they can get Kurt Bauer, we'll never be able to prove it.'

Suddenly Alex strode out of his father's bedroom, his face a mask of pure hatred. 'I'll fucking kill him,' he muttered, shouldering his way through their group.

As he took off down the hall, Stella lunged and grabbed him by the wrist, but it hardly slowed him down. 'Wait, Alex!' she begged. 'Stop!'

Alex turned around. His eyes were wild and unfocused.

'We need Jimmy to confess,' she said, forcing him to look at her. 'If you challenge him now, he'll deny everything and get away with it. You'll lose the title and the company and all the money to the man who killed your family. We have no evidence; nothing more than a theory. Are you listening to me?'

'We'll get Willy to confess,' Alex said, trying to pull his arm free.

'Willy is dead, Alex.'

That got his attention. 'What?'

'There's still a lot you don't know. Many people have died because of your brother's plotting.'

'Half-brother,' he said dazedly.

'Jack and I are lucky to be alive,' she went on. 'We've earned the right to see justice done almost as much as you have, and if you go rushing to Jimmy now, we all lose. But, Alex, if we do it right . . .'

His face softened slightly and he contemplated her with an expression approaching awe. 'You really are an extraordinary woman, Stella Sartori. What exactly do you have in mind?'

*

Kurt Bauer lowered himself easily through the window, pulling down the line behind him. It had been a close call. They would be looking for him, but there were hundreds of places he could be hiding in the rabbit warren that was central Rome. If he stayed calm, his escape would be assured.

But, for once, escape was not the highest priority. He'd listened to the conversation in the old man's office. It had been a constant distraction while he went about his work. But could it possibly be true? Had Willy really been duped into believing there was a prize of incredible proportions that did not even exist? And had he, Bauer, fallen under that same spell, willing to dispatch people for a pay-off that would never materialise? And was this Jimmy the same man who'd assured Willy that the evidence of Bauer's hit on Moretti would be collected and destroyed?

Disturbingly, he found himself believing the woman more than anything he'd been told by Willy. He'd never been happy that Willy had no access to the mysterious container. And he'd always been suspicious of the historian, who had seemed to think the whole thing was a game. Even the deaths he'd been paid for were galling, now he realised they were meaningless. He'd been treated as a fool and there would have to be a reckoning.

56

'This is reckless,' Jack hissed. 'The police should be handling it.'

'You heard the Grand Master,' Stella said with quiet determination. 'This is sovereign territory. He wants to handle it without the Italian authorities. The carabinieri will stay outside the palace. When Jimmy has confessed, the Order's men will hand him over at the gate.'

'I still don't like it.'

She gave him an impatient look. 'He's one priest, Jack, and there are armed men in all the adjacent rooms. There's nowhere he can go.'

She crossed the Grand Master's enormous office to where Alex was standing by the window, staring out at the dark sky with a melancholy expression. 'Are you okay?' she asked, her voice soft with concern. 'I can do it, if you'd rather sit things out.'

He managed a wan smile. 'I'll be all right. If he sees you too soon, he'll be suspicious and clam up. Should I struggle to find the right words, Fra Anthony will no doubt help me out. He's known both of us since we were boys. I doubt Jimmy will be able to sustain a lie with him.'

As if on cue, the Grand Master entered the room and moved

towards his desk. He, too, looked pale and apprehensive as he directed his ire towards the head of palace security, Colonel Wilder, who was following two steps behind. When his tirade was over, he dismissed the officer and came over to Stella and Alex. 'I'm sorry to report they've found no sign of the assassin. There is some evidence he travelled across the roofs but there are countless avenues for escape.'

'It will be easier in the daylight,' Stella said, feeling the need to keep the mood optimistic.

'These are for you and Jack.'

The Grand Master held out his palm to offer her two tiny flesh-coloured devices. 'Put it in your ear and you will hear the feed from my security team. The device receives only, so don't expect them to respond to you. Follow any instructions the colonel broadcasts and, in particular, if you hear the command to withdraw or take cover, do so immediately. Is that clearly understood?'

'Absolutely,' Stella replied, feeling a rush of adrenaline. 'Are we ready to go?'

The Grand Master nodded. 'Fra Sebastian is getting him now.'

She turned back to Alex. 'Just stick to what we talked about, and you'll be fine. Give him the bad news and gauge his response. Ask him about his intentions. Then Jack and I will come in, okay?'

Alex nodded and took a deep breath, as though preparing for a long swim. 'I must keep my anger in check,' he said, as if coaching himself.

'We are diplomats and men of peace,' the Grand Master said imperiously. 'Fra Giacomo will be seduced by our reason.'

'What's keeping him?' Jack said, looking at his watch. It was almost 1.45 in the morning.

The atmosphere in the small room was tense. Stella and Jack stood close to the door leading into the Grand Master's office. It was slightly ajar, so they could hear what was happening inside. Behind them stood two soldiers equipped with assault rifles.

'Stay alert. Target approaching.'

Jack glanced at the soldiers, but then remembered his earpiece. It was a weird sensation, hearing Colonel Wilder's commands directly in his ear.

Stella was chewing her lip again, going over the plan in her head and testing it for flaws. She could think of plenty. She put her eye to the gap but could only see another door leading to a room just like this one, similarly occupied. She positioned her ear closer to the door and went rigid when she heard a distinct knock.

Fra Sebastian opened the door but did not follow Jimmy into the room. The door clicked shut behind him. The Grand Master stood up at his desk. Alex stayed in his seat, his head bowed. Jimmy looked to the clock on the mantelpiece and opened his hands in a gesture of curiosity.

'Come in, my son,' the Grand Master said solicitously. 'Sit down.'

'What's wrong?' Jimmy said, his eyes moving to Alex. 'Why are you here so late? Has something happened?'

He was wearing a simple dressing gown that reached all the way to his ankles. Alex looked up at him with a pained expression but when he opened his mouth to speak, nothing came out.

'Fra Anthony?' Jimmy said, turning to the desk. 'What's happened?'

'We have some terrible news to share with you,' the elderly man said. 'Please, sit down.'

'What news? Just tell me, Your Highness, please!'

'Your father . . .'

'Yes, yes? What about him?' His voice was strained, like a man waiting for the results of a life-or-death blood test.

'He's dead,' Alex said, watching his brother's face carefully.

'Dead?' Jimmy said, his hands rubbing together in a gesture that could be interpreted as either distress or anticipation. 'How?'

'Heart attack, they think.'

Jimmy sat down heavily on the other end of Alex's gilded sofa and dropped his face into his hands. But when he raised his head, he wore an expression nobody had anticipated. He was grinning. 'What a pity,' he said.

'What?' Alex barked, his fingers forming into fists.

Jimmy gave him a look of mock sympathy. 'Oh, poor Alex, I really am sorry for you, but that man sidelined me from the moment you were born. And while you and our pathetic cousin got to splash around in the great big pool of family money, I was packed off penniless to work for a God I don't even believe in.'

'Fra Giacomo!' the Grand Master said, shock straightening the lines in his face.

'I'm sorry, Fra Anthony,' Jimmy said, sounding sincere. 'You've always been good to me, but this was never my calling. You must have suspected I was only doing it out of family obligation. Now I have other responsibilities.'

Alex sat up straight, straining to keep control. 'You killed him, didn't you?'

For the first time, a flash of doubt crossed Jimmy's face. 'What? Don't be ridiculous, Alex. You said he died of a heart attack. But if you think I'm going to honour his pathetic wish to put the family's future in the hands of a second-rate accountant like you, you need to think again.'

'You didn't sign the papers, did you?'

'I was putting it off,' Jimmy said casually. 'Something was holding me back. Perhaps it was destiny.'

'You selfish bastard.'

'Get over it,' Jimmy said with a sneer. 'You were never in line for the title until the jet went down, so what have you lost? You can still run the business, if you like. I won't deny it, you're pretty good with the numbers.'

There was a crashing noise from the end of the room and Jimmy leapt to his feet at the sound.

'You ungrateful piece of shit!' Count Charles roared from the doorway in the corner. He staggered forward, supported by a male nurse. 'I didn't believe them until this very moment. I said you could never betray your family like this. You would never condone the death of innocents just to claim a birthright that was never yours.'

Jimmy's face had turned ash grey, his eyes wide and blinking. 'Father?' he said, like a five-year-old caught stealing cookies.

'Too soon,' Stella muttered, uncertain how to respond. She turned to Jack. 'He's come out too soon.'

'Go!' he said.

She pulled back the door and they tumbled into the room, followed by the armed soldiers.

Jack registered the situation and felt his heart stop. A gun had appeared in Jimmy's hand. It was pointing at his father. When Stella and Jack appeared in the opposite doorway, soldiers rushing in behind them, Jimmy's arm dropped and suddenly the gun was sitting at the back of Alex's neck.

'Stop right there!' he commanded in a loud voice. 'Come any closer and Golden Boy's brains will be all over the floor.'

His dressing gown was hanging open and he was fully dressed underneath. 'I felt something was off,' he said, staring at Jack and Stella and shaking his head in disappointment. 'I should have known you two were behind it.'

One of the soldiers moved to raise his weapon. Jimmy grabbed his brother's hair and pulled his head back onto the barrel of the gun. His eyes shot to the Grand Master, who was frozen in horror by his desk. 'Tell them to put their weapons down, Fra Anthony, or I will shoot. The bullet will go through my dear brother's neck and straight into your chest.'

Colonel Wilder's voice crackled in Jack's right ear. 'Lower your weapons. The building is secure. Our first priority is to get the Grand Master clear.'

The soldiers obeyed, dropping their rifles to the antique rug on the floor.

'It's over, Jimmy,' Stella said, her hands extended in front of her. 'Too many people have died already.'

'Shut up,' Jimmy spat. 'You've caused enough trouble.'

'I've caused enough trouble?' she responded furiously. 'Did you ever stop to think about the blameless people who've been killed to feed your megalomania?'

'Son,' Count Charles said, arms wide in a gesture of appeal, 'please listen to me —'

'I will not!' Jimmy said, his eyes flashing. 'If you'd had the decency to die when you were supposed to, there would've been a lot less bloodshed.'

'I never realised how unhappy you were,' Charles said, his voice cracking. 'You should have talked to me.'

'Like Laura did?' Jimmy stared at his father with unfiltered hatred. 'She told you Moretti raped her, didn't she? And what did you do, darling Papa? You called her a whore and a liar, that's what you did. So don't pretend for a minute that you're a good father. On the contrary, you're a lousy father and an even lousier man.'

His rage and frustration seemed about ready to boil over. Jack sensed a crisis looming. 'What do you want now, Jimmy?' he said, as calmly as he could manage. 'You and I know how to put a deal together. It's how we both got our start, after all. You've missed out on the big prize this time, but any good trader needs to be adaptable. I'm sure we can find a way to end this peacefully.'

Alex made a small noise of pain as the gun barrel was pushed deeper into his neck. 'Don't patronise me, Jack,' Jimmy said. 'I like you, but spare me your patter.' He looked to the Grand Master, who seemed to have visibly aged. 'Fra Anthony,' he said, in a firm voice, 'here's what I need from you. A car, with the motor running, in the courtyard. Via dei Condotti is to be cleared, all the way to the Piazza di Spagna. And tell Colonel Wilder if I see a single soldier of the Order between here and the front gate, he will be responsible for the death of the chosen heir to the Aretino fortune.'

With shaking hands, the Grand Master lifted the phone on his desk and started speaking. Jimmy nudged Alex with the gun. 'Get up, brother, you're coming with me. Move slowly. Don't try anything stupid. You know I'm a good shot. If you shake yourself free, I promise you, our illustrious father's run of luck will be at an end – permanently.'

'It's all right, Jimmy,' Alex said soothingly, as he rose gingerly to his feet. 'I'll do whatever you want. Let's go for a nice drive.'

The terror on the Count's face only enraged Jimmy more. 'Losing Alex would be the ultimate punishment for you, wouldn't it, you fucking hypocrite?' He smiled maliciously. 'Can't imagine why I didn't think of it before.'

Placing his left hand on Alex's shoulder, he used the right to thrust the pistol into his back, at the level of his heart. 'Now,' he said brightly, as if planning a fishing trip, 'I think we need someone to lead the way, don't you, brother of mine?'

His cold eyes scanned the room. 'Stella!' he said. 'Why don't you join us? It wouldn't do for you to be separated from your boyfriend, now would it?'

57

As soon as the office door clicked shut behind Jimmy and his hostages, Jack turned frantically to the nearest soldier. 'Give me your gun,' he demanded.

The soldier's hand covered his holstered pistol protectively. Jack looked to the Grand Master, who'd sunk despondently into a chair. 'Please, sir, tell him to give me his gun.'

'No,' the old man said. 'He said —'

'He said no soldiers,' Jack insisted. 'He knows I'm a talker; he won't see me as a threat.' He took a step towards the door. 'I'm going after them, whatever you say, but I'd prefer to be armed.'

Count Aretino had been settled in a wheelchair by his minders. He still looked sickly but his voice was strong. 'Give him the damned gun, Anthony. Somebody has to stop Jimmy . . .' He brought his knuckles to his mouth, appalled by the image in his mind.

The Grand Master's face looked conflicted. 'Colonel Wilder and his men —'

'I can still hear them,' Jack said, tapping his ear. 'I won't get in the way of their operations, and I guarantee the weapon will be an absolute last resort.'

Fra Anthony sighed deeply and gestured to his men. 'Sergeant, give him your gun.'

The firearm was heavier in his hand than Jack had expected. 'Safety catch?' he said, pointing to a spot above the grip.

'That's right,' the soldier said warily.

'How many shots do I have?'

'Fifteen.'

'Okay.'

Holding the gun made him feel slightly more secure. He lifted the back of his T-shirt and shoved the gun into the waistband of his jeans. Without a second look, he pulled the door open and moved stealthily into the hallway.

'Units One and Two fall back. Clear the hallways and courtyard. Secure the perimeter and await orders. Unit Three, take up covered positions on the roof and confirm. I want the target acquired but do not take the shot without clearance. Lieutenant Rossini, inform the carabinieri and request their assistance on the surrounding streets. Unit Four, remain with the Grand Master.'

Colonel Wilder's orders and his troops' responses filled Stella's ear as she led the way towards the grand central staircase. The soldiers used English to communicate, but their accents ranged across the full breadth of Europe. It was of some comfort to know the soldiers were nearby, but the palace felt abandoned as they moved through it. Only the ghosts of long-dead knights observed disinterestedly from their gilt-framed portraits.

'Keep moving at a steady pace,' Jimmy called, as he pushed his brother ahead of him. His head swivelled left and right and his voice was rough. 'Hands where I can see them.'

She held her arms like a milkmaid who'd forgotten her pails. 'Where do you think you're going to go?' she said, as they approached the stairs. 'How can you possibly escape with all —'

'Don't worry about me,' Jimmy cut in. 'A high-risk plan like this always called for an exit strategy. The world is a big place.'

'I'll make damned sure they hunt you to the ends of the earth,' Alex said, with unquestionable resolve.

'I'd watch my mouth if I were you, brother,' Jimmy said menacingly. 'I haven't yet decided how long you have left to live.'

'Why threaten Alex now?' Stella asked, straining to keep her tone nonconfrontational. 'He was never on your hit list.'

'No, he wasn't,' Jimmy said, with a tinge of regret. 'He wasn't to blame for my father's failings. My intention was to cut out the dead-wood, not the fresh growth. But,' he added, with a shove in Alex's back, 'he is my father's most valuable possession, and everybody knows it. They're not going to risk the Count's wrath by putting his pride and joy at risk.'

As they came down the thickly carpeted staircase, the courtyard outside appeared beyond large glass doors. The brightly illuminated space was empty but for a white four-door sedan with the logo of the Order on the front door. Fumes rose from its exhaust pipe.

Jimmy was careful to keep Alex and Stella between himself and the doors as he guided them to the telephone sitting on a baroque credenza against the wall. He picked up the phone and stabbed at a button. 'Colonel Wilder,' he said. 'I want the lights out in the courtyard and the front gate opened completely. You have thirty seconds.'

Within moments the courtyard fell into darkness. Only the parking lights of the getaway car were still visible. Suddenly, Jimmy spun around and fired a shot up the stairs. A shower of plaster dust flew from the wall. Stella jumped as the noise echoed away.

'Come out now!'

Jack rose up cautiously from the landing where the staircase turned. He held his hands open at shoulder height. 'I'm unarmed,' he said.

'Shot fired,' a deep voice said into Stella's ear.

'Anyone see what's happening?' Colonel Wilder's tense voice said.

'Join us, Jack,' Jimmy said. 'Slowly, now!'

As Jack took a step down, he heard a voice in his ear. 'This is Three, no hit. Repeat, no hit. Subject has new hostage.'

'Damn it,' the colonel's voice said. 'Unit Three, do your snipers have a shot?'

'Unit Three, negative. No angle until subject exits building.'

Jimmy used the gun to direct Jack to a spot alongside Stella, who was watching with an expression of complete dismay.

'Couldn't help yourself, could you?' Jimmy said with a twisted grin. 'Always the risk-taker. Did you ever think you might be too brave for your own good?'

'I'm not giving up on you, Jimmy,' Jack said. 'Let's talk for a bit. There must be a way —'

'The time for deals has long passed, Jack. If you wanted to do a deal, you should've contacted me before blowing my plans to hell. I could've offered you a seat on the Aretino board.'

He dismissed any further discussion with an eloquent gesture of gun waving. 'It's time to get moving. Stella, I want you to go out to the car and check it. Make sure it has plenty of fuel and no hidden surprises. Open the doors so I can see inside. Open the boot too. Then come back here. Remember, one tricky move and you'll be back on the singles' scene.'

She moved to the heavy doors and pulled one open. The night air was mild. With a quick glance back to Alex, who was maintaining a stoic blankness, and Jack, who looked unnervingly calm, she stepped outside.

'Control to Unit Three. Snipers, report your position.'

'Sniper One, in position south side.'

Stella moved quickly to the car, resisting the urge to look up to the dark roof.

'Sniper Two, in position north side.'

She opened the door and the interior light came on. She moved aside to give Jimmy a clear view into the vehicle.

'Control, this is Sniper One.'

'Go ahead, Sniper One.'

'Please repeat status of Sniper Three.'

'Say again.'

'I did not copy Sniper Three's report.'

Stella leaned into the driver's side. The fuel tank registered full. She found the catch to pop the boot and stood up again. Then she heard Colonel Wilder's edgy voice. 'This is Control. We have no Sniper Three. Repeat, we have no Sniper Three. Sniper One, confirm sighting.'

'This is Sniper One. Gunman with rifle on west side. Wait one.'

Stella opened the boot and made a show of putting her hands inside.

'This is Sniper One. I can't see him now, but he was definitely there.'

Christ, Stella thought, it must be Bauer. A chilling sensation crept up her spine. Things were about to get ugly.

'Somebody get eyes on that shooter now!' The colonel's order was loud in her ear and she couldn't help but wince slightly as she walked back to the entrance.

Jimmy had arranged his human shields in front of him, shoulder to shoulder. When Stella approached, he instructed her to stand behind him. 'But don't touch me,' he warned. 'If you try a move, I will pull the trigger before I do anything else. It was good of Jack to provide me with a spare hostage, don't you think? I'm perfectly content to lose one. All right then, move!'

They shuffled forward in a tightly packed group.

'Sniper Two, no clear shot.'

'One, have you got eyes on that shooter?'

'Negative, Control.'

'Damn!' Colonel Wilder said.

'What are you going to do about Kurt Bauer?' Stella said in a clear voice. 'He won't be happy you conned him, you know. And won't he be expecting a big share of the payout from the non-existent treasure?'

'Shut your mouth,' Jimmy said, scanning the dark corners of the courtyard.

'What would he say if he knew you'd kept the evidence of his hit on Moretti? Was that your insurance policy, Jimmy? Your way of controlling him?'

'Sniper One, I have movement. Shooter is moving to fire.'

'Take him!' the colonel shouted.

'Get down!' Stella screamed, reaching past Jimmy to grab Alex's shirt.

Jack had already grabbed Alex by the arm to pull him to the ground but there was a sudden jerk and he lost his grip. Alex fell sideways, blood staining his shirt, and he rolled on the paving stones.

'No!' Stella shrieked.

Jimmy was momentarily stunned. His primary hostage had been taken out and he was suddenly exposed. He raised his pistol but couldn't decide on a target. A moment's hesitation was too much. He grunted and staggered backwards, his spare hand clutched to his belly. Falling against the car, he slid to his knees, his gun hand still flailing dangerously.

Jack leapt to his feet and grabbed the arm Stella was extending towards Alex. He dragged her bodily to the rear of the vehicle just as Jimmy started firing blindly. More loud reports followed, as a firefight broke out on the roof of the palace. Their earpieces relayed the sound of heavy breathing and terse orders and rapid firing.

Without warning, a body crashed down into the courtyard only a few metres from where they were huddling. 'Fucking hell!' Jack said, as he instinctively pulled Stella closer.

'This is Sniper Two. Sniper One is down! Repeat, Sniper One is down!'

Jack's attention was caught by a dark shape as it slithered smoothly down a rope in the corner of the courtyard. He shook Stella. 'Hurry! Get around the other side of the car.'

They scrambled on hands and knees to the far side of the sedan. The dark shape was moving so quickly it was impossible to keep track of it, until suddenly they sensed it approaching. Jack reached for the gun in his jeans and when Stella saw it, she gasped. He touched her leg to indicate silence, then tensed his muscles and lifted his head to peek over the car.

Bauer was reaching down to his left leg, from where he pulled a pistol. Jack ducked down again but Bauer had stopped in front of Jimmy, whose empty gun lay useless by his side. A deep-red stain was soaking his shirt.

'You must be Kurt,' Jimmy grunted breathlessly.

'Nice to meet you, at last,' Bauer said coldly, as he raised the gun and fired two bullets neatly into Jimmy's eyes.

'Courtyard,' Colonel Wilder's voice crackled over the airwaves. 'The shooter is on the ground in the courtyard. Move in.'

But it was too late. Alex Aretino was conscious and groaning in agony as he tried to roll over. Bauer contemplated him with a look of contempt. Raising the gun again, he walked towards the struggling man.

'Don't you fucking dare!' Jack shouted, leaping to his feet with the pistol held firmly in two hands.

Bauer's eyes met Jack's, and his gun turned. Jack pulled the trigger on his own gun and felt a kick and a wave of noise. The bullet hit Bauer in the shoulder but he didn't drop. Jack adjusted his aim and pulled the trigger again – and then again. He didn't stop firing until Bauer had keeled over backwards onto the stone paving.

58

'How are you feeling?' Stella asked, gently touching Jack's arm.

'Pretty woozy,' he said, 'but a whole lot better now.'

She smiled. 'They have remarkable medical facilities, don't they?'

'It's what they do,' he said drowsily, conscious of her fingers on his arm. 'I'm not sure what they gave me, but it's making me float. Or is that you?'

'It's the drugs,' she said softly.

'I can't believe things ended up this way. All the blood. And Jimmy's eyes . . .'

'Don't think about it.'

'Easier said than done. I liked the guy, too. He made me re-evaluate my whole opinion of priests.'

'I'm not sure he ever thought of himself as a priest,' Stella said with a melancholy voice. 'I think he saw himself as a son whose talents were never given due recognition.'

'It's a pretty fucked-up way to get attention,' Jack said, shaking his head. 'And for a few seconds there, he thought he'd done it. Did you hear the triumph in his voice?'

She shivered involuntarily. 'He came awfully close,' she said. 'If we hadn't turned up when we did . . .'

He put his hand on top of hers. 'We were right to keep going. That's down to you. I was ready to give up back in Milan.'

Stella looked him in the eye. 'I would've given up long ago, if you hadn't been with me.'

Jack smiled tiredly. 'Which just goes to prove what we already knew. You and I make a bloody good team.'

Fra Sebastian appeared in the doorway. 'Ms Sartori and Mr Rogers,' he said, with a polite tilt of his head, 'they'd like to see you now.'

Stella stood up and helped Jack to his feet. He shook himself briskly in an effort to clear his head of the drugs injected by an earnest doctor thirty minutes earlier. 'Too much sedative,' he said, reaching out with an arm to steady himself. 'That guy must have misjudged my weight by a hundred pounds.'

'He probably expected you to lie down for a while,' Stella replied wryly, offering him her arm. 'This way.'

She led him down a short, antiseptic corridor to the room indicated by Fra Sebastian. Inside, they found a private medical suite fit for a head of state. In the bed, Alex Aretino was lying naked from the waist up, his shoulder and left arm heavily bandaged. Count Charles was in a chair by the bedside but when he saw Stella and Jack, he stood up unsteadily and stepped forward.

'Stella, Jack. We owe you our lives,' he said, struggling to hold back tears. 'When I think what might have happened if you had not come along, well, it makes me . . .'

Words appeared to fail him. He compensated by pulling Stella, and then Jack, into an embrace.

Stella helped the Count back into his chair and gently touched Alex's right hand. 'What's the story?' she asked. 'You going to be okay?'

'Yeah, I'll be fine,' he said, managing a weak smile. 'The bullet went right through my shoulder. I'm going to have some scars that should look pretty impressive.'

'I don't think you need battle wounds to make yourself more impressive,' she said, but his eyes had already moved away.

'Jack, my friend,' he said. 'Come and shake my hand. You saved my life. I watched you shoot that animal while he stood over me. Anything you need, you tell me. I know how to repay a debt.'

Jack moved closer and took Alex's hand. 'A quick call to Giorgio Borboli to explain why we haven't made much progress with his report would be helpful.'

Alex laughed, then winced at the pain. 'Of course.' He glanced at his father and said, 'We feel terrible that you were sucked into Jimmy's terrible, selfish machinations. He and I weren't the closest of brothers, but I never thought . . .'

Tears filled his eyes and the Count took his son's hand and gave it a squeeze. 'It's my fault,' he said sadly. 'Alex and I bonded early, in a way I was never able to with Jimmy, and this developed into an easy working relationship. I never stopped to think about how Jimmy must have seen it. And when I encouraged him to join the priesthood, he obviously thought I was trying to exclude him completely.' He looked up at Stella and Jack with an appeal in his eyes. 'You must believe me, that was never my intention.'

Stella nodded sympathetically.

Jack said, 'He was diabolically clever, when you think about it. It's a pity his motivation got so twisted around.'

'The important thing is, he didn't succeed,' Alex said, 'thanks entirely to you. I have no doubt your partnership will be a big success. In fact, I can think of a project or two we could use your help with.' His smile grew warmer as he caught Stella's eye. 'Though I seem to recall there's a downside to becoming your client.'

She raised her eyebrows suggestively for just a second but said nothing.

'Let's get this job done before we move on to the next,' Jack said, his fuzzy brain still processing the implications of what he'd just seen.

'Is that what's next for you?' the Count asked. 'Back to Milan to finish your analysis of my companies?'

'Yes,' Stella said. The work still needs to be completed, although I'm sure Giorgio will be relieved to hear that we've established there was no external attack on the group.'

'Actually, my first stop is going to be Nice,' Jack said with a soporific smile. 'I owe Louis Ganet a visit. He deserves to find out who was behind the death of his father.'

The Count gave Stella a quizzical look. 'You'll have to tell us the entire sorry tale. We will take immediate steps to ensure the families Jimmy injured are given due respect and compensation.'

She nodded. 'We'll be very happy to do that. Personally, I'm looking forward to some peace and quiet. Life in the public eye is really not my —'

'Excuse me,' Fra Sebastian said from the open doorway, 'but I think there's something you need to see.'

He came into the room and turned on the large flat-screen television positioned across from the bed. As the screen came to life, it filled with the image of a large man in his underpants chasing a young, naked girl around a haystack.

'Late night TV,' Sebastian muttered disapprovingly, as he changed the channel. 'Here.'

He brought up CNN's global twenty-four-hour news service and a female anchor was at the desk. 'Repeating that in breaking news,' she said. 'There has been an exchange of gunfire at the Rome headquarters of the Sovereign Military Hospitaller Order of St John, otherwise known as the Knights Templar. This footage is exclusive to CNN.'

'Knights Templar?' Alex said. 'You'd think these reporters would do their research . . .'

His voice fell away as every eye in the room was drawn to the images on the television. The camera was across the street from the entrance to the palace and had a clear view through the open gates into the courtyard. A white car was sitting centre screen, clearly visible until the lights suddenly died.

'The press were there almost as soon as the carabinieri were,' Fra Sebastian said, by way of explanation. 'There was nothing we could do.'

The cameraman made some adjustment that rendered a dim but distinct image of the courtyard, even without the lights. There was an editing cut and then the sound of gunfire as two figures appeared, scrabbling around the end of the vehicle on all fours like frightened chimps.

'Shit,' Jack said, 'that's us.' Suddenly he was watching himself stand and shoot, the flashes from the gun illuminating his face as he fired bullet after bullet into the falling body of Kurt Bauer. Another edit and the lights in the courtyard were back on, as armed soldiers and medics moved around the bodies that could just be seen on the left side of the picture.

The network's correspondent started talking over the pictures. 'CNN understands that Stella Sartori, a Wall Street mergers guru, and Jack Rogers, a former star trader at Sutton Brothers and now business partner of Sartori, were involved in the gun battle. Sartori has also been recently linked to Italy's wealthiest and most eligible bachelor, Alex Aretino.

'Earlier this year, Rogers and Sartori founded a consulting group based in Manhattan. Initial reports indicate that they were instrumental in foiling a terrorist plot to assassinate the Order's Grand Master, the British academic and theologian Anthony Blanchard.

The bodies of three terrorists shot dead by Rogers were reportedly taken to the police morgue, but their identities have yet to be established. We will keep you up to date with any developments. Melanie Richardson, CNN Rome.'

Jack looked at Stella with wide eyes and she returned the stare. And as the implications sank in, she started to shake her head. 'This isn't good. I see stormy waters ahead.'

'Yeah,' he said, with a sigh of resignation, 'me too.'

'One thing seems certain,' Count Aretino said, with the wisdom borne of long experience. 'A quiet life is probably not on the cards for you two.'

Acknowledgements

One of the great joys in writing this book was doing the research. I am grateful to all who helped but particular thanks must go to Anthony Schiavo, a true friend and coach in all things Italian. Anthony's posting in Milan gave me the opportunity to experience the city like a resident and provide Jack and Stella with a perfect base of operations for their first European adventure. Thanks also to Sandra Sartori, who was an enthusiastic tour guide during my exploration of the villas and towns of the Veneto region.

My parents, Jill and Norman, and my sister, Jeneen, were, as ever, tremendously encouraging, as were Pat and Lesley Donohue. The importance of their support cannot be overstated and is only shaded by the love, advice and motivation provided by my partner Julia. She is the fuel in my tank.

The team at Penguin Australia was a pleasure to deal with. Their advice on plot direction and pacing was invaluable. My heartfelt thanks to publishers Bob Sessions and Belinda Byrne, but Arwen Summers deserves a special mention for her excellent work as both editor and adviser. Her investment in my characters and their story as complete as any writer could hope for.

ALSO BY BRETT HOFFMANN

THE CONTRACT

Wall Street star consultant Stella Sartori is very good at her job. So good, in fact, that she can't help but follow up a casual remark made during a routine company assessment. It leads her to a dusty old contract in the archives and within hours she is running for her life, taking the file and its cryptic contents with her.

Fellow Australian Jack Rogers is sent in for damage control, but when he finds Stella's notes, her realises she has stumbled onto a devastating secret. Suddenly, it's vital that he finds her before some else does.

Relentlessly pursued across the country, Jack and Stella uncover a shocking trail of corruption and murder dating back forty years, with an explosive secret at its heart. If they can prove their suspicions correct, they'll survive. But with the contract in their hands, the past threatens to destroy them.

'An intelligent insight into the dirty world of corporate takeovers and acquisitions ... Gripping.'
Launceston Examiner

'Business is indeed risky in this well-paced yarn.'
Weekend Gold Coast Bulletin